Advance Praise

"*The Impossible Why* is a powerful portrayal of childhood, not as a training ground, but an uneven, beautiful, and often cruel terrain. A country that must be crossed without a map.

Sixteen-year-old June Taylor grows up a Jehovah's Witness in the Arkansas countryside, where she learns early the choreography of survival: the Eggshell Walk around a mother whose storms set the household's weather.

June's safe places are humble and faithful: the McDonald's register that pings like order, Grits, the yellow lab who never asks for explanation, and the Clapping Tree where secrecy feels like prayer.

A story about the bruising tenderness of devotion, and how a girl learns which debts are hers to pay. It understands that coming of age often means the courage to love without surrendering yourself, and that the hardest part of growing up is not choosing between others, but choosing who you will be."

— J. A. Dailey, best-selling author of *Tough Rugged Bastards*

"I was totally absorbed in June's story from the first line, and at the end so sad, but also so happy, because I could see her path forward, out into the world. I would follow June's voice anywhere..."

— Robert Anthony Siegel, award-winning author of *All Will Be Revealed*

"*The Impossible Why* is a heart wrenching and healing, lyrical deep dive into the darker territory of mother-daughter relationships, religion, and family – a bright, riveting, love-filled story of one girl's journey to freedom.

Maternal abuse is a hard topic to confront but it has played out for generations behind the scenes, knocking girls and women sideways into shame, anguish, and confusion during their most crucial developmental periods, and sometimes for entire lifetimes.

It requires terrific grit and courage to step outside the contorted looking glass of a narcissistic family system and tell the truth. June does just this; her cycle-breaker determination and petrified-wood strength shatters through the twisted mirrors of generational trauma and cycles of abuse. June's story offers a roadmap to what healing looks like in real life: nonlinear, chaotic, punctuated by longing, denial, and grief.

At the same time, June's story, while veering away from an easy redemption arc, holds out hope. Love and refuge can be found in a sweet dog, a good book, a job well done, a tree that listens. And if you are brave enough to keep your heart wide open, a new family can Kintsugi its way into the cracks of your heart, transforming you into the golden version of your true self that has been there all along."

— Kathy Morgan, M.Ed., LPC Licensed Professional Counselor

The Impossible Why

Summer Hammond

First Edition

Library of Congress Control Number: 2025948872

Casebound ISBN: 978-1-62720-635-8
Paperback ISBN: 978-1-62720-636-5
Ebook ISBN: 978-1-62720-637-2

Permission for excerpts from *Christy* by Catherine Marshall granted by McGraw Hill LLC

Design by Caroline Corr
Editorial Development by Riley Mitchell
Promotional Development by Caroline Gerosa

Published by Apprentice House Press

Loyola University Maryland
4501 N. Charles Street, Baltimore, MD 21210
410.617.5265
www.ApprenticeHouse.com
info@ApprenticeHouse.com

for Aly, my tree
and for Grandma Millee,
who gave me sequin dreams

PART I
FAMILY

I've found that there is always some beauty left –
in nature, sunshine, freedom, in yourself;
these can all help you.

-Anne Frank

January 7th, 1996
Fayetteville, Arkansas

"Why are you here, June?"

Judge Sanders places his spectacles on the bridge of his nose. This action seems to signal his eyebrows to draw together, his mouth to turn downward, and his pupils to sharpen. He no longer looks like the sweet, sparkly-eyed gentleman who welcomed me into his home. He looks mean. And he's scaring me.

He knows why I'm here. He doesn't like it. He thinks it's outrageous. He wants me to look him in the eye, stand firm, and speak. Instead, my stomach clenches. My heart thumps in my ears. My palms sweat. *Help*. I steer my eyes to Judge Sander's wondrous golden floor-to-ceiling book shelves, packed with books. Scanning, my eyes catch on beloved titles. *Pride and Prejudice, Jane Eyre, Evelina*. My heartbeat calms, evens.

I remember something Dr. Freeman taught us: the blood pressure of a frightened ill person will almost instantly lower when a loved one walks into the room.

For me, the loved ones are books.

I breathe, and find my voice. "Your bookshelves are beautiful. They almost have their own spirit. They glow. I hope to own as many books someday. Only, I prefer old books." I look at him. "Don't you love the musty, dusty smell of old books?"

"I prefer the smell of leather," Judge Sanders retorts. "And fresh ink."

"Oh." He isn't softening. Why would he? To him, I'm just a young girl, out of her mind, sitting before him in an outlandish sequined dress, on the run. And partly, that's true. But that's not the whole story. I feel myself shrinking into my chair. How can I argue my case, when I'm not even sure what it *is*?

"June." Judge Sander's tone shifts to a slightly warmer key. I look to the side, blink tears.

"I understand, this situation is unsettling, to say the least. I apologize if I've frightened you. I don't want you to be afraid. What can I do, to put you at ease?"

My pulse taps in my throat. "Could you remove the spectacles?"

He blinks. "Say again?"

"Your spectacles. They make you look like a judge."

"I am a judge."

"I know. But I'd rather you didn't *look* like one."

He laughs, a deep vibrant sound that warms the room. "You got it." He slides off his spectacles and places them on the large, curved beak of a wooden owl figurine. He leans back. "Better?"

I lift my head. The sparkly humor in his blue eyes is restored. My heart is drawn out of hiding. "Much. Now the owl looks like the terrible judge, and you look like the wise grandfather."

"Grandfather! Jeez Louise. I hope not." He runs a hand over his face, chuckling. Then, far more gently, "June. Why are you here today?"

I take a breath. "Oh, Judge Sanders. That is a big *why*. Maybe, impossible."

"Indeed." He studies me for a moment, then turns to his

bookshelves. "So. You love books, do you?"

"More than love. They're my heartbeat."

"All right." He swivels back, decisive. "Let's do it this way. Tell me a story."

"Which one?"

"Yours. If June Taylor's life were a book leading up to this very moment, where she sits in knots before the terrible and ancient judge," he smiles, "where would you begin to tell it?"

"I'm not sure. With a life-changing moment?"

"If you had to pin-point that moment, what would it be?"

"Whew." I push my frizz back, and let my fingers trail down the side of my face, to my earlobe, to my earring. Amethyst, in the shape of a violet.

Our flower.

And I'm seared. So much pain. So much longing. If I breathe, I'll crack.

Do I start there, at two years old, with her in the garden?

No. Not there. I can't.

I undo my earring, hold it in the palm of my hand. It glistens. For a long time, I just look at it. Until a memory surfaces, grows vivid, and insistent.

Okay then. I'll start there.

I take a breath.

And begin, for the first time, to tell the truth about my life.

June 5th, 1995
Hopeton, Arkansas

violets

I'd spent too long in the shower daydreaming, and I knew it.

It had been a wild day at McStop, the truck stop McDonald's where I worked. Three busloads of kids coming back from a zoo trip on the last day of school when the worst had happened. We'd run out of Happy Meal toys. While Janet, my manager, neared the brink of meltdown, I'd gone scavenging in the back and found the box of children's books I'd bought from the Hopeton Library used book sale. I'd been meaning to bring them out to the play area, for the kids like me who might need a comfort book. As I lugged that box up front, Janet looked at me like I'd grown two heads. Well. I was used to that.

And at first, it was true, the kids who got a book instead of a Disney princess pitched a fit. Then, I started talking with them about the books as I rang up their order. I told them that Ramona was my best friend, and Matilda my hero. Paddington had taught me the gift of the "hard stare", which I demonstrated, winning some laughter. The kids with books ended up reading, with fries and shakes, all smushed together in a booth. And eventually, some other kids wandered up to the counter, plunking their Disney princesses down and asking, "Can I get a book?"

Janet actually smiled at me.

It was wonderful to come home, peel off my grease-and-sweat stained uniform, unleash myself from every inch of clothing. The shower on my skin, sweet relief.

Mom was gone grocery shopping and the very walls seemed to exhale. Her mood was precarious again, filling the house with razor sharp edges. When she was home, I stayed on high alert, closely monitoring everything from my tone and facial expression, to how I walked, and how loudly I closed my bedroom door. My sister, Rain, had christened this: The Eggshell Walk. She said it was the art form you mastered when you grew up on an island with a volcano you were afraid to wake up. But right then, Rain and I had the house to ourselves. Along with the water, I felt washed over by this exhilarating feeling of *free*.

And so, I started daydreaming.

About him.

The cowboy.

He hadn't shown up for lunch that day, and I'd found myself looking for him, missing how he'd work his way into my line, no matter how long it was. How he'd make sure to catch my eye, tip his hat. Oh, he was handsome. Tall, tan, and lean. Maybe I had the tiniest crush. Not enough to sin, just enough for some small, secret joy. There were no boys my age at kingdom hall. Besides, nothing would ever come of it. He was just a charming country boy flirt, and I was just a small town McDonald's cashier. Not even a very pretty one. There was no real danger. So, I allowed myself this little dream.

Clint's strong hand slipping round my waist, drawing me close. Closer still, until I couldn't breathe, and my heart beat so hard, it hurt. And so slow, so sweet, we danced...

"JUUUUUNE!"

I threw the soap in the air. It flew over the curtain, landed with a thud on the bathroom floor. Flinging the shower curtain aside, I scrambled out, dripping water all over the floor, collecting the soap, toweling off in a frenzy.

"June!" Rain rapped at the door. "What are you doing in there?"

"Just give me a minute." I wriggled into my cut-offs, threw on my oversized Hamburglar tee. Rain stepped back as I opened the door. She held a spatula in the air. I raised my hands. "Lay your weapon down. I come in peace."

She rolled her eyes, spun on her heel, and walked back toward the kitchen. The house smelled yeasty and rich. "You can't get out of this with a dumb joke."

I scurried after her. "Sorry! Big lunch rush at work."

She still didn't speak, her back to me as she worked at the stove.

I plopped down on a stool at the counter. "Third graders. Whew. I stunk!"

Rain's face hardened. "So you abandoned me."

"I didn't mean – "

She shook her head, hard. "I'm freaking out, trying to get everything perfect before Mom gets home, and you're *luxuriating* in the shower." The frying pan sizzled and popped as she shook it. "You have no idea what I go through. And you don't care."

I slipped off the stool, sidled up beside her, my hands in begging position. "Rain, I'm sorry. I mean it. I am. What can I do to help? Tell me."

“Stop making puddles!” Rain knelt, sopped up the water I’d dripped onto the floor. “Mom will blame me! She’ll get even more pissed.”

I darted back to the bathroom, snatched the towel, wrapped up my hair and ran back. “Here I am.” I saluted. “At your command.”

Rain rolled her eyes. “Whatever. Get the pink plates.”

“Yes, sir!”

“Don’t call me *sir*.”

I flicked the lights on, and caught my breath. The table was set like a five star restaurant, everything perfectly placed, and sparkling. Above, Mom’s beloved dream-catchers swayed, white feathers shining, dancing, more beautiful than any chandelier. I turned to the frosted glass cabinet where Mom kept her cherished collection of antique depression glass. I removed the key, folded into a lace doily in the top drawer, and unlocked the cabinet, gathering four ornate, cherry blossom pink plates. One slipped from my grip, fell to the floor.

“Oh hell!” Rain ran over. She snatched the plate up, examined it, revolving it in her hands. “If she finds a chip, *I’ll* be the one who gets it.”

Pissed. Hell. I supposed it wasn’t the time to mention her cussing habit. I was getting baptized in a month and, except for daydreams, trying very hard to be *no part of the world*. Rain was already baptized, but ever since starting classes at the University of Arkansas, she had grown lax. For now, I held my tongue, and eased the plate from her white-knuckled grip. “I’ll do better. I’ll be delicate and nimble, like a field mouse.” I tip-toed to the table, set each plate down with exaggerated grace. Then, swiveling to Rain, who had returned to cooking, I pushed my hand to my bosom, proclaimed, “Always resignation and acceptance.

Always prudence and honour and duty. Elinor, where is your heart?"

Rain flicked salt into the pan. "Your British accent sucks. Also, would you please quit using Jane Austen against me?"

I laughed, then gazed at her. She was stunning, my sister, with her long, thick curls, now pulled up into a fountain of a ponytail. Sweat beaded her forehead, tiny gems sitting above her lavish eyebrows. She melted my heart. And she didn't realize, I used Jane Austen to draw her closer. I tried again, this time shy, straightening Mom's heritage lace placemats. "*Sense and Sensibility* is out in theaters in a few more months. We're still on to see it together, right?"

Silence. I looked up. Rain was focused, wilting cabbage leaves into a pool of melted butter. But then, the tiniest smile broke through. "I guess. It's not like anyone else will go with you."

"Yes!" I shot my arm in the air. My towel unraveled and fell onto the carpet. I knelt, gathering it up while saying a quick prayer of thanks. Mom and her older sister, Rena, hadn't spoken in years. Sometimes Aunt Rena tried to call, and Mom slammed the phone down. Letters that arrived were quickly dispatched to the trash can, with the aid of scissors. That would not be Rain and me. Not if I could help it.

I returned to the cabinet, retrieved the candlesticks. We only used them on Mom and Dad's wedding anniversary, the one thing we celebrated as Jehovah's Witnesses. I set them beside the vase of fresh wild lavender, straight from Mom's herb garden. I leaned in for a long inhale – anxiety medication, Mom called her lavender – then lit the candles and dimmed the lights. I stood back. Candlelight made pink glistening pools of Mom's plates, and haloed her feathered dreamcatchers.

The slam of a car door jolted me.

Rain scampered to the window, stood on tiptoe. "She's here."

A few seconds later, Mom stepped into the kitchen with grocery bags. Her face was tired, lipstick gone. Still, she was striking. Plump and shapely. Her hair flowing loose, thick and black, down past her hips, so long she often sat on it. Her bangs, which she now flicked from her eyes, showed a new streak of silver. She set the bags down, straightened. Her dark eyes drifted, taking in the kitchen, the dining room, the flickering candles. "What are you girls up to?"

Rain stepped forward. "Mom," she held out the tray, and my heart ached at the sight, the rows of darling little dumplings my sister had so carefully crafted. "I made these for you."

Mom's eyes lowered to the dumplings.

Her face turned to stone.

Lifting her chin, she brushed past Rain.

To me.

"Juney!" she cried, a big smile lighting her up. "I got you something." She dug in the depths of her wrinkly, black purse. "It's a thank you gift for always being so helpful and kind." She withdrew a delicate white box. "Proverbs says, a good heart is *better* than beauty."

My eyes slid to Rain. She was still gripping the tray. Her face, shattered.

Mom said, "Go on, June. Open it."

I took the box, nudged off the lid. Nestled in cotton, a tiny pair of amethyst earrings winked. *Violets.*

"*Our* flower," Mom said.

With a harsh scrape and clatter, Rain dropped her tray onto the stovetop.

I struggled, alone with triangles, at my desk.

Erase, crumple, repeat. Over and over.

I gave up, shoving my geometry textbook away. I'd dropped out in 9th grade, two years before, when we'd moved from Wisconsin to Arkansas. I'd wanted to free myself from public school to focus on spiritual pursuits, preaching Jehovah's kingdom door to door, with my heart set on baptism. Dad had promised to help me with homeschool classes. He'd even bought a blackboard. It was dusty now, but not with chalk. It leaned, untouched, against the dining room wall. Dad had struggles of his own and lately, they took all his time.

We'd moved so he could take over a chiropractic clinic, Good Spine, run by a Jehovah's Witness brother who was retiring. But Dad was having a hard time attracting new clients. Or, as he liked to tease, he was having a hard time "adjusting". At first, the chiropractor joke had been funny. That was before we started running low on money.

Needing a lift, I reached for my butterfly planner with gold-trimmed pages, flipped to the big date.

July 15th, 1995 - Baptism!!!!!

One more month.

After baptism, I would apply to Gilead School for Jehovah's Witnesses in New York, where I'd train for a missionary assignment. Actually, this was something Rain and I had dreamed for years we'd do together. We would fantasize about the places we wanted to travel to as missionaries, and why. The Seychelle Islands, I said, for the giant coconut crabs. Paris, she'd said, for the fresh baguettes, the art, the everything. Then she'd changed her mind, choosing college over missionary work. Yet she still liked to claim that *I* was the one who abandoned *her*! My chest hurt, picturing her face as I took the present mom offered. Shaking the image away, I pulled my English homework toward me. I didn't need help with English. The teacher in Chicago had written instructions. *Write a poem, any length or style, about your most meaningful memory.*

As I sat there thinking, my hand went to my ear, found my new earring. I spread open my notebook, leaned in, and the words spilled out.

I am two years old. Mom dresses me in a lacy pink sundress and matching bonnet. She takes my hand, and we go outside for a walk. We sit in her garden in the sunshine. She picks two violets. One for her, one for me. She lifts her violet to her nose, closes her eyes, and breathes deep. I do the same. She brings her violet to her mouth, nibbles the petals. She is eating the violet!

And I awaken.

Alive to my own heartbeat, my own life, this woman. My mother is a goddess, her long hair black fire in the morning light. I nibble my violet, and giggle. We are laughing together. This goddess has given me life. She has awakened me to the world

in the most astonishing
and beautiful
way.

My door pushed open and Rain peered in. "Hey."

I moved my hand over my poem. "I'm studying!"

"Want a tetherball break?"

I checked her face. "Really?"

"Yeah. Come on." She stepped backward, waved for me to follow. "Let's play."

I jumped up, and together we tore outside, racing each other and whooping. Childhood came back, through the silky green grass, and the sunset, bright peach feathered with pink, making us glow. As kids, Rain and I had bickered endlessly. One evening, Dad put up a tetherball pole for us, within the cooling balsam firs of our Wisconsin backyard. We'd crouched, tattooing the wet concrete with a stick, christening our sacred ground. *Rain, 12. June, 9.*

Then we'd played for hours. The Elders told us not to join school sports teams. Doing so would take away from Jehovah. So Rain and I made our very own tetherball team. Except for meeting nights, we met faithfully after school in our tees and cut-offs. We named ourselves *Tetherball Warriors*. We played against each other, but really, with each other.

Now, June, sixteen, and Rain, nineteen, faced off on the circle of dirt round our Arkansas tetherball pole. Rain tightened her ponytail, rolled her sleeves over her shoulders, and grabbed the yellow nylon ball. Her fingers dug in. "Ready?"

"Ready!" I clapped my hands.

Her smile...like an animal baring its teeth.

My blood turned to icicles.

Rain tilted back on one leg, then smashed the ball. "Rawwwwrrrrr!"

I ducked just in time. The ball grazed the top of my hair. *Whoosh!*

Boom! Bash! Smack! My sister's fists struck that ball like a lightning storm.

I grit my teeth, fighting back, arms flailing in a cartoon blur. The ball zoomed at my face. I smacked it away with the fleshy inside of my wrist. “Ahhh!” I cried. We both knew, that was the worst place to take a hit. Usually we’d stop the game to recover. I staggered backward, doubled over.

The game didn’t stop.

Rain grabbed the ball and rushed me.

I looked up. Our eyes touched, held.

“Why...” Was all I could get out.

She flung the ball at my face. *Smack!*

I fell to my knees. Dirt rose in a puff around me.

Standing over me, Rain laughed. *She laughed.*

Adrenaline drove me to my feet. I screamed in her face. “You bitch!”

I went dead still. Never in my life had I cussed.

For a moment, Rain was stunned, too, her mouth open. Then she pressed her lips together. Balled her fists. The hairs on the back of my neck rose.

She lunged, and we crashed to the ground.

We rolled like animals on the grass, twisting, pinching, pulling hair. She went for my ears. She slapped them, relentless. The posts of my new earrings stabbed me, again and again, in the tender bone right behind the ear. “Stop! Stop it!” I shrieked, trying to wriggle free.

She straddled me, pinned my shoulders to the ground. She pushed her face into mine. Her eyes twitched. “You’re the bitch!” Her hot breath smelled like the cooked cabbage in her dumplings. She drove the words down, a fiery stake into the center of my heart. “Ugly bitch. You know that? You’re ugly. Frizzy hair,” she yanked it, “big nose,” grabbing and twisting.

I started to cry.

"Wah! Wah! Run to Mommy!" She shook my shoulders so hard my teeth knocked. "Mommy's little brat." She shoved me away, looked up at the sky. Screwed her eyes shut. "Nothing. No matter what I do. *Nothing* makes her love me." Her face split in two, and a cry, a deep guttural howl, worked its way up from her center, trembling at her throat, unleashing into the gathering dark.

One of my sister's tears dropped onto my cheek.

That single tear. More sharp, more exquisitely painful, than any punch could ever be.

I held very still.

I let her tears drop onto my face like punishment, like shame.

kingdom hall

The next night, when we piled in the car together for meeting at Creekwood Kingdom Hall, our fragrances mingled. Mom's lavender oil, my strawberry lotion, Dad's spicy vanilla aftershave, and Rain's peach-rose body spray, harmonious as a garden, one that I cherished.

That night though, Rain dropped her book-bag on the floor of the car with a thud. She jerked her seatbelt across her so it sliced the air, then adjusted the strappy red sundress mom hated so that it showed a little more of her shocking cleavage. Then she scooted as far from me as she could, pressing herself against the car door.

I closed my eyes. This was how it went when Rain got mad. She stopped speaking to me. She stalked out of the room when I came in. She slammed doors in my face. She left. In small ways, again and again.

Mom in the passenger seat, her voluminous black hair pinned into an elaborately braided up-do, turned over her shoulder. Eyes on Rain, her lips thinned. "You know I don't like that dress. You want the Brothers having dirty thoughts about you? You want to get yourself disfellowshipped? Shame us all? Cover up."

Rain crossed her arms over her chest.

"You know what I mean, missy. Don't play games with me."

Rain threw open the car door and flung herself out. She stalked to the house, curls flying a flag of defiance behind her.

Mom said through clenched teeth, "Ever since she started college that attitude is ten thousand times worse. And the way she dresses! It's like she's *trying* to humiliate me."

Dad set his hand on Mom's knee. "Remember what we talked about?"

Mom sniffled, let out a whimper. "I'm trying, Phil. I swear I am. But I don't know how much more I can take with her."

"Breathe, Abequa. Stay calm. Every time you let her push your buttons, you let her steal your peace."

Mom took a deep, shivering inhale. Once, then twice, and another time, as Dad coached her. Then she turned, studied me over her shoulder. "Don't think I don't know what she does to *you*, June. I know. I see." Her eyes narrowed at the bandage across my cheek. She shook her head with disgust. I'd told her I'd gone for a walk in the forest and gotten scratched by a thorn tree. Clearly, I didn't have her fooled. "Don't let her corrupt you and steal your sweet spirit. You hear me?"

I nodded, a strange feeling in my throat, like it had been numbed.

Rain stomped back to the car. She'd thrown on a cardigan, something pulled from the dredges of the dirty clothes it looked like, wrinkled, threadbare, and stained. Another slap in the face for Mom, who liked us to be neat and put together. Rain slid into the backseat, slammed the door and when I tried smiling at her, she twisted away from me, her back emitting wave upon wave of flaming retribution.

***

We attended five religious meetings each week, and the Theocratic Ministry School was my favorite. The whole congregation, small children and elderly alike, honed our public speaking and preaching skills, giving talks and acting out skits.

This was our training ground to follow Jesus' command: *Go forth and make disciples!*

At age five, I'd taken my first door in the preaching work. Wearing a frilly dress and shiny black Mary Jane shoes, I'd rapped on the door of an apartment. Dad had stood behind, letting me do the work. A man had swung open the door. Sleepy in flannel pajamas, hair sticking up, his bleary eyes had flown open at the sight of the little girl in pigtails, holding a Bible. I'd launched into my heartfelt spiel. *Jehovah God promises to return the earth to a perfect Paradise where no one will ever have to suffer or die!* At that, the man had slammed the door on me with such force, my dress flew up over my head. I'd burst into tears. Dad had taken me to a donut shop and bought me a strawberry one with sprinkles. On a napkin, he had drawn a skull with flames fanning out from the top. He'd slid it toward me. *This is how you have to see people like that man. Already destroyed at Armageddon.*

Dad was my role model. He kept knocking on doors no matter how many slammed in his face. He was a respected Ministerial Servant in our congregation, and well on his way to becoming an Elder.

That night, he was the one delivering the talk.

Dressed in his best suit, navy blue, neatly pressed and paired with a silky, gray-striped tie, he strode up to the stage. Standing tall behind the podium, he adjusted the microphone with a resonant crackling. The eyes of the congregation were glued to him before he spoke a single word. With his dark hair and sideburns, black, bushy eyebrows and strong, square face, my father cut a striking figure. The moment he launched in, everyone leaned forward in their seats.

"Guard Against Independent Thinking!" He thundered, holding one finger in the air. "When you question Jehovah's

Organization, you question Jehovah God! When you question the beliefs set forth in The Watchtower, you set yourself *against* God. Beware, brothers and sisters. Higher education is brainwashing our youth. In college classrooms, their minds are being eroded by the Devil's gospel. It goes like this: *Think for yourself. Be open-minded. There is no truth. Question everything.* This is the sin of Independent Thinking, brothers and sisters. This is how it seeps in. The process is slow, insidious – one doubt, one question...what's the harm? And yet, before we know it, we are knee-deep in the rubble of what was once our precious faith." Dad paused, let that sink in.

I looked around at the brothers and sisters. They nodded, solemn, soaking up his words.

Then I snuck a glance at Rain. Her mouth was twisted, eyes cast down. Spots of pink rose up in her cheeks. She'd just finished her first semester at The University of Arkansas after secretly taking the SAT's and applying. Against Dad's warnings. Against our Elder's advice. She glanced sideways, caught me looking at her. She bugged her eyes out at me, then leaned away, as far as she could without toppling over into the aisle.

After Dad's talk, his exhortation to *choose Jehovah and reject higher education!* ringing in everyone's ears, Rain grabbed her book-bag and shot to her feet. She stalked down the aisle, shoved out the door. The collective gaze of the congregation pinned to us. I could feel their eyes burning into the back of my head. Mom could feel it, too. She sat rigid in her favorite silky black blouse that matched her hair. Her red lipstick, immaculate, the beauty mark on her chin darkened with an eyebrow pencil. The smile on her lips, like brittle ice about to crack. After the final prayer, as soon as the brothers and sisters dispersed into fellowship, talking, laughing, shaking hands around us, she hissed into my ear, "Just wait until I get my hands on that witch."

Hot acid boiled up my throat, and pain seared my chest. Rain knew Mom hated having attention drawn to us, especially when it might stir up gossip. The worst sin against Mom was public display of a snit.

"And look, it gets even better," Mom said. "Here comes Jezebel."

Sister Jansen, a recent transplant from Miami, had electrified our quiet, stodgy congregation with her big, bleach blonde hair and fake tan. Not to mention how brazenly she violated the Bible's command to sisters – dress with modesty. She strutted our way in a low-cut blouse, her boobs jouncing like giant water balloons. Mom sat up straighter and forced a smile. But Sister Jansen wasn't coming to talk to us.

"Brother Taylor!" She bee-lined straight to Dad, poking his shoulder. "Now you, sir, why, I just have to fuss over you! Your talks are just so smart. So full of passion. You *inspire* me."

Dad grinned, looking both pleased and bashful. "Well, I appreciate that, sister."

"You know I have a touch of ADHD and I get bored so easy. But when *you* give a talk, Brother Taylor, you really hold my attention." She touched Dad's elbow. "I heard you're a chiropractor. Is that the truth? I might make an appointment with you. My back really needs some attention." She arched, hands on hips, water balloons pushed heavenward.

"Any time, sister." Dad's voice cracked, and he adjusted his tie.

Sister Jansen's gaze then slid to Mom. She smiled, nodded, but her face looked smug, like she'd won something. Mom stood and reaching for my hand, she yanked me to my feet. "Let's go, June."

"Where?" as she pulled me down the aisle, my hand in a death grip.

"Bathroom!"

I broke into a sweat that drenched the armpits of my flowered sailor dress. I should get Mom out of here. But where? Not in the car. Not with Rain!

At McStop, I knew what to do about messes, really bad ones like ketchup explosions and vomit. There, I grabbed a bucket and a mop and went to work. This though. How did I fix *this?*

Sister Finn reached out as we passed. Grabbing onto my arm, she forced me to halt. "Sister June! I've been wanting to ask you all night. What on earth happened to your face?"

Mom turned, stared at me over her shoulder. *Well?* Her eyes asked, sparking and defiant. *Sister Finn or me?* In the middle of everything else, a loyalty test. Before I had a chance to process, she wrenched her hand from mine and stormed off to the bathroom alone. I stood, torn asunder, split between two women like Solomon's baby.

Sister Finn went ahead and pulled me into the seat next to her. She took both my hands in hers. "Oh honey, your hands are ice cold." She rubbed my hands between her own. The warmth from her hands flowed straight to my heart. Sister Finn had four grown sons and according to Mom, she'd always wanted a daughter. I loved Sister Finn ardently. I loved the sunset of her red hair and her round apple cheeks. I loved her unhinged laughter. I loved, most of all, how she looked at me. "So. What's with the bandage, hm?" She peered at my face, lifting a brow.

I touched my cheek. "Oh. Me and Rain. We play tetherball. We get – kinda rowdy sometimes."

Nearby, a group of brothers erupted in laughter. Dad was at the center, holding court. They slapped Dad's back so hard, he was the one going to need a chiropractor. My spirit was provoked, watching him bask in the attention, totally oblivious to the mess.

"Tetherball! Aw, you and your sister. What a sweet relationship." She looked at me for a long moment, then squeezed my hands. "Are you excited about your baptism?"

I broke into a smile. "So excited. Only a month to go! I've got a brand new bathing suit. It's so cute."

"*You're* so cute." Sister Finn tweaked my nose. "You've worked hard for this." To get approved for baptism, I'd had to answer eighty Bible questions before a panel of Elders. I'd made flashcards, and Sister Finn had helped me study. "You planning anything special to celebrate?"

"Mom said I could have a pizza party after the baptism. Can you come?"

"Of course I can!" She beamed. "Is it a big gathering?"

"Oh, um, no." My smile faltered. "Just you."

She tilted her head. "Dear June. How I wish you could find yourself a friend. It's a shame. Such sweet, pretty girls like you and Rain, stuck in a congregation with a bunch of old folks like us." She studied me. "You know, sweetie, my offer still stands. If your mom and dad are too busy, I will gladly take you to Witness Skate Night. You can meet young people from other congregations. Who knows, you might even meet one of those 'kindred spirits' you talk about."

I smoothed my dress. "Thank you, but I don't want to put you out. Fayetteville's a bit of a drive." Mom did not like for us to take favors. She said once you did, people felt owed. From then on, that's how they treated you. I didn't want to risk losing Sister Finn's kindness.

"Only thirty minutes, my dear. A hop, skip, and a jump.

I would be happy to come and get you. Don't you know? Spending time with you is such a pleasure."

"Really?"

Sister Finn tucked a strand of frizz behind my ear. "Yes," she said. "Really," holding my eyes.

Mom emerged from the bathroom. She stood at a distance, watching us with her arms folded. I could see from here she'd been crying. I gave Sister Finn a quick, hard hug. "Thank you." I jumped up, rushed to Mom's side. She grabbed my elbow and steered me right out the door. My abdomen braced, tight as a fortress. I was in for it.

Miraculously, in the car, Mom winked at *both* Rain and I over her shoulder as she tugged on her seatbelt. "Guess what, girls? You will never guess. Jezebel Jansen can't get enough of your Dad. She's so – *inspired* – by him." She barked a laugh, then muttered, "She's not the one who has to clean his dirty underwear."

Dad winced, face turning a deep shade of red as he started the car.

Rain and I hooked eyes.

She grimaced. I grimaced.

She sunk low in her seat. I sunk low in mine.

We scooted close. Our knees touched.

Just like that, we were friends again.

mistake

Mom doled out one of her worst punishments: a week of the silent treatment for Dad.

He would call from work and Mom would smash the phone down, the sound reverberating through the house. Mom would cook dinner, talking and laughing with me and Rain, her face going blank as a dead woman's as soon as Dad walked in the door. Again and again throughout that agonizing week, I watched hope die on his face as she turned her back to him, slamming their bedroom door. He didn't look like a powerful man, crisp and formidable in a suit, on his way to becoming an Elder. He looked like a lost little boy.

The silent treatment was nearly as terrible to witness, as to endure.

Rain, Dad, and I ate at the dinner table and, aside from Dad's prayer, offered in a broken voice, no one spoke. Rain spread open her calculus textbook and worked out equations, pencil scritch-scratching across paper. I read *Wuthering Heights,* venting about Heathcliff in the pages of my English literature journal. I wrote that Heathcliff was not a hero, he was a bully, and all I wanted was for Catherine to sprint like an Olympic athlete, far and fast across those moors. While writing, I kept one eye on Dad. His elbow planted on the table, his forehead pushed into his palm, he forked food into his mouth mechanically.

One morning, at the end of that long week, Rain was bedridden with a bad cold. I tip-toed into the kitchen to make her some tea, and spied the bouquet left on the stovetop. Dad had picked them himself, I could tell. A rambunctious collection of goldenrod, Queen Anne's lace, blue sage with bent stems, and bugs still attached. I could almost see Dad, hopping a fence on his morning walk, wading through the weeds. My eyes caught movement. A tiny green inchworm had fallen from the flowers, onto a pink envelope where Dad had written Mom's name, framed by a heart. The little worm looped straight through the heart. It raised up, looking around, searching. It had a desperate, frantic air. The sound of honking startled me. Dad, on his way to work. Normally, Mom stood at the door in her robe, with her coffee, waving him down the road, blowing kisses.

Once again, Mom was a no-show.

Still, he honked. On and on.

I couldn't bear it. The little, searching worm. Dad, honking at a closed door.

I picked up the envelope and carried it, carefully, down the hall, out the door, onto the porch. Too late to wave to Dad, though it wasn't me he wanted to see, I held the card to a big leaf on one of Mom's potted plants, and gave the worm a tiny nudge. He got a foothold on the leaf and took off in tall arcs of joyful abandon. I watched for a while, hands tucked between my knees. How did something so small and tender even make it a day in this world?

A few minutes later, Mom appeared.

She unlocked the bedroom door and swept airily out, chin in the air. Her long black hair was neatly braided, the silver streak in her bangs curved and shining like a bird's wing. She wore red lipstick, her dark eyes dramatically outlined with liquid liner. This was a good sign. Sometimes that's how she came around, with a new haircut, outfit, or a makeover.

She grabbed her herb basket from the kitchen, called to us.

"Come with me, girls! Let's walk in the fresh air and sunshine. Let's soak up the beauty of the morning together." Rain shuffled out of her room, looking pale in her sweatpants and tee, coughing a little into her fist. Mom hooked our arms with hers, squeezing us to her like her best girlfriends. "We'll gather thyme for that cough," she said to Rain, who smiled.

This was a big perk of getting sick – Mom's caretaking.

Outside, we meandered the dirt path of her beloved herb garden. Mom had poured her heart into it and she had created something special, both carefree and calming, with winding paths, wooden benches, whirligigs and colorful ceramic birdbaths. The mint leaned in, tickled our elbows. Rosemary flirted with our bare feet. Bees zipped in and out of the sage. The earth exhaled cool sweetness.

"Girls, look, look at the light!" Mom stopped, and Rain and I followed where her finger pointed, to stripes of sunlight frisking on wide green leaves. I loved the way she saw the overlooked beauties of the world. Interesting light, funny clouds, strange bugs, her face wearing the kind of awe others wore before the big and showy. The way she made us stop. *Feel* the grandness of a small delight, right along with her.

Grits dashed in. She danced around us, yellow fur turning gold in the soft seep of morning sun. She leapt, knocked me right down, clambering all over me and licking my face with ardor. "Grits!" I laughed and laughed. *This dog!* She was the neighbor's dog, not mine. Yet she was my magic. The way she made my joy appear out of nowhere.

"Breathe in, girls!" Mom closed her eyes and inhaled. "Breathe with me, Rain," giving my sister's arm a coaxing shake. "A garden in early summer is nature's medicine cabinet."

I stood, brushing dirt off my bottom.

"June, no. Your shorts."

Mom's voice, the downward lilt, the sudden tightness, made my gut clench. I twisted around, trying to look.

"You leaked again. How many times have I told you? You need to change more often."

"Oops." Shame burned inside me. I hadn't told her yet. I didn't know how. My period had grown too heavy for the thin pads she'd given me when I first started. She'd been flustered, upset, when I'd come to her, biting my lip as I showed her the rusty stains on my underwear. I didn't want to bring it up again, or burden her more, so I'd taken to wearing two or three pads at once, stuffing toilet paper and paper towel down there. Trying to spare a mess, I'd made a bigger one. "I'm sorry," I told her now. "I'll do better."

She softened. "Soak your shorts in hot water and use the stain stick. Hopefully, it'll come out in the wash. Now that your father's business is failing," she added with bite, "we can't afford to throw clothes away."

Rain broke down coughing into her fist. Mom withdrew a sprig of thyme from her herb basket, crushed it between her fingers. She held it under Rain's nose. "Breathe."

The crunch of wheels on gravel made us all stiffen like we'd been struck between the shoulder blades by an arrow. Grits danced in circles, barking with glee – *Visitor! Visitor!* Carefully, Mom parted the marjoram. Her face darkened. "Why is *she* here?" Rain and I peered over Mom's shoulders. A glossy red minivan made its way slowly down our steep driveway. *Sister Finn!* I wanted to dance like Grits.

Mom felt otherwise.

"Hurry, girls, go, *go*!" Mom hustled us down the narrow garden path. She pressed her hands into our backs. We scooted faster, scaring up a cardinal from his bath, a flash of red wings and shining water droplets. I didn't understand why we were fleeing. But Mom wanted us to go, so we went. As we darted onto the porch, Grits raced the opposite direction, eager to greet our guest.

We scrambled into the house. Mom flicked off the lights. Together, we huddled in the hallway. High-heels clicked down the sidewalk, far off sharp points of sound getting closer. "Hi, doggie! Aw, sweet doggie! Beautiful one!" Sister Finn's sing-song voice. Grit's bark grew more high-pitched, getting love from this kind stranger.

"Damn dumb dog," Mom muttered.

Rain and I exchanged glances.

Click click click. Sister Finn, ascending the porch. The clatter of Grit's toenails on concrete. The doorbell, too sharp, too bright. "Hellooooooo! Anyone home?" A pause. And then, "June? You there, sweetie? I have something for you!"

Mom eyed me over her shoulder. I cringed.

One final door-bell jab, and then, high-heel taps fading away.

The symphony of leaving – car door slamming, engine starting, and the slow crunch of wheels up the gravel driveway – signaled that we were free.

Mom slumped with relief.

And then, the fatal error.

A giggle escaped me.

Mom turned with a glare. "What's so funny?"

"Sorry, it's just, everyone hides from Jehovah's Witnesses. Even us. We're Witnesses hiding from Witnesses!" I pressed my hand to my mouth, stifling another giggle.

Rain sucked in her bottom lip, averted her eyes.

"Oh yeah?" Mom stepped closer. Shoving her face into mine, she wagged her head and spat, "Laugh, clown, laugh!"

She threw her garden basket down between us, and the herbs sprung out.

Then she swiveled and stomped down the hall, braid bouncing on her back.

"Mom!" I chased after her. "I'm sorry! *Mom...*"

She slammed her bedroom door in my face.

So hard, I could feel the vibrations in my throat.

I stared at the door, touched my hand to my neck, and swallowed.

In the shadows, Rain pointed at me and mouthed *ha-ha-ha.*

daydreams and birthdays

Hopeton, Arkansas, population 800, was home to two sprawling truck-stops that seemed bigger than the town itself. Locals referred to the McDonald's where I worked as McStop, since it sat next to Love's Travel Plaza, and was frequented by truck drivers and tourists.

I hadn't learned how to drive yet, so I usually walked the mile there. On my right, fat belted cattle grazed in lush, green pastures. We called them 'Oreo cows' because of their broad white middles flanked by black bands. On my left, cars raced along the interstate. And in my hands, a glorious, old, perfectly tattered book of George Bernard Shaw poems fell open to "Oh the Dreaming". This was the gift Sister Finn had left for me, deposited in a shiny green bag on our welcome mat.

Lately, because of Sister Finn's Irish ancestry and the pictures, songs, and stories she'd shared, I'd fallen head over heels for Ireland. My new favorite daydream was to imagine that's where I *actually* lived.

Now, my sturdy work shoes crunching along the gravel shoulder, I imagined myself out for a saunter in the Irish countryside, laced with mist. I wore a long country dress and an apron, sprigs of wild purple heather blooming from the pockets. The moo-ing of the Oreo cows took on the quality of melancholy song. I walked, reciting out loud: *Oh the dreaming! The dreaming! The torturing, heart-scalding, never satisfying dreaming, dreaming...*

WAAAAAAAHHHHHH!

The blast of an air horn from an 18-wheeler roaring past

broke the dreaming.

I leapt into the muddy ditch and crouched in the weeds, legs shaking, heat creeping into my cheeks. The Oreo cows gathered at the fence line to stare at me, chewing on grass, like they were at the movies.

I was dumb today. So dumb! First, leaking on my shorts. And then *Witnesses hiding from Witnesses.* Why did I say that?

I swallowed again and again. I couldn't stop the swallowing.

Or the heartburn, searing my sternum.

I stood, then darted across a small, muddy patch of field toward the travel plaza, chrome-glinting trucks pulling in and out, talking to each other in little huffs and squeals. Up above, the McDonald's golden arches, the way they shone, pointing the way like my own personal lighthouse. I remembered, with relief, today I had tray duty. It was dark and calm at the cavernous sink behind the kitchen. I needed that. I'd get to wear a black rubber apron while spray-washing dirty trays. To me, there were few things as comforting or thrilling as watching big, sticky ketchup splats blossom, then disintegrate under the sharp burst of water.

In the soothing drizzle created by the spray, I'd close my eyes and return to Ireland. This time, I'd run to The Cliffs of Moher, open my arms wide, dance in the rain in my bare feet. One of my happiest daydreams.

But when I stepped into the restaurant, I walked right into the middle of my least favorite song.

Happy Birthday to you! Happy Birthday to you! Happy Birthday, dear Beckyyyyyy...!

I froze right there at the entrance.

My co-workers were gathered in the otherwise empty dining area. They clapped, hooted, and boot-stomp boogied in a druidic cowboy circle around the birthday girl.

Becky the pirate-y cook had scared me from day one. Like a pirate, she was blunt, crude, and unpredictable. Equally disconcerting was her bristly chin, scarred up face, and, if you made her mad, dentures she'd pop out at you, startling as a switchblade. My first day, she'd christened me Little Daydreamer, and ever since, she didn't miss a chance to yell it at me, while smashing a pan down on the grill.

At the moment, she was happier than I'd ever seen her, batting her eyelashes and beaming. Everyone quieted as she leaned in over a platter of pink-frosted cupcakes, candle flames dancing. She closed her eyes, puffed out her cheeks, and blew so hard – she farted!

First, a stunned pause. Next, an eruption of laughter. The riotous kind, my co-workers doubling over, smacking each other's backs, hee-hawing up one side and down the other. A perfect demonstration of why birthdays were evil, hedonistic revelries resulting in heads served up on platters. (Mark 6:14-29, detailing King Herod's murderous birthday party, always brought me to tears, as I harbored a secret Bible crush on John the Baptist.)

I tried my best to slink unnoticed to the back, but Janet caught me by the arm. "June! Where do you think you're going? Get yer little butt to the party!"

My co-workers all swiveled at once. They motioned me over. "Come on, June, come celebrate! Becky's turning the big 5-0! Today we can officially call her Gassy Grandma!" Any other day, Becky would've snarled, shot out her dentures. Today, she threw her head back and hooted. Then, she turned an actual smile on me. She looked so pleased and almost cute – in the way of a bulldog with a bow in its hair.

I wanted to run.

"Here, June," Janet said with a wink, holding out a cupcake. "This one's got your name on it." And oh Jehovah, it really did! A beautiful golden puff of cupcake with a delicate smear of pink frosting and *June* spelled across the top in bright beads of candy.

I didn't move or speak. The stares sharpened.

I was back in elementary school, facing the birthday firing squad.

First grade. I held out my palm to signal a powerful *no!* to the cupcake. "I am one of Jehovah's Witnesses," I'd said, lifting my chin. "Birthdays are pagan. I don't celebrate them." Bobby Danver's freckled face crumpling. His mother's eyes shooting fiery darts into mine. This was my version of Shadrach, Meshach, and Abednego. The cupcake was the false god. Rather than bow down, I chose the furnace. In that case, the furnace was sitting alone in the corner of the classroom, reading *Ramona Quimby, Age 8*, while the other kids belted out the birthday song, holding hands with our teacher in a big, rollicking group. I'd admit to peering wistfully, just once, over the top of my book. I was tempted by belonging, far more than cupcakes.

I'd been working at McStop for five months and still hadn't told my co-workers that I was Jehovah's Witness. Telling people always changed everything, but here, I was truly scared to reveal my faith. Arkansas was a buzzing hornet's nest of false prophets and pharisees. On doorsteps, Pentecostals tried laying hands on my head while praying gibberish. Mom believed Pentecostals were demon possessed.

Janet peered at me, forehead scrunched. "What's the matter, June? You've got no color."

"Well, I..."

"BUS!" Mikey, the drive-through guy, gestured wildly toward the parking lot.

In seconds, everyone was on their feet, yelling orders, scrambling to their places. Janet patted my back as she hurried by. "Never mind. I'll put your cupcake in the fridge, June."

I'd never been so thankful for a tour bus jam-packed with cranky old folks in western wear on their way to Branson, Missouri.

With only me and the new girl, Maggie, working register, my adrenaline kicked in. Soon I was in the flow, smiling, greeting, slapping down red trays one after another *smack! smack! smack!* Tapping in complicated orders—no tomato, extra cheese, hold the mayo, add bacon. Switching out Happy Meal toys for the ladies who wanted Cinderella-not-Pocahontas.

In these parts, people did not like Pocahontas. With unwanted Pocahontas' piling up, the managers had finally called a meeting and warned us not to switch out toys anymore. I still did it if the customers got too vicious. The old ladies sometimes got in my face, yelling, "I don't want this one! *I don't want her!*" throwing Pocahontas on the countertop. I guess they had no way of knowing I was a quarter Chippewa. Their words were like little lightning strikes burning right through me. The Pocahontas' hurt me every time I walked by them, discarded in a cardboard box. I wanted to gather them up, take them all home, love them and keep them safe. Their long, luxurious black hair reminded me of Mom's.

Mom.

I started swallowing again, compulsively. I got dizzy, then sweaty, my stomach churning. I dug the heels of my hands into the countertop, slowly drew in a breath.

A second tour bus enroute to Branson rolled in. Soon, two long lines snaked out the doors into the parking lot. At times like this, I was grateful for my surplus of adrenaline.

I rushed back and forth between my register and Maggie's, trying to help her. Tufty gray-haired men in Andy William's Moon River Theater T-shirts groaned with complaint, like old wood floors. At the same time, I expertly filled up and capped drinks with that soul-satisfying lid crinkle, shoveled fries into cartons, and handed them to customers like golden, greasy bouquets.

One by one, customers scooted from Maggie's tortoise line to my cheetah line. Satisfaction cards were filled out with a flourish, and winks. "This June girl is top-notch!" One of the ladies in a pink sequin Dolly Parton ball cap cried out, lifting my arm, champ-like. "Give her a raise!"

I felt bright and shiny. Precious, like gold.

Finally, we got them all fed, and they filed out to board their buses, rubbing their bellies and cracking jokes, festive moods restored. I fell back against the counter, plucked off my visor, and wiped my sweaty hairline with the back of my arm. "How are you?" I checked in with Maggie, who was slumped against her register.

She pushed her head into her hands, her braids frayed. "Oh, Lord, June! How do you do it? That was a *nightmare*."

I'd seen too many fragile newbies quit after their first bus group. I'd almost been one of them. I leaned into her. "If you stick it out, I promise it'll get better."

Janet swooshed out from the kitchen and shocked me, pulling me into a big, warm hug. She was a manager, not a hugger. "I had my doubts about you, June," she said. "We all did at first. But you've surprised us." She took hold of my shoulders and looked me right in the eye, beaming. "You're a real McDonald's girl."

I couldn't breathe. "Thank you, Janet." I hunted out a dish rag, dipped it in a bucket of fresh, soapy water, and began scrubbing the countertop to keep from flying to pieces.

"Maggie," Janet said, "keep watching June. She'll show you how it's done."

It was too much. My toes scrunched inside my nonslip restaurant work shoes. *A real McDonald's girl!* I scrubbed and scrubbed at the countertop, smiling, blinking back tears.

That's when he snuck up on me. "Howdy, June."

I jerked my head up. He rocked back on his heels, thumbs wedged in the pockets of his Wranglers, and grinned.

"Oh, hi, hello! Clint." My words, rocky ground I stumbled over. I wrung the dish rag between my hands, dropped my eyes. I didn't even like Clint! I mean, I didn't trust him. The way he got in my line, on purpose. Even when there were five people in my line and two in the other. And when the other cashier motioned him over, he'd shake his head and smile, making a point of planting his boots in place. The way he'd catch my eye and wink. Who did he think he was? Willoughby from *Sense and Sensibility* came to mind. A charmer. A cad.

Only Clint was full-blown Arkansas – dirty camouflage ballcap, ostrich skin cowboy boots, rusty blue pickup truck.

I raised my eyes and studied Clint as he studied the menu. His arms, tan and strong, every muscle a poem, his bulky shoulders and chest flowing into a long, narrow waist – and a butt that made blue jeans something breath-taking, glorious.

I said in a rush, "You know what you want?"

"Yes, ma'am, I sure do." He lowered his deep brown eyes, looked right at me.

A wildfire started in my neck. "I'm ready when you are." He smiled, and the wildfire spread to my face, cheeks throbbing with heat.

"Can I get a quarter pounder, no onion, extra pickle, and a large Coke to go?"

"You can. Of course!" I tap-tapped the register, grateful for a task.

And then, leaning in, Clint rested his elbows on the countertop. "How are you, Miss June? You happy?" It was a strangely intimate question, one he asked every time. Another reason not to trust him. He dug his faded leather wallet embossed with a saddle from the back pocket of his jeans. He flipped a five dollar bill onto the counter. I grabbed it, hating how my hand shook. My voice, my face, and even my hands – all betrayers!

"Oh, I'm good. I'm fine. Busy. Very busy." I swiveled to make his drink. Closing my eyes, I took a deep breath.

"You happy?" Clint pressed.

I gripped the cold, silver scoop and plunged it into the ice. The ice cubes rattled into the plastic cup. I jabbed the button of the soda machine and Coke whooshed out. The whole process of making a drink was so wonderfully loud, you could pretend not to hear anything. This was a great perk when serving lonely, loquacious truck drivers. Or a bold cowboy.

"'Cuz, you know," he said, "I always get happy when I come in and see you here, that sweet little smile you got, all them pretty curls." I set his drink down on the counter and he dipped his head, trying to find my eyes. "I bet you hear that all the time, don't you?"

"Oh, thank you, no, I don't." I took two quick steps backwards, yanked my visor down. Usually I abhorred my blue mustard-stained visor, but right now, I loved it. My hiding place.

"So, uh," he picked a piece of straw from his black t-shirt. "There's something I been meaning to ask you. I been wondering if..."

I shrieked, "You got that burger, Becky!"

Clint jumped, brown eyes going wide.

"Quarter pounder, no onion, extra pickle!" Becky yelled back. I scurried to the warming bin. Becky crouched, peering at Clint through the metal slats. "Grrrrrrr," she growled. "Bet *he's* got extra pickle."

Pretending not to hear, I plucked up the burger, warm and greasy, popped open a bag and arranged the food inside it with gravely exaggerated TLC. Then I folded the bag neatly once, twice, three times before delivering it to Clint.

"I love how you take your job so serious," he said, ensuring our fingers met as he took the bag. "I guess that's why everyone likes to get in your line. 'Specially the guys." His fingers lingered on mine. "Does your boyfriend ever get jealous?"

I coughed, gently sliding my hand from under his. "I don't have a boyfriend." It was time and past time to announce that I was one of Jehovah's Witnesses. *That* would get rid of him. It got rid of everyone! But I stayed quiet, compressing my lips.

"No boyfriend?" He straightened and laughed, a silly, boyish laugh, bordering dangerously on a whoop. "You know what, girl? You just made my day." He took off his dirty camo ball-cap, pressed it to his chest, and gave a little bow. "See you tomorrow, Miss June."

He swaggered out of the restaurant.

My eyes weren't the only ones glued to him as he left.

Maggie sidled up beside me. "*June!* I swear he was about to ask you out."

I waved her away. "I couldn't care less."

But inside my sturdy nonslip restaurant shoes, my toes scrunched, deeply.

make up cookies

Aside from my overly emotional toes, I'd lived sixteen years mostly unaware of my feet. Becoming A Real McDonald's Girl had changed that. Now I lived about 85% of my life keenly aware of my soles. *Oh, fiddlesticks. My bunions are talking to me.* Grandma's beloved complaint, back in Marsh Lake, Wisconsin, stretched out on her bed after a day of heavy duty chores or shopping. As a kid, I hadn't known exactly what bunions were, but they sounded glamorous, in an industrious way. If I couldn't have big boobs or great beauty, I had decided, I wanted bunions. I figured I'd have to wait maybe fifty years to be so blessed.

But in my job, I'd grown bunions, and they talked nonstop, keeping me company the whole hobbling walk home. When I arrived, Rain's old hand-me-down white Toyota Corolla was gone. She'd started summer classes at the university. Dad was still at his clinic, working overtime on advertising. So that meant, it would just be me and Mom. Together. In the house. Just the two of us. Alone.

I limped up the back porch, pushed my key in the lock.

Laugh, clown, laugh!

Door slamming in my throat.

I couldn't swallow the fear.

Turning my key in the lock, cramps flashed bolts of pain across my abdomen. Along with heartburn, this blinding stomach pain seized me a lot lately, even after my period was over. I dragged myself into the shadowy laundry room, twisted my legs, and bit down on my clenched fist to keep from crying out. And then, a sweet cinnamon aroma gathered around me like a warm embrace.

Make up cookies.

Sometimes after a blow up, Mom made cookies. She'd nudge your door open, and hold one out. You might be in the middle of crying, just heaving with sobs. But if she brought you a cookie, you had to gather yourself fast. You did not talk about what had happened. You did not ask questions. You did not try to tell her how you felt. You did only three things: take cookie, smile, forget.

***

Mom and I sat together at the kitchen table, a whole platter of freshly baked fennel-oatmeal-raisin cookies between us, along with a tissue box, and a pile of old photos she'd been combing through. Her glamorous eyeliner was all cried away. She passed me a cookie, asked about my day. I told her about the crazy chaos of the bus groups, how fast I'd gotten, and how I was, miraculously, A Real McDonald's Girl.

"No miracle about it," she said. "I'm not surprised. Remember when you wanted to quit? You said you were too slow, couldn't pick it up. I told you then, didn't I? You're a builder. You've got to give yourself time to learn. Remember?"

"I remember." I took a bite of cookie, crisp, sweet, and spicy with fennel seeds. Mom lovingly incorporated the herbs she grew into all her cookies, cakes, and breads. Rain and I always told her she should open a bakery with a big, flamboyant herb garden out back where people could sit and eat their treats. In response, she'd shake her head, say, *oh girls, you know what my name means in Chippewa? Stay at home. That's all.*

She believed in me, but not in herself.

Mom smiled. "Now look at you. A star. Like your name." Mom had given me the middle name Namid. It was Chippewa for Star Dancer. She said, she wanted me to have a name to aspire to. "The night I named you, your dad and I were on a beach in Florida, watching Rain hunt for seashells with her little flashlight. I felt so lucky. You know why? When I was a kid, my family never took a vacation together, not a single one. I looked up and thought, I must be dreaming all those stars. It was a warm June night. And in those stars, I saw you. I did! I saw your face. *June Namid*. Your name pierced my heart like a whisper."

I laid my hand on hers. "I love that story, Mom."

"Really?" She glanced at me. "Sometimes, I think you forget."

I blinked, setting my cookie down. "I never forget."

Mom ripped her tissue into fragments in her lap. "It's just, I see how close you've gotten to Sister Finn. She's really taken you under her wing. That's good, I want you to have a mentor. But *she's* not your mother." She looked at me, her face turned fierce. "That's me, June. I'm the one who gave you your name. I'm the one who rocked you when you were a baby, up all night with colic. I'm the one who knows you, all of you, your good *and* your bad. Who's here for you all the time, caring for you, encouraging you, setting you straight? Not your perfect Sister Finn."

I was so scared, just as we were making up, she would go away again. I got up from the table, went to my room, and returned with two things. The first was a Pocahontas doll. "This is for you," I said. "She's beautiful and strong. Like you are."

Mom smoothed the doll's hair. "Oh, June. She's much more beautiful than me."

"Read this." I held out a copy of the poem I'd written, about the violets. I fixed my eyes on her while she read, watched her face move from confusion, to wonder, to – her hand flew to her heart. "June, can I have this? I promise you, I will keep it forever. The way you wrote about me makes me feel like a real person." Her voice broke.

I whisked another tissue from the box, handed it to her. I wished I could hand her peace, just as easily.

She wiped her eyes, her face, then motioned to the chair. "Here, sit. I want to show you something." I sat, and she slid a photo toward me. I picked it up. Written in the corner was *Abequa, Age 6*. I had never seen this photo. My mother as a child, staring back at me, right into me it felt like, her eyes so big and dark, framed by her long black hair, parted down the middle. I glanced at her now, sitting beside me. Those same eyes watched me, anxious, full of hope. She didn't let people in too often. Showing me this photo, I understood, was an act of trust. I studied the details. Her stained, oversized overalls. No shirt. One bare foot resting on top of the other. Her little hand curled around the handle of a wagon. Inside the wagon, two dolls. Neat as could be, all dressed up in lace and ribbons. I pointed to the dolls. "Susan and Mandy?"

Mom's eyes widened. "You remember their names?"

"Of course I do." Every story she told about her past, I hoarded in my memory, hoping one day, I could make the stories fit together, like puzzle pieces, and finally understand her the way I needed. "Susan and Mandy were your favorite dolls."

Mom touched her throat. "They were my babies. My reason to get up in the morning. I made them those fancy dresses at Ma's sewing machine. I did their hair and kept them clean, no matter what. Every day on the school bus, the kids threw garbage in my hair and reminded me I was nothing but the town drunk's daughter. *Trash.* But they couldn't say a word about Susan and Mandy. Oh no. They were the best, the cleanest, the prettiest dolls in all Marsh Lake, Wisconsin." She glanced at me. "With the Old Man, you just never knew. After work, he'd head straight for the bars. When he came home, he might stumble in, pass out right there on the floor. I'd *pray* for that. Other times, he'd cry on the couch, making sounds like death. I'd stand there, shaking. And that wasn't even the worst part. The worst was, when he'd hunt me and Rena down. *Girls! Where you at, girls?* He couldn't remember our names, see. He'd fall on the stairs, hunting us down. That gave us time to hide. He'd tear the house end to end. The thing is, if he couldn't find us, he'd go after Ma..." Mom squeezed her eyes shut. "When I got between Ma and his fists, he'd grab me by the hair, yank off his belt, pull my skirt up and whip me."

I sat there in a horrified trance.

"Oh, June. What hurt most, what really killed me, was Susan and Mandy having to hear that. I tried so hard to protect them!" Mom took a breath. "You know what I did? I scrounged up some boards, some tools, and I made them a cradle. Way up in the leaves of my favorite tree. When the Old Man staggered home, looking for a fight, I knew what to do. I gathered up Susan and Mandy, crawled out the window, and climbed my tree. I tucked them into their cradle, hidden in the leaves. No matter what happened to me, at least I knew, *they* were safe."

I could see it, the wood cradle in the tree, Mom's dolls gazing up at the sky. It hurt me so much that Mom had no one to protect her. I hesitated, then said, "Mom, if I could go back in time, you wouldn't be alone. I'd help you. I'd be your friend."

Mom tucked her fingers under my chin, held my eyes with

her own. "I know you would. And you would have been the *best* friend. What would I ever do without you, my sweet June Namid? If I'd had a friend like you, my life would have turned out different. Better." She dropped her hand. "The thing about your dad was, he was so different from the Old Man. So kind and upright."

My head spun with this sudden jump to Dad.

"Look." Mom slid another picture my way. "This was me and your dad our senior year. Can you believe it?" I leaned in close. I had never seen this picture either. Dad, so tall and dashing in a tux. Mom, breathtaking in a strapless gown, long hair streaming down her bare shoulders and back. In the picture, they danced, holding onto one another and gazing into each other's eyes as though lost to the world. They were two people I knew, and also two people I had never met.

Mom said, "Your dad was the one person in my life I could relax with, feel safe. He went off to college, and right before he graduated, a month before our wedding, he started studying the Bible with Jehovah's Witnesses. He pushed me to get baptized. He told me, Jehovah will heal your past." She made a face. "Ma warned me to break it off with him. She said I'd have to give up Christmas and go knock on doors. None of that mattered to me. What mattered was, he didn't drink. He didn't even swear. I thought I could trust him with my life." Mom turned to me, her face red and shaking. "June, you should know. I found out something today. Your dad's not who he says he is. I am *never* going back to that kingdom hall. Not after what he did."

She got up, stormed to her room, and shut the door.

Leaving me to guess what Dad had done now.

***

That evening, I eavesdropped when Mom called Grandma back home in Wisconsin.

I pushed open my door, sank to my knees in the hallway. *Ma, won't you visit? It's been two years. The girls miss you so bad. I'm not doing so well, Ma. I'm about to die. I'm so lonely out here in the backwoods. I should've listened to you a long time ago. I don't know how much longer I can keep going like this.*

I was sick with worry. I went to my room and pulled my favorite comfort book from my bookshelf. I headed outside, looking for Grits. If only I could hug Grits, kiss her kind yellow head. But I didn't see her. I couldn't call her because she was the neighbor's dog, and he was home.

Everything hurt.

I sidled around the corner of the house. The garage door was raised. Inside Dad paced, phone pressed between shoulder and ear. "Evening, Brother Manning. This is Brother Taylor." I fell into a crouch, listening hard. "I'm calling to let you know, we won't be at kingdom hall for a little while. A couple weeks, maybe longer. Something's come up in the family. I have to take care of it." Pause. "I'd appreciate that, brother. Please keep us in your prayers." His voice was thick.

We, he had said.

I wandered off, kicking through the grass, lost in my own backyard. My feet took over, took care of me, guiding me to clapping tree. I climbed, pulling myself branch by branch, deeper and deeper into the silver-green sea of her leaves, settling at last into my nook, a perfect valley in her sturdy trunk. She greeted me the same way she always did, with a joyous rustle that sounded just like clapping.

In the warm bath of late gold light, I opened my comfort book, a dear, raggedy copy of *Anne of Green Gables*. The book that had seen me through everything. Anne Shirley had arrived in 4th grade, telling me I was not the only weird, lonely girl. She said imagination would rescue me, time and time again. Back then, I had dreamed of myself at sixteen. I wouldn't be alone with my books anymore. I would find that kindred spirit. But look at me, sitting up here, crying in a tree. Anne turned to me now, her red hair aglow, like firelight in the treetops. She said, *You'll find your place in the world. You'll make your place. And there, in that place, will be so much love.*

For the first time, I didn't believe her.

From up in the swaying branches, far-off moos of cattle reached my ears, a plaintive chorus. I pictured my world, spread out below. The dark sweep of woods, the aching green pastures. Oreo cows swishing along, eager to get back to the barn for dinner. I pictured our neighborhood, the houses spaced far apart, everyone cut off by trees, backyards steeped in thick, wild country gardens, birds dipping and darting, rusted out trucks on blocks. In my mind, I searched, roving the town, the small brick high school I didn't attend, the two big truck stops, full of trucks that came and went.

Not a single kindred spirit in sight.

I hurt us

The next morning, I paused, whispered a little prayer, before slipping into the garage.

Dad's long legs in holey, grease-stained blue jeans stuck out from underneath Mom's red Subaru. He hammered away. *Clink clink clink.* Her car had been acting up, and she'd complained about not having the money to take it in for repairs.

I leaned against the doorway, watching. We'd moved a thousand miles, from Marsh Lake, Wisconsin, to Hopeton, Arkansas, because of Dad. His practice was doing well in Wisconsin, but when he got the call from the brother in Fayetteville about taking over Good Spine, he said it was an offer he couldn't refuse. He wanted to expand, he said, grow, learn new healing therapies. One night though, before we moved, Dad had revealed another, bigger reason for the move. I was wandering the yard, saying goodbye to the house I'd grown up in, hugging each kind balsam fir, weeping into their bark. Dad had found me, and pulled me close. . . *June, I want you to know, we wouldn't leave if I didn't believe this move will change all our lives for the better. You know Marsh Lake is full of bad memories for your mother. If she gets out of here, and far away, I think she'll heal.*

Would he really bring her here, just to hurt her?

Clink clink, and this time, something clattered loose and rolled across the floor of the garage. I scooped it up. A greasy silver washer I rotated between my thumb and forefinger. Dad pushed himself out from underneath the car. His eyes were wide, face pale. When he realized it was me, his whole body relaxed. "Oh, hey. Morning, kid." He raked a hand though his thick, dark hair. "You work this early? Dumb question. Truckers are always hungry, right?" He tried a smile. It wobbled, and he looked away.

I plunked down on the cold cement step, held out the washer. "Here, Dad."

He glanced at me, then took it. "Thanks, June Bug." My childhood nickname. He hadn't called me that in so long. I didn't even know I had missed it, but now I choked up watching him rotate the washer between his thumb and forefinger, the same way I had. As June Bug, I'd loved helping Dad in the garage. Once upon a time, I'd even had my own little stool. I'd hand him the tools he needed. Black-handled screwdrivers and tiny wrenches. I'd spin on the stool with my legs stretched out, talking his ear off. He never seemed to mind.

"Dad," I said now. He looked up. "Do you still have that old work stool I used to sit on?"

He tilted his head. "You remember that?"

"Of course I do." I wrapped my arms around my knees. "Those were some of the best days."

The way his face lit up, like a sunrise. He jumped up and strode to the corner of the garage. I took in his workbench, newspaper spread out. Laid on top, a wood post, freshly painted white. Dad's beloved project, a work in progress, not yet complete. He was building Mom a white picket fence.

Dad tugged the stool free from where it was wedged behind his workbench, tore off the plastic covering, and with a flourish, spun it my way. I caught it. The black vinyl seat had cracked. Stuffing poked out like a puff of white beard.

"Take a seat," Dad said. "See if it still fits! Or if you do." He winked.

I sat, and yes, still a perfect fit. I looked at Dad, and the brave, frank nine-year-old in me came pouring out. "Dad, I heard you on the phone yesterday. You said *we* wouldn't be going to kingdom hall for a while. This is my life, too. I need you to tell me what's happening."

Dad's face shut down. He leaned back against the wall, folded his arms across his chest. "You shouldn't be listening in on conversations," he said. "There are things that are private, that don't belong to you."

"This does," I pushed. "I'm getting baptized next month. Remember?"

"Of course I remember!" He shouted it, his face turning red.

"How can I get baptized if we're not going to kingdom hall?"

He turned to the side. The muscle in his jaw twitched.

"Well, Phil. Are you going to tell her?"

I hadn't heard the garage door open. The hairs on the back of my neck stood on end as Mom approached from behind. Dad looked up, blanched. He tried to hold his sternness. "Abe, not now. This isn't the time or place."

Mom stepped beside me, bringing the scent of sweet lavender. She gathered her robe in her hands, her hair wrapped up in a towel. "How much longer am I supposed to shut my mouth and protect you, Phil? Your daughter is sitting here, asking you to be *honest* with her, and after everything, you can't do that?" She scoffed. "You really are a coward."

Dad tilted his head back against the wall. He breathed in, long and slow.

"That's right! Breathe, Phil, breathe!" She coached him in a mocking voice. "It's hard for you, huh? What do you think it's been like for me?"

"Hon, please..."

"I'm not your hon! I'm not your anything. Don't you get it? I'm sick of playing the good wife! Expected to cook, clean, and stay quiet. If I speak up, I'm a monster. And you? Off you go to your failing clinic, playing hero to your *clients*," with venom. "Oh, you're a real hero, all right. What are you going to do, Phil? Are you going to tell your daughter what you did?"

My gut roiled, stomach acid frying my throat. "Dad...?"

"June." He met my eyes. "I made a mistake..."

"Mistake?" Mom lurched forward, pointing at him. "You *cheated!*"

Dad strode over, eyes flashing. "I didn't cheat!"

"You did!"

"Lust isn't cheating!"

"Tell that to your God!"

They screamed in each other's faces right over my head.

"Tell her, Phil!" Mom said. "Tell her about your darling Jezebel."

Dad dropped to his knees, right on the floor in front of me. "I did. I hurt us, June. I did."

"You hear that, June?" Mom's voice was soft now, almost meek. "Did you hear what your father said?"

I nodded. Up, down, up, down. My teeth chattered.

"What did he say?"

"He hurt us."

The garage door flew open, cracking against the wall.

"June!" Rain jangled her car keys. "You're late for work. Let's go. *Now.*"

I was grateful to Rain. I don't think I could have walked to work without getting smashed by a semi-truck, the last words in my head: *Cheating! Lust!*

We pulled up in front of McStop. I tried to get out of the car but Rain grabbed my arm, yanked me back. "Listen to me." Her hazel eyes shone with intensity. "That's their drama. Not yours. You can't fix it, or them. You've just got to shake it off."

Was it that easy? Maybe for Rain. Not for me. *I hurt us, I did. Did you hear what your father said, June?* The words rolled over and over in my head, blinding me to everything else.

Not helpful in my line of work.

"What the hell is this?" My first customer of the day, a burly, bearded truck driver, gaped at his McNuggets meal. He looked up at me, stricken. Then he surged his gigantic belly over the counter, and shaking the bag in my face, roared, "I asked for the twenty piece, not the ten, you dimwit!"

I froze, clenching the countertop for dear life. Maggie ducked, pretending to search wildly for ketchup packets.

"Hey!" In the kitchen, a pan slammed onto the grill. "Hey, you!"

Becky stalked to the front, stood right beside me. She jabbed a finger in the trucker's face. "You, sir, need to take a seat before I kick your hairy wild boar's ass clean out of here! You think you're a big macho man, bullying this sweet little girl? I'll tell you what you are. A piece of shit! I will bring you your precious 20-piece as long as you sit real nice and quiet in that corner over there and *zip your pants*, sir, you might be able to go commando in your big boy truck but right now you are vandalizing our eyes!" She had to yell this last part, since he was already fleeing (and zipping), right out the door. "Well, looky there." She swiped her hands together. "Ol' bouncy got himself some cardio today."

I turned to her. "That was my fault. I wasn't paying attention." My eyes filled, and I didn't look away. I let her see.

Becky's wiry eyebrows lifted. Her bristly jaw softened. "Hey, now, Daydreamer. Don't go beating yourself up. Everybody has off days." She paused. "Well, almost everybody. Not me. But if you compare yourself to me, you'll drive yourself nuts." She laughed, with a little snort.

I tried to smile, but then pressed my hand to my mouth. One warm tear let go, shimmied down my face.

"Oh boy." Becky tilted her head back, checked out the ceiling. "Listen. Whatever's going on, it'll get better. I know 'cuz I've been through lots. Yes, ma'am. Lots and lots and lots." She rapped the warming bin with a fist. "I've been rough on you. But the truth is..." She lifted her visor with a knuckle, scratched her forehead. "Even with all your weird-ass ways, you kinda brighten this place up."

I stared. Because right then, Becky-the-pirate-y-cook was my very own Marilla Cuthbert. The moment she told Anne, crustily, but with affection, *the trial is over, you will stay at Green Gables.*

I wiped my face with the back of my hand. "Thank you, Becky." If only we were allowed to say, instead of a tiny, polite *thank you*, the truer *you just saved me*. If only, in moments like that, we could fall to each other's feet.

Outside, an engine thundered. Becky clamped her visor down hard. "BUS!"

We rushed to our positions.

The chaos was exhilarating.

The Branson bus group poured in. Hungry, stiff-limbed, and glowering, they were eager to unleash their resentment on the lowly McDonald's girl. I looked each customer in the eye. I shone my warmest, most welcoming smile.

Here, at least, I had some power. I could make things better. This, along with Becky's kindness, this saved me, too.

***

After the bus groups, a rambunctious military convoy pulled in, jeeps and tanks, one right after the other, strewn across the parking lot. Loud, blustery boys in camo lined up, chanting *McRibs! McRibs!* Next, a big party of Amish arrived in a caravan of horse-drawn buggies festooned with yellow smiley-face birthday balloons. Our McStop offered a neat row of hitching posts for the local Amish community. They were polite, but fastidious, insisting on direct-from-the-fryer fries.

The one person in the entire town who hadn't come in today was Clint.

See you tomorrow, Miss June.

Isn't that what he'd said? With a little gentlemanly bow. Or had I imagined it?

What a cad.

The restaurant door pushed open. I jerked my head up from counting change at the register. It was only Drive-Through Mikey, returning from his smoke break. As he strode past, his headset beeped. "And so it begins," he grumbled. He pushed down on the button, singing with great cheer, while rolling his eyes, "Welcome to McStop! May I take your order, please?"

After a minute, I stood on tip-toe and craned my head,

looking this way and that out the window. Not a single rusty blue pickup truck in sight. The parking lot was dead.

Slowly, I sank back to my feet.

"Wake up, Daydreamer!" Becky rapped her knuckles against the warming bin. "Janet wants to see you in her office, pronto."

"Oooooooh, June's in troooouble..." The cooks crowed as I headed to the back. I jammed my visor down over my eyes, wishing for just a moment I could flip people off. I knew what this was about. My anti-regulation ice-cream cones.

Small cones were three twists. Large cones were six. For old Farmer Henry, I made cones with seven twists.

No one else but Farmer Henry!

Because he was so bashful, his thumbs wedged in his overall suspenders. And sweet, his gray handlebar moustache twitching with joy when I handed him a masterfully swirled, supersized cone. Janet had warned me twice already. But I'd broken the rule again today. How could I resist? Farmer Henry had bumbled right into the maelstrom of burly soldiers chanting for McRibs. He'd winced and stumbled backward, toward the door. Then, catching my eye, he'd flashed me a desperate look. I'd smiled, waved him forward. *You can do it, Farmer Henry.*

After waiting in line with all those army guys cracking dirty jokes and cackling, how could I not reward his bravery with an *eight* twist cone? And oh my, was it a thing of beauty. A frosty spiral staircase of ice-cream.

Who'd been heartless enough to tell on me? Although, I'd heard there were cameras everywhere. I imagined Janet watching me on a security monitor from her office. *June Taylor, at it again.* I wanted to run away. But not home.

I knocked on Janet's office door. "Come in."

I stepped inside. Janet, filling out paperwork, looked up.

"June." She set down her pen, tilted her head, and frowned. "Why do you look like that?"

"Like what?"

"Guilty!"

"Do I?" I wiped my sweaty palms up and down my pant legs.

"And terrified. Like I called you back here to fire you."

"Well." I blinked back a sudden surge of tears. "You never know."

Janet studied me. "Actually, I called you back here to *read* to you."

"Read to me?"

She tapped a small stack of cards on her desk. "No one ever fills out the customer satisfaction cards unless they want to bitch. Boy hallelujah, do I ever get sick of the bitching." She set her spectacles on her nose. "Let me tell you. This is such a refreshing change of pace." She plucked a card from the pile, straightened, and read, "*I'm traveling down from Minnesota on my way to a conference. It's a hot day, my AC dies, and I'd kill for an ice-cream shake. There's a big bus group in your store and they're all thinking the same thing. And your shake machine dies. Everyone's getting pissed, a manager's trying to fix the damn thing with no luck. Then one of your cashiers, June, jumps in and starts offering everyone Coke floats. The mood totally changes. Saves the day. And that was one hell of a Coke float. I sure hope you aren't going to let that girl go to waste. I run a business in St. Paul. I know a leader when I see one.*"

Janet leaned back. "There's a whole bunch like that, customers bragging on you. Of course, I don't need to be convinced. I've seen with my own eyes. You know, June. Once upon a time, I *did* think I'd have to call you back here and fire you. You took such a dang long time getting the hang of things! We all secretly thought you were slow in the head." She chuckled. "Now look.

A leader. Well? What do you think?"

Think? I didn't even know how to breathe, or where to look, or what to do with my arms. "I've never...sorry. I've never thought of myself as a leader."

Janet eyed me. "Well then you best start rethinking yourself. You're nervous as a little deer, but you step up when it matters most. You care for people. You make them want to come back." She smiled. "*If* an assistant manager position were to open up, let's say, in the next few weeks – would you be interested?"

I pulled off my visor, scratched my head. I had to dig out my voice.

It said, quietly...yes.

Janet leaned across her desk, hand cupped around an ear. "Come again?"

I coughed the word into my fist. "Yes."

"Oh, Lord. I'm signing you up right now for the next assertiveness training." Janet scribbled on a pad of paper. "In the meantime, go home and talk it over with your parents."

I turned to go. My hand was on the doorknob when she said, "Just bear in mind, June Taylor. Managers *have* to make regulation cones. Even for sweet old farmers."

***

"What do you think you're doing? You can't go home yet." Becky snatched my time card right out of my hand as I attempted to clock out. I stared at her. Her eyes were shining. "This way, girlie." She took my shoulders, swung me around. "You got one more big order today. And I do mean *big*." She steered me past the kitchen.

Shoveling fries into a carton, Maggie swiveled. She flashed

a thumbs up, bounced on her feet. What in the – ?

Becky shoved me around the corner. And I froze.

He stood at my register with his head bowed, all decked out in a tan suede cowboy hat, pale green western shirt, and big, silver belt buckle engraved with a bucking bull, shined to a sweet polish.

Shaky-legged, I made myself step forward. "What can I get you?" My voice, pitched a few notches too high.

He lifted his head. Our gaze locked. For the first time, I noticed the little points of gold in his brown cowboy eyes. "I ain't here for lunch, Miss June. I'm here to ask you..." Clint stopped short. Usually so suave, his lips were trembling. He swiped off his cowboy hat, gripping it between rough, tan hands. "Will you go line-dancing with me on Saturday night?" Clint's knuckles whitened, squeezing the life out of his cowboy hat.

And then, I did it again.

Only louder this time.

"Yes."

dumb dog

I walked home hard and fast along the gravel shoulder, head down, backpack thumping between my shoulder blades. A tanker roared by, whisking my frizz this way and that, tickling my face. The smile I'd been biting back unleashed.

I squeezed my backpack straps, and right there on the side of the highway, surrendered to the kind of squealing little hop-dance a normal girl might do. The Oreo cows stopped, lifted their heads, and stared. Instantly, my rapture plummeted. They were right. Of course they were.

I couldn't go on a date.

It wasn't even that he was a worldly boy. After all, I had no plan to marry him. Instead, it was something much more confusing. Memories I had never really made sense of swam up into my mind. The time in 3rd grade when I wrote about a crush on a classmate in my little red diary with the lock. I'd come home to find Mom mysteriously enraged, ready to swoop as soon as I walked in the door. I could still picture her, vividly, shaking the diary in my face, the broken lock jangling. Another time, in 6th grade, I confided in her that I liked a boy in my class, a fellow reader who read out loud to me from *A Wrinkle in Time*. We'd been driving, and she slammed on the brakes, swerved to the side of the road where we slid on gravel before coming to a standstill. Then she exploded. Nothing about the boy – but about how much I had failed her in countless little ways she ticked off, right there on the side of the road, one wheel nearly hanging in the ditch.

I readjusted my backpack, and trudged on, eyes downcast.

Will you go line-dancing with me on Saturday night?

I pressed my hand to my heart. What was line-dancing? Was it like a square dance? Most importantly, could I wear sequins? Anne of Green Gables had dreamed of puffed sleeves and I'd always dreamed of going to a dance decked out in a sequin dress that looked like the wings of a dragonfly I'd once marveled at for at least fifteen minutes in the garden, glittering gold in the sunlight.

The Oreo cows rolled their heads back, bellowed loud enough for the whole world to hear. *It doesn't matter, June Taylor! Don't you get excited! You can't go!*

Nearing my house, I spied Dad sitting on the front porch. And I knew. He was waiting for me. *I hurt us, I did.* No! I wasn't ready to lose my beautiful dream to my real life. I scampered down the road, cut through a small, ragged field into a patch of woods that led directly to our backyard, then sprinted to clapping tree.

My pant legs were a collage of gravel dust, seeds, and burrs as I scrambled up into her branches. I sank into my nook, caught my breath. "Guess what?" I said. "You will never guess." I looked around, then whispered, "I got asked on a date. For the first time ever." Her little leaves rustled together, making that clapping sound. I rested my cheek against her sun-warmed bark. I could always count on her to celebrate with me.

I dug my book out of my backpack. I was reading *Poets In Love*, a play based on the epic love story of Robert Browning and Elizabeth Barrett. The last time Dad had taken me to the library in Fayetteville, he'd had to run errands and pressed me to make it quick. Quality book selection could *not* be quick. Hence, I'd been stuck with this cheesy 1960's melodrama. Even so, the book was steadily growing on me. Though I'd read the

Browning's poetry for my home-school English class, I didn't know much about the poet's lives or how they'd met. I had no idea that in her forties, Elizabeth still lived at home with her father. Treated like a hopeless invalid, she spent seven years secluded in a dark upstairs room, her beloved Spaniel, Flush, her constant companion and only friend. She poured her pent-up life and dreams into writing. Her work drew the admiration of fellow poet, Robert Browning, who began writing her the most passionate letters. *I love your verses with all my heart, dear Miss Barrett, and I love you, too.* Their story was captivating! I opened to where I had left off and soon, sunk deep into a book trance.

Mr. Barrett (stern): This man. He's been coming to see you frequently, Lizzy.

Elizabeth (smile fading): He's a poet, father. We share our work.

Mr. Barrett (pacing): You're lying to me. I see the way he looks at you. I see the way you encourage it. It's shameful, and I won't have it (swiveling). You have given me your word, Elizabeth, you will never marry. I have *trusted* you.

Elizabeth: Let your heart be at ease, father. You know how greatly I love and respect you. My promise to you is secure as ever. Mr. Browning is my friend only.

Mr. Barrett: It is my duty to keep you safe. I forbid you to see him.

Elizabeth (clasping her hands): Father, if you care for me at all, please, I beg of you. For so long I've been here, sick, alone, without hope. And now, this unexpected joy has entered my life. Father, please, I beg, do not take this single joy from me.

Mr. Barrett (shaking his head): How I pity you, Lizzy. Now you have a choice to make. This man's fleeting friendship, or your father's life-long devotion?

Elizabeth (burying her head in her hands): You know who I choose, father. You. Always you.

I let the book fall to my lap.

"No, Elizabeth!" I cried into the leaves. "Don't give in. Be brave. Choose *you*."

"June?" Dad's voice from below, threading up through the branches. "You up there?"

My impassioned plea had betrayed my hiding spot.

***

Dad and I sat side by side on the front porch stoop. He wore his red Good Spine polo, *Phil Taylor, DC*, embroidered in shiny white thread above the pocket. On his head, his favorite hat, the one he'd worn in Wisconsin and seemed to have worn my whole life. Straw, with a brown velvet band, and a graceful brown and white-spotted quail feather. He wore that hat when he crouched in the garden, scooping up earth in his hands, making space to nestle in his beloved tomato and pepper plants. He wore that hat when he mowed our yard in careful, mathematical stripes. He wore it when he took me fishing and we sat in lawn chairs, dangling our bare feet side by side in the water, tickling crawdads with our toes.

Everything I loved about my dad seemed to gather in that hat.

He turned, and our eyes snagged. A small smile tugged at the corner of his mouth. "What have we here?" He reached out, gently untangling something from my frizz. I expected a twig or leaf, the usual fare. He held it up, so the evening light set it aglow. A small french fry!

I clutched my head. My mind raced. With Janet in her office. With Clint. Some of the most meaningful moments of my life and I'd had a french fry in my hair!

"Hey," Dad said, fighting laughter, "you know what this reminds me of?"

"Please, not the worm..."

He chuckled. "You tried to cast out, and your hook was bare. I said, 'June, where'd your bait go?' and when you spun around..." He slapped his knee. "The worm was in your hair!" He laughed, full on, then dug his handkerchief out from his jean's pocket and blew his nose, an exuberant honk. After a minute, he said, "You know, I keep wanting to dig out our poles, take you on another fishing trip. I can't believe how fast it's all going. I'm sorry I've..." His voice caught. "I don't know how..." he rubbed his face. "I hope you know..." He set his hand on my knee and squeezed, once, twice, three times.

My heart hurt. "I know, Dad."

Grits galloped over from next door. She clambered up the steps, planted herself between us. Dad and I sank our hands into her coat, both of us welcoming the distraction. She melted, leaning first one way, then the other. She never got this love from the villainous neighbor, her owner, the man I called Mr. Bad Flannel based on his fashion choices.

Dad took a breath. "Mom says, I should tell you everything."

My hand curled into Grit's fur. "Okay."

"Sister Jansen came to see me for a spinal adjustment. At the end of the appointment, she requested a massage. And... I gave her one."

A shock zinged through me as I pictured his hands, groping Jezebel Jansen's water balloons.

"She has a lot of neck tension from her desk job."

It took a second to register. "You...gave her a *neck* massage?"

He stared straight ahead. "I know it was wrong. I should have referred her to another chiropractor, or a massage therapist."

"A neck massage." I tried to process. "Is that cheating?"

"I looked at...I liked..." He shook his head, fast. "The scriptures are clear. If you look at a woman with lust, you've committed adultery in your heart." His chin quivered, and he tugged his hat down over his eyes.

His shame left me stricken. I latched and unlatched my fingers. *Pat his back. Tell him it's okay, and you love him.* That's what my heart told me to do but....I peered over my shoulder, checked the windows. I wasn't free to do my heart's bidding. If Mom saw me, she'd think I was on his side. Then I'd be in her line of fire, too. And I already had my own guilty secret to worry about. I wedged my hands between my knees, and deliberately leaned away from him.

He made a sound then. A small choking cry he did his best to stifle. It was horrible. Even so, I didn't move to comfort him.

After a minute, Dad gathered himself. "June, I am just so sorry that because of what I did, you're going to have to put your baptism on hold."

My face prickled and stung like I'd been slapped. "What?"

He dropped his voice. "We can't go back to kingdom hall right now. You have to understand that, until I fix this, we can't go back."

"Dad," I strained to keep my voice steady. "Why can't I go? Rain has a car. She and I can go together."

"People will talk. They'll try to pull you in and pry. Mom wouldn't like it."

"But what if Sister Finn could pick me up, even just once a week..."

Dad side-eyed me. "That's another thing. Mom's not too happy about you and Sister Finn."

"But why? What did I do wrong?" I started to cry. Grits snuggled into me. Her closeness, her warmth, holding my splinters together.

"Shh," Dad said. "Hush." He turned, checking the windows, just the way I had.

I took a breath, pressing the pain down deep into my guts.

"Listen," Dad whispered. "Grandma's flying out Friday. I paid for her tickets. It's a surprise for Mom." A beat passed. "I'm going to fix this, June. But I need you to work with me. Whatever you do, I beg you, don't fret, don't cry, don't bring *any* extra stress to Mom. You understand?"

"Yes, Dad." I quickly wiped my face.

Just then, there was the ugly prowling growl of a monster truck and sweep of headlights across the lawn. Mr. Bad Flannel, home from the bars. With a sharp scrape of toenails against concrete, Grits flew from my side. She zigzagged up the hill, toward his truck, yipping like a puppy.

He'd stumble out of his truck, drunk, decked out in one of his many ripped flannel shirts. Grits would dance at his feet. He'd kick her aside and curse. He'd fling his beer bottle onto the gravel, just to watch her flinch.

My beautiful Grits.

Running, always running, to the person who could never love her back.

Dad glanced at me, shook his head. "Dumb dog."

In my room, I sank down at my desk. I was painfully conscious of Mom in her room. Conscious that she knew Dad and I had spoken. Conscious that she was conscious of me and any sound I might make. Though a wall separated us, it was like she was watching, waiting for me to react. I knew, as Dad had directed, it was crucial not to cry. I had to somehow anaesthetize the brutal swirl of disappointment, frustration, and fear.

I closed my eyes, pinched the skin on my arm hard, until it took my breath, made me dizzy, made sparks dash behind my eyes. When I opened my eyes again, I saw what I had missed before, the manila envelope on my desk, addressed to me.

Grandma. How did she do it? The last two years, since we'd moved here, Grandma's letters had arrived like life rafts, spinning my way out of the blue when I needed them most.

Thankful, I pressed the envelope with both hands, savoring its strange, unruly shape. Grandma loved to send me what she thought was contraband.

I tore the envelope open and sure enough. Three pairs of extra-silky pantyhose, a handful of slightly melted Slo-Pokes, and a mixtape. Grandma was Catholic (on Easter and Christmas) and clung to the belief that Jehovah's Witnesses were a cult with wacky prohibitions. *I heard your leaders won't let the girls wear pantyhose! Is it true they won't let you-all listen to music?* Grandma relished sneaking me what she thought were "forbidden" pleasures. I flipped the tape over. In her flourishy cursive she'd penned *Glen Miller Orchestra, for my little Romantic.*

As the pinch on my arm lost its burn, I slipped the tape

into my cassette player and pressed play. My room grew dreamy with saxophone, weepy with bassoon. In my work uniform, blue McDonald's polo, black trouser pants, and sturdy black nonslip restaurant shoes, I stood, closed my eyes, and swayed.

Fantasy worked just as well, if not more than a hard pinch, to make me forget.

It was World War II. I was at a USO dance, in a sailor dress with little flashing sequins, bows on my shoes. My golden hair styled in soft, inviting waves. He approached, in his uniform, tall and strong, yet sweetly shy. He held out his hand. I took it. A shock zipped through me. I wanted to hold that hand all night. All my life. He pulled me to him. So close. Then closer still, his other hand clasping my waist. We moved like one creature, hips locked in rhythm, across the room.

I opened my eyes, and my beautiful dream burst.

I stood before my closet, doors flung wide. I ran my hand across my kingdom hall dresses, in a tidy row. And there. My hand rested on my brand new baptism bathing suit. Vintage 1940's-style, like the music. Black with white polka dots, a big, adorable bow in the back. Mom had helped me pick it out.

I gently slid it off the hanger, pressed it to me. At the Jehovah's Witness convention in Little Rock, almost 15,000 brothers and sisters would gather for three days of Bible talks and instruction, a spiritual feast. Three baptism pools would glisten under the arena lights. And I...

Would *not* change excitedly into my bathing suit during intermission.

Would *not* line up, giddy with the other baptismal candidates.

Would *not* dip under that winking blue water, and rise up new.

Would *not* be eligible for full-time door-to-door preaching.

Which meant, when I finished home-schooling, I could *not* pursue my dream, and apply to Gilead Missionary School.

Mom's not too happy about you and Sister Finn.

I was so careful not to make errors. And lately, it seemed, that's all I could do. I had attached myself to Sister Finn. And Mom had been hurt. Jealous even. Was it supposed to be that way? Was every mother threatened when her daughter had a crush, or made a friend?

There would be no line-dancing for me. Absolutely not. I'd have to take back my *yes*, turn it into what it should have been in the first place. *No.* No, no, no. Always no.

A weird little blaze started in my chest. At first, rubbing between my breasts, I thought it was the heartburn again. But this was a different kind of burn, one that made me almost wild. I yanked off my work uniform, first the shirt, kicking off the shoes, then the pants, until I was stark naked and trembling.

I pulled on my bathing suit.

I wanted to wear it, just once. I sank to my knees and crawled to the back of my closet, digging out a pair of sleek black high-heels. Mom had bought them for me on clearance, so marked down she couldn't resist. On one condition, she told me. I wasn't allowed to wear them until I turned eighteen. I pushed them fiercely onto my feet.

I rose, wobbled across the carpet to my full-length mirror.

My breath caught. Slowly, I turned side to side.

Had the bathing suit looked this sexy in the dressing room? The fabric clung to my every curve. I leaned in, pressed my shoulders together. My breasts rounded into full, milky white moons. This was not the body I saw every day in a McDonald's uniform and kingdom hall dresses. This different body was a different self, a different life, with a whole set of other possibilities.

On Grandma's tape, the song switched.

In a sweet clear voice, a lady sang about a walk with a lover beneath fragrant apple trees on a moonlit night.

Nothing was safe, and everything could be taken.

Except my dreams. My dreams were all mine.

I held myself, closed my eyes, and swayed, returning to the dance.

Clint pressed me into his lean cowboy body. *June*, he whispered, breath hot in my ear. *You're so beautiful.* With a fingertip, he lightly traced the curve of my breast. *June, can I kiss you there?*

My crotch tingled and warmed. *Wait, Clint, wait.*

Heart beating fast, I kicked off my heels, flipped off the lights, and crawled excitedly into bed.

First a lengthy courtship, then marriage. We had to do it the Watchtower way.

I closed my eyes and for a long time, beneath the blankets, savored a movie reel of images while touching myself gently in different places. Clint reaching for my hand, the warm rush of our palms, pressed together, as we ambled side by side through a shower of autumn leaves. Clint reading poetry to me, his tender brown eyes lit by flickering candlelight, his hand trailing the length of my arm, leaving a stream of goosebumps. Clint dropping to one knee, cowboy hat pressed to his chest, rain dripping down his tan, strong jaw as he pulled me close, pressed his face between my breasts. Me in a flowy white dress, wildflowers laced in my hair, lifting on tiptoe to kiss him.

In our own room, alone at last.

Me in lace lingerie, breasts full and rounded, dancing against him, so I could feel all of him, so he could feel all of me.

Clint, I've waited for you, for so long.

June, I can't wait a single second more.

Clint kissing me, deeply, with heat.

I pushed my pillow to the side, now wet with kissing, and rolled onto my belly. Heart thumping, skin hot, I quickly folded the blankets into a mound, until the blankets beneath my crotch felt solid, full, like what a man might feel like.

Clint and I were married now.

I thrust my hips and drenched my swimsuit in sweat.

I filled the night with *yes, yes, yes.*

the girls

Three long days before Grandma swooped in like a superhero, red lipstick instead of a cape.

I believed every bit as much as Dad that her presence was a necessary gift, one that would begin to set things right for us.

I also knew Grandma feared long trips.

She feared a lot of things.

At fifteen, during the Great Depression, she'd had to quit school to clean homes for wealthy families, polishing their silver obsessively, frightened they wouldn't pay her if they found a single spot. She sent the money back home to her folk's ailing farm. While at work, she was stricken with rheumatic fever. She lost consciousness for days. The doctor predicted her death. Though she'd pulled through, to this day, she suffered the effects of an enlarged heart. She obsessed about keeling over with a heart attack. She backed out of plans, worried she'd *kick the bucket.*

So, I waited. I went to clapping tree. In the sanctuary of her branches, I prayed.

Friday morning came.

The scent of perfume awakened me.

A familiar bright sweetness, like rose petals basking in morning sun.

I threw the covers off, scrambled out of bed. Creeping down the hallway, scared to hope, I peeked around the corner. My hand went to my mouth, tears stinging the back of my throat.

Her.

Sitting at our dining room table, wrapped up in a silky pink and gold kimono dressing gown, lucky pearls, mass of bleach blonde hair pinned and piled high.

Curling her eyelashes, she unleashed her signature booming belly laugh. *Oh ho ho!*

And my knees went weak with love.

"June!" Mom spied me first. She waved the spatula. Specks of grease bounced off, bright dots like tiny shooting stars. "Look who it is, Ma!"

Grandma swiveled. Her jaw dropped. "Juney! Is that you? No. It can't be. Our sweet little June? Not so little!" She threw her arms open wide.

I danced into them, burying my head in her giant, pillowy bosom. In that moment, I knew. Home wasn't Wisconsin. It wasn't a two-story soft blue Colonial left behind in the balsam firs. Home was the warm, freckled space between my Grandma's breasts, which smelled most richly of her. "I miss you, Grandma. Oh I miss you."

Rain dashed in, circular waving. "Hi, Grandma, Hi!" Then she burst into tears.

We three drew into the most tender knot.

Our hair caught between each other's fingers, pulled gently.

Our tears, on each other's cheeks. "My girls, oh I'm here, my girls..."

"Breakfast is served, girls!" Mom sang from the kitchen.

Girls, girls. My heart danced that word around. There was nothing better in the world. Warm fire, sweet song, all I wanted.

Giddy and giggling, we lined up for eggs, bacon, and Mom's homemade lemon rose-geranium tea cake. Golden brown, sprinkled with powdered sugar, and topped with a sunburst pattern of geranium leaves. "Abe, you outdid yourself!" Grandma crushed a geranium leaf between her fingers, taking a whiff.

"Such a good baker, ever since you were a girl."

Mom, dressed in a blue and white flowered sundress, almost stood on tiptoe, incandescent, haloed by Grandma's praise. When she'd discovered the surprise visit, she was so overcome, she'd broken down weeping into her hands. Dad had tried to make his move, attempting to hold her. With a vicious look, she'd shaken him off. Their fights had stopped though. Things were moving in the right direction. And now, in Grandma's presence, Mom bloomed, serving up her artful cake, laughing, dotting our noses with powdered sugar. This was all so good. *So good.*

Then I remembered. Grandma would have to go home.

It had only just begun, and already – I dreaded the end.

I shook Grandma's arm. "Grandma. You should stay for Rhubarb Pie Day." Also known as Fourth of July, which Jehovah's Witnesses didn't celebrate. We'd reinvented the holiday around Mom's most famous pie. What birthdays and Christmas were for other people, Rhubarb Pie Day was for us. It was tradition for Mom and me to bake her pie together, a blissful daylong ritual.

"Oh, I wish!" Grandma said. "Your pie, Abe, is the only time I'll eat a lick of rhubarb."

"Then *stay*," Mom coaxed. "We have room. Stay as long as you want." She pulled me under one arm, and Rain under the other. "Come on, Ma. Stay here with your girls."

Grandma set her hands on her hips. "Oh, now. That's not fair. All your big eyes looking at me. I would, but Abe, you know how I am. What if I keel? I don't want to kick the bucket in your guest room!"

Rain and I caught each other's eyes and cracked up.

Back at the table, I scooted my chair between Mom and

Grandma. "June, what happened there?"

Grandma eagle eyed the pinch mark I'd made on my arm, which had bruised. Mom saw it, too. For just a split second, she looked scared, her eyes on my face, widening. Like she knew what it was.

"Oh, nothing," I said, waving my fork. "Just from climbing my tree."

"You and your trees!" Grandma took a bite of cake. Her eyes fluttered. "Heavens to Betsy, this is good, even better than it looks. Why don't you open a bakery, Abe? You could make a damn fortune."

"Oh, Ma, stop." Mom fiddled with her napkin. "You know I don't have the smarts to run a business."

"But you've got Phil. *He's* smart. He could help you."

Mom's face soured. "He could help me, all right."

"I can't tell you how good it is to be here." Grandma looked around at us, oblivious, adoring. "Every day I pray to God, bring my beauties back home. Without my girls, I'm just a lonely old crow. Abe, why'd you let Phil drag you so far away?"

"More of my stupidity, I guess."

"No, I get it. He's making the dough here. But I do wonder – how do you let him go off every day to give back adjustments? Putting his hands on other women...all these blonde bombshell southern belle types! Do they even have their clothes on? Can you trust him, Abe?"

Across the table, Rain bugged her eyes at me.

Mom threw her napkin down. "You're right, Ma. I can't compete. Who do I think I am? I'm no Marilyn Monroe! I'm just some dumb half-breed trash."

"Jeepers, Abe. Christ. You know I didn't mean it like that." Grandma threw down her own napkin. "I can't say anything to you. Not a damn thing. You take it all so personal."

Now I recalled the dark side of being with Grandma. No one could make Mom so giddy, so eager to please. But in the next instant, Grandma's words could shift like weather, strike Mom like lightning, kindling a wildfire that engulfed us all.

I hadn't forgotten how to intervene. I tapped Mom's foot with mine under the table. She swung her blazing eyes to me. *Love you*, I mouthed. Mom set her hand on mine, squeezed. Ticking her chin up, she rallied. "Ma. June here is so successful at her job. Her customers just love her. Her manager thinks she's a dream."

Grandma spun to me, clasping her hands. Her rings clacked, one of my heart's favorite sounds. "Look at you, Juney. Working your way up in the world."

I peeled off my sock and kicked my foot up, hovering it over the table. "Look, Grandma, I've got bunions, too!"

Grandma leaned in to inspect while Rain flipped out. "Oh my God, June! Get your nasty McFeet away from our food!" She shoved my foot, while Mom laughed into her fist.

"And what about you, Rain? I hear you're a college girl now."

Rain dropped her gaze, tucked a curl behind her ear. "I've got a 4.0, Grandma."

I set my fork down. I didn't know that.

"You've got it all, my girl, haven't you? Beauty *and* brains."

"Ma, stop." Mom turned to Grandma with a glare. "You'll give her a big head. She's far from perfect. Go look at her pigsty of a room, if you don't believe me."

Rain's smile disintegrated. She hung her head. With her finger, she moved crumbs around on her plate.

Grandma shifted gears. "What about boyfriends? Either of

you? 'Fess up, girls. This old lady risked her neck on an airplane. You owe me *all* the juicy gossip."

Simultaneously, Rain and I picked up our drinks, took long swigs.

"Come now, Rain. I was married at your age. You don't have a feller?"

Rain plunked her glass down. "I do, Grandma. We spend every minute together." She batted her lashes. "His name is Calculus."

"You're no fun." Grandma flicked her hand, then turned to me. She waggled her drawn-on eyebrows. "Juney. What about you? I know you too well. You're all about the romance. Remember when we finally got you potty trained? We threw a Potty Party, bought you a record player. Remember that, Abe?"

Mom smirked. "Who could forget the Potty Party?"

Grandma shook a finger at me. "Robin Hood. That damn record you listened to over and over. Drove us all up the wall. You were so in love! I tried to break it to you. *He's a cartoon fox*, I said. You know what you did? You yelled at me. You stomped your little Mary Janes and said *no, Grandma, he's a real man*."

Rain said, "I think she's moved on, Grandma."

Grandma rubbed her hands together. "Tell me everything."

"He's a bad boy and a poet. Oh, Johnny Cade." Rain swept her hand to her forehead, and fell sideways in a swoon. "Stay gold, Ponyboy."

"Shut up! I was thirteen." I balled my napkin, threw it at her. She snatched it out of the air in one slick move, grinning like the Cheshire Cat.

"I *have* moved on actually." I lifted my chin. "To Colonel Brandon."

Grandma leaned in, bright-eyed, playing with her lucky

pearls. "Ooh, a military man?"

"Ma, quit," Mom snapped again. "These two have better things to think about than boys."

"But, Abe. They're young. I'm worried about them. They shouldn't be locked away in the countryside with their books and Bibles. They should be out once in a while, having fun."

Mom's face darkened. "Who says they're 'locked away'? Is that what you think? There's more to fun than parties and boys. My girls have fun reading and improving their minds. Don't you, girls?"

Rain and I nodded eagerly. *Oh yes, fun, so much fun, too much, please save us from all the fun.*

"And anyway, Ma. Where did fun get us? Like you said, they've got smarts. They can be more than a couple of housewife drudges."

"Good God, Abe. I'm not telling them to run off and get married..."

"But that's what happens, isn't it? And then what? No money, struggling, babies before you're ready. A mean old drunk for a husband. Or a *cheater*," she spat.

No one spoke. I glanced at Grandma. She looked stunned. I got the feeling she didn't know about the illicit neck massage.

She didn't know, she was here to save us.

Mom laughed, cutting the tension. "Well, if there's one perk to living in the backwoods, I don't have to worry a minute about boys. Can you imagine? June running off with some redneck?" She leaned into me, winked. "Why, she knows I'd never forgive her."

***

After breakfast, as I scurried down the hallway to get ready for work, Grandma cracked open the guest-room door. "Psst! June." I pulled back. She waved me inside, shifty-eyed, like a spy. I hurried in. Grandma closed the door, twisting the lock. Pressing her hand to my back, she hustled me to her suitcase, flung open on the bed. "Here," she said in a whisper, thrusting a package into my hands. "I got this for you. And do not, do not, swear it to me, June, that you *will not* tell your mother. Christ, she'd have my head!"

"I promise, I won't." I smiled. More of Grandma's funny contraband. But when I opened the package, the gorgeous bright glinting shocked me. "Grandma," I said. "Grandma! You got me *sequins*!"

"Sssssh," she pressed her finger to her lips.

"Sorry, sorry," I whispered. I lifted the shirt from the crinkly leopard print tissue paper. It was sleeveless, silky pale green, and stippled in flashing silver sequins. "Grandma, oh my gosh, it's stunning, oh, I love it so deeply." I danced in place, holding the shirt to me.

Grandma's eyes, watching me, grew shiny, more deeply blue. "Ever since you were itty bitty, you fancied sequins." She reached out, touched the tip of my nose. "My little ostrich. Wish I could have gotten you a whole dress of 'em. But this was all I could afford."

Grandma, divorced from my alcoholic grandpa for years, lived on government assistance. As a little girl, I'd been fascinated by what I thought were pink carnival tickets she used to buy groceries. When we went shopping, she'd sweep up glamorous clothes on clearance, then wow us with a dressing room fashion show. She looked like magic in everything. But then, she'd grow discontented, finding small, silly reasons – loose thread here, nicked button there, slightly uneven cuffs – to take everything back the next day. Only recently, Mom had revealed that even on clearance, Grandma couldn't afford those clothes. She bought them to pretend for a while.

Maybe it was Grandma who had taught me how to daydream.

I threw myself into her arms. "Grandma, you made all my sequin dreams come true." I kissed her powdery cheek, again and again.

She laughed against me, a sweet rumble in my own chest. Then, catching my face between her smooth, dry hands, she made me look her in the eye. "Promise me one thing," she said. "If you get the chance, Juney, go. Have a little bit of fun. Make your *own* sequin dreams come true."

McDate

I was in trouble. So much trouble.

"Rain!" I'd run straight home from work, fast as my sturdy work shoes could go. Breathless, ribs heaving, I pounded on my sister's bedroom door. Mom and Grandma were out shopping. Dad was still at work. I didn't have much time before they all converged, and fire rained down on my head. "Rain, please. Let me in!"

She didn't respond. I threw her door open.

Rain's head snapped up. She sat cross-legged on her bed, jabbing at a calculator. She wore her new tortoise shell glasses, curls flowing free. She looked like Harvard Brooke Shields, only outraged. Little Sister, breaking one of Big Sister's Holy Commandments. "What do you think you're doing? I didn't say you could come in. Get the hell out." She swept her arm to the door. "*Out!*"

I dropped to my knees on the carpet.

Rain's eyes popped. "What the hell is wrong with you?"

I turned my face up to her, beseeching. "Rain, help me."

Her face went gray. She slid from her bed. Kneeling beside me, she placed her hand on my arm. "June, what is it? What happened?"

I sank my chin to my chest, let out a harsh sob. "Come here, come here." She pulled me into her. I wept into the soft creases of her t-shirt. After a minute, she took me by the shoulders, pushed me back and looked into my eyes. "Talk to me."

"I have a secret McAdmirer. He's picking me up in two hours."

Behind her glasses, Rain's pupils sharpened. "What?"

"I have a *date!* I was going to cancel. But I didn't." I jumped up and ran. She followed, hot on my heels. I tried to shut my bedroom door in her face but she jammed her foot in sideways, shoved it open with her fierce Tetherball Warrior arms. She cornered me. "Did you tell Mom?"

"No!" I backed up, shaking my head, pressing myself against the wall.

"Shit." Rain tossed her glasses onto my bed. She rubbed her eyes, raked her hands through her curls. "Seriously, June. Now you rebel? In front of Grandma? You know Mom has to make everything look perfect for Grandma."

"I'm not rebelling. I just didn't want to say no, Rain. I just didn't want to..." I tilted my head back against the wall, opened my mouth, unleashed a wail.

Rain grabbed hold of my shoulders, shook them. "Stop. Would you stop, June? I can't help you if you don't get calm." She spun, snatched a box of tissues off my desk, shoved them at me. "You've got to breathe. Breathe with me. One, two, three..."

I inhaled, and exhaled a big blast of snot. Rain sputtered, clawing the air. "Oh my God, gross! Blow your nose." She whisked a tissue out of the box. "You crazy ball of McSlime."

I laughed, and blew, and laughed, and blew some more, wobbling like a drunk.

"Okay," she said, "okay. Where's he taking you?"

"Line-dancing. I don't know what that is, but I want to go, Rain. I want to go *so bad.*" I took another tissue, pressed it over my face, squeezing out more tears, and more. My eyeballs were like juicers.

Rain didn't mince words. "Soon as Mom gets home, you have to tell her."

"No." I shook my head. Slow at first, then faster. "No, no, no."

"You have to, June."

"I don't even know if I'm going. Maybe I won't go!"

Rain and I both swiveled at the sound of car doors slamming, followed by Mom and Grandma's laughter. Rain shook my arm. "Go now. Tell her. It'll be worse if you wait. Worse if she's surprised. You *know* this."

I pushed my face into my hands. "I wish I hadn't said yes. I shouldn't have said yes."

"But you did." Rain peeled my hands away, held my wrists, looked me in the eye. Her expression changed. She blinked, like she was seeing someone new. "You did."

For a moment, we held each other's gaze. Then I pushed past her, out my door, scrambling down the hallway, into the bathroom. On tiptoe, I pulled the blue-checkered curtain back, peered out the small square window. Mom, in a sleeveless yellow shirt and blue jeans, her black hair twined in a long loose braid, purse slung over her shoulder, shopping bags at her feet. She was showing off the garden we'd planted this past spring. Our first garden together. Small, but a beginning.

"June planted the petunias because she remembered they're your favorite," Mom said, her hand on Grandma's back. Grandma, all dressed up in a leopard print blouse and black skirt, leaned in to *oh* and *ah*. "She planted the pansies for me because I love their sweet little faces. The bleeding hearts are Rain's favorite, and the moss roses are June's. She says her garden's how she keeps her girls together. Isn't that the cutest thing you ever heard, Ma?"

Their tangled up laughter, and love. I dropped my forehead to the screen, squeezed my eyes shut. *The girls.*

Footsteps pattered past, down the hallway. The back door opened, slammed. I heard Rain calling them.

I spun away from the window, yanked the bathroom door shut, and slid, back against the door, until my bottom hit cold tile. I held my head in my hands, and listened to the soothing sounds of the countryside. A goldfinch singing, a breeze floating, leaves clinking, silky, like water over pebbles. A dog barking...

Door slamming.

Feet pounding.

Fist smashing.

Smashing.

Against the bathroom door. Reverberating my spine, rattling my ribcage.

Boom! Boom! Boom!

I leapt to my feet, flung the door open.

Mom lunged.

I stumbled backward, fell to the floor, scooted away, banged my funny bone against the toilet. I clasped my elbow, rocked it like a crying baby.

Mom dropped into a crouch. She pushed her face into mine. "How could you!" A whisper-scream. Saliva bubbling at the corner of her mouth. Her pungent coffee breath hot in my nostrils. Her lips a red slash. "You dirty little rat!" I winced as her spit flew into my eyes. "I thought I could *trust* you." She jabbed her finger into my sternum, then pressed deep, deep, deeper still, her sharp fingernail boring in.

I started to cry but it wasn't crying. Deep down guttural heaves.

Mom wrenched her finger back. "Aww, there, there, baby. Did I make you sad?" Patting my head, she stood. Her hand wrapped around my ponytail. Twisting hard, she jerked me to my feet. I shrieked, and she jabbed her finger in my face. "Shut your mouth." She'd pulled out my scrunchie. I saw it there, crushed in her fist, my soft dandelion frizz clinging to it.

"Mom." I looked deep into her eyes. "Mom." I reached for her.

She jerked away. "Oh no you don't. Too late for that, little girl." She yanked me into the hallway, pointed at the carpet. In my panic, I'd forgotten to take my shoes off at the door. On top of everything, I'd tracked big ugly mud prints through the hallway.

Mom stomped to the supply closet. She threw the door open so hard it shuddered against the wall. She wrenched out the vacuum, charged toward me. I shielded my face as she threw it. The vacuum crashed on the floor, toppling sideways at my feet. Parts rolled helter skelter. I dropped to my knees, gathered them with shaking hands.

"You think you're so grown up? Clean your filth before you go on your *date*." She spat the word.

Hugging the vacuum, frizz flying, a dirty rat facing my mess.

Burning alive with shame.

***

Rain found me inside my closet balled up on the floor.

Balled up tight with my work shirt pulled over my head.

Not crying, not moving. Not praying, not thinking. Not asking, not hoping, not dreaming, not seeing, not believing, not wanting, not nothing, not anything.

Breathing. But not alive.

She shook my shoulder. "June, he'll be here in an hour.

You've got to get ready."

Her hand on my shoulder made my nerves stir, made me tingle back to life. My elbow. My sternum. My scalp. My heart, my mind, my life. It all hurt. Every bit of it, at once. "Go away." *She'd* done this. *She'd* told on me. Why had she done this to me? Why had she told on me?

"Come on." Tugging at my shirt sleeve.

"I'm not going," I said.

"Get up." She tugged and she tugged and she tugged.

I was on my knees. Then my feet. Rain took my hand. She pulled me into the hallway. The house smelled lovely. Like one of Mom's vanilla spice bundt cakes. Yes, that's what it was. The one with the lavender flower icing. The stove banged shut. Grandma cracked a joke. Mom's high-pitched giggle rang out. *The girls!*

"I can't, Rain." I tried to twist my hand free. "I can't!"

Rain pressed her knuckles into the small of my back. She steered me into her room. She pulled open the door to her bathroom, pushed me inside, pressed me down onto the toilet seat. "Oh jeez." She studied my face. "This is bad, and I've got less than an hour." She swiveled, flinging drawers open, makeup containers rattling as she scrounged.

My scalp throbbed and burned. I touched my head. "Mom grabbed my hair. She never..." My voice cracked.

"Is that right?" Rain smiled, a hard little smile. "How nice it's been for you all these years. How lucky. Well," she shrugged. "Welcome to *my* world."

There she was. My bitter, jealous big sister. The one who'd beat me up with a tetherball. She'd wanted to turn Mom against me. Wanted me to suffer the pain she'd had to feel all these years. That's why she'd told on me.

But if that was true, then why was she popping one compact, then another, so determined to help me? I made a decision. "Rain. I'm not going. If I go, Mom will hate me forever."

Rain leaned in. She planted her palms on the countertop. She gripped my eyes in the mirror. "And if you don't go? You'll hate *yourself* forever."

I swallowed. "That's okay. I can live with that."

Then, she was there with us. I could see her clearly.

Elizabeth Barrett Browning (gazing upon me with great sadness, and great love): *Don't give in, June. Be brave. Choose you.*

I shook myself, looked up.

I met Rain's eyes in the mirror.

She was holding two lipsticks.

"That one," I said, and pointed to the pink.

June Namid

Line-dancing: *a group of people dancing together in one or more lines or rows, facing each other or the same direction, performing the same steps at the same time. Mostly dancers keep their hands tucked in their pockets. This is something to be grateful for if your hands won't stop shaking.*

That night, Clint took me home on twisting backroads, and I couldn't help but notice the sky, romantically brush-stroked with stars. Every star, every firefly, every little sweet, beautiful thing bloomed, an ache inside me. The night was over, and eventually this peaceful country road would run out. What awaited me at the end of it?

Soon enough, I'd find out.

Just a few minutes later, Clint flicked on the turn signal. The sharp *tick tick* snapped me from my reverie. Turning onto my neighborhood road, I said to Clint, "Would you mind dropping me off here?"

It was a weird request. After tonight though, he couldn't have a doubt. June Taylor was a very weird girl.

Clint pulled to the shoulder, switched off the engine. Silence. The crushing kind. I curled against the door, hugging myself. I didn't know a lot about dates. But I knew, this one was a flop.

Tonight though, I'd stunned myself. On the way out the door, I'd paused, hesitated. In the kitchen with Grandma, Mom's voice had sharpened, followed by the smack of a cupboard, the bang of a pan on the stovetop. She'd shouted, "Oh, I really don't care!" followed by a loud laugh. Whatever she was responding to, I knew what was beneath it. A warning to me. If I turned around, she was saying, if I came back, I'd still be punished, oh yes. But only for a while. One day, there'd be the metal trill of the tray from the oven, the house warm and honeyed with make up cookies. I'd follow the drill: take cookie, smile, forget. She'd swat my butt, playful and cute, pull me to her, and whisper *Juney*. My world, set upright again.

What would happen – if I didn't turn back?

Perched on that threshold in pink lipstick and sequins, my heart pumped so hard my whole body vibrated. I wasn't going on a date. I was jumping into an abyss. As Clint's blue pickup rattled into view, I sucked in a breath, and leapt.

Scrambling out the door, off the porch, stumbling, racing up the hill, tearing the threads between Mom and I, *tearing them*, screaming through my teeth. I didn't stop, didn't turn. Clint had hopped from his truck, striding toward me in dark jeans, cowboy boots, fancy black shirt embroidered with shiny silver lassos. He'd held out his arms with a big grin...

...and I'd swooshed right past, throwing myself into the passenger side of his truck.

It was all downhill from there. At the dance-hall, a big red barn, all lit up, sparkling and shimmering, alive with fiddles and banjos, the swirl of skirts and the stomp of boots, Clint stood close, tried to teach me the steps. I couldn't think straight. I kept messing up. Gently, to guide me, he'd touched my forearm. I'd flinched away. He'd followed my edgy eyes to the bank of windows. With an uncertain smile, he'd glanced from the windows, to me. "Dang, girl. Is someone after you?"

He couldn't feel the savage raw ache of my scalp. Couldn't see the ragged explosion wounds, pouring blood. No one could see the way I was hurt, without my words.

For just a moment I had considered speaking up.

What if I told him the truth?

Instead, I'd put my shaky hand in his, tried to dance.

Now, it was all over. Clint rolled down the window a crack. The sudden sweet chirping of frogs relieved the painful quiet. I swept my gaze to his face, noticing for the first time how clean-shaven and smooth, the care he'd put into our date.

A warm rush, and I felt like, I wanted to give him something. Gathering up tiny crumbs of courage, I spoke across the gulf. "Clint, can I tell you something?"

He lifted his head, turned his face, just slightly. "Sure."

I twisted the ring on my finger. "My middle name is Namid. It's Chippewa for Star Dancer. Which is funny because, truth be told, I've never been to a dance in my life. Until tonight." I captured his gaze, and held it steady. "Thank you, Clint."

A little wisp of a smile. He picked at the steering wheel. "My pleasure. I, uh, hope you had fun."

I clasped my hands, leaned in. "I did! I'm sorry if it didn't seem like it. The truth is I was just...I was so nervous." Did I sound like a regular girl? For extra impact, I fluttered my hand to my chest, glanced at him, shy. "This was my first date."

That got his attention. He sat up straight, turned to face me fully. "Is that right?" Before I knew it, he'd swept up my hand. The warm press of his lips made my pulse beat hard and fast in a most unlikely place. No boy had ever touched me like that, in real life.

He lowered my hand, looked at me earnest. "Can I call you?"

I held my breath. I imagined Mom answering, hearing his voice, smashing the phone down. Averting my gaze, I said, "Well um, see, the thing is, we don't have a phone."

His face fell. "I see." His hand left mine.

That was that. I pushed on the door handle. "Well, goodnight, Clint."

"Goodnight...Miss June." He tipped his hat.

I hopped from his truck. The engine fired up. I stepped back, watching as Clint backed into a driveway, spun the wheel, then roared off down the road. I waved him away, even as I longed to lasso him back. *Miss June.* No one would ever call me that again.

I turned toward home. At least I had a little bit of a walk between me and my house. I walked slow, ambling alone inside the crushed velvet of a backwoods night. I opened my jacket, shimmied side to side. My sequins glitter-glittered. I was my very own star-filled sky. At the top of the hill, I paused, looking down at my house, engulfed in blackness. Not even the single shine of our porch light. I let out a breath.

My worst fear was that Mom would be up, waiting for me.

I jogged down the hill, then stepped up, leaden-legged, onto the porch. I held onto one of the stone columns. My eyes skipped from window to window. Dark, dark, and dark. I dropped my forehead to the cold stone.

My worst fear was that Mom would *not* be up, waiting for me.

I stepped to the door, breathed, turned my key in the lock slowly, oh so slowly. I crept in, picked my way on ballerina toes to the bathroom. I wasn't prepared, when I opened the door and flicked on the light, for the shock of my scrunchie.

It lay on the floor.

I knelt, picked it up. My dandelion frizzies, clinging to it.

My hand went to my head.

The ache and throb of skin was gone. But the pain hadn't

evaporated.

It had seeped inside. Where no one would ever find it.

A door creaked. I shot to my feet, eyes flying everywhere. *Hide, hide!*

"June? That you?" Grandma poked her head around the door. Her face, scrubbed clean of makeup, was pink, wrinkled, vulnerable as a baby bird. This shredded me. "Sorry," I said, wiping my face of tears. "Gosh, Grandma. I am so so sorry."

Grandma's eyes fluttered closed. "Himmel, Himmel." The German word for heaven, and Grandma's favorite thing to say when confronted with a mess. With a little huff, she reached out, curled her hand around my wrist. "Come with me." I let her pull me down the hallway. In the guest room, she pointed to the bed. "Sit."

I plunked down on the rumpled quilt. Grandma locked the door with a sharp twist and whipped around, roughly fastening her robe as she strode toward me. She hauled herself up on the bed, perched her admirably bunioned feet on the sideboard beside mine. "So," she leaned into me. "Who's the lucky feller?"

My head spun. "I...he...Clint?"

Grandma's hands flew together, rings clacking. "That's a hunk's name! Where'd he take you?" Her eyes bright in the dark.

"Line-dancing."

"Juney! You got to dance with a real cowboy?"

"Yeah. I did." A little geyser of joy unleashed. How surreal to be sharing my first date with my *Grandma*.

"Oh, honey," she pinched the fabric of my jacket, drew it aside. "You wore your sequins." Her expression grew so tender, I thought she'd weep. "You're made for them. Just made for them." She ran her hand through my frizz. Well, she tried. Her fingers locked in a tangle. Gently tugging them free, she smiled. "You and your kooky curls." Then, conspiratorial, "Sooooo... when's the next big romantic date?"

I drew my knees up, tucked my chin between them. "Never, Grandma. He doesn't like me anymore."

"Oh, pshaw. Of course he does! You're June."

Her underlying belief. *To know June is to love June.* I smiled, even as I hurt. "Oh, Grandma."

"Clint's a keeper, too. Handsome. Nice. Good dancer. And such a glorious young butt!"

A laugh burst from me. "Grandma! How do you know?"

"I might have snuck a peek."

I gazed at her. She'd seen me off. And where had Mom been? Where was she now? *She* was the one I wanted. The two of us. Mom's hands tangled in my kooky curls. Mom and I whispering together side by side, until we fell asleep.

There I went, dreaming again. Always dreaming. *Never ending, heart-scalding dreaming, dreaming, dreaming.* You know who I hated? Marmee, the mother in *Little Women.* I'd despised that book since sixth grade. I'd wanted to chew it up and spit it out. Marmee! Who in the whole world had a mother like that? What a fantasy! What a fake! Now I was sobbing. Now my hurt was out, spilling all over the place.

"Aww, there, there," Grandma said, rubbing circles on my back. "What's the matter, sweetheart?"

"Grandma, I...I acted funny. On the date. Mom wasn't happy with me, so. I just...I had a hard time...having fun." I peered at her. How much did she know? The line between telling the truth, and betraying Mom, so very thin, and edged in fire.

Grandma sighed. "Oh for Christ's sakes. Such a fuss over

nothin'! I tried my best to calm her down. I said, *it's not about you, Abequa, it's about June growin' up!* If you ask me, it's about damn time, too." She latched and unlatched her fingers, rings flashing. "I try to stay out of your folk's business. But truth is, I've been worried about you and Rain. All alone out here in the sticks, your Dad pushing that strict religion of his. And your Mom, well." She leaned in, spoke out of the side of her mouth. "Just between you and me, June. I do *not* agree with your mother's ways."

My mind went wild with questions. What 'ways', Grandma? Do you see something wrong? What do you see?

Grandma took my face between her hands. "I need to know something, June. Do you swear on the Lord's Holy Bible to tell me the truth?"

I broke into a dire, drenching sweat. "I swear, Grandma."

She tipped her forehead to mine, eyes piercing. "Does your mother hit you?"

It took a second to register.

Then I recoiled.

"No, Grandma!" My hairs stood on end. "She doesn't hit me. No! Never." I shuddered and rubbed my arms.

Grandma exhaled, slumped. "Oh, God. Thank you, God." Her hand found my knee, squeezing. "Now when I go home, I can rest easy."

i'll get you

Two days later, I snuck out to the garage, picked up the dusty green phone and dialed work.

"Daydreamer!" Becky's pirate-y cackle greeted me through the line. "How was the sex, ahem! I mean, date?"

Beep! Beep! Beep!

"Fries are ready," I said in response to the beeps. "Hey Becky, can I talk to Janet, please?"

"Well, hell. I'm not enough? JANET!" *Shick, shick!* That was the fryer basket. The music of crispy, greasy french fries, shaken up. "But listen, you. You'd better not hold out on me. I been waitin' to hear about the big..."

Janet swiped the phone away. "June, where you at, girlie? Have I got a surprise for you! Oh, I'm just about to bust. But never mind, I'll wait til you get here."

"Shoot, Janet. Just tell 'er!" *Whisk, whisk.* The broom, the poetry of stray fries flying into a neat golden pile on the floor. "Do it before you pee yourself and I gotta clean up that mess, too!"

Janet's voice, muffled. "Shush, Becky. We gotta make it special." Then, "Sorry, June. What was it you were calling about?"

I sank to the grimy concrete of the garage, curling my fingers into the cord. "Well, you see. My Grandma's extending her visit. I was wondering, can I take a week off, starting today?"

A startled pause. "A week off? Starting *today?* That is really short notice."

"I know it is. I'm sorry, Janet. It's just, when she leaves, I won't get to see her again for who knows how long. She has heart problems. So…" My voice cracked.

"Oh, June. Well. Of course you can. Take the time you need. Sure, honey, sure, we'll make it work." But, clear as the fryer, the broom, and all the sounds of my beloved McWorld, I heard her disappointment.

Almost like she knew I was lying.

***

Grandma wasn't staying.

Grandma had a flight back to Wisconsin that very evening. Her suitcase was packed, resting on her immaculately made bed. Better get out, it seemed to say, while the getting is good.

I need to take time off because my mother hates me was not a truth I was willing to confess to Janet. Or anyone.

The good news, the lone sliver of light. Mom was happy with Dad again. Not just happy, almost beside herself. And even though Dad hadn't spoken a word to me since my date, I was relieved for him.

During Grandma's farewell lunch on the screened-in porch, Mom scooted her wicker chair right up next to his. Dad, freshly shaven, dark curly hair carefully styled, poured Mom's hibiscus iced tea, which glowed amber in the late afternoon sun. He'd dressed up in khakis, and a navy blue kingdom hall blazer. Mom touched his arm, held his hand, giggled at his jokes. She lavished him with praise. *Ma, look at the tomatoes Phil grew! Aren't they the best you've ever seen? He could win trophies!* Beaming, Dad salt-and-peppered the tray of fat glistening tomato slabs with extra flair. He gazed at Mom, melting and grateful. We'd switched places, him and I. He was in paradise. I was in the grave.

Grandma, in a silky bright purple blouse, blonde hair

whipped into a high, girlish pony-tail, plied Rain with questions about college. Well, about the professors. "Any good-looking old farts? Not for *you*, Rain," eyes flicking to Mom, "For *me*. What, Abe? What's that look? Hells bells. I'm not dead yet. I'm still hot stuff. I'm a vintage Camaro!"

"Yeah, Ma, sure you are." Mom lifted the tray with Dad's tomato slices, turned toward me. As soon as our eyes met, her face slammed shut like a steel trap. She twisted the *other* way, passed the tray to Rain instead. "Here, sweetheart, first dibs." While Rain pushed two tomatoes onto her plate, Mom lifted my sister's thick curly hair, holding it up in a bunch. "Ma, would you look at this mane!" she crowed. "Rain got the good looks, the good hair, the big boobs, all of it."

My skin went cold.

"Like I said, beauty *and* brains." Grandma winked at Rain, who smiled, wary, stunned by the sudden deluge of praise. Carving into her chicken, Grandma plunged into a boisterous story about Aunt Rena, Mom's estranged older sister. I'd only met Aunt Rena a handful of times. I remembered her jet-black hair teased to the sky, dramatically freeze-sprayed. I remembered her chain-smoking with a deep, crackly laugh, and long, glossy red fingernails like bloody spears. According to Mom, Aunt Rena was Satan's soul-mate.

"Abe, you won't believe this. That witch, Rena, is back to her tricks! She's telling everyone she's got cancer. Cancer my ass. She's getting those suckers pumped up." Grandma made squeezing motions by her boobs. Dad, taking a sip of tea, choked. Mom dissolved into laughter. "Jeez, Ma. Have some couth!" She patted Dad's back.

"Well, Abe, for Christ sakes. Cancer." Grandma scoffed. A small white butterfly that had found its way onto the porch flit like winged starlight around her ponytail. "She's a liar. A pity whore! Speaking of which, did I tell you the Old Man showed up again?"

Mom's head jerked up so fast the little white butterfly zoomed off. She set her fork down. "No. You didn't."

Grandma shook her head, lips compressed. "Passed out dead drunk on the porch. I couldn't even get my damn door open! And I had an appointment for my heart."

Mom's face reddened, her voice shook. "Next time, call the cops. He's caused us enough misery. He's not our problem anymore."

Reflexively, before I could stop myself, my hand reached for hers.

She whipped away like my hand was a rattlesnake, then shoved her chair out and stood. "Ma! More potato salad?" She shouted it over my head.

I pulled my hand back, set it in my lap. My face and gut just burned.

Grandma said, holding out her plate for another helping, "You know me, Abe. I always get taken in. I feel sorry for the old bastard. When he's not drunk, he's got a soft heart. And boy, he's had a hell of a life. I called 911, covered him with a blanket, and sat there with him til the ambulance came. Three broken ribs this time."

"Let me guess. You sat there with him and missed your heart appointment."

Grandma didn't say anything. She wiped her lips with her napkin.

"He used to beat you, Ma. He beat all of us."

Heavy silence. No one moved.

"Remember? I stood between you and his fists, when I was

five."

"God, I know it, Abequa. I've been told before. I'm sorry for being a romantic old fool." Grandma's gaze lowered, then snagged on my untouched plate. She tucked her napkin back in her blouse. Her eyes flicked from me, to Mom, to me, like she had thread, and was trying to knit us back together.

Finally, smacking her palms down on the tabletop. "So! What about that rhubarb, eh, girls? I went down this morning and took a look. The stalks are so big, a giant could climb down from the clouds." She chuckled. "Fourth of July, I mean, Rhubarb Pie Day, is right around the corner. Don't you two make that pie together? Isn't that your mother-daughter tradition?" More glances, more knitting, back and forth.

"It's my favorite day," I said, gazing at Mom, heart in my throat.

Mom stared straight over my head, glassy-eyed, like a wax figure.

Grandma shifted, cleared her throat. "What about that job of yours, sweetheart? Any news?"

Desperation drove me over the edge. "Grandma, my boss has a surprise for me."

"What?" Grandma craned toward Mom. "Whatever could it be, Abe?"

I said, "I think it's about a promotion. She mentioned an assistant manager position. She says, I'm a leader." I looked right at Mom.

And this time, finally, Mom looked right at me.

She rolled her eyes back, wagged her head, and ugly-mouthed *blah blah blah*.

I stared, in shock.

A glass thunked down on the table top, and I jumped. "I'm

proud of you, June," Rain said fiercely. "*You* should be proud of yourself." She skewered Mom with a dirty look, and my fear doubled.

"Oh heavens, we're all proud, aren't we, Abe?" Grandma spun to Mom.

Mom's sneer morphed into a smile. She lifted the tray. "One more tomato, Ma. It's all yours."

"How 'bout that home-made ice-cream!" Grandma waved her spoon. "We'll have a toast to June's success."

"I'll get it." I shot up from the table, darted into the house. Rain followed. Together, we skittered through the laundry room, into the garage. I swung the freezer open and grabbed the frosty, stainless steel bowl. The cold was a shock. I drew back, crying out. "Here." Rain tossed me a greasy towel from the garage floor. I used that to grab the icy bowl. I bowed my head, panting. "What's happening, Rain?"

Rain squeezed my shoulder, hard. She whispered, "You have to be strong, okay? You have to prepare yourself. After Grandma leaves, Mom might come after you. She'll burst into your room. She'll bring gifts you've given her, and break them. She'll tell you that you lied, that you never loved her. She'll scream, and keep screaming. Even if you go mute. Even if you curl up in a ball. Even if you crawl under the bed. She'll sweep everything off your desk. She might rip up your stuff to lure you out. Don't come out! Don't fight back." She advised me on and on, like an old war veteran.

"Okay, okay," I mumbled, while inside, I resisted. I'd make amends. I'd figure out how. I'd never let it get so bad it was unfixable.

As we hurried inside, there, amidst the drifting shadows of the laundry room, the back door flew open. Mom stepped in, clutching a small bouquet of Lily of the Valley. Rain and I stumbled backward, together. We pressed into the wall like one creature, shoulder to shoulder. Mom edged in. I caught the sharp sweetness of the delicate white flowers, crushed in her grip. Pushing her face close to ours, her lips tore away from her teeth. “I’ll get you,” she hissed, eyes darting rapid fire between us. “I’ll get you both.”

I knelt at the top of the hill, near the road, by the unfinished white picket fence. To the neighbors, I must have looked like I was praying. I crushed lavender flowers between my palms. I rubbed the sweet-spicy flowers on my wrists, my arms, my neck. I pictured Grandma, her plane flying over the last of the tall, slim Arkansas pines. *Stay*, I'd whispered, a plea, into the soft, sweet wrinkles of her neck, locked in our last embrace. My tears had fled into the valley between her breasts. The place that smelled most richly of her. *Home*. Holding my face between her hands, thumbing my tears away, she'd whispered, "Give her what she wants, June. Will you do that? Swallow your pride. Smooth her ruffled feathers. She'll come around."

Rain had offered to take me with her to class, but I knew. Leaving with her would make us look like a team, an alliance against Mom. I closed my eyes, sank into a daydream. I imagined Sister Finn driving down the lane in her shiny red van, finding me there on my knees. I imagined her kneeling, caressing my hair, gently collecting me from the grass. I imagined her taking me out to eat, looking at me kindly, telling me how happy she was to be with me. Then, an intruder bursting into my dream, Mom appeared. Sliding into the booth beside Sister Finn, she made terrible faces at me. "Go on, June," she taunted. "Tell your favorite person what you did. Tell Sister Finn who you really are, running off with some worldly boy, and see if she looks at you the same."

Dream turned nightmare, I fell sideways in the grass, pulled my knees to my chest, my teeth chattering like it was the middle of winter.

A minute later, a warm face nuzzled my arm. "Oh, Grits." My beautiful yellow angel friend, arriving in the nick of time. She sank into the grass beside me. I wrapped my whole self around her. I shivered into her. Her heartbeat, her steady panting, a lullaby. The shivering stopped. My body calmed, settled into hers.

Footsteps yanked me upright.

Dad, walking up the hill. He stopped beside me, hands wedged into the back pockets of his jeans. He tilted his head, squinting. A sudden strong breeze flipped the leaves onto their silvery backs. Dad's hand flew to his straw hat, holding it in place. "Storm kicking up." The brown and white-spotted quail feather in the brown velvet band, bent this way and that. Then, without looking at me, he said, "I had a plan. You agreed to it. You broke our contract."

His first words to me in two days, and he was talking like a businessman.

A surprising surge of heat straightened my spine. "I didn't do anything wrong."

"You didn't?" Still not looking at me, he set his hand on one of the three posts he'd managed to get in the ground for the white picket fence. "You ran out the door. You took off with a strange boy. Mom says, you'd never even mentioned a boy. You ambushed her."

"I was scared..."

"And *I* had a plan!" He brought his fist down on the post.

I rose to my feet, faced him, heart pounding in my throat. "*You* lusted after another woman. *I* went on a date. Which one of us sinned?"

He didn't skip a beat. Pointing at himself, "Do ye not lust

in your heart after her beauty." Then, turning that same finger on me, "Be ye not unevenly yoked with unbelievers."

My jaw fell. "I didn't marry him!"

Two fingers in my face. "Bad associations spoil useful habits."

"He's not bad! He took me line-dancing!"

"Honor thy father and mother." Three fingers, waving them in my face.

I ducked away.

"You have no idea, do you? No idea what you've caused. I was making headway! She was getting better. Now she thinks we're all against her." He buried his face in his hands and groaned.

I was crying now. "Why is it my fault! Why is it yours! Why does she get every excuse! She hurts us! She *hurts* us!"

"*She's* hurt!" Dad lurched at me. "And you're too selfish to see!"

Grits jumped on Dad's leg, barking. Dad raised his hand.

"No!" I grabbed his arm, bit down hard on his wrist. He wrenched away. Saliva fell down my chin. Grits cowered behind me.

Cradling his arm, breathing hard, Dad said, "Look at you. You're out of control."

He was right. Wiping my mouth, arm shaking, I was a wild animal.

Dad stared at me, got very quiet. "Tell me something. Do you love your mother like you love that dog?"

"You know I do."

"No, I don't. Because when it came right down to it, you didn't care about Mom, what she was going through." He let his arm drop to his side, heavy. "You only cared about what *you* wanted."

"But she..."

He waved me off, turned on his heel, started walking.

"Dad! Wait!" He halted, but kept his back to me. I had to get control or he wouldn't listen. *Breathe, June.* I raked my hands through my hair. "Dad, I...I have to tell you something." He turned slightly, looked at me over his shoulder. "She said... to me and Rain..." I tented my hands over my nose and mouth, gasp-cried. I lowered my hands, took a breath. He had turned to face me. I met his eyes. "She backed us into a corner. She said, *I'll get you both.*"

Dad blinked hard. I watched his Adam's apple bob up and down. I had never told him what Mom did or said to us, in one of her rages. We never talked about it. The breeze lifted, sweeping my frizz across my face. Dad looked down. I started shivering again.

When Dad raised his head, the anger was gone, and whatever else I had seen on his face, shock, maybe fear, it was all smoothed away. "First Corinthians 13: 7-9," he recited. "Love bears all things, believes all things, hopes all things. Love... *endures* all things."

He held my gaze. And I broke. Doubling over, I wept hotly into my hands.

As the wind tore loose, leaves fluttering down, Grits pressed herself into the backs of my legs.

Dad's voice was soft, but merciless. "You want to get baptized? Become a missionary? First, you have to learn how to love."

mom's goodbye

I woke up stunned, even before I saw the doll.

She was lying face down on my floor, long, black hair splayed around her.

As I crept closer, I saw bits and pieces of something in her hair.

I wanted to think they were flowers. Something desperate in me wanted to see something else, something other than what was real. But when I knelt beside her on the floor, bending down to look, not wanting to touch her, I saw that the pieces were torn up bits of paper with words. Words I recognized. My handwriting. My words. *Violets*, I saw. The poem that had poured out from me at my desk. The poem I had given her, the one she said she would keep forever, now confetti in Pocahontas' hair.

And beneath the doll, a note was wedged.

Dear June,

I am sorry we had to stop going to kingdom hall. I know you blame me. I guess that boy was your revenge. Well, I want you to know. I've always supported your dreams. I was the one who bought you that expensive swimsuit, remember? I wanted to see you get baptized. That special day was stolen from me. Your dad broke me, carrying on with that Jezebel. How could I sit in a place of worship, where I should feel safe, watching them flirt. Everyone gossiping, laughing behind my back. Don't you think I wish things were different?

I told you things about my life that I never shared with anyone. I trusted you when I couldn't even trust your own father. What happened to my sweet June? You were so kind. You cared about everything, and everyone. Remember when I told you that your heart was like a garden? I watched you let the weeds in. It started with that job. You changed. You got a big head. You weren't the humble, selfless June I knew. Then that boy. You hid things. You shamed me in front of my mother.

Now you listen to Rain. I see her turning you against me. That hurts worse than anything. I can't live with liars who pretend to love me. It's time for me to finally have a life of my own.

Goodbye,

Mom

blue suitcase

"To June and Rain. Sisters. Free at last." Rain's eyes shone bright as the wine in the glass she raised.

We clinked, side by side on the front porch swing, legs pressed together.

It was a muggy evening, almost July, the sky steeped in shades of sherbet. I wore overall shorts and my favorite McDonald's shirt, Grimace peeking over the pocket. Inside the pocket, the note Mom had left for me, folded and unfolded, and folded again. No one knew. No one but Grimace and me. We knew that note by heart.

My bare feet scraped the warm concrete as we gently swung back and forth. Thumb tucked under my suspender, I took my first ever sip of wine, and winced. Oh, it was bitter. Gone a week. And she wouldn't tell Dad where she was. The night before, I'd spied him through a crack in the door, on the phone, begging her on his hands and knees to come home.

My sister wanted to celebrate.

That day, she'd driven us to Fayetteville. We'd joined the gym.

"We need to learn how to swim," she'd said. "We can take lessons together. You can wear your new swimsuit."

"Okay." It was like I'd signed the gym membership with a mechanical arm. Nothing felt real.

Now, Rain took a luxurious drink, wiped her mouth with the back of her hand. "Delicious. Don't you think?"

I gave a half smile, didn't disagree. Dad's home-made blackberry wine was meant only for rare special occasions, and never for me and Rain. I'd followed her, creeping and sly, down into the dank depths of the cellar where Dad stored the bottles. Mom had warned us all our lives to stay away from drink. *You have Native blood*, she said, *and we can't hold our liquor.* You could see it in her face, when Dad poured a glass. *Stop, that's enough*, she'd say, holding her palm out. It showed in her eyes, how scared she was for us to even look at it, see how pretty it beamed in the glass. Once, when Dad brought the wine out, she'd run to her room and in a comical flurry, returned with her dream-catchers, hanging them on the dining room wall. *What are you doing, Mom?* We'd all laughed, but underneath, it wasn't funny. She'd cut the Old Man out of her life, and kept him away from us. The last thing she wanted was her daughters gathering dreams about the thing she called, like some dark fairytale, *the beast in the bottle.* That's why her dream-catchers still hung in the dining room. The only artifacts of our heritage on display, because she feared these things were idols, an insult to Jehovah.

I took another sip, cherished the fantasy that Mom hadn't run far. Reveled in the feeling that she was nearby, spying. I wanted her to see her daughters drinking wine. I wanted her to fear for us, and come flying back. I wanted her to rip the drinks out of our hands, fling them across the lawn, smash the bottle on the pavement, cuss us out so the whole neighborhood could hear. *My Mom caught me drinking and boy, did she get mad!* I got tingles, wanting that. For her to be our dream-catcher.

"Why do we need to swim?" The question emerged out of nowhere.

"What?" Rain lowered her glass.

I focused on Rain's toenails, freshly painted a glowy peach. We'd done each other's nails, too. She'd painted mine in purple glitter to match Grimace. I edged my fancy toes closer to her fancy toes. I crept my toes over hers. A toe hug. "Why do we need to swim?"

She studied me a long time without speaking, then seemed to make some decision. She jumped to her feet, plucked up the wine bottle, and with it, motioned for me to follow her. "Let's go!" She hopped off the porch.

I hesitated, then slowly rose. "Where?" I was sick of adventures.

She wiggled her brows. "On a sight-seeing tour." We tripped side-by-side through the long whispers of unmown grass. Not mowing was Dad's form of not shaving. I looked this way and that for Grits, without hope. Mom had left, and I hadn't seen Grits since. The thought kept intruding. When Mom packed up her car in the middle of the night, had Grits shown up to dance at her feet? Had Mom swung open the car door, taken Grits away on purpose, to hurt me? It was terrible to think that. And yet – the doll, the pieces in her hair, what my mother could do – the vision was so real, it raised the hairs on my neck.

Rain stopped at our driveway, swung out an arm. "Where's your car, June?" She took a drink, right from the bottle.

I tried to swipe it from her, and she twisted away with a laugh.

"Rain! Are you drunk? You know I don't have a car."

"Why not? You're sixteen, aren't you?" Another swig.

"Yes, but I don't have my license. I don't even know how to drive."

Rain thrust my arm high in the air. "Ding, ding, ding!"

I felt like a champion, without knowing why. "You've had too much. Give me that."

"Only if you promise to drink it." She batted her eyelashes and grinned, purple-lipped.

"Fine, Grimace Lips." I took a small drink, trying to laugh.

She threw her head back, pounded her thigh. "Grimace Lips! Please call me that forever." We lingered together at our tetherball, the ball glowing orange, like a setting sun. It made me think of our childhood, long summer evenings in bare feet, cut-offs and rolled up sleeves, making muscles at each other, slamming the ball back and forth until it was too dark to see.

"Tetherball Warriors." Rain said the words in my mind, and grabbed my hand.

Like kids again, we flew up the back porch steps, through the laundry room, into the kitchen. Rain flipped on all the lights. She flung open the cupboards and drawers, one by one. I hung back, resting one foot on top of the other. "Now what are you up to?"

She widened her eyes, barked a laugh. She looked so young. Like I'd never seen her before. Prancing in bare feet, curls swept up into a rambunctious side ponytail. She hauled off, and smacked one of the cupboards closed. *Bang!*

I jumped. "Shh!" My head snapped to Mom's room. "What's wrong with you?"

"Nothing. Everything." Rain shoved a drawer shut. *Crash!* Gleeful, bouncing on her toes, she motioned for me. "Come on. Why are you looking at her room? She's gone. We can make noise!"

A nightmare feeling oozed inside me. Yet my sister's brimming joy was infectious, and swept me up. I grabbed a handle, threw a cupboard closed. *Smack!* Rain jumped up and down. "Yeah!" She cried.

Rain flipped on the radio, switched it from mom's favorite Oldies station, cranked up pop music instead. We latched hands and crazy-danced through the kitchen, kicking up our heels, making a god-awful racket. *Slam! Bang! Crash!* "We're nuts!" I looked down at my shirt. Wine had dribbled down the front, so it looked like Grimace was bleeding. I grew deeply concerned. "Are we, Rain? Are we nuts?"

"Yes." She smiled, pulled me to her, hooked her chin over my shoulder. My sister and I, slow-dancing in the kitchen to Mariah Carey, Dreamlover, her voice a cry. "For the first time in a long time," Rain whispered, "it feels like we could be friends."

A heart shock. We weren't friends? I knew we had our troubles but when had we stopped being friends?

She broke away, twirled me once. "Ugh, *don't*, Rain. I might puke."

"No time for puking," she said, pulling me by the hand. "Onward, to the dining room." Like a game show hostess, she swept her hand across the long rectangle leaned up against the dining room wall. She swiped off the sheet. "Behold, the infamous home-school blackboard."

It stared at us, blank, smooth. A brand new eraser and two fresh, pointy chalks rested on the ledge. I blinked at her. "Why are we beholding the blackboard? We don't even use it."

She raised one of her thick, dark brows, now comically askew. "That's right. Explain that to me. Didn't Dad promise to help you with home-school?"

"Yeah."

"So you know everything? You don't need help?"

"Well, I'm struggling with geometry." I scratched my elbow. "Triangles hurt my soul."

"Okay, but, you have to hurt your soul to get your diploma. Have either one of them checked in with you about your school-work?"

I pressed my lips together, shook my head.

"June. Are you even doing your school-work?" She looked at me closely, with real concern.

"Kind of. Mostly? I mean, not geometry. Or biology. Or Spanish..."

Rain's face just kept falling.

"But I'm almost done with Wuthering Heights. I've finished my journal entries. I don't like Heathcliff at all. He's not a hero. He's a warning. A giant, bloody red flag in human form..."

"June." Rain held up her hand, stopping me. "Are you on track to graduate next spring?"

I grimaced, like my shirt. "Can we play something else? This game isn't fun anymore."

She closed her eyes for a second, took a breath, then opened them. She pressed the wine bottle into my hands. "Here's your fun." She turned on her heel, headed down the hallway. "And up next, if you keep playing, there's a prize."

"Really?" Following her down the hallway, I dipped, furtive, rolled the wine bottle out of sight, beneath the dining room table. We halted outside the bathroom. Rain ducked in. I heard the closet door squeak open. She reappeared. "YOU WIN!" She tossed me a package. I caught it, and screeched. "Pads? This is my prize?"

She smirked. "Aren't they every woman's?"

"Haha." I was confused, and more than a little embarrassed. I squeezed the package. "These things are gigantic, like pillows. I didn't even know they made them this big."

Rain leaned on the door frame. "I got them for you."

"You did? Why?"

"Your period is heavy. You leak a lot."

I bit my lip. I didn't know where to look.

"It's not your fault." Her voice, too gentle. "Mom didn't

want to deal with it. With you. I saw, June. She threw a box of panty-liners at you, then stopped paying attention. She doesn't want you to grow up. She doesn't want you to date. She wants you to be a sweet child forever. So you'll always adore her without question. And never fight back."

Where was this coming from? Her intense stare, everything she was showing me on this 'tour', was beginning to feel deliberate, like it was all leading up to a point she had to make. I began to feel trapped. Me and Mom weren't her and Mom. She didn't know the first thing about me and Mom. But I'd never say that. I dreaded a fight. I shook the package at her, distracting with a joke. "How am I going to wear them? They're like great white whales."

Rain burst into laughter, draping herself around the door. "Oh my God. From now on, when you're on your period, I'm going to call you Captain Ahab." She laughed so hard, she fell against the wall.

Laughing and laughing, bumping into one another, it didn't sink in, until she was twisting the knob, where we were going next.

The moment I realized, I grabbed her arm. "Rain, stop. We can't go in there."

Rain shook me off. Stepping inside, she looked at me over her shoulder. "She's *gone*, June."

I watched, stricken, as she crept to Mom's bed.

Without a moment's hesitation, she crawled up and patted the space beside her. "Come here. I want to tell you a story." She looked a little frightened. "Will you please come here, June?"

I went, skulking and wicked, desecrating holy ground. Mom would *hate* us in her room. I held myself rigid. Even to look at Mom's stuff felt like treachery.

Rain hugged her knees as I climbed up, my stomach twisting and turning snakelike.

"Sometimes," she said, "I think that you think it's only been like this since we moved. Mom's gone off the rails because we moved. Because Dad's been having a hard time getting his clinic going and we don't have as much money. Because she doesn't like it here. Because she's lonely. Sometimes I think, that's the story you tell yourself."

"I don't know what you're talking about."

"But it's always been happening, June," she went on like I hadn't spoken. "It just wasn't happening to *you*." She turned to me. "You remember Mom's suitcase?"

"The blue one?"

Rain nodded. She set her chin on her knee, picked at her freshly painted toenail. I pictured the suitcase. 1970's-style, hard body and powder blue, with gold clasps, gold lock, and a tiny gold key. When it popped open, the inside pockets were satiny, like water. I knew right where Mom kept it. On the top shelf of her closet, between two stacks of shoeboxes. "It was her honeymoon suitcase, wasn't it?"

"I don't know. I only know I hate it. More than anything."

I stared at her. "Why?"

Rain closed her eyes. "The first time I remember making Mom mad, I was five. Maybe I talked back, I don't know. She grabbed me by the arm, pulled me into her room. I thought she was going to spank me. Instead, she marched me to her closet, flung open the doors, and pointed at the blue suitcase. She said, *You see that? If I pack that and leave, you did it. It's your fault.*"

The hairs on my neck rose. "What?"

"You don't believe me." Rain jerked her head up, eyes wounded. "Dad didn't believe me."

"I believe you," I said. And again, "I believe you, Rain."

She breathed. "Once, she made me watch." Rain's long fingers latched and unlatched in her lap. "She forced me to sit in the corner. She carried her bras, her shorts, her shirts from the dresser, tucking them into the blue suitcase. She said, *This time you've done it, you've pushed me over the edge. Now I have to leave!* I cried, June. Until I was hoarse. I wrapped my arms around her legs. I begged her to stay. *Sorry, Mom, please, don't leave me! I'm sorry!*"

I opened and closed my mouth. Where was that wine?

Rain lay her head on my shoulder. We breathed together. She tilted her face up to mine. "Why, June? Now can you tell me? Why do we need to swim?"

My gut burned. Here was the destination. She had plotted it all out in her head, a 'tour' leading to this room, this story. Rain's version of the truth. But Rain's story wasn't the only one. I pictured that cradle, hidden up in the tree. I pictured a little girl, terrified, finding a way to protect her dolls. No one in the world to protect her.

I knew what Rain wanted me to say.

But I had my own story, too. *Rain, on our tour, we didn't go to the rhubarb patch. Rhubarb Pie Day's next week. I don't want to swim with you. I want Mom's floury hands tangled in my hair. I want to chop the ruby red stalks in our matching aprons side by side. I want to bake our pie, watching together as the crust turns gold, and the sweet jeweled juice bubbles out. I want my mom. More than anyone or anything in the world, more than a driver's license or a diploma, or baptism, or swimming lessons, or my own two hands, or my very own heartbeat. No matter what she's done, or hasn't done. For the rest of my life, I want my mom.*

I thought I might die, hugging my package of great white

whales.

Rain pulled away from me. She slid to the floor, tip-toed to Mom's closet. She opened the doors. A beat passed. And then my sister's voice, chilled, hushed. "June. Look."

No. No! I did not want to look.

"June."

Full of dread, I raised my eyes.

My sister pointed to the empty space, between two stacks of shoeboxes.

The blue suitcase was gone.

abraham

Crouched just outside, I listened to the phone click.

A minute later, Dad stalked from the garage, face grim. He held a book. Gripping my own book, I sprung to my feet. I started to follow him, then remembered something, and turned. I dashed into the garage, grabbed his straw hat from its hook. I held it in my hands, just for a moment, held it tight, before chasing after him. "Dad!"

Head down, he stormed up the driveway, kicking gravel.

"Dad!" I called again.

He kept going, taking a sharp right onto the neighborhood road.

I knew he heard me. I sprinted, tugging my shorts up. I had lost weight. "Dad!"

At the bottom of the hill, he veered, plunking himself down in the long grass by the creek. He picked up pebbles, flicked them sharp-wristed into the water. I lowered myself next to him, gathering breath, and courage. Finally, I held it out to him. The quail feather in the velvet band of his hat trembled between us in the soft breeze.

Dad stared as if he didn't recognize it. When he finally took it, I saw the bandage on his arm. What had happened?

I had bit him.

A pit of horror opened in my gut. I looked away, to where Dad's Bible lay in the grass. The pit only deepened, churning. Even though we couldn't go to kingdom hall, he still read his Bible, faithfully, every night. I loved his green Bible with the gold lettering. At meetings, I loved to lean in, against him, read from his Bible instead of my own. I loved his notes, his insights inked neatly in the margins.

He turned, and to my surprise, slipped my book from my fingers. "What's this?"

"It's just...a play I've been reading."

"About?" His glance was sharp.

"The poet, Elizabeth Barrett. Her life, her poetry. Her love story with Robert Browning." I had just read the part where Elizabeth's doctor ordered her to Italy for her health. He'd warned her she would die if she didn't go. But her father forbade her from leaving. Robert was furious, frantic, trying to convince her to go anyway. She hated him for it, and they'd fought.

Dad flipped through the pages. "Did it start with these books, June?"

I curled my fingers around my knees. "Did what start?"

He looked at me hard. "Your disobedience."

I swallowed. Picking my lip, I scoured my brain for a starting point. Where had evil leaked in?

"Was it your sister?"

I shook my head, but didn't speak.

"I know you look up to her. But she's choosing the world. She swears. She's defiant. She dresses immodestly. She puts herself first, before family, before Jehovah. You see that, don't you?"

"Yes," I said.

Dad set his hand on my back.

At his touch, the longed for reconnect, tears spilled down my face.

"I don't think either of you girls realize what your mother's been through. Just how much she's overcome."

"I know about the Old Man."

"Not much, you don't. Know why?"

"She's kept him away from us."

Dad nodded. "She wants to protect you and Rain, the way she couldn't protect herself." He flicked another pebble into the creek. "I met your mom in high school, June. I know things about her you can never know."

"Like what?"

He glanced at me. "Like the night I brought her home from our first date. Her father was sitting on the front porch. From a distance, he looked like a normal dad, waiting up for his daughter. I remember Abequa, rising with hope. Because she always hoped. But when we got close, the mirage dissolved. We saw his blood-shot eyes, his trembling hands. The pile of crushed beer cans. It wasn't, *hey kids, how was your evening? Do anything fun?* No, he spit at her. He called her a whore. Asked her if she'd gotten herself knocked up. Has your mother ever done anything like that to you?"

"No, Dad." I balled my shirt in my hands. "Never."

"That's because your Mom chose a different path. She studied the Bible with me. She stopped swearing, stopped smoking. Your Aunt Rena fell into sin, started drinking, made a mess of her life. Your mom got baptized. She keeps our home clean, beautiful, filled with flowers. She cooks, bakes wonderful things for us, takes care of us when we're sick." He tapped my book. "She's the one who taught you to read. Remember?"

More than a memory. A cherished vision. Mom and I at the kitchen table, poring over Mom's childhood copy of *Dick and Jane*. I'd struggled with the word *look*. Every single time, my brain got stuck on that word, and frustration brought me to tears. *It's okay, June. Look.* Lovingly, every time, Mom leaning in, sketching eyes with extravagant eyelashes in the two *o's*. *Look*.

No matter what, she'd kept believing in me.

"When your mother gets upset, June, when she lashes out, you have to switch your lens. You have to see her differently. You can't see her as *Mom*. You have to see her as the little girl who was, who still is, afraid."

I hugged myself. "Why won't she come home? What can I do?"

"She wants change. She wants to know you love her. By your *actions*, not your words."

"Tell me!" I cried, twisting to him. "Tell me how to love her better."

Dad picked up his Bible, opened to the place he had marked. And like when I was little, and I'd curl up in his lap, my cheek resting against the warm, wrinkled cotton of his t-shirt, he read me Bible stories. This time, he read to me about Abraham.

"Sometime later God tested Abraham. He said to him, 'Abraham!' 'Here I am,' he replied. Then God said, 'Take your son, your only son, whom you love—Isaac—and go to the region of Moriah. Sacrifice him there as a burnt offering on a mountain.'"

Abraham obeyed, Dad said, thereby giving us a model of selfless love.

The sky folded itself into twilight lavender and the bullfrogs *whop-whopped* in the reeds.

I closed my eyes, leaned into him. I sighed, the hum of his deep voice against my cheek as he read to me about love, and sacrifice.

And after a while, in the gathering dark, it came to me.

I knew exactly what to do.

on the altar

The moment I stepped into McStop, Becky whooped and rushed me.

Becky the pirate-y cook *hugged* me. She lifted me right up off my feet! She set me down, yanked my visor over my eyes. Then stuck her fingers in her mouth and whistled.

"Look who's back, everybody!" Then, "Little Daydreamer, it has not been the same without you." She snickered, poked my shoulder. "This place actually ran smooth for once."

I lifted my visor, working hard to smile. Maggie scurried over, gave me a shy little side hug. "Gosh, I missed you, girlie. We had tons of buses. I almost quit three times! But I remembered what you said about sticking it out. You were right. It's better now."

Mikey the Drive-Thru guy high-fived me. "I had to sub for you at register. I *did* quit three times. But like a dumb ex, they just kept taking me back."

I grinned, surrounded on all sides. They'd *missed* me.

I flashed back to the moment, six months before, when I had first stepped into McStop on a winter day during a snow flurry. Hands wedged deep inside my coat pockets, I'd approached the counter and asked for an application. My terrifying interview with Janet, sitting across from her in a booth as she took notes, appraising me through her sinister spectacles. How I wished she'd take off those spectacles! They'd made her look like a manager. My first couple months on the job when, slammed by buses, trucks and military convoys, not to mention Becky's endless parade of insults and eruptions, I thought I'd either die, or get fired. Now here I was, wrapped up inside the biggest welcome party of my entire life. "I missed you all, too," I said, my voice full of gratitude, and brokenness.

Becky waved her hands. "Okay, okay! Back to your places! Shoo!" She threw an arm around my shoulders, marching me to the back to clock in. "How was your visit with dear old Granny? Did she spoil you?"

"Yes, ma'am. She surely did."

Becky leaned in. "Guess who's been here asking for you?"

Mom. Hope got my heart pounding. "Who?"

She shoved my shoulder. "Your *cowboy*, dumb-dumb!"

"Clint?"

"You got more cowboys?"

"No..." I pressed my hands to my face as Becky stalked ahead, past the kitchen. *Clint.* I'd thought for sure he was long gone. I scooted up beside her. "What did he say?"

She snorted. "Prying, that's what. I said, *tough luck, buck.* If he couldn't get your digits, after all that boot scootin' dirty dancin' hot tonguin'..."

"There was no hot tonguin!"

Janet poked her head out of her office. "Well, what kinda vacation is that?"

Becky cackled. "Ain't that the truth."

Janet waved. "Welcome back, June! I'm swamped, but give me a sec, and we'll chat." Flashing a thumbs up, she retreated. She was downright giddy, and I remembered. She had a surprise for me.

I closed my eyes briefly. I was going to have to tell her.

Becky elbowed me as I clocked in. "Why, you little tease. No number, no tongue." She leaned against the wall. "Your loss. I betcha that boy's got a tongue like a lasso."

"Becky!" I shoved my time card back in its slot. "We didn't even...it didn't even...the date was..." I don't know what showed up on my face, but Becky's naughty laughter fizzled.

Her eyes narrowed. "What's goin' on with you, huh? Don't lie to me, girlie. I saw it the minute you walked in. Something *bad*."

The truth was so close, on the tip of my tongue, I tasted it.

Becky's face grew dangerous, one eye widening, the other squinting. "If that cowboy perved on you. I swear, June. I will carve his heart outta his chest, slap it on the grill, and sear out every last drop of blood. *Ssssss*."

Oh, she meant it, too.

"It's not Clint," I said. "It's my – my stomach hurts." This was true. I'd woken up with it. A deep, steady ache. "I think I caught a bug."

"June..." She reached out. I shook my head, pushed past her.

First, I had a highly emotional reunion with my register. Then, I focused on my work. Pressing down the button. The ice-cream machine reverberating, rattling, sighing, clunking. That poor old ox, always on the verge of break-down. Moving the cone in slow careful circles. The frosty vanilla swirls, one after another, spiral after shimmering spiral, five, seven...I stepped away, beheld the glory. *Ten* gorgeous, glorious anti-regulation swirls! In my time away, I certainly hadn't lost my touch. I whipped three napkins from the dispenser, wrapped up the cone snug, and with pride, presented it to him across the counter.

Farmer Henry's eyes were baby blue, and when he took that cone, they rounded with sheer delight. In spite of that gray handle bar moustache, he looked ten-years-old. I memorized that sweet old hand, wrinkled and gnarled, but still embedded with boyish freckles. With bashful glances, and nods, Farmer Henry turned to go. Then he stopped, turned around. Eyes pointed to the ceiling, he hemmed and hawed. Then he said, so quiet only I could hear, "You're my favorite."

I pressed my hand to my heart, waving as he shuffled in his overalls out the door. *Goodbye, Farmer Henry.*

"You have a fan club."

And there he was.

Sneaking up on me like always.

Making my breath catch, my pulse patter. Like always.

Brown cowboy eyes, shining from beneath a dirty camo ball cap. He leaned in, planting rough, tan hands on the countertop. His slow smile that still made my toes scrunch inside my sturdy nonslip restaurant shoes.

I flung my drawer closed and ran.

Diiiiiiinnnnnggg!

The cry of my beloved register, following me as I shoved out the door.

***

Next morning, soon as I looked out the window, I could tell.

It was going to be a beautiful Rhubarb Pie Day.

I dressed and went outside, down to the rhubarb patch, alone. I carried a notebook and pen. Grandma was right. The rhubarb was taller than ever, grand and gleaming, big leaves bouncing in the warm burst of breeze. I shook my head. I couldn't do it. I couldn't. I couldn't be there alone. "Grits!" I called and I called, sinking down, knees pressed into earth. I tore out big handfuls of grass, threw it. "GRITS!" voice rising to a shriek. I buried my face in my hands.

Things that were supposed to love you, left you. Knowing that, how could *anyone* survive this world? I cried and cried and cried, my knees sinking ever deeper, planting themselves.

Nearby, my clapping tree rustled. I couldn't raise my head. I couldn't look at her. And my stomach hurt and hurt and hurt. That low ache now spreading, drilling down deeper.

The summer I turned ten, Mom made her first rhubarb pie. It happened to be the Fourth of July. That evening, Dad propped a ladder against the side of the house. *Let's have an adventure.* We climbed onto the roof. Dad, Rain, then me. Mom brought the pie up, nestled within a backpack. We circled around her. She lifted the towel, revealing her masterpiece. Sunset glow, rich ruby juices. *Mom, it's beautiful. Mom, it's art.* She carved the pie into thick, luxurious wedges.

We dipped our spoons in, blissful. Sitting together on the sun warm tiles, cross-legged. A rooftop picnic, sugared crust and sweet tang of rhubarb. Fireworks, a whole meadow of flower sparks, blooming over our heads.

We were Jehovah's Witnesses. We did not swear our loyalty to any human government. We didn't vote. We didn't serve in the military. We didn't sing the national anthem, or any patriotic songs. We didn't say the Pledge of Allegiance. We didn't celebrate Fourth of July. That night, we celebrated the pie. We celebrated being *happy* together.

Rhubarb Pie Day.

The ritual persisted, and grew. Even though the kitchen was Mom's dominion, I wedged my way in. Soon, I had my very own apron. Blue gingham with lace pockets, just like hers.

In the morning, every Rhubarb Pie Day, Mom and I held

hands, swishing bare-footed through the dewy grass to the rhubarb patch. Together we knelt like worshippers before the thick, red stalks, slicing them at the base, gathering them in her basket. Rolling out the dough in the kitchen, Mom danced me around. She smudged flour on my nose. *Happy Rhubarb Pie Day, Dear Juney!*

I could hear her. I could hear her singing to me.

I wiped my face, and flipped open my notebook. There, I had inscribed the scripture Dad read to me: *Genesis 22:15: The angel of Jehovah called to Abraham from heaven a second time and said, 'I swear by myself, declares Jehovah, that because you have done this and have not withheld your son, your only son, I will surely bless you...because you have obeyed me.'*

It was time to follow through on my plan. I wrote hard and fast.

Dear Dad, please let Mom know, when you talk to her, my love is more than words. Here is the sacrifice I promise to make...

***

I stood before a stone-faced Janet in her office, dirt gritty between my toes. I was pretty sure it was on my face, too, but I'd run out the door the moment she called me in.

And now I couldn't move a muscle, pinned in place by her fury.

"June, what happened yesterday? Running out of work? I have not a clue why you did that, and frankly, I don't know if I care. I just can't believe..." She pressed her fingertips to her temples, shook her head. "You left your register hanging wide open!"

"I thought I'd shut it – "

"You didn't even answer the phone! You run out of work, and don't think to call? To explain or at the very least, let us know you're safe? A truck could have run you over. I was beside myself."

I fell apart. I couldn't take in one bit more of someone's anger, couldn't cope. My face flushed, throat tightened, pulse pounded. Not one rational thought could form, much less an adequate response. I gripped the back of a chair, just to stay upright.

"June. Sit down, would you, please?"

"No, ma'am, thank you."

I sat.

I swept off my visor, crunched it between hot, sweaty hands. "Janet, I'm sorry. I've let you down. I've let McDonald's down. There are no words sufficient to express my remorse. I hope, I only hope that someday, you'll be able to forgive me."

She blinked, set her palms flat on the desk-top. "June..."

"It was so *bad* of me." A little squeak of a cry, like a wounded field mouse. I pressed my hands to my face, peered at her between split fingers.

"Oh, dear Lord. Help." Janet closed her eyes. She breathed in, slow. Then, dropping her shoulders, she leaned back. "You know, June. It was Becky who leapt to your defense. She *likes* you! I've never seen her like anyone, and she's been with us over a decade." She tapped her pen on the desk. "Becky told me you haven't been yourself this past month. She says you come to work anxious, in tears. She wanted me to ask...is something going on at home?"

I held her gaze. "There is no excuse for what I did."

Janet nodded. "Alrighty then. Maybe you don't want to tell me. That's okay, for now. It has to be, I guess. And I have to respect you taking full responsibility. Now, by no means am I letting you off the hook," she wagged a finger at me. "Upset as I am, I have faith in you. I'm certain we can untangle this knot, whatever it is, as long as we keep talking. I'm willing, if you are?" The way she looked at me. Hopeful, almost shy.

"You're not going to fire me?"

"No, I'm not. And in fact..." Janet slid open her desk drawer. "Remember that surprise?" She removed something, held it cupped in her hands. "I get it, June. Believe me, I do. Leaders have bad days. They make mistakes, like everyone else. The difference is, leaders don't blame, or try to wriggle out with excuses. They *own* their mess ups. I hold to what I said before. I see a leader in you." She smiled, and then, her hands bloomed. There, in her palms, shone a beautiful gold badge.

June, Assistant Manager.

My hand flew to my mouth.

Janet winked. "I take it that's a *yes?*"

I couldn't look her in the eye. "No." Gently as I could, I lay my crumpled blue, mustard-stained visor on her desk. "I quit."

***

I power-walked along the gravel shoulder of the interstate. The Oreo cows stared. *Mooooooo!* They called to me. Oh, how they wanted me to look. One last time, they cried, just look. *Mooooooo!* Like they were bawling their eyes out.

A car pulled over behind me, skidded a little on the gravel. I sprinted ahead. Then the honking started, urgent. I spun around. *Rain!* I jogged toward her old white Toyota Corolla, climbed in. "I thought you were a kidnapper," I told her.

"Don't you wish."

Dazed, I pulled the seatbelt across me, clicked it in place. In Janet's office, I had forgotten my stomach pain, now it roared back, a dragon breathing fire all the way up, scorching my eyeballs. I doubled over, holding myself as an eighteen-wheeler whooshed past, rocking the car side to side. "What's the matter?" Rain said. "June, are you in pain?"

"My stomach hurts. Why are you here?"

"I was coming to get you." Rain's voice sounded funny.

I snapped my head up. My sister was pale, her pupils huge. "What is it? What's happening now?" I started to shiver.

"Dad said, he read Mom some note you left? About sacrifices?" She tilted her head.

"What's happening?" I gripped the seat. "Just tell me."

"June." My sister's face looked so fragile. "Mom's in the kitchen. She's making your pie."

***

The car was still moving when I flung open the door.

Mom. Mom.

I slipped and fell on the gravel, picked myself up, tore around the side of the house, slipping on the long grass, falling again, getting up, driven and wild. *Mom. Mom.* I raced up the back porch steps, threw the door open, into the laundry room, into the kitchen. She stood at the sink, back to me, thick black hair unloosed, flowing down, down, down. She wore her apron, blue gingham with lace pockets. She scrubbed a bouquet of ruby red stalks under the rush of water.

"Mom!" I shrieked it.

She turned. She opened her arms. And I flew.

"Mom, Mom, Mom." I cried the word into her apron, her

neck, her skin. I inhaled her skin, her ears, her hair. I drank her, the being, the realness of her, into all my cells yearning to hold her, my mother, for eternity. She cradled my head with her floury hands, the holiness of my mother's hands, woven into my hair. "I'm here, June. I'm here."

I sobbed and couldn't stop, did not want to, ever.

Then gently, lifting my chin with her finger, she looked me in the eye, and she sang. "*Happy Rhubarb Pie Day, Dear Juney...*"

The pain brought me to my knees.

Dearest Juney,

I hope you like the roses! I hope they're the first thing you see when you come out of surgery. As soon as your Mom called from the hospital, I ordered you the biggest bunch of red roses I could find! I didn't know what else to do. Fourth of July and your appendix explodes. The biggest firework show of them all!

I'm sorry, honey. That's a bad joke.

The truth is, I've been terrified. When I was a little girl, people died from burst appendixes all the time. There were no antibiotics back then. Every week, seemed like, there was another funeral. I was told your religion made you sign a 'No Blood' form before the surgery. I did not like that one bit. I've been praying for you nonstop, baking cakes and then eating them all by myself. I'm going to be a damn hippo in a tutu by the time you're better!

You'd better get better! You have to do everything the doctors tell you to do. Even if it goes against that religion of yours. You promise your old Grandma? Your life is more important than that religion (don't tell your Dad I said that).

The girls would be lost without their June.

Love Always, Your Grandma

P.S. Mark my words, you are bound for great things. You'll be rich and famous!

P.S.S. I should just keep my mouth shut but I sure thought that cowboy was awful cute. Your mother said it didn't work out? Well, phooey.

P.S.S.S Just in case, I'm sending more pantyhose!

PART II
LOVE

Only once in your life, I truly believe, you find someone who can completely turn your world around.

-Bob Marley

January 7th, 1996
Fayetteville, Arkansas

I fall quiet.

Judge Sanders and I look at one another.

Just him and me, and the gentle light flickering across his golden bookshelves.

All this time, he hasn't spoken. Only listened. Now he hangs his head, chin to chest.

My heart is pierced. I wonder what he's thinking. I wonder what he'll say next. When he finally looks up, his eyes are richly blue. He smiles. "You survived."

The word shakes me.

Survived.

Is that the truth? As I think, I fall into a dream. My clapping tree, her leaves gilded by autumn light, clattering music made for me. Her golden leaves shift, and become Grits. Warm sunshine of my life, she is shimmering, dancing beside me. Her eyes send me love. I reach out to touch her face, and beneath my hand, Grits changes, becomes our tetherball. Orange as a setting sun. I smack the ball, and Rain leaps, her beautiful, long curls flying behind her. The tetherball is curling round and round the pole. And then, in my hand, there is an ice-cream cone, twisting into a perfect sparkly spiral. A beloved hand, both wrinkled and freckled, reaching. Gray hair, and then, the gray of a suede cowboy hat, clutched in rough tan hands, crushed to the chest. And another hat. That hat, the dearest of all. Straw, with a brown velvet band, and a white and brown-spotted quail feather. There, I pause, and zoom in. I'm five-years-old, and I'm dancing on Dad's feet. We're outside, near a white tent where pink wedding cake is served. Dad wears a suit and tie, and his straw hat. The quail feather bends graceful as a dancer in the breeze. I reach for it. Dad grins, takes off his hat, sticks it on my head. It falls over my eyes. Fairy lights twinkle in the trees, and we dance.

Survived. I blink, and look around.

If you're falling to pieces – have you survived?

A sound makes me look up. Judge Sanders is pushing a box of Kleenex toward me.

Am I crying? I touch my face, and yes. Without a word, I whisk out a bunch, wipe my face, blow my nose. I honk like a goose. Just like Dad. That makes me cry harder, shoulders shaking.

Judge Sanders is quiet. He waits. Sometimes the best gift in the world, the most needed thing, is someone who sits with you, and waits.

"Thank you," I say, finally. "You know, you're actually quite nice...without the spectacles."

He chuckles. "I'll keep that in mind." Then he leans back, laces his hands across his red and white Razorbacks sweatshirt. "Your story isn't over, June. As with all good stories, there's a turning point, isn't there?"

"Yes," I say. And then in my chest, a glow, like a fire. Not the kind that burns holes in your heart, and turns your insides to ashes. Instead, the kind that draws you close, warms you. The small fire of *home*. I latch and unlatch my fingers. "I don't even know where to begin."

"A prompt might help. How about, *One day I turned the corner and...?*"

"One day I turned the corner and..." I take a breath, smile. "I wasn't alone in the world anymore."

Judge Sanders pinches the bridge of his nose. "Good grief." He reaches for a Kleenex, one, then two. "Best get prepared. I may look like a mean old judge. But I'm a sucker for a love story. Especially," he looks me in the eye, "for a character I've grown to care about."

scar

At the end of my hospital corridor was a shower room.

My favorite nurse, Magda, had walked me there, helped me undress. My first shower, after two weeks of sponge baths. I had finally that day been freed, unhooked from the IV catheter.

Now, wobbly and weak, I turned on the water with a sharp squeak. Swathed in goosebumps, I stepped in. The bar of soap silky in my hand, I traced it over my bony hip, up the ladder of my ribcage, to my chest, grazing the sore part, where the IV had fed me a steady flow of antibiotics. Then down, skimming over my breasts, to my belly. The appendix, my surgeon had explained, was a small finger-like organ. When it popped, it unleashed poison, like a deadly balloon. *You were one very sick little girl*, he'd said, holding my hand. I slid the soap down, to the newest part of me.

A three-inch slash, red and raw.

One touch, feather light, and I jerked away. The soap escaped, fell to my feet, spinning in the water. I hugged myself. Was it supposed to hurt?

It was only a scar.

I wanted out of this cold, white place. I wanted to go home. In my head, I roved around my beloved personal map. Clapping tree, my books, my garden, Grits...the place behind my register. No longer mine. But my heart would go there anyway. I sank down, wrapped my arms around my knees. Huddled at the bottom of the shower, I let the warm water bury me.

A soft knock on the door. "Juney? Are you there?"

"Mom." Slowly, shakily, holding onto the bar, I rose to the sound of her voice. "I'm here."

seat #25

"June, smile! It's your first day!"

I smiled so big it hurt.

Standing on the front porch, the day already drenched in late August heat, Mom knelt with the camera, taking picture after picture. Dad leaned against the house, arms folded across his chest, watching. Rain waited for me in the car. I was painfully conscious of the fact that no one had taken her picture, her first day of college. She'd gone off alone, trailed by our disapproval. And I wasn't even an official college student, with a full load of classes like Rain. I was a dual enrolled high school student, only taking one class.

Yet, there was such a fuss over me.

"Hold up your bag." Mom was eager to send pictures to Grandma, who, Mom said, was a mess of nerves, and needed more convincing that I wasn't dead. I also suspected that Mom wanted to show her that I was not a prisoner at home. Here was the proof.

I clutched my brand new messenger bag, army green and big enough to house an army. Silly, because all it held was one textbook, a notebook and pen, and the book my favorite nurse, Magda, had gifted me in the hospital. One night, coming in to take blood, she'd found me immersed in my raggedy old copy of *Anne of Green Gables*. I told her it was my comfort book, which made her smile. The next day, she'd brought to my bedside the equally well-loved copy of her comfort book, *Christy* by Catherine Marshall. Sitting beside me, Magda told me what the story had meant to her when she'd first read it in 9th grade, the most lost and lonely year of her life. She said Christy's story had inspired her to become a nurse. *Keep it*, she'd said suddenly, pressing the book into my hands. *I have a feeling you'll love this book the way it deserves.*

I'd only known her for two weeks, but I knew then, Magda was a kindred spirit.

Now, Mom rushed me with a sack lunch, stuffing it in my bag. "I made your favorite lavender sugar cookies."

"Thank you, Mom." I hugged her, my hand sinking into her thick coarse hair, twining my fingers through it. My eyes moved to Dad. "Bye, Dad." I lifted my hand in a wave, and was rewarded only by a head shake.

It was Rain who'd talked Dad into letting me dual-enroll at the University of Arkansas. She sold it by telling him I would be eligible to receive free tutoring on campus. Someone there would help me finish home-school so I could graduate on time. Dad had agreed, since he was busier than ever, building up his chiropractic clinic. He'd driven me to campus to enroll, but the whole drive, he had fired warnings at me about the many spiritual dangers of higher education. Atheism, drug abuse, fornication. College was a seething den of sin, like a dance club, or worse. Now, he put his arms around me, a little stiffly, and said, "Remember what we talked about. Everywhere you turn, you'll be exposed to worldly behavior and philosophies. You'll have to stay on guard, and pray for protection constantly."

"I know, Dad." I looked up at him. His thick eyebrows were pulled together, forehead a knot. "It's only one class." I shook his arm. "*One*." His face relaxed a bit, and he allowed a smile. As close as I'd get to his blessing.

Rain pressed the horn. I shouldered my bag and headed off the porch. As I stepped down, there was my yellow friend, galloping across the grass, haloed in late summer morning light. I fell to my knees and we had a joyous, slobbery reunion. One of many since I'd come home from the hospital.

Grits had reappeared on Fourth of July night, the same night I was rushed into surgery. When Mom and Dad returned from the hospital to pack my things, there she was, waiting on the porch. They told me later her coat was caked in dirt, and a rope, frayed, was looped round her neck. She'd broken loose, from wherever it was she'd been held.

Now I cupped Grit's face between my hands and looked deep into her eyes. "We made it," I whispered. "We're here." She set her big paw on my knee.

I wished I could take her with me everywhere, forever.

***

The University of Arkansas sprawled like a city on a hilltop, with a view of the rolling Ozarks, laced in mist. And my sister knew her way around like it was nothing, walking fast, her stride sure. I could barely keep up with her.

We passed by an immense building, grandiose brick, flanked by towers and banked with windows, like a country estate in England. Any minute, Mr. Darcy might step out on the walkway in his top hat, pulling on his gloves. I stopped to stare, hopeful. "June!" Rain yelled. "Move it!"

I hurried to catch up. "I was stopping to wait for Darcy."

Rain spun around, kept walking backwards. "What are you talking about? Darcy?" She palmed her forehead. "Please don't be weird."

I jogged up beside her. "What do you mean, weird?"

"I mean, this is college, June. The real world. No one's

going to get you if you talk like you do at home. Don't tell people you're waiting for Darcy. God!" She rolled her eyes. Her big curly ponytail swished back and forth with every stride.

I wished she wouldn't say *God*, a growing habit. I especially wished she wouldn't say it *at* me, a spit of contempt. Since I'd come home from the hospital, it had been like this. Either she was cold and distant, or impatient and snappish, poised for a fight.

We passed by a bright building with a fountain out front. "What's that?" I asked quietly, pointing.

She shrugged. "I don't know. Arkansas Union. You can get food and stuff." She then blithely ticked off every restaurant, shop, and all the amenities on every floor.

I marveled. "You know this place. This place is like, *your* place."

"Well, yeah. I had to figure it out, didn't I? All by myself." An edge of bitterness. We stopped before a formidable stone building, and she hefted her backpack, full of books. "Well, here it is. Statistics. One of the most notoriously failed classes on campus." She didn't say this with trepidation. In fact, she rubbed her hands together, practically beaming. "Wish me luck!" She saluted and started up the concrete steps.

I grabbed her arm. "You're going in there?"

"It's a building, June. It's not going to eat me." She eased her arm from my grip. "Okay? I'm going. Here I go. Bye!" She swiveled, darted up the steps.

"But, but, but!"

She stopped, peered over her shoulder. "What?"

"Do you have to?"

She hesitated, then slumped, jogged back down. "C'mere." She dropped her backpack, opened her arms. I collapsed into her. We hadn't hugged since – I didn't want to think about when. "You'll be fine, country mouse." She laughed into my hair. "If I can do it, you can. And like you keep saying, it's only one class."

"I haven't been to real school for two years. I'm scared." It hit me then, the truth of that.

She said, "I'll tell you what I did, to survive my first day."

"Should I take notes?" I reached for my notebook.

She swatted my hand. "Stop it. Now listen. You're going to get to your class early. A half hour early. Got it?"

She was so bossy. I soaked it up. "Okay. And then?"

"What's your building?"

"Um, Hill...something...?"

"Oh my God. Let me see your registration sheet." She held out her hand. I withdrew it from the side pocket of my messenger bag. The sheet was now a thin paper tube, I'd rolled and unrolled and re-rolled it so many times.

Rain shook her head as she flattened the sheet on her leg. "You are a mess." She studied it, then broke into a grin. "Hiller. The same lecture hall I was in my first semester."

"You weren't scared?"

"Terrified. I puked."

"I think I'll skip that step."

She smirked, handing me my sheet, which promptly rolled into tube formation. "Then I washed my face, marched in, and I sat third row, center. Seat #25. I still remember. My first seat in college." Her dark eyes shone. "Today, when you get to class...how early?"

"Half an hour."

"You're going to find that seat. And you're going to sit there. Which seat?"

"Seat #25."

We fist-bumped. "And remember, don't be weird!" She turned, raced up the steps, and pushed through the doors. Leaving me there.

A bell sounded, deep and resonant. I blinked at the doors where my sister had disappeared. Before I could process, I was swept up in a wave of people, college students, pushing me I had no idea where. I wasn't new to big crowds, but they'd always been in neat, controlled lines behind a register. Now, the crowd surrounded me, like I was one of them, but I wasn't. I walked fast, head down, my giant messenger bag thump-thumping against my hip. A guy on a bike, headphones spilling rap, raced by, too close. I stepped to the side, bumping into a group of girls in tight, bright spaghetti strap tank tops, shoving each other, laughing too loud. I veered, and found myself walking side by side with the world's tallest human wearing a Razorbacks basketball jersey. The crowd jostled me into him. He grinned down at me and waved, his hand fluttering like a leaf atop a mighty Oak. "Hey, munchkin. What's up?"

I swerved, off the path, burrowing into a huddle of flowering crepe myrtle bushes. I sat cross-legged on the ground, in a pool of wrinkly hot pink blossoms. I parted the branches, more flowers shaking loose, flitting around me. I peered out at all the shoes rushing past. This was the perfect shadowy fort, aside from the little bee zipping around my face. "Shoo!" I got on my belly. My heart thudded like a mad-woman against the ground. I rolled over on my back, pulled *Christy* from my bag, and instantly felt calmer with a book in my hands.

Still, my hands trembled a little as I opened the book. The pages were brittle and slightly yellowed. I sniffed them. They smelled a little burnt, with a note of lemon, and maybe just a touch of pine forest. Every book had its own perfume. An aromatic history. I pressed pink crepe myrtle blossoms into the pages. A reminder years from now, of this moment, hiding in the bushes before my first college class.

So much for not being weird.

***

A half hour early, I picked my way down the steps of Hiller Hall into the dimly lit basement. I rounded the corner, stood before tall double doors. This was it. Psychology 101. My one and only class. I wiped my palms up and down my shorts. *Seat #25.* I pushed through the doors, and...

Himmel, himmel!

I swept my gaze around. This was a concert hall. An arena! There were easily a few hundred seats in semi-circular rows leading down to a lectern. I tried to breathe. My sister had been here. She'd felt this fear. She'd puked, and then she'd returned. I could do this.

Seat #25.

I scanned the rows and...

I wasn't alone.

One other person had arrived early. And out of hundreds of seats – where was he sitting? Third row, center!

All my fear turned to fury. Who did he think he was? Whoever he was, he wasn't going to chase me away. I would get my seat. Shouldering my bag I marched down the aisle, straight to the third row.

He was sitting in my seat.

I screamed in my head, threw down my bag, and plunked down in Seat #20.

I clenched my jaw against tears. How dare he.

He turned to me. I stared straight ahead, steely. *Seat Thief!*

He leaned in. "Hey. Did you know..."

I whipped away, turning my back to him.

"...you have flowers in your hair," he said, softly.

Heat rose into my face.

The doors opened. Students streamed in. The empty lecture hall burst into vibrant commotion. A squall of chatter, laughter, squeaking seats, and backpacks hitting the floor.

From my peripheral, I monitored Seat Thief. He pulled something from his backpack, onto his lap, followed by the rich crinkling of pages. *My siren song.* I didn't want to look, but my eyes were pulled, against my will.

It was a large book, leather bound. One I instantly knew.

Fayetteville was packed with churches, yet this was the first time I'd seen anyone pull out a Bible and start reading. Maybe it was the way Seat Thief ran his finger beneath the lines, like they meant something to him.

I lifted my gaze to his face, and...*oh.*

dressing room

It was September, and Mom took me shopping for school clothes.

Dad's clinic was gaining momentum, and Mom said, she wanted to treat me.

Side by side, Mom and I perused clearance racks, elbows bumping. "Ooh, Juney. Look!"

Mom whipped out a jacket, soft pale green with shiny silver buttons. She pressed the jacket to me. "Oh yes. With your eyes? Stunning. And with this..." She held up a chocolate brown shift dress. She clutched my arm, led me toward the dressing rooms. "Let's try on. If we like it, we can hunt down a necklace, some tights, a pair of ankle boots, and make a whole outfit for fall."

In the dressing room, I turned this way and that. Mom fussed and adjusted, pulling at the jacket cuffs, straightening the shoulders, tugging at the sides of the dress. I soaked up every little touch. At the same time, I was frightened, nearly to the point of paralysis. If I moved the wrong way, I might elbow this dream, knock it into splinters, fragments I couldn't catch.

At last, she stood me still in front of the mirror. My reflection startled me, as it did these days. I hadn't recovered the weight I'd lost in the hospital. My face was more angular, cheekbones carved out. My reflection was the only reminder of what had happened over the summer. Otherwise, everything had clicked back into normality. *Better* than normal. Better... than I could ever remember things being.

"Look at you," Mom said. There were tears in her eyes. "Look how *beautiful* you've become." A crooked smile formed.

"Even with a price tag in your hair." She removed the slightly crumpled paper rectangle, holding it up.

I patted my frizz. "Is it on sale?"

Mom burst into laughter. She laughed so hard she dropped her forehead onto my shoulder. I laughed with her, leaning into her. Behind us, a silver-haired woman, waiting for her friend, watched. She tilted her head, smiled at us. *Ah, the sweetest love, a mother and daughter*. That's what she was thinking.

I wished I could build a house in that moment, and stay there with my mother forever.

***

Mom and I hooked arms and meandered down the shiny mall corridors, swinging our shopping bags. Mom was overly tired and hungry. I was starting to see the signs, her mood dropping. I steered her toward the food court and a cup of hot coffee. I couldn't control the glimpses she caught of herself in store windows as we passed by, her face becoming a steady glower. "June," she said, "look at you, and look at me. You're so petite. So pretty. You can wear stylish clothes. Me, I'm fat. Nothing looks good on me." She stopped before a mirror, and beat her thighs with her fists. "Built like a dump truck."

"Come on, Mom." I pulled her from the mirror. "You're gorgeous," I said, bumping her hip. I smoothed her river of black hair with my hand, fantasized about being able to brush and braid it. Something that, for some reason, she would never let me do. "You have princess hair. I only wish I'd inherited it."

"Oh, that." She waved my compliment away, roughly pulled her hair from under my hand, over her shoulder. "I should cut it all off. It's nothing but a pain, really. I sit on it all the time.

And *princess hair* looks plain ridiculous on a fat piece of trash."

After what felt like a year-long trek through a mine field, we finally made it to the food court. In the booth, I took my time, peeling the crinkly wrapper away from the cheeseburger, listening to the music it made. My hands remembered, the tin foil, the grease, the swift *tap-tap* of register keys. *Extra cheese, hold the onion!* Like a song that would always be part of me. Grief pressed hard, behind my eyes.

Across from me, Mom took a sip of her coffee, let out a sigh. "Much better." Her eyes fluttered. She took another sip, leaned back, hands cradling her cup. "So. How do you like your class? You sure haven't said much about it."

"I like it. I, um..." I smiled, and bit back the truth. Two weeks in, I *loved* the immense lecture hall that had at first frightened me. *Loved* my shiny textbook, the glossy pages, new words in bold. *Loved* Dr. Freeman, our cool, eloquent, force-of-nature professor. I'd utterly lost my heart to the velvety skim of highlighters across text. Instead of saying these things, I took a drink. Let the love pile up, guarded in my chest.

"Well," Mom said. "I hope you get *something* out of it. What about tutoring? How far along are you to being done with home-school?"

"I'm halfway through geometry. After that, I only have biology." After class, I met with a tutor on campus at the learning center. Finally I was making headway, if not peace, with triangles. It looked like I would be able to graduate the following spring.

"Look what I found half price." Mom pulled a gift box from her purse. She opened it, held it out to me. "You think your sister will like this?"

I took the box. The necklace inside, lustrous dark silver-gray beads on a sleek silver chain. "Oh, she'll love it! Hematite is her favorite mineral. Remember?" I laughed. It was great fun, teasing Rain for having a favorite mineral.

Mom's eyebrows drew together. "Of course I remember, June. That's why I got it." She took the box back, sighed. "These days, honestly. I don't know what to do to please her. Nothing seems to work. She's got this strange idea in her head that I love you more. I wish she'd snap out of it. You've been sick and need more..." Eyes flitting up, her face froze. "Oh no. Don't look now. We've got a visitor." She smoothed her hair, touched a finger to the beauty mark on her chin she'd darkened with eyebrow pencil. Between her teeth, she hissed, "I don't even have my lipstick on."

Peering over my shoulder, it took me a minute to register the figure, the face, the person approaching with a huge smile and arms open wide. And then, when I did, I jumped to my feet. "Sister Finn!"

My old friend swooped me into a hug. "Sister June, how are you!" She rocked me side to side. "I saw you from behind, your big, wild hair! I *knew* it was you." I pulled back, and oh, drank her in. Her red sunset of hair, round apple cheeks. The way she beamed pure joy at me. "Just look at you," she said, taking my face between her hands. "How we've missed your sweet smile at kingdom hall." Her eyes lingered on mine, and then, moved to Mom. "Sister Taylor, hello. It's so very good to see you. How are you?"

"Doing well. Good to see you, Sister Finn." Mom sputtered a laugh. "I'm so embarrassed. You've caught us. We've made such a mess..." She swept lettuce and empty ketchup packets onto her plate. I saw her hand trembling, and wanted to catch it in my own.

"June, I heard about your surgery. The Elders said you were very brave and loyal." Sister Finn squeezed my hand. "Brother Michaels told us that you signed the No Blood form without a moment's hesitation." Her blue eyes glowed. "You are an example of true faithfulness. You've made Jehovah's heart so happy. Mine, too."

I recalled the form delivered to me as I was rushed to surgery. Dad had called our Elders to alert them to the medical crisis. One of the Elders, Brother Michaels, had shown up in the nick of time. He had sprinted down the hospital hallway, waving the form, flagging down the nurses transporting me to the operating room. Drawn up by the Watchtower Society Legal Department, the document ensured that a transfusion would not be forced on me in case of blood loss. Signing it meant that I chose to die on the operating table, rather than break Jehovah's blood law. There on the gurney, I had raised one leg, set the form on my knee, and signed, handing it back to Brother Michaels. It was the last thing I did before losing consciousness.

"Well, I should leave you girls to your lunch," Sister Finn said, glancing at Mom. She seemed to be awaiting something, maybe an invite. Mom merely smiled and nodded. Pulling her purse strap higher on her shoulder, Sister Finn hesitated, then said, "We sure do miss your family at kingdom hall. We've been worried, and keeping you all in our prayers. Any idea – when you might be back?"

Mom wouldn't like this. Sure enough, I watched her hands tighten around her coffee cup. Her eyelids dropped, just slightly. I saw the strain to stay polite, pull at her mouth. I saw it all, the tiny things no one else would notice. "I can't say right now," Mom said. "June's been very sick. The infection was severe. She needs to rest."

"Of course!" Sister Finn smoothed her skirt, now looking nervous herself. She took a breath. "Sister Taylor, I'm just going to say, I would love to come out to your house and study the Bible with June – just once a month even, just to keep her progressing in the faith, toward baptism."

Mom stirred her coffee, took a sip, said nothing.

"Whatever you think is best." Sister Finn's warm smile faltered.

Mom said, with hard, frozen politeness, "Why, that's very kind of you. I'll talk it over with Phil, and let you know."

With a final hug, Sister Finn left. I slid back into the booth, wrapped up the rest of my cheeseburger. Mom watched me. "Huh. Looks like you have a fan club. Sister Finn's the president."

I shrugged, kept wrapping my burger with painstaking care, like a gift.

"Would you want that?"

I startled. "What?"

"A Bible study," Mom said. "With *her*. The president of your fan club."

My armpits prickled with sweat. "I – do miss studying the Bible." In my lap, I tore my napkin into tiny shreds. "I still want to get baptized." My mouth went bone dry, speaking this wish.

Mom's shoulders slumped. "I know. It's so sad. Your darn appendix sure put a wrench in your plans." She looked at me gently. "I'll think about it. How about that? We'll see how things go."

"Okay," I said, letting the pieces of napkin fall to the floor, onto my feet, like confetti.

the voice

The last week of September it rained.

And I was getting over a cold.

Rain parked in Student Lot C. We stayed where we were. The deluge rolled in waves down the windshield. I checked my messenger bag. "Oh no," I said. "Where's my umbrella?" I sneezed three times, great air horn blasts.

"Oh my God. Look at you! A month into school and you're still a mess. Here," Rain thrust her umbrella at me.

"Rain!" I was never allowed to borrow anything of hers without bent-knee supplication. And this was her lucky umbrella, the black one with the red fire-breathing dragon. "Are you sure?"

"I don't want you to get pneumonia..."

"Aww..."

"...and make me lose beauty sleep because you're hacking up a lung." She topped off her lip gloss, smacking her lips in the rearview mirror. She drew her hood up over her hair, tightened the drawstrings. She set her hand on the door handle, and turned to me with a practiced and highly effective death glare. "If you lose my lucky umbrella, I will eat your face."

"What! I would never lose it." I clutched her umbrella to my bosom, like a first-born.

***

I had to complete a paper for home-school biology, so my first stop was the computer lab in Kimpel Hall, the English building. The steady clicking of fingers on keyboards mingled with the soft tapping of rain on the window made a quiet symphony. Therefore, when I had to blow my nose, I tried to do so with gentle grace, like an oboe.

I alternated between tedious writing about cell structure, and sneak-reading *Christy*. I was indebted to Magda, my nurse. It was like she was still here, caring for me through the pages of her comfort book. As I turned each page, I found myself seeking, rooting as if for treasure. What in this story had helped Magda navigate her darkest of days?

I was immersed in Christy's first journey up into the wild Smoky Mountains to meet her new students. She was an affluent teenager, raised in the city, and though she had never been away from her home and parents, she felt called to teach. On foot, she followed the intrepid mailman, Mr. Pentland, ever deeper and higher into the mountains. They reached a makeshift log bridge, six feet above a large, roaring creek. *I was forced to look at my feet lest I trip...and then in spite of myself I saw the water, too. The logs were swaying, tilting...I dropped to my knees and began crawling. I hadn't thought it would be this bad!*

I was deep in the book trance, barely breathing, reading hard.

The campus bell sounded from the clock tower and I jumped. Around me, a new symphony. The click-tap of students logging off, chairs sliding out, the rustle of jackets and backpacks.

With a regretful sigh, I closed my book.

I had written exactly three lines of my essay.

Outside, the rain had ebbed into a soft drizzle. I sneezed twice. A sudden breeze whisked my Kleenex out of my hand, danced it away. I wiped my nose, barbarously, on my jacket sleeve, then shouldered through the heavy doors of Hiller Hall.

Heading downstairs, I patted my hair, an extra-large rain-induced poof. *Supersize,* I thought, and smiled.

In this drift, not paying attention, I stepped down each stair to class until – one step felt different. I stumbled back. "Oh, gosh! Excuse me!" I'd stepped onto a pair of legs, stretched out.

A boy sat there, reading on the steps.

Seat Thief.

He looked up at me. His auburn curls were darkened by rain, damp, pressed to the planes of his face. He smiled, and a dimple deepened in his left cheek. "You're the girl who sits by me. What's your name?"

Rain's lucky umbrella.

"Crap!" I wheeled around and fled. Up the stairs, out the door. Running. Drizzle in face. Sneezing, spluttering. Careening around the corner, into the computer lab. Rain's lucky umbrella leaned, unmenaced, against the wall where I'd been working. I snatched it up.

On the way back to Hiller, I replayed events.

I'd stepped on Seat Thief.

He had asked my name.

I'd yelled *crap!*

Happily, there were two stairwells that led to class.

I slunk down the *opposite* one.

I found an empty desk, hidden in an alcove. I slumped into it. I slid my textbook from my bag, spread the book open on the desk. Uncapping my beautiful pink highlighter with a delicious click, I leaned in to study a bit before class started. I couldn't let Seat Thief get ahead of me.

He's sitting right behind that wall.

I raised my head, listening. A voice. Not in my ear.

You could talk to him.

I looked around. I fidgeted.

You want to. You want to know his name.

My knee bounced under the desk.

Go find out.

My heart thumped. My stomach gurgled. My palms broke into a sweat.

You've got this one chance.

Go talk to him.

Now!

I rose as commanded, quivering from head to toe. I peered around the corner. There he was, long legs stretched out on the step, reading. *I couldn't.* I whipped away, pressed my back against the wall.

Then I saw her.

Christy, on that harrowing mountain hike.

I watched her terror as she crawled across that log bridge.

I picked up my bag, and Rain's umbrella.

I stepped out from behind the hidden alcove.

Step by trembly step, I walked my entire terrified self, right up to him.

"Hello," I said. "What's your name?"

keegan and june

"Keegan," he said.

I extended my hand. "June."

When our hands met, it felt like this. *Click click.*

"Hi, Keegan."

"Hi, June."

We shook, looking into each other's eyes for a long time.

Then, "Hey, here, sit down." He drew his legs up, patted the space beside him.

I sat. Then promptly sneezed into my balled up Kleenex. Three times.

"Bless you. Bless you. Bless you."

"Thank you times three." I smiled, and studied him. He wore a dark blue shirt, same color as his eyes, rolled to his elbows. A gray vest and nice pants, shiny shoes. He didn't dress like the other college boys with their hoodies and backward baseball caps. He didn't look like them either. His dark auburn curls framed his strong, square jaw, the dimple in his chin. "I love your name," I told him. "Keegan. Strong, but also warm. Like a fire."

His eyes opened with surprise. "Keegan is Gaelic for *small flame.*"

"That's beautiful!"

"We both have warm names. June," he said. "Like a summer day." His gaze lifted, and I watched as his dark blue eyes danced around my frizzy, supersize hair.

Stricken, I clamped my hands over my head. "I'm getting over a cold." As if that explained my hair. "I'm afraid I don't look much like a summer day."

Keegan smiled. "You look like one to me."

I dropped my hands from my hair. "Gaelic, you said. Are you Irish?"

He rolled his shoulders back. "That I am. Keegan Patrick Brennan Callahan." In this totally dorky and awesome Irish accent.

"Wow! You are Irish in every last syllable. But..." I wrinkled my nose. "Your accent kind of sucks."

"I'll work on it. What about you? Are you Irish?"

"Me? I'm German, English, a quarter Chippewa, and," patting my frizz, "a wee bit dandelion."

"That's an amazing combination."

"In my daydreams, though, I'm Irish."

He put his head to the side. "Say what now?"

"In my daydreams, when I'm dancing on the Cliffs of Moher, in the rain, in bare feet..."

"That sounds dangerous."

"Dangerous and wild and *magical.*" I pressed my hands to my heart, and my Kleenex puffed out between my fingers. "With the sea foaming and crashing beneath, in the distance the cry of a flute, making my heart wistful..." I stopped myself, bit my lip.

His elbows were perched on his knees, chin propped on folded hands. "Wistful," he said. "I love the words you use."

"Thank you," I said, while inside, my heart threw flowers at his feet.

"So you like to dance on cliff-sides," he said. "And read."

"Do you like to read? I mean, something other than the Bible."

"The Bible is my favorite, but there are others. Hold on, I'll show you." He bent, rummaging through his backpack. My eyes were drawn to his forearm, to a tattoo there, dark and glistening. I knew the image. It was a Celtic cross, ornate and elegant, with tiny script I couldn't read.

Seeing that tattoo, it was like a cold finger touched my heart. In my faith, we believed that Jesus was crucified on a stake – no cross beams. The traditional symbol of the cross was plucked from false pagan religions. In any case, it was unimaginable to decorate our homes, much less adorn our bodies, with the symbol of Christ's crucifixion – his *murder*. But Keegan wasn't a Jehovah's Witness. Of course he wasn't. Maybe when I first saw him, reading his Bible with such careful attention, I'd wondered, even hoped. But compared to the churches in Christendom there were so few Witnesses, what were the odds? I sucked in a breath, said, "Well, look at that. You have a tattoo."

"Oh. Yeah." He sat up, rotated his forearm. "My first. I got it not too long ago." He wore a bewildered expression, as though he'd forgotten it was there.

"Cool! What denomination are you?" Catholic, Lutheran, Methodist, Baptist, I ticked them off in my head, and *prayed* that it wasn't...

"Pentecostal," he said – I winced – and then, "Check it out." Keegan held up a book. He peered at me, his forehead crinkling. "Oh wait, you've got – what's this?" He plucked something from my frizz. "Kleenex? How did you get Kleenex in your hair?"

"Oh gosh." I snatched the shred away, stuffed it in my pocket. "My hair catches everything. Bugs, twigs, leaves...small kitchen appliances."

Keegan burst out laughing. "You're hilarious."

He loved my words. He thought I was funny. This was the

best day of my life.

He had a cross tattoo. He was Pentecostal. This was the worst day of my life.

Keegan placed the book in my hands, a gentle, sacred weight. "*The Lion, the Witch and the Wardrobe*," I read.

"My dad read to me from this book every night when I was a kid. I've been re-reading it lately. It makes me feel close to him."

"Oh!" I beamed. "This is your comfort book."

"My what?"

"Your comfort book. That's what I call the books from our childhood that we just keep turning to throughout our lives."

He gazed at me, thinkingly. "Yes," he said, "this is my comfort book."

I opened it, and the pages crackled, the best sound in the world.

"Isn't that the best sound in the world?" Keegan said. "I found that copy at Dusty Books. The used bookstore near campus. That's why it's a little beat up."

I looked up, into his eyes.

He shrugged. "I have a thing for old books."

"So do I! In fact, if I didn't have a cold, I'd sniff each one of these dusty, delicious pages." Then, scrunching my face – "Is that weird?"

"Yes," he said, nodding. "Yes, it is."

We smiled at the same time.

And it felt like this.

Click click.

tacos

The next morning, Grandma called.

In the kitchen eating breakfast, Mom handed off the phone to me, ruffling my hair.

"Juney! It's your Gran-maw-maw!" Grandma's booming belly laugh went straight to my heart, an arrow of love. "Mom says you had a checkup. What did Doc say? You all better now?"

"I'm getting there, Grandma." I twined my fingers through the phone cord.

"You better be! I'm trying not to kick the bucket myself. I gotta give daily pep talks to my old heart. I say, listen up, you crank, we've got more adventures! More shopping. More food," she whispered the next part, "More *dances*..."

In my laugh, a strained, cracking note. My eyes darted to Mom, washing dishes at the sink. I could tell by her back, she was listening. Thankfully, Grandma turned the talk to weather, rhapsodizing on the colorful Wisconsin fall. "It's like a carnival for the eyes! If only you girls were here," she said, "we'd pile into the car, go on a trek. Like the good old days. Remember, Juney, how we'd stop and get those big ol' pumpkin ice-cream cones?"

"Of course I do," I said. "Ice-cream isn't the same without you." Nothing was.

"Awww! How's sister?"

"Good. Busy with school."

"She have a feller yet?"

"I don't think so, Grandma."

"Darn it. How's pops? I hear he's the Clint Eastwood of chiropractors."

"Yep. He's the local spine-adjusting superhero."

"That's what Mom says. The cracking backs business is booming!"

Dad had bought Mom a fancy new vacuum cleaner, one that wouldn't fall apart, and the new living room furniture she'd always wanted. "He's taking night classes, too. He just got certified in reflexology."

"Whatever *that* is. Sounds like voodoo to me. And what about his white picket fence? Did he finish it yet?"

"He's still working on it, Grandma."

"Half a damn fence." She chuckled. "How's the weather down yonder?"

"Yesterday, it rained." *And I met him. Seat Thief. We talked so long, Grandma, we missed class.* If only I could tell her!

"This old lady's so happy," Grandma said. "All is well again. I hear it in your voice. Your mom sounds good, too. Strong. Best I've heard her since you folks moved. See? I told you so. Hope and faith, Juney. Something good comes out of something bad."

***

"Ouch! What are you doing? STOP!" Rain shoved me, slapped her hand over her eye. "June! Did you seriously just grab my eyelash?"

Across from her in Arkansas Union, I fell back in my chair. "I had to know!"

"For God's sake, know *what*?"

"If they're real." I crunched into my overloaded taco. Guacamole, sour cream, and clumps of cheese spilled out. I giggled.

"Piglet!" Rain threw napkins at me. "Yes, they're real. Amazing what an eyelash curler and some mascara will do." She crunched into her taco, and *everything* fell out the side.

"Ahahaha!" I pounded the table.

Rain narrowed her eyes. "What's up with you? You're downright giddy."

"I talked to Grandma this morning."

"Lucky! What did she say?"

"Oh, you know. A scintillating mix of nostalgia, hypochondria, and snooping."

"The cocktail of Grandma." Rain's hand went to her necklace, playing with the dark glossy beads. The hematite necklace, I realized. The one Mom had bought for her.

I eyed her, sly. "She asked if you had a *feller* yet."

Rain grimaced, raking her hands through her curls. "No, Grandma. Sorry! And furthermore, Grandma, just so you know, I don't want a boyfriend. And I never want to get married! NEVER."

I set my taco on the plate. "You don't?"

She threw down her crumpled napkin. "Hell no. It looks like the worst thing in the world. Marriage, kids, all of it. Nothing but grief. Remember Sister Henderson's wedding last spring, when she tossed her bouquet? It came toward me and I ducked and covered, like it was a bomb. Honestly, whenever someone at kingdom hall got married or had a baby, I wanted to send them a sympathy card."

"Really?" I clinked the ice in my drink. I'd taken for granted I knew her. My sister had a secret interior. I leaned in. "What *do* you want?"

"What do I want?" Rain blinked. "I want..." She looked around as though lost, searching. "I want..." She set her jaw.

"Statistics."

"You want statistics?" I laughed.

She nodded. "And I want..." she took a breath, "to be free of religion."

"What?"

She was on a roll. "I want...to graduate with honors. I want...to get a good job. I want...to move far away and live on my own." She gripped the table-top, white-knuckled, like she was on a roller-coaster.

"You – you don't want to go back to kingdom hall?" I was stuck on that, shock zipping up and down my arms. "I thought – remember when we dreamed about becoming missionaries together?"

Her eyes lit, widened, like something was coming to her. "I want...to be an actuary."

"What's that?" My hairs stood on end. I thought it was another religion.

"It's someone who has to deal with uncertainty, and risk management, which I think – I think I have the skin for because, God knows, I've had to practice." She gazed over my head, and her eyes traveled. "An actuary is someone who makes good money and can buy their own house, and if they want, some land. Or they can live in the city, whatever city they want, and they don't have to have anything they don't want. They can have a quiet kitchen to cook in, filled with light. They can never do dishes, and make a big fat mess. If that's what they want. No one bothers them. No one yells. No one tells them they're bad. And it's bliss, June. Being left alone. It's...*peace*." My sister's chin wobbled, then scrunched. "Dang it." She picked up her napkin, pressed it to her eye. "There go my fake lashes."

***

Across from Hiller Hall, I sank into the grass beneath a small tree covered in ivy. A good place to collect myself. I hadn't been able to focus during Dr. Freeman's lecture. Keegan hadn't shown, and I was convinced he didn't want to see me, had dropped the class so he would never have to see me again. What had I said? What had I done? My mind circled and circled, trying to locate the terrible error that had turned him away. How had I so quickly messed things up? I told myself it was for the best. Jehovah's Witnesses and Pentecostals did *not* mix, not even as friends.

This thought summoned the troubling conversation with Rain. I was pleased she'd opened up to me, a rare event. But her wants...it was like my question had opened some Pandora's box inside her. Isn't this what the Elders had warned us about? The slow seduction of higher education? If my sister left Jehovah to become an actuary, Jehovah would destroy her in Armageddon. I would have to live in the New Earth without her. I pulled at the grass, overwrought, making myself sick. I reached for my bag, pulled out my book.

Christy's first day as a teacher.

Her prim, fancy shoes crunching through the snow. Her little school-house. Her students, twisting to stare, scrutinizing her from head to toe, lingering on her shoes. Her sharp realization: *they were barefoot*. They'd walked through the snow, and their feet were red and raw. Christy's drenching shame, her desire to run. And then, Little Burl Allen, scampering up to her. His freckles, his big eyes. His red hair with a cowlick. He offered his hand to her, said, *Teacher, I've come to see you and to swap howdys.*

I pressed the book to my heart.

Crunch-crunch-crunch. The music of shoes, landing on crisp leaves. I startled, looked up.

And up, and up. "You are tall!"

Keegan grinned. "Are giants invited to the party?"

I patted the ground beside me.

Keegan lowered himself onto the grass. *He'd found me.* I took him in. The mid-afternoon light twining gold through his dark auburn curls. His strong jaw, faintly stubbled. Dark green sweater, sleeves pushed up to his elbows, a collared shirt beneath. He leaned in suddenly, closing the space between us. My breath hitched. He plucked something from my hair, opened his hand.

An acorn!

I laughed. "That's a new one. I'm glad the owner didn't come looking for it."

Keegan said, "Someday I'm going to untangle a squirrel from your hair, aren't I?"

Someday. I plucked at the grass, gazed at him from beneath my lashes. "Why weren't you in class?"

"Big rush at work. I'm trying hard to get promoted. So I decided to stay."

"I see." My eyes snagged on the measuring tape round his shoulders. I pointed to it. "A favorite accessory?"

"Ah! I wondered where that went." He swiped the measure off his shoulders, looped it expertly round his finger. Then winked at me. "Bet you can't guess my day job."

"Crane measurer?"

"You really do think I'm tall."

"Mortician?"

"You're good."

"Please tell me you're not a mortician."

"For now, I only measure the living."

"Hmm." I considered, then snapped my fingers. "You sew swim trunks for seals?"

"*Swim Trunks for Seals*. That's a million dollar business idea. But my current job is way more prosaic." He held up his palms, shrugged. "Wedding tailor."

"That's not prosaic. That's romantic!"

He beamed, leaning back on his palms. "Do you have an occupation?"

I produced my book. "Reading. Unpaid as of now."

"What are you reading?" Keegan searched my eyes. "Something that made you tear up."

I showed him my book. "It's about this girl, Christy Huddleston, who leaves her home to teach in the poorest part of the Great Smoky Mountains. I was crying because of Little Burl, one of her students. She feels out-of-place, overwhelmed, ashamed, and the way Little Burl rushes to welcome her...it's just...it's *beautiful*." I pressed the book to my heart again.

Keegan watched me. "You're so real."

I sat back. "What do you mean?"

"I mean, you don't hold back, do you? You don't pretend, play it cool. You don't speak and act to impress. You're...you. Sitting in the grass, crying over books, with acorns in your hair."

"You don't think I'm a mess?"

"Sure." He smiled, and I laughed. "I think you'll be an amazing teacher, with a bunch of Little Burls who think the world of you."

"I'm not going to be a teacher. I mean, I will be, in a way. I'm going to be a missionary."

"Really?" He sat straighter, the light in his eyes rising.

"That's my dream, too."

He held my gaze, and I swallowed, realizing what I'd done. I braced myself for the inevitable next question.

"What church do you go to?"

I wasn't ready. I wasn't ready to lose – whatever this was.

I jumped to my feet, swooped up my jacket. "Guess what time it is?"

He looked up at me, squinting and bewildered.

"Time to skedaddle!"

I took off.

tacos part two

"June!"

I should keep running. The truth was, running was the only right thing to do.

Instead, what did I do? Like Lot's wife, I looked over my shoulder, back at the forbidden. His fitted jeans. His tall, lean, muscular body. Coppery curls tumbling across his forehead as he jogged toward me.

I stood there, staring. Fixed to the ground. Soon to be a pillar of salt.

"You in a hurry?" Coming up beside me, he switched his backpack to the other shoulder.

"How could you tell?"

He grinned.

"My mom's picking me up soon."

"I'll walk with you." He checked my face. "If you want me to, that is."

"Oh, I do want, I mean," I cleared my throat, "sure." As we walked, I squinted up at him. "How tall are you anyway?"

"Six four. How short are you?"

"Ha! Five two." I swung my messenger bag, said, "And the twain shall be known throughout the land as the giant and the garden gnome."

"1st Samuel 3:15," Keegan said.

"Actually, it's Deuteronomy 3:15..."

We laughed, and then, he looked at me like I was his Pentecostal dream girl.

A sick feeling washed over me. He'd told me I was real.

And here I was, letting him think something about me – about us – that could never be true. I was perpetuating a sham. I had to tell him. I should be used to doors slamming in my face. But I had to work up the courage to hold the pain, when the door slammed shut between us in his eyes.

In a fit of mental agony, I sank down at the burbling fountain outside the School of Arts building, where students went to paint, draw, and sculpt. A girl with shiny purple pig-tails pushed through the door, hefting a massive art portfolio case. "This building always makes me think of my little brother," Keegan said, sitting beside me. "He could study here someday."

"Is he an artist?"

Keegan whistled. "Is he ever."

"That good?"

"Genius! Actually, hold on." Keegan dug in his bag, curls falling into his eyes. Retrieving a small sketchbook, he held it out to me. "He just gave me this for my nineteenth birthday. I take it with me everywhere now."

Carefully, I took the sketchbook from his hands. I smiled at an elaborate colored-pencil drawing of a globe, straddled by a very tall man with familiar curly hair, and in bubble letters: *Keegan's Intrepid Adventures*.

Keegan said, "Like you, my dream is...*was*...to be a missionary."

"Was?"

"My plans have kind of halted, for now." He looked at me, with a torn expression, then shoved a hand through his hair. "Let's just say, it's not something I can do right now." The sadness in his voice, his face, called to my own.

"My dreams are on hold, too."

I opened the sketchbook. On each page, elaborate drawings showcased iconic places around the world. In every picture,

Keegan was a superhero, with a measuring tape instead of a cape, in the midst of some grand, daring escapade: scaling the grid-work of the Eiffel Tower decked out in a tux with a measuring tape round his shoulders. Keegan in goggles, parasailing over the top of the Taj Mahal's turrets and minarets, his measuring tape like a wind-blown scarf billowing out behind him. Keegan leaping Stonehenge, like a Paul Bunyan high-jumper, Bible in hand. The Bible, I noted, was very lovingly drawn, with a name printed in tiny letters in the lower right corner. *Patrick*. Who was Patrick?

Turning the page, I broke into a huge grin. Keegan, depicted as a guard outside the Queen's palace. He saluted, face stoic beneath a towering bearskin hat. Standing tall atop the hat, a turtle. Not just any turtle. A turtle wearing his own bearskin, also saluting, with a miniature measuring tape unfurling behind him in the breeze. Across the tape in flowing letters was another name: *Intrepid*.

"These are wonderful," I said. "Your brother is truly an artist. Who's Intrepid?"

"Rory's pet," Keegan said. "He wanted a dog. He got a turtle. He's taken it very well. In fact, Rory might be the most devoted turtle-owner ever. He's currently training Intrepid to come out of her shell."

"Aren't turtles meant to hide in shells?"

"Rory has his own carefully cultivated philosophy about that. When you meet him, I'm sure he'll tell you all about it."

"Who is Patrick?" I pointed to the name on the Bible.

Keegan's face fell. "Well, that's our..."

The campus bell sent me to my feet. "I have to go."

Keegan stood, taking the sketchbook from me. "I'll walk with you."

"No!"

He stepped backward with a puzzled look. "Okay?"

"I'll be...I mean you...*you'll* be late for class."

He shrugged. "It's English Lit. Dr. Mason loves me. I can be late one time."

"English Lit! What are you reading?"

He pulled *Jane Eyre* from his back pack.

"No way. I'm so jealous." Now we were walking together and, blinded by book-envy, I'd forgotten the awful predicament.

"Lot A?" Keegan pointed to the stairs leading underground, through a tunnel under the main road, rising up to the parking lot on the other side.

"Yeah, but..."

"Cool." He walked ahead.

I skittered up beside him, tugged at his sleeve. "It's English Lit, Keegan. You might miss the discussion."

"It's okay," he said. "Just this once."

"No, no. It's *never* okay to miss a single second talking about *Jane Eyre*."

He laughed, and kept walking. I followed him downstairs, through the tunnel, which was not nearly as dark as my soul just then. Climbing up, I clutched the hand-rail. I was going to faint. I was going to die. We stepped out into the blaring sunlight of Lot A. I looked every which way. Mom's red Subaru was nowhere to be seen.

I spun to Keegan. "Now get thee to class." I tried to sound playful. I gently shoved his arm. "Go on. Go!"

"I don't mind waiting." Keegan lowered himself onto the cement ledge, parked his backpack between his feet. "Even if I skipped, it wouldn't hurt my grade."

He was determined to stay with me.

It was beautiful. It was shattering.

I plunked down beside him, and twisted my legs together. My stomach gurgled. My bladder pressed. I had to go to the bathroom so bad.

"Do you live around here?" Keegan asked.

"Hopeton."

"That's out in the boonies!"

I lifted an eyebrow. "I believe the polite term is *in the sticks*." A red car rounded the corner. I shot to my feet. The car veered, parked.

I sank back down, heart going mad. I was short of breath, my ribs were tight. I felt like I'd just run a sprint. And I was about to pee my pants. "I thought that was her."

"I'm working late tonight," he said. "I'm tailoring a bunch of tuxes for a huge wedding party. May I..." he looked off to the side, then at me. "May I call you?"

Her car rounded the corner and I was off like a rocket, leaving a blaze behind me. I flung open the passenger door, tossed my bag on the floor, swept into the front seat. I smiled, breathing hard, my lips trembling. "Hi, Mom. Don't you look stunning!" Her black hair was braided into two braids which were pinned into an elaborate up do. She wore dark red lipstick, the beauty mark on her chin freshly penciled. She edged her sunglasses down her nose, and stared at me. She didn't say a word.

"What?" I tucked my hands between my knees.

"You look beautiful, too. Radiant, in fact." Mom pressed gently on the accelerator. The car rolled slowly forward. "Well, well. What is this? Who do we have here?" She slowed, dipped her head to peer out the window. "Someone out there is trying *very* hard to get your attention."

Cringing, I looked. Keegan stood there, all innocent,

waving at us. What was wrong with him?

Mom poked my leg with her fingernail. "Don't be rude, June. Wave at that boy. Before his heart breaks."

I waved, gritting my teeth. Then fell against the seat. My back, slick with sweat.

We drove on. Mom lifted her gaze to the rearview mirror. "My, my. What a handsome young buck. So tall. So dashing." Her eyes slid to me.

"He's in my class," I said. "I loan him my notes."

"Is that right?" Mom's mouth flickered. "You must think I'm dumb."

I dug my nails into the vinyl seat, bladder about to lose the war.

We glided to a standstill at a 4-way stop. "Isn't there a taco place on campus you girls like?" She didn't wait for an answer. She lifted her chin and granted me a smile. "If you want, June. You can get tacos with that boy sometime."

"I can?"

"Sure you can."

I sat there, holding my breath. Too much emotion, one way or the other, might nudge this unprecedented gift right over a cliff.

So I stared straight down the road, heart a dazzling fireworks show, and said nothing.

steak

"Tacos?" Keegan's eyebrows drew together.

"Would you like to? Eat them?"

Keegan and I sat facing each other beneath the poetic little tree, draped in ivy, outside of Hiller Hall. We were studying for our first exam. I'd discovered, much to my surprise, he was struggling to maintain a C average in every class but English Lit. I'd asked him if he knew about the magic of flashcards. Next thing you knew, we were sitting under the tree together with our books and my trusty pack of cards. One minute, Keegan was defining *cognitive dissonance*, and the next, I'd invited him to lunch, which seemed to be afflicting him with the very term he'd just defined.

I thought maybe I should clarify. "You know. Tacos?" I made my hands a cradle, which I hoped conveyed a taco shell.

Keegan looked up into the tree. "I'm not feeling tacos."

"You...you aren't?" Translation: *he didn't like me.*

"Nope." He plucked up a leaf, twirled it. "Not really."

"Okay! That's okay." I shuffled the flashcards, and they flipped out of my hands, spilling across the grass. We both reached to collect them, and our hands met. I pulled back, my heart hurting.

"What about steak?"

"What?"

Keegan went on, gathering up the cards. "I know this place. Flamaggio's. It's really special." He handed the cards to me, and held my eyes. "June, will you have dinner with me tonight?"

I blinked. *Steak.* That sounded less like tacos, and more

like – a date.

He cleared his throat. "I could, um, pick you up?"

I shook my head.

Keegan's face fell. "I could...not pick you up? I could..." he raked a hand through his curls, looked at me. "Do you not like steak? I should've asked. Because we can totally get something else. Anything you want. Tacos! Do you want tacos, or...for me to shut up now?"

"You need to know something."

"Okay."

"I'm a Jehovah's Witness."

Keegan and I stared into each other's wide open eyes.

Then, in one quick movement, he turned from me.

He actually turned his back.

I stared at his back, stricken.

He was hunched, his hand under his chin, not speaking.

A bright yellow leaf fluttered down between us.

Finally he turned to face me, his jaw set. "June. Will you have dinner with me tonight?"

"Yes," I said.

***

I'd been given permission to have tacos.

Not steak.

In my room, I lay flat on my stomach on the floor, looking under my bed.

Eye to eye with a discarded Pocahontas, shredded bits of poetry in her hair.

This is where I had hidden her, this past summer, and forgotten. But she was still there. Everything that had happened, even if I didn't think about it, was still there, a nightmare hidden.

I knew very well that steak was not tacos. I had said yes because...tacos were halfway to steak? Weren't they?

I jumped to my feet. I paced. I was cold. My teeth chattered. I was hot. My shirt stuck to my skin. I peeled my shirt away, fanned air in. I was cold. Goosebumps swarmed. I was hot, like a fever, like the plague.

I marched to my door, threw it open, then stood in the hallway shivering.

Again, she was there.

Christy dropped to her hands and knees, crawling her way across that log bridge, high above a mad, roaring creek, eyes squeezed shut, determined not to turn back.

I would go find Mom.

I crept down the hallway, into the kitchen. The timer on the oven dinged. I slipped on the oven mitt, pulled the pan of lasagna out, and set it on the stove-top. The cheese bubbled and glistened.

I started at the *whump!* of the dryer, snapping to life in the laundry room. The dryer thrashed, bumping against the wall. Mom had nick-named our dryer Bucking Bronco.

I peeled off the oven mitt, stepped to the laundry room door, clasped the cold knob.

Across the bridge, June!

I pushed the door open. Mom was bent over the ironing board, long black hair swinging loose to one side as she ironed one of Dad's work shirts.

She didn't hear me approach over the rumpus of Bucking Bronco. I stepped closer. "Mom!"

She jerked her head up, hand flying to her heart. "June!

You scared me!" She propped the iron up, looked at me. Her forehead creased. "What's the matter?"

"Remember that boy, you said – we could get tacos?"

"Yes?"

"Well, he said not tacos, steak, so we're going to get steak."

She stared at me, a flat look on her face.

"Tonight," I added.

"Steak?"

"That's right."

"Steak." With a strange little smile, she met my eyes. "Very clever, June," she said.

But she didn't say no.

holy cottonwood

"I recommend the ribeye." Keegan spread the menu open between us, and I tried to pin my frantic, wandering attention there. "It's so rich, and the spice combination is phenomenal. They keep the recipe top secret. Believe me, I've tried everything short of selling my soul to get it."

I nodded, sweeping my gaze around again. This place was unreal. Like a castle. Dimly lit, with a soft golden glow emanating from wall sconce candles. Across the walls, a sweeping mural of birds and vines and flowers. A real fountain, tall and bubbling, in the center of the restaurant. I'd been dropped into another world.

My eyes drifted to Keegan across from me. And the astonishment deepened. He was breath-taking in a crisp white button down shirt, the top button open, revealing a glimpse of manly clavicle. Candlelight flickered on his cheekbones, his faintly stubbled jaw line. He looked like he belonged here, as elegant as the place.

I grew keenly, painfully aware of the butterfly hairpins attempting to restrain my frizz. Mom's handiwork. She'd insisted on doing my hair. "Don't bother Rain," she'd said, closing the bathroom door and twisting the lock. "She already got to help you once. It's *my* turn now."

What did she mean by that? Her words tangled up my brain. I couldn't make sense of them. She ran a comb through my hair, tugging at the knots, so hard I winced. "Steak." She'd chuckled, jabbing in the pins left and right, though I didn't want them, thought they were childish. "Fancy, fancy. This boy must come from money. He sure looks like he does. So tall and well-dressed. What does he want with you? Why not some cute, perfect little sorority girl? Be careful, June. You trust too easy." I'd sat there, gripping the sides of the cold toilet, unsure whether to feel loved, or hurt.

She'd driven me to the mall, dropping me off at the entrance nearest Luca's Formalwear, where Keegan worked. "What do you want me to tell Dad? You know how he gets about you and boys. That man. He's so dang uptight." She'd rolled her eyes, then nudged me. "I'll tell him you're at school, in a study session. I won't give you away." She'd pinched my cheek, a little too hard. And then, eyes roving me up and down, "I should have helped you pick an outfit. That dress makes you look backwoods." Pulling a face, she'd plucked a loose thread.

I sat here now, smiling on the outside, but writhing on the inside. I felt wrong for the place, wrong for the boy across from me. Wrong in my own skin. My knee bounced under the table. Keegan glanced up from the menu. "Everything okay?"

"Oh, yeah. Everything's, wow." I squeezed my lemon wedge over my ice water. Lemon juice squirted outward with startling vehemence, and reach.

"Oof!" Keegan flew back, rubbing his eye.

"Oh my gosh. I'm so sorry! Here," I plucked up my white linen napkin and threw it at him. It landed on his head, like a sun-bonnet.

With perfect timing, our server arrived. He did a double-take at Keegan, tried not to laugh. "Rough night, man?"

Keegan removed the napkin from his head. He blotted lemon juice from his chin. "Actually, it's a great night." He caught my eye, held it, and my whole body softened in the warmth of his gaze. My fingers uncurled from their death grip on the tabletop.

"I see that, man. I see that." The server glanced between us, chuckling. "I'm Greg." He stuck out his hand. Shook mine, then Keegan's. "Y'all know what you want?"

Keegan ordered the famous rib-eye. While he tried coaxing and flattery to procure the secret recipe, I pretended to scan the menu. I already knew what I was going to order, not because I wanted it, but because it was the only thing I could eat.

Greg turned to me. "And for the lady?" Pen poised over pad.

"I'll have the garden side salad, please."

They stared at me like I'd broken a commandment. "What? What's the matter?"

Greg leaned in, planted the heels of his hands on the table. "This is Flamaggio's, my dear. We serve the best steak in Arkansas. In the USA. Maybe even the world. This is not the time to be dainty!"

I straightened. "I am *far* from dainty. My sister calls me Piglet." Greg's eyes widened. I looked at Keegan. "I'm ordering salad because I'm full. I, um, already ate dinner."

Greg dropped his pen. He rubbed his face. "You *ate* before coming to Flamaggio's?"

"My mom made lasagna." This was another strange thing. She had insisted I eat dinner before going out to dinner. And she'd served me a mountainous portion. *Go on*, she'd said, *eat up*. I knew not to protest, and definitely not to mention the steak. She had smiled, watching me, making sure I finished every bite. I'd had the dizzying sense we were playing some sort of game.

Greg swiveled to Keegan. "You hear that? Mama Bear didn't trust you to feed her daughter." He chuckled, collecting our menus. "You two college students?"

"U of A," Keegan said.

"Whoop whoop. Class of '92, Go Hogs! You see how that MBA is working out for me." He shook his head, doleful. "Where y'all go to church?"

This was a normal get-to-know-you question in these parts, I'd learned. I focused on stirring my demolished lemon, deep into the icy depths of my water glass.

Keegan said, "Glorious Pentecostal. What about you?"

"Holy Assemblies, man. On *fire*! Praise Jesus!" They high-fived each other. As if their churches were football teams.

Greg turned to me, expectant. I was Daniel in the Lion's Den. "I go...to this place..." I took a quick drink of terribly over-lemoned water, grimaced, then blurted, "Church of the Holy Cottonwood."

Greg click-clicked his pen. "Sounds Baptist. Where is it?"

"Hopeton."

"Out in the boondocks! The woodsy woods. That makes sense. Church of the Holy...what'd you call it?"

"Cottonwood," I said. "It's a safe place, for *everyone*." I glanced at Keegan. He took a drink, avoiding my eyes.

"Sweet!" Greg scribbled on his pad. "They have good music? That's key to me. A really rocking worship band."

"Oh yes. There's lots of...clapping."

Greg threw a fist in the air. "The Lord is *moving* that congregation! I'll be back with your bread." He darted off, and I exhaled.

Keegan met my eyes. "Alone at last."

"I was about to invite him to pull up a chair."

"You almost got him going to church with you." Keegan paused. "In a tree."

I choked, started coughing. Greg dashed over with a basket of piping hot bread. He saw me coughing, threw down the bread basket, rolled up his sleeves like a prize fighter. "Good thing I just got re-certified." He made terrifying thrusting motions by his chest.

"No! No, please. I'm fine." I waved him away.

Keegan broke down laughing. His auburn curls fell across his forehead.

I would've laughed, too. But I was ashamed. I had failed my Daniel moment. I thought about Jehovah's Witnesses imprisoned in Nazi concentration camps, prisoners of conscience, those who refused to surrender their faith or fight in the war, identified by an upside down purple triangle worn on the left side of their striped jackets. *Bibelforscher*, they were called. Bible Students. In the face of certain death, they continued to meet in the camps, singing praises to Jehovah, even preaching. And I couldn't tell my bubbly Pentecostal waiter that I was one of them? I grumbled as Keegan laughed. "It wasn't a lie, exactly."

Keegan raised an eyebrow. "You go to church in a tree?"

"I read in a tree. And that's holy." I bit the inside of my cheek, rubbed my forehead with my knuckle. "You wonder why I didn't tell him I'm one of Jehovah's Witnesses."

"No." Keegan met my eyes. "I wonder why you didn't tell me."

The breath kicked out from between my ribs. "I wanted you to know me first."

He didn't say anything.

"The moment I tell people my religion, that's all they see. It felt good, when we talked, that you saw *me*. I wanted to keep being seen by you. I know, believe me, it was a wrong desire, a selfish one."

Keegan said, "It makes sense though."

"If I had told you I was a Witness, that first day we talked on the steps, would you have wanted to get to know me better?"

"Probably not."

Again, the air punched out of me. He looked me in the eye, and without even trying to be polite, he told me the truth. I hated that truth. It hurt me. And yet there I was, leaning in for more. "When I told you today, you turned away from me. What were you thinking?"

"That I should get up and leave."

I winced. But then I remembered. "When you told me you were Pentecostal, my first impulse was to run as fast and far as I could go."

"Okay." He took a swig of water, rolled it around in his mouth like whiskey. It was clear he thought it was natural to be repelled by my religion, but bizarre to feel the same way toward his. He said, setting down his cup, "A couple years ago, a Jehovah's Witness knocked on our door. My dad said he wasn't interested, but the guy kept talking, and when my dad tried to go, the guy wedged his foot inside so my dad couldn't close the door. My dad said that level of aggression showed who the Jehovah's Witnesses are ruled by – and it's *not* the Lord."

My chest burned, but I stayed steady. "I have anecdotal evidence, too." Dr. Freeman had introduced this term and it was one we had studied for our upcoming exam. She explained that anecdotal evidence was based on personal observation, and therefore, it was not scientific, not verifiable, and not the truth.

Keegan caught the reference, and raised his water glass in acknowledgement.

I said, "I've learned to fear Pentecostals more than any other religion when I go door-to-door. Before I've even introduced myself, they're on the doorstep, putting their hands on my head – without permission – and praying for me in words that make no sense."

"Speaking in tongues. They do that because they want you to be saved."

"I could say the same about the man who put his foot in the door to keep talking to your dad. They both think what they're doing is an act of love, but aren't they both forcing their way?"

Keegan considered. "Maybe so."

This was surreal. Everything had melted away. The fancy restaurant. My self-consciousness. Other people. Time. The only thing left was the only thing that mattered. Our conversation. Just like the first day. "And yet," I said, "in spite of our mutual dislike..."

"Not dislike."

"Okay, distrust."

He didn't argue.

"In spite of our mutual distrust, here we are. Together. Why?"

"Good question. I have a lot going on right now." Keegan's eyes were heavy with something. "It was dumb of me to start school. I can barely keep up. I promised myself, the first day of class, not to take on more. And then, you show up. Out of all those seats, you sit right next to me! With these little pink flowers in your hair. And totally blow me off." He smirked. "I was intrigued by you from day one. Ever since we talked on the steps, talking with you is the highlight of my day. I've been praying about it, and feeling at peace. Like God brought us together. Then you tell me you're Jehovah's Witness. So what's *that* about?" He shook his head, eyebrows lifting. "I turned away from you, to get quiet inside, to think. My dad always said, *an emotion isn't a decision*. I was scared. Your religion scares me. But I didn't want *fear* to make my decision."

"Why did you ask me to dinner?"

Keegan said, "I like you."

The simple words filled the space between us.

He said, "Why didn't you run from me?"

I smiled at him. "I like you."

We held eyes. Then Keegan took a slice of warm bread from the basket. He lay it on his plate. I watched as he buttered the slice with great care, his wrist moving with strength, with grace.

He raised the bread up, and across the table, offered it to me.

The butter glistened in the candlelight.

As I took it, our fingers gently brushed.

I set the bread on my plate.

Then, I lifted a slice from the basket.

I buttered it with great care.

I held it out to him.

He took it.

And together, we ate.

get away

Keegan drove me home and we talked, nonstop.

He told me he hadn't declared a major yet. He wanted to transfer to Fayetteville Bible College, study church management, and one day, pastor his own church. I told him that I was dual-enrolled at the university, finishing my senior year of home-school. As soon as I was baptized, I'd commit to full-time door-to-door preaching, then apply to Watchtower School of Gilead, in New York, for missionary training.

Keegan shook his head. "Want to know what's crazy? I accepted a missionary assignment from my church in July. If things had worked out, I'd be in Guatemala right now..." he trailed off. Looking left, then right, he said, "Am I going the right way?"

Instead of Guatemala, here he was in Hopeton, Arkansas. Here we both were.

I popped back into reality.

I hadn't noticed the flow of highway, or the lights of Fayetteville receding. I hadn't absorbed the *Welcome to Hopeton, population 800* sign. I hadn't even seen the glitzy, lit up18-wheelers, pulling in and out of the neon-flashing truck stops. Talking with Keegan was the equivalent of a good book trance.

"You'll turn here." I pointed to the turn-off that led to my neighborhood road. We passed the pasture, cloaked in darkness where, during the day, my old friends the Oreo cows grazed. "There," I said, and we turned down my road, down the hill, past the sleeping creek and bullfrogs, then climbing up, until the road leveled off. As soon as his headlights illuminated our unfinished white picket fence, the posts sticking up, one slanted from the recent storm, my self-consciousness flew back. "That's a fence," I said. "Well, it's meant to be. Dad hasn't quite finished building it yet."

Keegan craned to look. "Your dad builds things, too. My dad's a furniture maker." At this, he went quiet, and in my own body, I felt sadness gather. Deep and dark. I wondered about it as the car crunched down our long, gravel driveway. I noted, with relief, that Dad's car wasn't there. He was still at night class. In the house, the kitchen light was on, a single burn in the darkness.

The light was on.

I nearly died from happiness.

I still belonged.

At the bottom of the lane, we glided to a standstill. Keegan switched off the engine. In the sudden quiet, I took a breath. What would happen next? My heart started to thump, a low buzz filling my head.

Keegan took the keys from the ignition, opened his door, and climbed out.

I gripped my seat-belt. What was he doing? He couldn't get out.

He did not understand the rules of my world.

Neither did I, but I knew them.

I knew, without being able to explain why, that he could *not* get out.

I knew, he could not be in our yard.

I unbuckled and threw off my seatbelt, flung open the door.

Keegan leaned back against the car, gazing up. "I forgot," he said.

“Forgot what?” I looked around for what it might be.

“What stars look like.” Face pointed to the sky, he wore a rapturous look.

“Ohhh.” I drew up alongside him. I tilted my head up, gazing with him at the immense swath of glitter. We looked together, for a long time, and I let myself settle beside him, into quiet comfort.

“My dad used to take us camping. That was the only time I got to see the stars like this.” He smiled. “The quiet in the countryside. It’s big as an ocean. So deep.” He looked around, eyes shining. “Stars, trees, and silence. You’re so lucky to live out here.”

His captivation, combined with his tallness, the aroma of his aftershave reaching me in the darkness, the beauty of him, all of it together made me lose my mind. “Would you like to walk?” I wanted to take him to my garden.

“I would love that.”

Leading him across the grass, my pulse beat in my fingertips. I kept one eye on the house. Mom’s bedroom stayed dark. “This is my garden,” I whispered. Moonlight shed silver on the entangled flowers. Keegan knelt, so I did, too. Very near him. He pressed one of the petunia’s soft, silky petals. My whole body lit up.

I wanted to touch him. I wanted him to touch me. I wanted our bodies to tangle like the flowers under the moon. The heat of my want poured from me. And he responded. He turned to me. He reached out. His fingers trailed down the side of my face, my neck. I closed my eyes, and leaned in.

Wsssht!

I jerked away, falling backward, my palms planted in the chilled grass. My eyes zipped to Mom’s window. I swore I saw her face pressed to the screen, a ghostly flash. There, then gone.

I swung to Keegan. “We can’t. Get away!”

***

I let myself in and huddled in the darkness of the laundry room, hugging myself, for a long time. My body, melty warm, zinging, still feeling Keegan's fingers, feather light, tracing, traveling. Imagining where they might go next. What would that feel like, his fingers on me, every little secret place. My underwear grew warm, wet. Mixed with this new excitement, was sickness, fear, and dread.

Get away, I'd told him. His face, horrified at first, had then grown cold. *Get away*, my mind kept repeating now, urging him psychically down the road, back to the city, back to safety.

I gathered myself, and then stepped up, into the kitchen. It was empty, dark. The hallways were dark. The house was still. My belly, held tight like a fortress, released. I fell against the fridge, and my eyes surged with tears. I tented my hands over my nose, my mouth, told myself, *you are safe.*

"Hi, how are you?"

I jolted upright.

Mom's voice, coming from Dad's study. "This is Sister Taylor calling."

I crept to the door of the study, opened a crack. I nudged it wider, peered in.

No light, except for moonlight, shining on Mom who stood in her robe, hair twined in a long, messy braid, looking out the window. "I'm sorry for calling you so late. But I wanted to let you know, I've been thinking about the offer you made. To come out and study the Bible with June."

My blood turned to ice.

"I'm going to have to say no."

I walked right into the study.

Mom must have heard. But she kept her back to me.

I clasped my hands, prayer-like. *Stop.* I formed the word, but couldn't make the sound. *Stop.*

"Yes, I'm disappointed, too. Believe me, it was not an easy decision, Sister Finn. But something happened tonight. I should probably tell you about it. I know how much you care for and respect June. But there are some things about her you don't know, and probably should."

The dizzy feeling returned.

I *was* in some sort of game.

One that I was losing.

She was going to tell Sister Finn about the garden. Tell her what she saw. What had nearly happened. What I'd *wanted* to happen. How bad I really was. With a boy, an unbeliever, in the garden, at night. Touching.

And Sister Finn's face would fall. The light would go out of her eyes for me. She would go away. I wasn't courageous enough to bear it. I backed out, stepping into someone. *Dad.* How long had he been there? He held his briefcase, his face drained and worn. He must have just walked in. Mom started talking again, and something in her voice – his eyes sharpened, his whole body went rigid. Then he looked at me. What he saw in my face, reinforced what was in his. We exchanged a message. He crept one way. And I crept the other.

In my room, from my window, I spied Dad's car, driving up the driveway, then down the road. His headlights were off, trying to get away, unseen. Leaving me here with her, alone. I was shocked, and not. Some terrible knowing cracked through its shell. This wasn't the first time he'd escaped.

I undressed, crawled into bed, pulled the covers up to my chin.

Keegan was right.
The countryside was full of silence.

friends

Rain flicked off NPR news. "What happened last night?"

I shook myself. I was half-asleep in the passenger seat on our morning drive to campus. Flashcards in my lap, I was attempting a final cram session before my first college exam. I rubbed my eyes, started to speak.

Rain talked over me. "Last night, I was studying in my room with headphones on. At dinner, you weren't there. Mom acted funny. Like, keyed up. Her eyes were all bright. She said you went out to a fancy restaurant with a guy? She was all coy and smug, telling me about it. She said you'd come to her, told her all the details, asked her for help." Rain clenched the steering wheel. "I don't even know what the hell is going on!"

"I went out for steak."

"Like on a date? Mom was giddy, bragging about how she'd met him, some tall, rich guy from your class."

"She didn't exactly meet him..."

Mom showing off to Rain. Mom calling Sister Finn. What was happening?

The rules of this game were all over the place, and kept morphing. I started to cry. "I don't know, Rain. I don't know what's going on either."

"You met someone? In your class? Is that why you've been even more weird than usual? How come you never told me?" Rain's voice cracked. She pushed down hard on the gas. We shot past an old pickup, white-and-brown speckled bull-horns arched across the cab. "Whatever. Fine! You know what? Don't tell me." She smacked her palms down hard on the steering wheel. Then, furiously, she rolled down her window. "I'm *done* with this family! I fucking give up!" She grabbed her necklace, tore it off her neck. Hematite beads fell onto her lap, dropping onto the floor, rolling. "Fuck her and fuck her gifts!" She whipped the necklace right out the window. In the next instant, we swerved, hitting the shoulder. My flashcards spilled off my lap.

"Rain!" I shrieked, covering my eyes. Bumping, rattling, teeth clacking, brain jumping.

When I opened my eyes, we were in the ditch, facing down an electrical pole inches away. We sat in silence, breathing hard, staring out the windshield for a long time. "Fuck," Rain said. She dropped her forehead to the steering wheel.

"Stop cussing," I said. At first, under my breath. And then, kicking the dash, smashing it hard as I could with my fist. "STOP CUSSING!"

***

The tow truck driver kindly delivered us to school. Rain's car was un-drivable but we were fine. Or at least, I would tell myself so because nothing was going to get between me and my first college exam. I'd collapse *after*.

Dad was securing Rain a rental car so we'd still be able to get back and forth while her car was in the shop. Mom cried on the phone when we talked to her, mostly *me* doing the talking because Rain was huddled, pasty white with terror, less about the accident, more about Mom's reaction. Rain was sure, she was in for it.

But Mom said she loved us and that she was so grateful, that we'd had Jehovah's angels looking out for us, and she was just so grateful. She asked to talk to Rain and Rain cringed and cowered, taking the phone. But Mom cried telling her the same things, and Rain cried back to her in the phone.

I barely had time to make it to my first exam. I slid into Seat #20, five minutes late.

I felt him look at me.

But I couldn't look at him.

***

Dr. Freeman was quite possibly the coolest person I'd ever met with her pixie cut and dark, square-framed glasses. That day, pacing the aisles as we labored over our exam, she wore baggy trouser pants, a puffy-sleeved shirt like a Romantic poet, and a vintage vest with a gold pocket watch. She stopped near me, flipping the watch open with a soft click.

Even with ragged nerves, I tore through the multiple choice. I hadn't taken a real exam in a real classroom for so long. And I was doing good. I could feel it. I was pumped. Then I arrived at the essay question, and paused. *Write about a life-altering experience, accurately and insightfully incorporating at least 5 of the psychology terms we've discussed this semester.*

Mind blank, I pressed my pencil down onto the page. I willed it to think for me. *The Old Man*, my pencil wrote. I stared at the words, stunned, and a little frightened. It was like my pencil had called forth some black magic. What did I have to say about a man I never knew?

Apparently, a lot.

> *My Grandma says there are different kinds of drunks. There are funny drunks and weepy drunks, sleepy drunks and mean drunks. Like a rhyme from my old Mother Goose book. Grandma says that the Old Man is a mean drunk. Mean as*

they get. He'd beat up Grandma, then win her back, every time, with gifts.

He'd beat on his daughters, too.

My mom, Abequa, and her older sister, Rena.

Mom says he'd chase her down with the belt, hold her down, whip her lash after lash. I can't think about this too much or I go crazy. Mom would show up at school with bruises. The teachers would see, and pretend not to. Mom says, she wasn't important enough to see. The town drunk's daughter. Trash.

Now, when she looks in the mirror, my mother's face fills with hate. She looks like him. Does she see him? Is facing her reflection a kind of stimulus generalization? I'm not sure. All I know is, the Old Man doesn't have to hurt her anymore. She does it for him. She tells herself all the ugly things she thinks she is. She beats her own thighs with her own fists. It reminds me of Freud's theory of self-punishment. Like she's so ashamed, she can't give herself an inch of mercy.

When my sister and I were born, she vowed to keep the Old Man away from us, even though he lived in the same small town. Rain and I grew up in Marsh Lake, Wisconsin. The town drunk's grand-daughters. The kids at my school knew all about him. He was small-town famous, stumbling from bar to bar, wearing a bib. He always wore a bib on his drinking sprees. He had a whole collection of them, like some men have ties. I know, because I saw him many times from the car window, and he always wore a different bib. Maybe the bibs were part of the gentleman persona he crafted to try to maintain some dignity. Sometimes he wore military uniforms to bars, too, but my Grandma says, that was a ploy to pick up women.

Mom made good on her promise to keep him away. He didn't know who Rain and I were, even when we crossed paths with him in town. Once we found him outside the post office, passed out in a mud puddle. Rain tore inside, called 911. Our Grandpa, she told the operator, pushing her hand through her curls, squeezing them hard, our Grandpa's hurt, he's unconscious, please help.

Our Grandpa.

She said it with anguish, and urgency, and tenderness.

She owned him, at his worst.

That stayed with me.

I set the pencil down. Maybe I'd fail the essay part because I'd only used three instead of five terms, but I had to go. I was in tears. I was sinking. I was a leaky boat that couldn't hold a single drop more. This whole day. This whole month. No, *this whole life.*

I stood and hurried down the aisle, handing my exam to Dr. Freeman, who leaned on the lectern, gold pocket watch flipped open in her hand.

She straightened, looked at me closely. "Are you okay?"

I hugged myself. "Yeah. The essay part, that was hard." Head down, so I wouldn't be tempted to catch his eye, I made my way back up the aisle, then out through the doors, into the overwhelming sunny and crisp October day. I sank down onto the step, the feel of chilled concrete seeping through my jeans. My head hurt, and I wondered if now a concussion from the accident would take me down. I'd pass out cold, right there on the steps. Would that really be so bad? I thought back to my time in the hospital. I'd hated it. I'd wanted out. And yet... Mom had been so worried about me. So frightened. She'd slept by my bed in a chair. Would it be so bad, returning to that?

The doors pushed open and there he was.

Seat Thief.

I braced, but he swept past me, jogging down the steps, and away down the sidewalk.

Watching him go, I thought, I don't want a concussion. Don't want to be in the hospital. Don't want to be sick anymore.

What do you want? The question I'd asked Rain. I remembered the way she grit her teeth, struggled with it. *I want...I want...*

I jumped to my feet. "Keegan!"

He hesitated, then stopped, keeping his back to me. I ran to him. "Hi," trying to catch my breath.

He turned. "Hi."

"Can I tell you something?"

"Sure." His face was guarded.

"I have bad anxiety. And when I'm anxious I – do and say weird things."

"Really?"

I looked up at him. He smiled.

"Haha," I said, smiling back.

"June, I'm..." He took a step toward me.

I stepped away. "You're Pentecostal. I'm Jehovah's Witness."

He stepped toward me. "I'm aware."

I stepped away. "This is serious! We'll walk into bars and instantly become a joke."

Keegan threw his head back, laughed. "You're the funniest

person I've ever met."

"I am?"

"Hands down." He stepped toward me.

I stepped away.

"June. Why do you keep backing up?"

"Do I?" I looked at my feet. I'd walked right off the sidewalk, into the grass. I clapped my hands to my face. "Because we can't!"

Keegan shook his head. "Can't stand close to each other?"

"No. Yes! I mean. Not *too* close. Not close-close...like last night."

That hit a nerve. His face went still.

"2 Corinthians 6:14," I said. "*Do not be unequally yoked with unbelievers.* That's a command. There's no way around it. As much as we disagree, this is our common ground: we both believe in the Bible. We both love God. And neither of us want to sin."

The muscle in his jaw jumped. "You're right. You're being wise. No matter how much I don't want it to be true, it is. I – wanted to touch you last night, be as close to you as I could."

"I wanted the same." We locked eyes. My face warmed.

"Ahh, this sucks." He tilted his head back, raked a hand through his curls. "What are we going to do?"

"I don't know." I gripped the straps of my bag. "But we started a conversation that I don't want to lose."

He looked at me, tenderly. "Well, I don't think there's any scripture that says we can't talk." He smiled. "June. Will you be my friend?"

All my life.

I flew forward, hugging him so hard, he rocked backward on his feet.

"I think that's a yes," he said.

"How old is your brother?" I swept my gaze around at the other cars, mostly minivans and sedans, parked along the curb of Weaver Elementary. I latched and unlatched my fingers. I was supposed to be at tutoring but I'd canceled the appointment. Just for today, I'd skipped. I'd almost died and then took my first college exam. I could skip. I was giving myself that.

"Rory's nine. Only in fourth grade and already, he's embarrassed by me. One of these days, when I get around to installing the stereo, I'm going to blast Stryper when I pick him up."

"What's Stryper?"

Keegan lowered his sunglasses, stared at me over the rim. "Um. Stryper is only *the* best Christian heavy metal band on the planet. Maybe the only Christian heavy metal band on the planet? Check it out." He pressed play on the tape deck. A screaming guitar, and a voice shrieking *to hell with the devil!*

It was all I could do not to clap…

…my hands over my ears.

"We'll have to check out a concert sometime." He nudged me.

"Probably not," I said. "Definitely not."

"You don't like it?"

"Jehovah's Witnesses don't listen to interfaith music."

"Oh, oops. Sorry about that." He clicked the tape off. Drummed his fingers on the steering wheel. "So. What do you rock out to at your church?"

"Not church. Kingdom hall."

He cleared his throat. "Kingdom hall."

"We sing kingdom melodies."

His face went blank.

"From a songbook?"

"Oh, hymns you mean. What's your favorite?"

"This one." I sang, while gently marching my feet on the floor, "*We're Jehovah's Witnesses! We speak out in fearlessness. Ours is the God of True Prophecy, what He foretells comes to be!*"

"Oh, wow, that's..." Keegan's eyebrows reached all the way to his hairline.

"When I was little, I'd belt it out in public restrooms while peeing."

Keegan's smile was feeble, I thought, for such a funny story.

We looked away from each other. An awkward silence bloomed.

Outside, I watched fall leaves drift from trees, spiraling to the ground.

A bell shrilled. Shortly thereafter, a bounding, leaping stream of small humans in bright, cartoony clothing and bouncing backpacks poured from the building. Shouts and laughter filled the air.

"There he is." Keegan honked, waved.

My eyes riveted on a boy, a center of calm in the chaotic swirl of kids. He had wavy chestnut hair and sported a Ninja Turtles t-shirt tucked half in and half out of faded jeans. He gripped a long cardboard tube in his hand, staring at it, absorbed in thought.

Keegan honked again. This time, his brother looked up, waved with the tube. Seeing me in the passenger seat, his smile disintegrated. His brows drew together. Now he looked formidable, like the scrutinizing and never pleased middle-aged Dad.

"I'll sit in the back." My hand, already pushing on the door handle.

"June, you don't..."

I threw the door open and clambered out.

Keegan's brother eyed me sourly, up and down.

"Hi!" my wave was a little too exuberant, and I lost my balance. I wheeled my arms around, righting myself in the nick of time.

"Whoa," he said, with a stunned look. "You almost fell."

I held out my hand. "Want to swap howdys?"

He stared at my hand. I marveled at the spill of freckles across his nose and cheeks, watching as they moved into little constellations when he smiled. "Sure," he said. "Why not." He stuck the cardboard tube under his other arm, took my hand. "Howdy, I'm Rory."

"Howdy, I'm June."

We shook. Kept shaking. We swung arms, back and forth, and then we were laughing. This moment, I knew instinctively, was one of those pure, beautiful ones you remembered forever, no matter what other memories were lost.

When we climbed in the car, Rory up front, me in the back, he said, "Are you the girl with Kleenex in her hair?'

"It's not always Kleenex. Sometimes it's a leaf. And once, a worm."

"Eww," Rory turned, studying me. "You do have funny hair. It floofs, like a sheep."

"Rory, be a gentleman." Keegan threw him a stern look as we pulled away from the curb.

I laughed. "I've heard rumors about you, too."

Rory glared at Keegan. "All lies."

"You're not a genius artist?"

"I don't know about *genius*..."

"You don't have a fearless turtle?"

"Intrepid!"

"I have a question. How can a turtle be intrepid?"

"Annnnd we're off..." Keegan smirked as we turned out of the school parking lot.

Rory stuck a finger in the air. "I, too, was once a skeptic. But here's the thing, the turtle's lack of bravery is – no offense, Lord – a product of bad design."

"How so?"

"Think about it. How can you be brave with a built-in hiding place?"

"Hmm. So you're saying, the shell offers the turtle immediate physical protection, but is psychologically crippling. It fosters cowardice."

"Oh my God!" Rory threw his hands in the air.

"Hey now..." Keegan warned.

"Sorry. I mean, *gosh*. That's what I've been trying to explain to numb-skull here for months." Rory jerked his thumb at Keegan.

"Who you calling numb-skull, numb-skull?" Keegan rumpled Rory's hair.

I hooked my chin on Rory's seat. "How do you make a turtle brave?"

Without missing a beat, Rory answered. "Flying lessons."

skeletons

I'd thought Keegan was rich.

I had imagined him living at the end of some quiet, upscale cul-de-sac, in one of those tall, stately stone houses with the curved oaken doors, always intimidating to knock on as a Jehovah's Witness, though most of the time, no one was home.

We turned down a side street, then into a neighborhood. These houses were small, squat, and looked beat up, like they'd taken three rounds in the ring, and were trying to wobble back to their feet. Wire fences. Rusted out trucks and tired work vans. On the sidewalk, a gaunt, scruffy dog rooted through an overturned garbage can. A police car zoomed by, followed swiftly by two more, sirens shrieking.

Rory swiveled to watch. "Ooh, another meth bust, I bet."

Keegan flicked the turn signal. We pulled into a driveway, rutted with potholes. Keegan's car bounced over them. I held onto the door, staring at his house. Two story, worn but pretty, painted light blue, with lace curtains in the windows. But not rich. Not even close. My eyes snagged on a weird green stain, winding snake-like down the side of the house. Moss? We parked beneath a big mulberry tree, unruly branches overhanging the driveway. Keegan pushed his sunglasses into his curls. I noticed that his hand shook slightly. My heart rate ticked up. I wondered about his parents, if he was nervous about introducing me, the unbeliever girl with Kleenex in her hair. He leaned into Rory, said, "Hey, is that the top secret masterpiece you've been toiling over?"

"Yeah!"

"Show us, man. Come on. I've been waiting for the big reveal."

"Okay, but don't judge. It's not *quite* done." Rory unfurled the paper slowly. I sucked in a breath. The pencil drawing was both elaborate and haunting. A skeleton-man. Eerie, other worldly, yet so real. A Halloween project? Rory had captured eyes, irises aglow, yet sunk down deep, disappearing as though being consumed, into dark hollows like caves. Cheek bones sharp, carving through flesh, colored an unsettling yellow. A thread of a smile. Long, thin neck, the withered flesh there also colored that same yellow.

"Oh. Whoa." Keegan whipped away, staring straight ahead.

Rory looked wounded. "I told you it wasn't done."

"It's captivating," I said quickly. "I've never seen a skeleton look so...*alive*."

Rory turned to me, forehead wrinkled. "That's no skeleton. That's my dad."

***

My mind was a blur as I followed Keegan and Rory up the cracked cement steps, through the battered screen door. The musty entryway was a tumble of shoes, stacks of paint cans, toppled umbrellas. Rory tore up the stairs. "I'll get Intrepid!" He yelled over his shoulder.

"Snack first!" Keegan shouted after him. "And clothes picked up! Laundry in the basket!"

Thwack! The sharp defiant slam of a door made me jump. Keegan raked his fingers through his auburn curls. "That boy thinks dirty underwear is fine decor." He turned, saw my face. "Come on. Let's talk." I nodded, and hugging myself, followed Keegan through a workshop. The lights were off, but the windows, though dirty, let in enough sun to let me see the concrete floor, golden with wood shavings. The workbench littered with tools. In the corner, a toothy band-saw, gleaming. On a table, a blocky industrial sewing machine, green like sea foam. I paused near a partially built rocking chair set up on a platform. It was lovely, wood the color of a deer. Most of the pieces had been shaped, and joined together. Except for the seat. My gaze fell. In a neat row on the platform lay a roll of cord, some nails, a tiny metal hammer. Waiting.

Keegan slid his hand between two tall, grand doors. Antique pocket doors. They moved apart on rollers in the wood floor. Beside him, I stepped into a room so luminous, it was like walking into the sky. Deeply soft blue carpet. White lace curtains in floor-to-ceiling windows. Keegan took a seat on a satiny blue couch. I lowered myself next to him, wedging my hands beneath me. He set his elbows on his knees, stared into an empty fireplace. Outside, the muffled sounds of traffic, bass thumping, dogs barking.

Finally Keegan spoke. "This was my dad's room. He worked all day in the shop, making furniture. This room is where he read his Bible, hung out, talked with us about life, God, everything. He..." Keegan looked around, confused. "He...passed... the day before school started."

I closed my eyes. The boy who stole my seat, out of all two hundred seats. *Seat Thief.* His Bible. His finger tracing the lines. Like they meant something to him. That boy had just lost his dad.

Upstairs, thumping feet. A door whined open, then shut. More thumping.

I turned my eyes to the ceiling. "What about your mom. Is she here?"

"Yeah, June," Keegan said. He turned, met my eyes, waved.

“It’s me.”

bean showdown

Keegan was cooking. He wore an apron, and stirred a pot of soup.

I sat at the kitchen table with Rory, and the legendary fearless turtle.

Rory sat beside me, while Intrepid sat on a woven placemat across from me. She nosed a tiny bowl, craning her head this way and that, as if to inquire after the whereabouts of her meal. She was not only brave, but beautiful. Her shell rich in orange and yellow, like she'd been dipped in sunset.

Rory had been ordered to finish his homework. Like me, I noticed, he had the tendency to procrastinate in favor of more interesting pursuits. His English book was dutifully open, yet his sketchbook peeked out from beneath. He was in fact hard at work on a character sketch: Keegan chopping celery in an oversized chef's toque that leaned sideways. Rory wrote inside the hat *Tower of Peasa*. He looked up, caught me watching, and we shared a stifled giggle.

"What's your opinion of Rochester?" Keegan scooped a handful of diced celery from the cutting board, let it fall into the pot.

That question alone was worth skipping out on tutoring. No one had ever asked me my opinion about Rochester. Such were the drawbacks to home-schooling. I drew up in my chair. "The first time I read *Jane Eyre*, I was twelve. I could hardly understand the book, but I swooned over Rochester. He was dark, intense, and fascinating. But last year, when I read it again, he repelled me. The way he manipulates Jane, plays with her head, lies to her. He *uses* her. He exploits her loneliness, her craving for love, to secure his own happiness."

Keegan adjusted the flame on the stove, fire flaring under the pot. "I see your point, but wasn't Rochester in a bind? He was in love with Jane, and married to a madwoman. A madwoman he was forbidden by law to divorce."

"That's true. And the laws were atrocious. I'm not arguing that. But the fact is, he chose to marry – and Bertha Mason was more than a *madwoman*, Keegan. She had a name, a whole other life and story before he entered the picture! Rochester chose to marry Bertha when he didn't love her. He didn't even know her. He admitted that outright. Jane should not have had to suffer because of *his* bad choice. He was a man in denial and it hurt him. It hurt everyone."

Silence.

My eyes darted to the chair at the head of the table, a blue-checkered cushion tied to it. When I'd tried to sit there, Rory had yanked me away. *Not there,* he'd said, in an urgent whisper. *That's Dad's chair. He needs that cushion because his butt's gotten bony.*

Maybe ranting about denial was not the most sensitive thing, considering.

"I'm sorry," I said. "I never get to talk about books. I might get a little carried away."

"Never!" Keegan said at the same time Rory said, "You do!"

I looked back and forth between them.

"Don't listen to my brother." Keegan flicked salt into the soup. "He doesn't even like books."

I whipped to Rory, making a horror-stricken face, like that painting, The Scream.

Rory threw his hands in the air. "Books are boring! Why do

you people like to read? It's just staring at words." He bent over his English textbook. "Blah blah blah. See? Just words. Who cares."

"Cover your ears, June."

"Too late. They're already scorched."

"Speaking of scorched," Rory returned to his drawing. "Wait til you try Keegan's food."

"Don't start, bro." Keegan stirred the bubbling pot. "For one night, how about you lay off your new career as kitchen table critic and just let me show off my cooking?"

"Whatever. You're not gonna impress her with your bean concrete."

I made a face. "Bean what?"

"Could you *not* bring up the split pea soup? That was weeks ago."

"Yet the trauma lingers."

I smiled, with a pang of sympathy for Keegan's position. Rory was quick. And relentless. He turned to me now and said, "You should know something about my brother's cooking if you're planning to stick around. Okay? Here it is. Keegan's soup is so thick, you can lay sidewalks with it. You can make houses with it. You can build a whole city with it!"

"Cut me some slack. I've been *practicing*." Keegan ladled soup into bowls. He placed one before Rory, and one before me. Slinging a dish towel over his shoulder, he bowed, face flushed from the stove, curls slick against his skin. "Mademoiselle."

I looked down into a golden beany concoction swimming with glistening chunks of ham and celery. "It's lovely."

Rory scoffed. "Watch out, June. Satan comes disguised as an angel of light."

I couldn't help it. I laughed.

Rory did, too, this great high-pitched giggle.

And then Keegan busted up.

I looked to the head of the table, where their dad had sat only two months before, and missed the man who must have been, considering his two sons, someone really special.

Keegan pulled out the chair beside me. Before I knew what was happening, he took my hand on one side, and Rory took my other hand. Keegan bowed his head, and began to pray. *To Jesus!* I stared straight ahead, in shock. At last he raised his head. He rubbed his hands together. "Alright. Let's eat like Saint Pete!"

Rory looked at me, rolled his eyes. "Some goofy thing Dad made up and always said before we ate. Keegan thinks he has to say it now, too."

No one spoke. Intrepid munched on her lettuce shreds.

Rory spooned at the soup without taking a bite. "Here's what I want to know. How does Saint Pete even eat? Isn't he in heaven? Do people in heaven have mouths? Or stomachs? What are souls made of? How do they touch things, or think? I have all these questions, and Dad never..."

Keegan took a loud slurp of soup. "Ah! My best yet."

I tasted a spoonful. It *was* a bit thick. Maybe just a tad concrete-y. "The texture needs some work..."

"Ha!" Rory said, pointing his spoon Keegan.

"But the flavor is *inspired*."

Keegan's fist shot in the air. "Yes!"

Rory scowled. "June, your taste buds are traitors." And then, stirring the soup. "Here's another thing I want to know. How come you didn't pray with us?"

"What?"

"You stared straight ahead with your eyes open like this." He pried his eyes open with his fingers so they looked enormous.

I turned to Keegan. "Have you told him?"

"Not yet."

Rory almost fell out of his chair. "Are you a Satanist?"

"Rory!" Keegan glared.

"What? Pastor Pitts showed us a film about Satanists. They have pet lions!"

I spoke calmly. "I'm one of Jehovah's Witnesses."

Rory stared. "Jehoso-bibi-ma-*what*?"

"Je-ho-vah's Wit-ness." I enunciated each syllable. It had been like this since grade school.

"Do you worship Jesus?"

This kid was sharp. He went right for the biggie. "No, I don't. I worship Jehovah."

"Who's that?"

"I believe God has His own name. Jehovah. Every time you read *LORD* in the Old Testament, over six thousand times, that's where Jehovah's name should be. But it was removed by superstitious scribes."

"What the heck? I didn't know that. Did you know that, Keegan?"

Keegan pointed his spoon at Rory. "Quit stalling and eat your dinner."

Rory turned back to me. "Then who do you believe Jesus is?"

"God's literal son. His only-begotten. Like, the first angel God made."

"Wait, whoa, what? My head's gonna explode. You think the Lord Jesus is just some *angel*?" Rory pushed his spoon around and around in his soup, then snapped his fingers, excitedly. "I remember now. You're the people who knock on doors and don't celebrate Christmas! We watched a whole documentary about cults in Vacation Bible School."

***

I wrapped my wound in a Ninja Turtle band-aid, admiring the fierce, embattled turtle in a red mask. I appreciated the irony, seeing as I'd been bitten by a turtle. Rory had claimed that it was Intrepid's way of making lifelong friends, like blood brothers only...sisters.

Turtle bites drew a surprising amount of blood.

"June, I don't even know where to begin."

Keegan sank beside me on the satiny blue couch, downstairs in his dad's room. "If Dad were here...well, first off, Dad would never have allowed a turtle on the kitchen table. I can't imagine what you must think."

I held up my bandaged finger. "I think I'm lucky."

"Lucky?"

"How many people get to be blood sisters with a fearless turtle?"

Keegan smiled at this, and his forehead smoothed out. He grew thoughtful, and after a minute, he stood, strode to the fireplace. He plucked a picture from the mantel. He sat beside me and his sleeve brushed my arm as he placed the picture in my hands. Keegan and Rory, standing on either side of a good-looking man. It was the man in Rory's drawing, only robust, with a dark swoop of wavy hair like Rory's, and a trim, rusty red beard. They were all dressed up in suits and ties, a church steeple rising in the background. Keegan's dad clutched a large maroon leather Bible. "That's your Bible," I said.

"Dad's Bible." Keegan rotated his arm, showing the Celtic

cross tattoo. I now saw the name, inked in tiny cursive. "Patrick Brennan Callahan," Keegan said, in that dorky Irish accent. He laughed, but it fractured. "He wasn't supposed to go." He bowed his head.

I watched him, holding my breath. The unfinished rocking chair, all the tools laid out neatly in the workshop. The cushioned chair upstairs, Rory not letting me sit there, speaking about *Dad* in present tense. Keegan, not telling me any of this to begin with. Neither of them had accepted, come to grips. "Keegan, your dad was, *is*..." I couldn't comfort him from a place of shared belief. I didn't believe in an immortal soul that went to heaven. So what could I give? I looked at the picture, studying the small, handsome family of three. "You know something? You have your dad's dimple. The one in your left cheek."

He grinned. "Yeah. And the same butt chin. He thought it made him irresistible to women, and he didn't want to remarry. So he grew a beard to hide it."

"Butt chin?"

He tapped the cleft in his chin. We laughed together.

"Where is your mom?" I asked.

"She left when Rory was a baby. I don't like to talk about her. She has problems. She was never really part of our lives." His face shut down.

"Oh. Okay." I bit my lip. "Is there anyone... to help?"

"The rest of the family are scattered, not close, in any sense. Rory's godparents offered to take him. They wanted to take him. They're wonderful people. A pastor and a missionary. But they live in St. Louis. Rory and I can't be separated. Nothing made sense after Dad...but *that*, I knew." His fingertips, pressed into his knees. "Dad's best friend has really been there for us. He's a judge. He's helped me figure everything out. Insurance, bills, house payments, social security. After lecturing me non-stop, and realizing I wouldn't budge, he helped me become Rory's legal guardian."

Tap-tap-tap on the floorboards above our heads. Rory, still sitting at the table, an hour later, staring down his bowl of bean concrete.

Keegan's eyes shifted from the ceiling, to me. "The battle lines have been drawn, June. I'll admit. I make a lot of soup. And it's not five star. *Yet*. What Rory doesn't know is, we're still paying off Dad's hospital bills. Dad had...it was pancreatic cancer. And Dad didn't have health insurance. The bills are... let's just say, Mt. Everest would quiver in a face off." He shook his head. "The judge talked to dad's surgeon and he blessed us with a generous payment plan. But I work at a tuxedo shop. You know?" His eyes went back to the ceiling, and he rubbed his face. "Dad never let him get away with bean showdowns, or talking about Satanists at the dinner table." Keegan laughed, and side-eyed me. "Still feel lucky?"

***

I went to say goodbye to Rory and found him perched on the sill, kitchen window thrown open.

Just as I stepped in, he tilted his bowl over the side.

Bean soup streamed down, into the bushes below. I tried creeping back out, but the floorboard creaked beneath my foot. Rory swiveled, and seeing me, his brown eyes grew huge. Even his freckles looked guilty. "Sssh!" He pressed his finger to his mouth.

I made the zipped-lips gesture.

And I remembered. The weird, green, snake-like streak

down the side of the house. The one I'd noticed when we first drove in.

Moss, of the split pea variety.

I leaned back against the wall, giggling.

Then got strangely choked up.

Yeah. I thought. *Lucky.*

woodsy ramble

I woke up at five, and couldn't return to sleep. I wanted to be awake. I wanted to feel my thoughts.

I crept into the dark hallway, then padded to the window, looked out at the porch. Everything my eyes touched, our porch swing, Mom's potted plants, the herb garden, all of it felt new, infused with sweetness. I smiled to myself, looking out at the sky, still faintly star-specked. My eyes snagged on a shape, curled up on the welcome mat. "Grits," I whispered, with wonder. This was a first. As far as I knew, she'd never stayed with us overnight.

Slowly, quietly, I opened the front door. She jumped up, slinking off the porch, tail tucked between her legs. Tears rose up, hurt me. "It's okay, girl. It's okay. It's just me." I stepped onto the cold porch in my bare feet, crouched down. Her whole body changed. She darted up the steps, into my arms, knocked me right over. I kissed her head. I held her. Her fur was chilly. She was ribby. "I'm going to get you some food," I said, holding her face. "Okay? Okay?" Her tail shush-shushed back and forth against the concrete. I padded back inside.

I'd thought I was the only one up. But in the dining room, candlelight wavered across the walls, flickering across Mom's dream-catchers. Mom, hunched over something at the table, jerked her head up. "June! What are you doing up?"

"I'm sorry," I said, stepping back. "I couldn't sleep."

The night before, after I'd met up with Rain, we'd driven the rental car back home, both of us sick to our stomachs because maybe Mom had changed her mind, and on second thought, was angry with us. Maybe we'd have to pay after all. But Mom had greeted us, gathered us up, hugged us hard. Buried in the softness of her chest, I understood that nothing more would be said about the treachery of steak. Nonetheless, I said it again. "I'm sorry."

In the candlelight Mom's face changed, softened. She had her hair in two braids, hanging over either shoulder, no makeup, looking very young. "Come here," she said, patting the chair next to her. I went, sat down. "Why are you sorry? You don't have to be sorry. Why do you look so cowed, June? When you and Rain came home last night, you both looked at me like that. Like I was some mad dog, about to bite your heads off. Why would you think that?" She searched my face.

So many memories sprouting at once, it was a fountain of pain. I felt nearly crazy with it. Didn't she remember? How could she not remember? How could she not know why we were scared? The look on her face, so genuinely puzzled and wounded, made me feel suddenly ten times bigger than her, and mean, unjust. I said, gently as I could, "I think, after the accident, we were both jumpy." I dropped my gaze, and took in glue sticks, stickers, colored pencils and other craft supplies, spread out on the table. "What are you doing?"

"You caught me red-handed." She laughed, and opened her palms, which were marked up with red marker. "All summer, I've been getting up early to make this for you." She pushed a scrapbook toward me, pages spread open. "It's your graduation present." She smiled. "I just finished gluing that picture there, and drawing those leaves." The photograph, black and white, looked upward into a tall, mighty tree, branches sprawled against the sky. She'd begun sketching fall leaves, in red marker, outside the borders of the photo, so they looked like they were flying from the tree in a wind.

"You were working on this all summer..."

"Soon as I'd hear you get up, I'd hide all the stuff."

In the nightmare tapestry of this past summer, I had to somehow weave in this beautiful thread: my mother, rising early to make this graduation scrapbook for me. She pointed to the photo. "That was my favorite tree. The one I've told you about."

"This is your tree?"

She nodded. "Such a good, old tree. Such a friend." She gazed at the picture, wistful. "I'm putting everything in this book I can think of that you might like to take with you someday. I want to draw you a family tree, with photos and stories. I know how you like the stories."

The question was right there, so I took a chance. "Grandpa's story, too?"

Mom went quiet, took a sip from her coffee. Finally she said, "His mother, your great-grandma, died when he was little from tuberculosis. She wasn't even forty yet, and she wasted away inside a sanitarium. He adored her. His father was grief stricken and turned to gambling, lost it all. The house, the furniture, everything she'd ever touched and loved. The Old Man was only able to save his mother's favorite mirror. He hid it in the barn." She took another drink. "Her mirror hung in our house when I was a kid. He broke a lot of things. But never that mirror."

She called him the Old Man, even when talking about him as a child. It struck me first as funny, then as tragic. That's who her father had to be to her – *Old Man* – in order to protect herself. He hadn't always been a mean drunk, hunting her down with a belt in his hand. Once he'd been a little boy, grieving, with enough noble instinct to save his mother's mirror. But he wasn't able to save himself. Or his own kids.

"Look, June. You'll like this. Here's Ma at ten-years-old." Mom slid another photo toward me.

"This is Grandma?" I picked it up, hungry to see, and was confused by the little girl in a thin dress with stick legs and knobby knees, badly cut hair, standing on a rickety wood porch. "This is Grandma?" I said again, trying to make this girl, with her frown, her haunted eyes, match up with the flamboyant Grandma I knew, her blonde hair and red lipstick, the one who belly laughed and brought me magic pantyhose. *Her shoes!* Electricity zinged through me. Her shoes were beat up boy's shoes, far too big for her feet, and they yawned wide open in the front. Her toes were pushed out into the cold. "What's happening here?"

"The Great Depression, that's what," Mom said. "Her family lived on a farm in Wisconsin. They really suffered. That's why she dropped out of school after eighth grade. She had to go to work. She went to keep house for a well-to-do family, sent the money back home to her folks."

Those shoes, her toes – Grandma's melting look, the tears in her eyes, when she gave me the sequin shirt. *Wish I could have gotten you a whole dress of 'em.*

My heart broke.

One piece for the Old Man.

One piece for Grandma.

One piece for Mom.

Aunt Rena, too, in and out of rehab, an alcoholic herself.

The limbs of this family tree were soaked in sadness.

***

"I didn't even know this place existed."

At the Fayetteville Nature Center, I turned in circles, gazing up at the red and yellow canopy of leaves, holding light, like lanterns.

"I'm so happy I could be the one to introduce you." Keegan smiled beside me in his hiking vest and long-sleeved shirt, auburn curls lifting in the breeze. "You have a real backyard. This place is my adopted backyard."

We reached the top of the hill and paused together, peering down upon a mountain creek, the playful kind, rushing and tumbling. The whole forest floor was jeweled in autumn leaves. They kept falling as we walked, drifting around us, landing with the softest *tick* at our feet.

"Your backyard is enchanting. Thank you for sharing it with me." His hand was so near mine as we walked, my whole arm tingled with the desire to reach for it. "We moved here from Wisconsin almost three years ago, and I've only ever been to the mall and the library."

"Are your parents homebodies?"

"You could say that." I didn't really know what they were.

We picked our way downhill, on slippery rocks, until we met face-to-face with the rambunctious stream. The breeze kicked up, lifting my ponytail, and sending down a whole glimmering shower of leaves. I spread my arms out, and the leaves *tick-ticked* against my jacket. "Don't you sometimes feel rich?"

"Lately, all the time."

The way he looked at me.

I turned my eyes to the stream, and Keegan knelt, plucked up a small, flat stone. "Once you finish home-school, will you register at the university full-time? You're good at school. You love it." He tossed the stone into the white, burbling water.

“I’m skipping class with you right now.” Laughing, I knelt beside him, gathered cold, gritty pebbles in my palm. “Jehovah’s Witnesses don’t go to college. Well, some of them do. But it’s frowned on.”

“By God? Or your leaders?”

A sharp bright flash moved across my chest, like lightning. “Leaders?” I looked at him. His expression, so happy a moment before, was tight and sour. “You should see your face.”

“Sorry.” He looked down, poking at the dirt, moving leaves around with a stick.

“You and Rory. You talked about it. You both think I’m in a cult, don’t you?”

He hesitated. Then raised his head and said, “Yes.”

“Are you serious? You just look me in the eye and say *yes*?” A huffy little scoffing sound in the back of my throat.

“Do you want me to tell you the truth about things?”

He held my gaze. I recognized, past my hurt, there was something vital here, like a pulse. “Yes, I do want that.”

“Truth isn’t polite.”

I threw my fistful of pebbles in the water. A heron startled, flapping her wide, gray wings. We lifted our eyes, watched her soar over the trees. “Wow,” we breathed the word into the air at the same time. Then I said, “You only think I’m in a cult because of what you’ve heard from *your* leaders.”

“Touché.”

“You don’t even know what I believe. Shouldn’t you find out first, and draw your own conclusions?”

We both rose to our feet. I watched the struggle on his face, with satisfaction. “Probably,” he said. We started walking again. “I’ve heard a lot of disturbing things about your religion.”

“Well, here I am. A real live Jehovah’s Witness. Ask me

anything."

"You got it." Keegan drew in a breath. "Why don't kingdom halls have windows?"

A laugh burst from me. "What kind of question is that?"

"It's something I heard. The other day, I drove past two kingdom halls. It was true. Neither of them had windows. It's secretive. Like there's something to hide."

It bothered me that he had clearly sought out kingdom halls, driving past them on purpose, with the goal of confirming his negative views.

"It's not that we want to *hide* the human sacrifices exactly, it's more like, the rituals are sacred..."

"Sacrifices?" Keegan turned to me, aghast.

"You really believe it, don't you?" I shook my head. "I'm sorry to disappoint. There are no altars, no robes, no chants. No pet lions. Just a bunch of friendly, ordinary folks, studying the Bible together."

Keegan thought. "Is it true that Jehovah's Witnesses refuse blood transfusions?"

"Yes, that's true."

"Haven't many Witnesses, including children, died?"

"Yes, they have." I said this with pride.

"Those aren't sacrifices?"

I stared at him. "Oh, come on. You know as well as I do that's different. Christians since early times have given up their lives to uphold God's laws." I glanced at him. "This summer, I signed a No Blood form before an emergency appendectomy."

"Wow, you say that so easy." There was real pain in his voice. "You'd rather die than take blood?"

"Leviticus 17:14," I recited. "*You must not eat the blood of any sort of flesh, because the soul of every sort of flesh is its blood. Anyone eating it will be cut off.*"

Our footsteps hit the dirt path in unison, harder and harder. "So you're arguing that a blood transfusion is *eating* blood. But are those two processes really the same?"

"The process doesn't matter. Taking blood into your body is the sin, because blood is sacred."

"Why is blood more sacred than life?"

"Blood contains the soul."

"You believe the human soul actually resides in the blood?"

"No." I was a little flustered. "I actually don't believe in a soul as a separate entity. The Hebrew word for soul means *breathing creature*. A soul is the whole living, breathing person."

"Then how is blood, specifically, life?"

"Blood keeps you alive. Without blood, you die."

"Exactly!" He threw his hands in the air. "Give people blood so they don't die! Blood is a symbol. Like a wedding ring. A wedding ring isn't *love*. It's a symbol of love. When you make the symbol of blood more sacred than the act of being alive, how does that honor God?"

I didn't respond. My mouth was parched. A pulse beat, hard, like a little stone in my throat. We crossed a wooden bridge arching over a pond. We leaned together, gazing out over the water. Yellow leaves scattered across the surface, shimmering like fallen stars, swirling away. How could everything look so idyllic, yet feel so awful. I had invited the questions, confident in my ability to answer them all. Because I couldn't, my whole body felt unglued, like it was falling apart.

Keegan was quite close to me, and I wished, right now, he wouldn't be. I moved away.

"Are you upset with me, June?"

"No!"

Below, a stout clan of turtles sunned on a log. I swung my arm out, and they all ducked into their shells.

I wondered how many of them had any real hope of being intrepid.

I pressed my boot down on the shovel, leaned into the beautiful breakage of dirt.

I knelt, scooping up the rich, black soil, letting it stream silky through my fingers. Reaching in, and there! The lumpy gold of a potato.

I whisked the dirt away with a small brush. Held the potato out to Grits, who inspected with hearty sniffs. Grits-approved, I tossed the potato toward the bucket at the same time as Dad, digging at the opposite end. Our potatoes collided with a *thunk!* before landing in the bucket.

"Hash browns!" Dad slapped his knee.

I burst into laughter. Grits darted back and forth between us, nosing my boots, Dad's, then spinning in crazy circles. We laughed harder. Dad whipped his hanky from his back pocket, blew his nose with a great honking. "My goose call," he said. "See? Here they are!" He pointed up, at the V of geese flying overhead with perfect synchronicity. My belly hurt with laughing. We returned to digging.

When I looked up again, it was the feather in his straw hat, swaying, that caught my heart. Soon, he'd put his hat up for the winter. The thought of that speared me straight through. "Dad," I said. I squeezed the words out, past the lump in my throat. "I've missed you."

Dad dropped his shovel, sat down on the ground. His back against the garden bed, he patted the space beside him.

I went over and sank down. Grits, seeing our hands unoccupied, raced over to take advantage.

Dad stroked her fur. "Can you believe this dog? She thinks she's ours."

"Isn't she?"

"I think we're *hers*." He was so gentle with her. I loved him for that.

Something then, boiled up in me. I pulled at the grass. "Say, Dad. This summer, when I had surgery, what if I had needed blood? I mean to say, what if there had been an emergency?"

Dad looked at me. "You signed a No Blood form."

"I know it. I was just wondering." I drew my knees up, hugged them. "How you would react if the doctors had come to tell you, I would die without a blood transfusion?"

"I would firmly remind them that you signed a No Blood form." His hand went on, petting Grits, while she soaked it up.

"Would you struggle with that?" My voice was quiet. I was frightened to hear his response.

"If you mean would it be hard, to think of losing you, absolutely. But would I accept that? Absolutely, yes. I would insist to the doctors, no blood. Obedience to God's laws comes first. Losing someone is temporary. I would see you again in the New Earth. Jehovah's disfavor is permanent, however, and cannot be reversed."

He sounded like he was giving a talk at kingdom hall, behind the podium, in his suit and tie. Rather than truly considering my death, what it might be like, living with that loss. The way Keegan had to face all the days forward, without his dad. No wonder he had said to me, with a cry in his voice, *you say that so easy.*

It put a chill in me, experiencing that same feeling now, with Dad.

"Where is this coming from?" Dad studied me, uneasy.

"That college class?"

"No. It's just something I wondered." I stood, grabbed my shovel, and went back to digging, hoping to ward off the reminders and reproofs about the grave danger in asking questions.

***

"You've got to put your fingers, here, like this, and hold onto her here. And here. You got her, June?"

Rory had declared, it was my turn to give Intrepid flying lessons. I knew this was an honor he was granting, a trust given, as he checked to ensure my fingers were spaced correctly and clamped securely around Intrepid's shell, like a carnival worker testing the safety belts before the ride. Finally he straightened, freckles bright in his pink cheeks. He flashed a thumbs up. "Off you go!"

"Now?" My feet stayed glued to the ground.

"Yeah! Look at her. She's ready." Intrepid's scaly orange legs paddled, beating the air. "Go, June, go!" Rory pumped his fist, jogging backwards to the porch where Keegan sat. They sat side by side, clapping and whistling. We had a cheering section.

I took off. My hands found the rhythmic dipping and diving motion. *You're giving her the wings, but she's the one flying.* Rory's wisdom played in my head.

I ran, swooping her this way and that. Instead of hiding, she stuck her head out, far as she could, her long neck painted in the same vibrant sunset colors as her shell. She swam the air in sure, powerful strokes. I laughed out loud, loving a turtle that defied her instincts, the easy retreat.

Rory and Keegan burst into whoops and shouts, jumping to their feet, clapping, as we sailed past.

"Look, June!" Rory called. "She's smiling!"

He was right. Intrepid's pointy mouth had parted, a beaky grin as she flew.

***

I rested beside Keegan on his front porch steps, facing the dirty sidewalk and street. A car shot by, bass thumping, and behind us, the windows rattled. This was a far cry from the garden, and yet the city had its own weird beauty. I thought this, just as the giant cross flickered on at the Southern Baptist church across the street. "Whoa!" Startled, my leg swung out, right against Keegan's. Instant warmth, heat. I drew away.

Keegan threw his hand out. "Welcome to my version of a star-filled sky."

"It changes colors." The cross threw pink, yellow, and green flashes across the lawn.

"Tell me about it. Every night, I'm treated to a spectacular light show." He leaned back against the railing, facing me, his curls wind-swept and wild. "You should know," he said, "not everyone gets to fly Intrepid. Not even me. Rory trusts you, June."

I pressed my hand to my heart. "That means so much to me. Intrepid is my new hero." I steered my gaze back to the road. "I want to be just like her, when I grow up."

In the silence, a heaviness grew.

Keegan's voice, when it arrived, was soft. "What are you thinking, June?"

My eyes followed cars as they pulled into the church lot, one after another, for the late service. I bit my lip. "Can a turtle learn to drive?"

The beauty of this arrangement was, I could say I was at tutoring, and it wasn't a lie.

To compensate for what was sure to be a scarring experience, I'd brought Keegan a Tupperware container of Mom's soup. "For my tutor," I said. He didn't have to work until around the same time I was due to meet Rain, so this rendezvous worked out perfectly. We sat in his car, in the empty parking lot of a vacant grocery store, on the outskirts of Fayetteville. Outside, steely gray clouds piled up in a mountainous heap. In his car, with the heat running, it was warm and cozy.

"It's from my mom," I said, as he peeled back the lid.

"Your mom made this for me?"

I hadn't meant to imply that. But now his face was saturated with such open joy, how could I tell him, my mom didn't even know I still saw him, and furthermore, I planned to keep him a well-guarded secret for the duration of our friendship, even if that was our whole lives?

He took a spoonful.

"What's the verdict?"

He groaned, melting into the seat. "Your mother puts me to shame. She is the Soup Master." He sat back up, intently examined a spoonful. "Perfect chunks of potato luxuriating in a rich, creamy broth, with tender celery and..." he lifted a brow, scrutinized the spoon like a scholar. "Is that thyme and a dash of...rosemary?"

"You got it." I beamed. "Mom grows all her own herbs. Have you ever tried a lavender sugar cookie with lemon-basil icing?"

"Come on. She's making me that next, right?"

"She's so inventive! She could open a bakery. We always tell her that."

"I need to meet your mom. I need to take classes from your mom." He took another rapturous spoonful while my eyes drifted around his car, fixing on the small ornate cross hanging from his rearview mirror. "That's a Celtic cross, isn't it? Like your tattoo."

"My dad got that in Ireland, shortly before dancing barefoot on the Cliffs of Moher." He winked at me, unhooked the cross from the mirror, held it out. "It's real jade."

I held up my hand. "No, thank you." A prim note entered my voice, as if this were an after school special on drugs.

"What? You don't like crosses?" He was offended. Though he tried to hide it, I could hear it in his voice as he replaced the cross on the mirror. "Is that because you don't believe in Jesus?"

"I do believe in Jesus. I just don't believe that Jesus and God are the same person."

"So what's the issue?"

"For me, handling a cross would be 'touching the unclean thing'."

He barked a laugh. "For real?"

"Yes." I sat for a minute, and thought about it. "Here's something I genuinely don't understand. You say you love Jesus. Why would you prize the weapon that murdered him?"

Keegan's eyes went wide. "The cross is used in worship, to honor Jesus' sacrifice."

"The Bible is clear, don't use idols in worship."

"I don't bow down to it, June..."

"So you'd honor your dad by wearing an image of what

killed him?"

Keegan shook his head. "His cancer. Is that what you're saying? You're comparing the holy cross to my dad's cancer? That's a horrific analogy. The cancer was this – random terrible thing, not a beautiful, noble sacrifice he made on our behalf."

He was very visibly rattled, nostrils flaring. He couldn't even look at me. I experienced a sharp moment of panic, and following that, an almost irresistible urge to apologize and shut up. This was the crossroads, I realized, where what you did determined whether the other person stayed, or left you. I imagined continuing to speak, and Keegan saying, "You know, this really isn't going to work out, not even as friends," and then returning to my old lonely life. I imagined swallowing my voice, the easier choice. I was used to doing it. He and I would remain friends, but what would be lost in that scenario? Something, or rather *someone* I would have to send away, time and time again. It would be better to lose our friendship immediately, than persist in that slow, excruciating erosion of self.

Having made my choice, I turned to face him, and asked him the same question he had asked me: "Do you want me to tell you the truth about things?"

He looked at me sharp.

"The other day," I continued, "you questioned my beliefs about blood, and it was very hard to hear – "

"This is different – "

"Let me finish."

Keegan went silent, and I surprised myself with the strength I could summon. This was a different June. Someone I wasn't, with anyone else. "If we're going to do this, it's going to feel awful sometimes. We're not going to have a normal kind of friendship. We can't. This is why people with different beliefs stay away from each other, isn't it? To avoid this kind of pain. But maybe if we stick with it, there's something here for us, in the pain. I think there is. I don't know what, but I still think it. Do you?"

Keegan sat quietly and I didn't look at him, let him privately reckon with that, and reach his own conclusion. "Yes," he said, finally, and drew a breath. "Okay. Lay it on me. What else you got?"

I charged in. "Let's say instead that your dad saved your life from a gunman. He stepped in front of you and Rory, and was shot. He sacrificed himself to save you. Would you wear the image of a gun on your body? Decorate your home with images of a gun to pay him tribute?"

Keegan thought, then said, "It wouldn't even occur to me to do that. It would seem sick. I couldn't do it."

"Now you understand how the cross feels to me. I love Jesus, too, and his death wasn't romantic. It was brutal. Have you ever read what it's like, being killed like that? The victim dies, inch by inch, sometimes over the course of days, first exhaustion, then asphyxiation..."

"Okay, okay." Keegan held up his palm. "Point taken." He turned, looked out the window. "You know, this is a really strange conversation. In my church, it's more important to feel than to think, if that makes sense. I have never in my life thought this deeply about the cross."

I couldn't resist adding, "The Greek word *stauros* refers to an upright post – not a cross. The two-beamed cross image was a religious symbol, used centuries before Christ, to worship false gods and engage in pagan sex rites. It was probably assimilated by the church, like a lot of pagan symbols and rituals."

Keegan side-eyed me. "I can see you have some heavy

conversations at your church."

"Kingdom hall."

He threw his head back on the seat with frustration, but also kind of laughing.

I felt the tension break.

"At least after this," I said, "a driving lesson should be easy."

***

I screamed.

Keegan's car shot ahead, my foot mistakenly pushing the accelerator.

I smashed the brake and we lurched forward. Keegan grabbed the dash.

"Sorry, sorry," I said, clutching the steering wheel, hyperventilating. The Intrepid June was gone, replaced by the June who desperately wanted to put her shell back on. Keegan put the car back in park. "I'm not good at this," I said. "And also I hate this."

"June, you've been driving for approximately," Keegan checked the clock, "three minutes."

I unbuckled and threw off my seatbelt. "Let's stop. Let's switch back."

Keegan set his hand on my knee, which I stared at. Clearing his throat, he pulled his hand away. "Haven't you ever been bad at something to begin with, then ended up rocking it?"

A memory surfaced, a girl I once knew. I saw her, vivid and bright. Decked out in a blue Polo shirt, black trouser pants, a pair of sturdy black nonslip restaurant shoes, blue mustard stained visor like a crown on her head. In my mind, I watched that girl *tap-tap* the register and smack down trays. In my mind, I admired her. A *real McDonald's girl.* "I guess," I said, tracing the cracked vinyl on the steering wheel. "But that was a long time ago."

Keegan said, "Put your seatbelt on. Let's start again."

I drove around and around the parking lot. Braking, accelerating, backing, signaling. I held my breath the entire time. But I didn't smash a single thing. After an hour or so, Keegan said, "I think we can venture out into the big wide world now."

I turned to him. "What? I just started!"

He adjusted his seat-belt. "You're very conscientious. You can do it."

I stared out the windshield. "I'm not sure about that."

"No highways or interstates. I promise. Just a sleepy rural road. The most dangerous thing might be a tractor zipping along at two miles per hour." He paused. "It's your call. But I believe in you."

I gripped the steering wheel with clammy hands, exhaled. "Okay."

"Just go slow. Take your time. I'm right here with you."

"Okay Okay Okay." I eased the car out of the parking lot, onto the road.

"Good job. We're going to turn right. See that sign? Go ahead and hit the signal."

I did. "Okay!"

The road was two-lane, surrounded by farmland, empty for miles.

I clenched the steering wheel, my shoulders drawn up around my ears.

"So," Keegan said. "Let's have a chat about that granny posture."

***

I was late to meet Rain. A whole half hour.

She would definitely be upset, and ask questions.

I pushed through the doors of Arkansas Union, fingers-crossed-hoping.

I crashed to a halt. Everything in me crashed to a halt.

Because there was Rain, standing under the stairwell.

With a man.

I stared and stared as the two of them talked, laughed, smiled at one another. He wasn't young. He had gray streaks in his black wavy hair and beard. He had to be fifty, at least. He carried a large black case, which I recognized, from watching students go in and out of the School of Art, as an art portfolio.

Rain didn't take art.

They fell into a hug, then broke apart. She waved, and he waved. He walked backward, watching her with a lingering smile as she turned. I scrambled around the corner, to the long, orange couch sitting against the wall where we always met. I pulled *Christy* from my bag, drew my knees to my chest. When she found me, there I was, like I'd been there all along. Fake-reading with a passion.

"Where were you, June?" She strode up to me. "I waited. I got *scared*. I went looking for you!"

I lowered my book. "Did you?"

She swallowed, backed up. "Just – whatever – don't let it happen again."

She hoisted her bag over her shoulder, turned, and walked away, fast.

I followed behind, jogging a little to keep up.

Rain. Rain.

It wasn't just me.

My sister had secrets, too.

loyalty picnic

With a loud scraping, I retrieved the bubbling, cheesy pan of burritos from the oven and set it on the stovetop, then scurried to the window, standing on tip toe looking out, down the road. No sign yet.

I gathered plates, and small bowls for the salsa.

Mom wasn't there. Dad had secured a vendor's table at some kind of state-wide health convention in Little Rock. He'd persuaded Mom to travel there with him and sell her herbs and home-made essential oils at the vendor's table. She'd been in high spirits all week, preparing little jars of dried marjoram, oregano, and dill, vials of lavender tied with ribbon. They were staying overnight.

The doorbell rang. Holding the tray, I stepped down the hallway, then, setting the tray on the mantel, I smoothed my hair, my shirt, my jeans. With a breath, I swung open the door.

Keegan knelt on the porch, laughing as Grits lavished him in kisses. He looked up at me, eyes full of light. "You didn't tell me you had a dog."

"Keegan, meet Grits. Grits, Keegan." My hand on my heart.

"Hi, Grits. Hi, girl. You're beautiful. You're the most beautiful, golden girl." Keegan scratched her face and behind her ears, then stood, moving toward me for a hug. As soon as he stepped over the threshold, into our house, I grabbed the tray from the mantel and shoved it into his midriff. "Oof!" Using the tray, I pushed him backward, onto the porch. Grits jumped on him, wagging her tail like a maniac.

"Fun surprise. We're having a picnic." I grabbed the door

handle and slammed the door shut behind us. "An autumn picnic."

"Okay?" He looked around, pulling his pea coat around him. "You don't think – it's a bit cold?"

"I'll get a blanket and make some cocoa." I turned back to the door.

Keegan followed. "I can help."

"No!" I pressed my hand to his chest, shoved him back. "Stay here."

Keegan held up his hands. "No problem. What do you want me to do?"

"Sit. Sit down." I gestured to our rustic porch swing, which I'd already neatly arranged with fluffy pillows. I dashed inside, where I stood in the entryway, back pressed to the door, heart pounding. I was doing it again. The weird anxiety-fueled behavior. It was bad enough I had invited him over at all. He could *not* come in. He could *not* be in her house. I'd even lowered all the blinds so he couldn't peek inside.

In the kitchen, I whipped up two mugs of hot cocoa, then snagged a blanket off the living room couch.

Outside, Keegan had settled onto the porch swing. He petted Grit's head, stroked her long nose. She locked eyes with him, totally adoring. "Rory's been begging for a dog," he said. "I keep telling him, not yet. We're not ready. But this girl. This girl could change my mind."

"She's taken."

"I suppose so." He laughed.

I served up the burritos, guacamole, and chips. I sat down beside him. We spread the blanket over our knees. I picked up my fork.

Keegan cleared his throat. "So, I don't know how it works

for you, but I usually pray before eating, so, yeah, I'm going to do that now. Pray."

"Of course! Same here. Me, too." Abashed, I dropped my fork, folded my hands. "But, um, you pray to Jesus and – I don't." We traded awkward glances. "Independent prayer," I said. "Like independent reading in school?" I angled away, bowed my head. He did the same.

Instead of praying silently, he whispered his prayer, and I found myself not able to focus on my own, eavesdropping on his instead.

"Dear Jesus," he said, "I thank you so much, Lord, for every good thing, for this food, and most of all, this friend..."

Against my will, my whole being warmed.

"I love you so much, Lord."

I shifted, uncomfortable. That's not how you talked to God. It wasn't respectful. Jehovah God was a force to be reckoned with. From the time I was little, I had pictured Jehovah in a suit and tie, with a big moustache, sitting behind a massive desk, CEO of the world. When you entered Jehovah's office, you stood before His desk and trembled. I was so absorbed in my critical analysis of Keegan's prayer, that I never got to my own.

He said, "Amen," and picked up his fork.

I picked up mine.

The hot, bubbly burritos were already cold. The cheese, rubbery. I set my fork down. Keegan shivered, pulled the blanket up a little more. I glanced at him. "Okay, fine. You're right. It's too cold out."

"Well," he said, "I have a solution."

"What?"

"We could go inside."

"We can't. No one's home."

"Oh." He looked puzzled, then, eyes widening, seemed to reach some understanding. "When we're inside, Grits could be our chaperone." He winked.

My face warmed. He thought I was scared to be alone with him, about what might happen between us. If only it could be normal like that. "I can't. It's kind of hard to explain." I latched and unlatched my fingers. "My mom's very nervous about – the way her house looks. She thinks it's a mess. She would be very upset if I let you see it."

"Why? It looked perfect in there."

"You *looked?*"

"When you opened the door, I caught a glimpse."

I winced. "My mom's out of town and I'm still concerned about her feelings." This part was true.

His face changed. "That's pretty amazing."

"It is?"

"I think it is. Your mom would never know if you let me in. You take *honor thy mother* to a new level. Even when she's not here, you honor her feelings. That's real loyalty."

I was grateful to him. I stood, and without thinking, held out my hand. "You want to walk?"

He looked at my hand and then at me. "No. I mean, yes. I mean, I would love to hold your hand and walk, you have no idea, but..."

I let my hand drop.

He stood with the blanket, tucked it around my shoulders, and then followed me.

***

She was at her most showy in October.

"Here she is," I said, swinging my arm out from beneath the blanket. "The legend."

"Holy Cottonwood." I watched Keegan's face as he looked up and up. He set a hand on her trunk, with reverence. "I can feel her heartbeat."

"Yes! You can, too? I call her clapping tree." Her leaves, a rolling, shimmering yellow sea, above our heads, clattered gently. "She's where I go to read, to think. To pray. To dream."

Keegan looked at me. "What do you dream?"

"You." I said it without thinking.

"Me?"

I choked up. "I thought I was alone. And then one day, you stole my seat."

"I stole your seat?"

"Seat #25. That's where I was going to sit. Out of all two hundred seats, there you were. For the longest time, I had this name for you," I laughed, then stopped, seeing his face. "What's the matter?"

He kept shoving his hands through his hair, and shaking his head. "June. You have no idea. That is so wild. That is the wildest thing."

"Why?"

"Before school started, I checked out all my classrooms. I picked out my seats, always in the front row. I thought sitting in the front row would help me pay attention and get good grades. But the first day of class, when I walked into the lecture hall, I changed my mind. It was bizarre. As I walked to the front, I stopped. I don't know why. Something made me stop."

I stared at him. "Was it a voice?"

"A voice?" He considered. "It was more like a feeling. The

kind of feeling I've always thought of as God. I turned around. And I went where it felt right." He met my eyes. "Seat #25."

I stepped closer to him. I reached up, cupped his warm cheek in my palm. "Seat Thief." I said it, soft. And he leaned in, slow.

Clapping tree clapped.

And it started to rain.

We raced up the yard. Grits bounded alongside us like a cold, hard rain was the most delightful thing. We jumped onto the porch. Keegan peered out through the slanting downpour, his face falling. "Hey, June, are those your mom's plants?"

Mom's prized Monstera, tree philodendron, and snake plant stood in giant pots in the yard. She'd asked Dad to bring them in before they left. He must have forgotten.

Keegan said, "If it freezes tonight, they'll die."

My mind went haywire. If I didn't do anything, she might blame me. But if they were in the house, she'd wonder how I managed it. She'd get suspicious. I was stuck. There was no safe direction.

"Come on." Keegan leapt from the porch. "Let's get them inside."

I gave in. The rain pelted my face. With a heave, he picked up one side of a pot, and, grunting, I picked up the other. We tottered like an unwieldy creature, rain and leaves in our face, across the yard, up the steps. Opening the door, I said, "Close your eyes."

From behind the plant, "Are you serious?"

"I told you. She doesn't want you to see her house."

"You are really committed." Keegan hefted the pot, squeezed his eyes shut.

We delivered each plant to its place. Once, I saw his eyes

flutter. "Don't look!"

"I'm not looking!" He huffed and puffed, lowering the tree philodendron. He crouched, set his hands on his knees, rain dripping down his face, eyes screwed closed. "What is it again your mom doesn't want me to see?"

"Her mess."

"June. You're scaring me. Is your mom in the Mafia?"

I headed to the bathroom to grab us towels.

Schriiick.

I froze at the sound of the key turning in the back door lock.

Please let it be Rain.

"Hellooo! I'm baaack!"

I stood ramrod straight. My body spit, hissed, and crackled.

The laundry-room door opened a crack. Mom peered in. I could hear her taking off her shoes. She saw me, not Keegan, who was still crouched down. "Oh, there you are. Dad's van broke down. I don't care how much he begged, I wasn't about to sit all day in some dirty shop, waiting on repairs. I got a cab and boy, let me tell you, that was some kind of..." She stepped in, peeling strands of wet hair from her face.

Keegan rose. His eyes were still closed. "Hi...June's mom."

With his eyes closed, he couldn't see.

The way she looked at me.

The way her eyes burned me to the ground.

The way she lifted her finger, pointed it at me, jabbing, her lips fierce and white.

I peed a little.

"Mrs. Taylor." Keegan cleared his throat, eyes still closed. "I apologize. June told me I wasn't allowed inside. I insisted. I thought your plants might die, so I launched a rescue mission.

As you can see though," Keegan pointed to his face, "I haven't opened my eyes once. June made me promise to keep my eyes closed."

Mom shifted her gaze to him. She looked him up and down, her face twitching.

"By the way," he said, offering a wave. "I'm Keegan. The one you made the potato soup for? I loved it. It was the best soup I've ever had. And I'm no soup novice."

Mom's eyes darted to me, narrowed.

I stayed very straight, very still, expressionless, like a soldier.

Keegan laughed. "My brother dumps *my* soup out the window."

I turned to him. "You know about that?"

He threw his hands in the air. "Of course I know. I don't always walk around with my eyes closed. I see the split peas down the side of the house!"

Mom laughed. She actually laughed. "You can open your eyes, Keegan."

He opened his eyes. They looked at each other.

And at the same time, they smiled.

cooking lesson

My phone was transparent plastic. When it rang, the colorful wires lit up, flashing like a neon lightning storm. For the first time since we'd moved to Arkansas, my phone was ringing for *me*. I grabbed it. "Hello?"

"Well?"

I fell back on my pillows. "She thinks you're wonderful." *He's a doll!* Her exact words.

"And I didn't even have to bring out the Irish accent."

"That might have worked against you. Do you...like her?" I picked at my lips.

"So much! Your mom's so cool. A bit of a control freak but still, she's amazing. Those citrus basil shortbread cookies she gave me? They're my dinner tonight." He crunched, and in the background, a steady whir started. It stopped. Then started again.

"What's that sound?"

"The music of my sewing machine." He sounded so proud. "I'm at Luca's, sitting on a stool in the back room, tailoring a bunch of crazy purple tuxes for a wedding. I'm talking with you, I've met your golden dog, your holy clapping tree, and your mom. Life is good." More whirring.

"Mom wants you to come to dinner tomorrow night, if you can. She wants to give you a cooking lesson." A single warm tear ran down the side of my face, into my pillow. I knew all about dreams turning into nightmares. But the opposite? This was a first.

"I'll be there," he said.

***

The next night, soon as I spied Keegan's car, I flew outside to meet him.

Grits ran with me, barking her most rapturous of all barks. She sounded like a child. The moment Keegan climbed out, she launched herself at him. He stooped, hugging her close. In one hand, he held a bouquet of roses, the same yellow as Grits. I had to stop, just look, just take it in, the beauty.

Keegan straightened, and brought me the roses. I dipped my face into the petals, breathing in the rich gold, rosy aroma. "Thank you! They are gorgeous. What does yellow mean?" I bit my lip.

"Friendship." He smiled into my eyes.

My spirit eased. That was good. That was exactly right. We walked together down the sidewalk, Grits bouncing between us, licking our hands. I stopped, hit by a sudden thought. "Would you mind giving these roses to Mom?"

Keegan held up a grocery bag. "Have no fear. I brought a hostess gift, just for her."

"That's so good!" He was a natural, doing everything right. "Would you also give her these?" I held out the roses. No one but Grandma had ever given me roses. I didn't want to part with them, but securing Mom and Keegan's relationship was more important. "Yellow is one of her favorite colors."

"June, I picked them out just for you..."

"Please, Keegan?"

He hesitated, then took them back. "Okay, sure. That's really sweet of you." We started walking again. As we reached the porch, I broke into a sick sweat. I placed my hand on his sleeve. "Could you make sure to tell her how nice everything looks? She's freaked out about the house. She thinks it's a mess."

His eyebrows shot up. "How? It's immaculate."

"I know. But she always thinks it's a mess. Just tell her. And take your shoes off."

From next door, the sharp slap of a door. "SADIE ANN! Get your dumb dog ass over here! NOW!"

Grits tore off, galloping next door.

Keegan turned to me, his face stunned. "Sadie Ann? I thought...?"

Mr. Bad Flannel stared us down, snake-eyed, as he took Grits by the collar, dragging her into the garage.

"Hey!" Keegan yelled. "Don't you touch her like that!"

He started to walk over there, eyes on fire, and I grabbed his arm. "Keegan, don't. It's a whole story but – she's *his* dog."

Mr. Bad Flannel shoved Grits into the garage, brought the door slamming down. Her barks from within were high-pitched and plaintive.

"I hate this," Keegan said.

"I know," I said, holding onto his arm. "I know."

***

Mom sliced into the fresh loaf of bread. Keegan's hostess gift. She leaned in close, breathed, fluttered her hand over her heart. "Heaven! Fennel is my favorite."

"Hmm. How did I know that?" Keegan tossed me a wink.

Mom threw him an apron. "Hope you don't mind gingham and lace pockets."

"I prefer it." He tied it on. Behind him, in a vase on the windowsill, Mom's yellow roses soaked up all the light.

"Tonight, young man, you're making acorn squash roasted with maple, parmesan, onion, and a pinch of fresh thyme."

Keegan's face lit like the skies had parted. He held up his hand and Mom stood on tip toe to give him a resounding high five.

Rain and I exchanged looks. Was this our dining room, or dinner theater in an alternate reality? I hated to think it, but I was relieved things had worked out so that Dad was out of town. *Everything* depended on Mom. If Mom liked Keegan, it didn't matter how much Dad didn't, the battle was won.

In the kitchen, Mom instructed Keegan how to cut the squash. "We want to keep all our fingers so we're using our sharpest chef's knife, and making our first cut on one side of the stem, straight down...yep, that's it. Put your muscle into it, Keegan!" Mom swiveled. "Juney, would you grab a couple onions from the garage?"

Rain and I caught eyes. We slid our chairs back in unison.

In the cool secrecy of the garage, we sat cross-legged on the concrete, conferring over the basket of onions. "What is happening right now?" Rain whispered. "How did he get past the fortress? What spell did you conjure?"

"I'm not sure. Mom caught us in the house together..."

Rain fell across the basket. "*You brought him into her house?*" She sat back. "And now he's in her kitchen." She shook her head. "This is unprecedented."

"I know."

"What'd he do? Turn on the charm? Load her up with compliments?"

"He saved her plants."

"Ah, I see. He's the foliage hero." Smiling, she sorted through the onions. "Does he treat you like he looks at you?"

"Remember George Knightley?"

"From *Emma*. How could I forget? Your book crush, beating out Johnny Cade, a close second, and Gilbert Blythe, coming in third."

My heart ached. My sister was the only one in the world who knew my hierarchy of book crushes. I said to her, "Keegan reminds me of Mr. Knightley. It's the way I can talk with him. From the very first day. He's so honest. He speaks his mind. I never thought I could be friends with someone who believes so differently. But I like it. I like the way he challenges me. And... it's safe to challenge him. I can tell him what I really think. We can argue, and things don't blow up into a million pieces. At least, not yet." I smiled.

"So you talk." She looked up, studied me, her eyes glistening. "Have you kissed him?"

"What? No. No, Rain." My face grew hot, and I ducked my head, searching through onions. "He's only my friend. My – very good friend." I was grateful for the concealing dark.

"A very good friend whose bones you want to jump."

"Rain!"

She wiggled her brows. And then, "I'm sorry I almost killed us the other day."

"I know you didn't mean it." We kind of laughed. Rain's car was fixed, and here we were, making our own repairs.

"I was stressed," she said. "I'm better now. I'm acing statistics. I didn't know how smart I was. I thought it was wrong to be smart. You know, almost a sin. Now I think, maybe I really can cobble some kind of life together, outside of the fortress." Her eyes roved around, returned to me. "If I tell you a secret, will you promise not to tell?"

"Promise." I thought about that old guy I saw her hugging. I didn't know if I wanted to know. She leaned in to whisper, and I felt queasy. "I have magazines under my bed."

"What?"

She bit her lip. "*Seventeen. Vogue. Cosmopolitan.* I've been reading them, and I think you should, too."

This was unexpected. "Why?"

She plucked up an onion, weighed it in her hand. "What do you know about your body?"

"I mean..." I scratched my neck.

"Do you know what happens during sex?" She held up two onions, knocked them together.

"I think so."

"Liar." Then, earnest, "We should know, June. No one's ever talked to us. We've learned everything from the Watchtower, and they censor what's real. They don't tell us the truth. We should know about bodies, what they do, and not feel bad, or dirty." She raised an eyebrow. "Do you still think men's things look like hotdogs?"

"No!" *They didn't?* I decided to put *her* on the spot. "What about you? Have you kissed someone? Someone besides Calculus?"

She giggled, held the two onions to her cheeks, and giggled.

The hairs on the back of my neck rose. *She had!*

From the kitchen, laughter, the oven door slamming. "We should get back," I said.

Rain put her hand on my arm. "I'm glad you like a Knightley, and not a Heathcliff."

"Heathcliff! I don't get it. How can anyone like a Heathcliff?"

"Maybe they don't know," she said, and her face grew sad. "Maybe they've never had to live with a Heathcliff."

We avoided each other's eyes, rising with our onions.

A week later, after class, I was driving down a country back-road, smooth as could be.

Like this was normal life.

Like it had never been any other way.

The tall, curly-haired boy by my side rolled his window down, letting in a strangely warm and glowing early November. He stuck his elbow out, singing along to Bob Marley. The magic was in how he drummed his knee, lifted his dimpled chin to sing. How he looked over at me, said,"You're getting so good at this. I could take a nap." How he tilted his head back, let out a loud snore.

How I yelled, "Don't you dare!"

How he sat up, drummed the dash. "Let's go to town."

How I said, "What?"

How he said, with perfect ease, "You can do it, Intrepid. Turn here."

***

First, we went to the library.

The stoplights and traffic and roadwork, sensory overload.

My heart beat too fast, my eyes blurred. Palms so sweaty, sliding on the steering wheel. *Breathe.* Keegan, steady, talked me through each step. And when we arrived – it was even more thrilling to pick out a book because...*I'd driven to the library.*

Next, I drove to the grocery store. This time, back straighter, breaths fuller. Not quite so grim and sweaty.

In the parking lot, engine off, Keegan turned to me. "June, that was beautiful. Well done. Now can we look at our exams?"

I'd been putting it off. I was scared to look. Keegan thought I was being a nut. "Do you really think you bombed? Have you no faith in the power of flashcards?"

I grimaced as he shoved the folded up exam in my hand. "You go first," I said. "Please."

He unfolded the paper, and his fist shot in the air. "Yes!"

"What? What'd you get?" I leaned in, and he showed me the 88 in red. "This is the highest grade I've gotten on a college exam so far," he said. "See what I mean? You and your flashcards." He put his hand on my knee, warm. "Thank you." I looked at him. "It's a huge deal for me, with everything I've got going on. Thank you very much for helping me focus, and study."

"You're welcome. Thank you very much for helping me drive."

"My pleasure." He took his hand from my knee. "Now quit procrastinating. Get to it. Go on..." nodding at my exam.

I unfolded it slowly. This was it. My very first college exam. I covered my hand with my mouth, stomped my feet on the floor of the car. I held it up.

"A 98! You're a rockstar!" Keegan high-fived me. Then again. We high fived until my palm was red and stinging.

Dr. Freeman had written something, too, in red ink, by my essay. "*This is one of the most insightful and heartfelt essays I've read while teaching this class. Excellent work!*" I read that part aloud. And kept this part silent. *I'd suggest researching Adult Children of Alcoholics, and look into a program called Alateen, for you and your sister.*

Keegan said, "That's amazing, June. That's so great. What

did you write about?"

He craned his head to look, and I quickly folded the exam, stuck it in my coat pocket. "The Old Man," I said.

He looked confused.

"My mom's dad. My...grandpa." And then an overwhelming flood of feeling, rising up from the depths. "I don't know him." My chin wobbled. "But I do. I think in a way, I do." I wiped tears with the back of my hand. "It's my mother. It's...so hard to explain."

"C'mere." With a tender look, Keegan opened his arms.

I unbuckled my seatbelt, and fell into him, resting my cheek against his scratchy pea coat. He smelled woodsy and sweet, all at once. I bit back what had been right there, on the verge of breaking loose.

"I'm proud of you," he whispered into my hair. "I'm so proud of my friend."

***

Hefting groceries into Keegan's house, he stopped short. "What's that smell?" He sniffed the air.

I caught a delicious pepperoni whiff. "Pizza?"

From upstairs, roaring motorcycle sounds.

Keegan's jaw set. "Rory!"

I followed him as he marched up the steps, shoving the door open into Rory's bedroom. Rory leaned into the computer, so engrossed in his game he didn't hear us. His hair stuck up in the back, and he already had pajamas on. Clearly, he'd settled in for the night. Beside him, an open pizza box emitted the saucy cheesy pepperoni good-smelling-ness. He reached for a slice with one hand, clicking the mouse with the other.

Keegan let the groceries fall to the floor.

Rory jumped. "Aw, crap!" He spun in his chair. "You made me crash!" On the screen, a motorcycle slid on its side, veering this way and that down a highway, flames shooting up.

"Are you kidding me right now?" Keegan pushed his hands through his hair. "*You* are supposed to be at Young Warriors."

Rory shrugged. "It was canceled. Pastor Pitts had a family emergency."

"When did you know? Why didn't you call me at work? You know you're not supposed to be home alone. This is a rough neighborhood. How did you even get in?"

"Uhhh, my key?" Rory made big eyes. "Remember? Dad made me a key. Even though I never had to use it. Dad never locked the doors. Not even in a *rough neighborhood*. Dad had a force field around our house."

"Would you stop saying *force field*? You don't even know how insane you sound."

"Whatever!" Rory kicked his foot out. "Whatever it was, Dad had it, and you don't."

Keegan strode over, smacked the lid down on the pizza box.

"Hey!" Rory cried, grabbing the edge of the box. "That's mine!"

"No." Keegan pushed Rory's hand away. "You didn't get permission."

"I don't need permission. I have my own money."

Keegan's face flamed. "You know what? No more allowance. I got a call from your teacher today. You're falling behind, Rory. Your grades suck. You should be doing homework."

Rory's eyes shot to me, stricken. "I did it already. I'm doing good. Back off!"

"Never." Keegan picked up the pizza box, carrying it into

the kitchen. "I'm making us dinner."

"I don't want your crap food." Rory pushed away from the desk. "I'd rather starve." He ran from the room. The door slammed so hard the walls shuddered.

***

I sat at the kitchen table filling in Punnett squares for biology, a task I found nearly as heartbreaking as measuring triangles. Keegan cooked, silent. I'd asked if he'd rather I go home. But he said no. He wanted me to stay.

"The force field." Keegan's voice startled me. I looked up, at his back, as he ground pepper over sausage sizzling in the pan. "You're probably wondering what that's all about."

"It did sound a little *Star Trek*."

Keegan laughed, shaking the pan. "Dad believed that prayer created a kind of spiritual fortress around our house. He never locked the doors. He said leaving them unlocked was an act of faith." He removed the lid from the pot of pasta. Steam escaped. He salted it the way mom had shown him. "It was an act of faith not to take aspirin. Or go to the doctor. We didn't know about the cancer until Dad's face turned yellow, he was in screaming pain, and ninety percent of his pancreas was tumor." Keegan turned. Avoiding my eyes, he leaned back against the stove, wiping his hands on his apron. "The surgeon called us into his office, gave Dad six months. Dad called us into his hospital room right after, told us not to listen to the surgeon. He said he'd had a word from the Lord. He said, Jesus would heal him. We believed him, Rory and me. I mean, in all the years we lived here, no matter how many break-ins or drug busts went down around us, *we* were always safe, so..." He shrugged.

Down the hall, the bathroom door opened, slammed. Keegan met my eyes. "The point being. I'm not Dad. It's true. I don't know what I'm doing."

"You're doing great, Keegan."

He closed his eyes. "Would you mind getting Rory? I don't think he wants to see my face."

***

Sullen, sitting beside me at the kitchen table, Rory pointed to my textbook. "What's that?"

"Biology."

"Boooring." He fake-yawned.

"Boring? Really? I thought you'd like biology."

"I told you. I don't like books."

"Keegan said he's been reading you *The Lion, The Witch, and the Wardrobe*."

"That book sucks." With his most fiery glare, Rory burned holes in Keegan's back. Keegan went on, grating cheese into the pasta. "Some prissy British kids tromping through a closet, talking to some creepy faun. Who talks to fauns? I don't even know what a faun is!"

Keegan stopped grating, rolled his head back. "We've been over this. A faun is a man with goat's horns, ears, legs, and tail."

"Lame," Rory muttered.

"I got this for you." I set the library book on the table. "For my first ever driving expedition, I drove to the library, and I picked this book out, just for you."

"For me?" He gazed at me wide-eyed. And then his eyes narrowed. "What is it?" He sat up, read the title. "*The Philosophy of Turtles*."

"It's written by a naturalist named Dr. Schroeder. Look." I turned to the back, pointed to the author photo. A young woman with a ponytail, freckled face like Rory, holding up a turtle. "Studying turtles is her life's work. Did you know you could make studying turtles your life's work? I didn't either, until I found this book. Then I thought of you because you're already doing that. You're developing this fresh, innovative way of thinking about turtles and..." I kept rambling, my eyes following his hand as he reached, reached, reached and...touchdown!

The book was in his hands.

***

"You're lying! This is not yours." Rory eyed the decadent home-made macaroni and cheese with fennel sausage that Keegan spooned, with deliberate grace, into Rory's bowl. Rory leaned in, sniffed. "This is an imposter."

"June's mom taught me. She's a five-star cook."

Rory swiveled to me. "Please verify."

"It's the truth." Keegan's back turned, Rory snuck a bite. His eyes opened wide. He pantomimed dying from shock. I laughed. Things were smoothing out a little.

And then, the gut-wrenching prayer to the false god.

While they prayed, I kept my hands laced in my lap, staring at an oil painting of Jesus on the kitchen wall. Even our faith's depictions of Jesus were nothing alike. The Watchtower's illustrations of Jesus portrayed a strong man with dark hair and beard, brown intense eyes. Keegan's Jesus was very blond with glassy blue eyes, like a stoned Scandinavian surfer, a lamb stuck under his arm like a wooly surfboard.

Again, I found myself eavesdropping on Keegan's prayer.

*Dear Jesus, Lord, we ask that you be with us, Lord, because we're really going through a lot right now, and Lord, we need your tender hand on our home...*He confided about how much he needed a promotion at work to cover the medical bills, and Rory needed help at school. He even prayed for me, asking his delicate, blond Jesus to hold me close, like a daughter. It was really sweet, although still weird to pray to the Almighty as though He weren't someone who could strike you down dead for accidentally touching the Ark of the Covenant.

Amen, and we all dug in. Rory ate, swinging his legs beneath the table, very nearly happy. He asked for seconds! Keegan jumped up so fast he nearly toppled his milk. As he served another helping, Rory glanced between us. "So, Keeg, you've met the parents. Does that mean you two are finally boyfriend and girlfriend?"

Keegan and I both grew laser focused on eating.

"Have you kissed?"

"Rory!" Keegan's head snapped up.

"I know, I know. You don't believe the same. You're crookedly yoked." He rolled his eyes. "Sucks, too. June's *way* cooler than Abby." He went back to eating.

Abby? My stomach flipped. *Abby!*

"Hey June. When's your birthday?"

"January." I sipped my milk. *Abby.*

"Hear that, Keeg? Two more months."

"We'll have a party." Keegan winked at me.

"Yeah!" Rory did a little dance in his chair. "Balloons. Presents. Cake! Keegan, get June's mom to teach you how to make a cake. What's your favorite cake, June?"

I straightened. "I don't celebrate birthdays."

Rory's eyes shot open. "You don't celebrate your own

birthday?"

"Nope."

Rory's jaw dropped. "Has anyone ever wished you a happy birthday? Or sung you the birthday song?"

I shook my head. "Never."

"Not even your parents?"

"Not one time."

"You've never gotten birthday cake in your hair?"

"The *only* thing I haven't gotten in my hair."

"Oh my gosh." The way Rory looked at me, spoon stuck in his macaroni and cheese. "*June.*" I thought he might cry.

Keegan said, "How come?"

"Birthdays started with worship of false gods and goddesses. The Greeks made round cakes to worship Artemis, goddess of the moon. The lit candles made the cake look like a glowing moon. They'd blow out a candle and make a wish. They believed the smoke carried their wishes up to the gods."

"Whoa!" Rory dropped his spoon. "That's so cool."

"Paul said in Galatians that a little leaven ferments the whole lump. When false religious practices seep into pure Christian worship, they contaminate it, like poison."

Keegan fell silent.

"Good one, June," Rory said. "She got you there, Keeg."

Keegan fired back, "When Christians blow out the candles, we aren't worshipping Artemis."

"The traditions are still tainted," I argued. "Where's the evidence that early Christians celebrated birthdays? There's only one mention of a birthday party in the entire Bible. Evil King Herod. And we all know how that ended."

Rory made a slicing motion across his neck. "A head on a platter instead of a cake."

Keegan shook his head. "Sorry. Don't buy it. Paul was talking about maintaining the purity of church doctrine. He doesn't say anything about birthdays or other celebrations. And just because King Herod was a bad guy, *birthdays* are bad? That's a stretch. If you think God's not tough enough to handle a few pagan traditions, you must not have weddings in your religion either."

"What does a wedding have to do with anything?"

"The wedding dress. The veil. The exchange of rings. Almost every part of a wedding is lifted from pagan religion and superstition. Do Witnesses have weddings?"

I shifted in my chair. "They do."

"Then they're hypocrites."

I exploded. "Don't be arrogant!"

"Don't be defensive."

"You're attacking my faith!"

"No, I'm attacking your belief!"

Rory's eyes bounced between us. "Oh man. This is *so* much better than Young Warriors."

Keegan said, "What about honoring your own conscience? What happens if a Jehovah's Witness chooses to celebrate a birthday?"

"It's a sin. If you don't repent, you'll be disfellowshipped."

"What does that mean?"

"Cut off from the congregation."

"Shunned?"

I didn't say anything. I felt the weight of Rory and Keegan's combined stare.

Keegan said, "June, do you seriously believe God would abandon someone for celebrating a birthday?"

I stared into his eyes. My throat went numb. "I don't know."

rhubarb magic

At two in the morning, I was up, with a flashlight and a burning mission.

This had to stop.

I couldn't keep saying, "I don't know."

The problem was, I hadn't been to kingdom hall in so long, my arguments were rusty. Maybe Dad was right, and here was the proof that higher education was insidious, a distraction from The Truth. I should spend less time with flashcards, trying to make A's in the only college class I would ever take, and more time sharpening my Bible knowledge.

I sat cross-legged on the floor of Dad's study, scrounging through his comprehensive collection of *Watchtower* and *Awake!* magazines, organized in pristine leather-bound anthologies stretching all the way back to the 1940's.

I came across an *Awake!* article from 1994, one I remembered vividly: *Youths Who Put God First*. The flashlight beam illuminated a haunting collection of photos on the magazine cover, most of them school pictures, featuring twenty-six Jehovah's Witness children who had refused blood transfusions.

In the foreground, three pictures were posed side by side: a twelve-year-old a girl with short, curly hair, twinkling eyes, and a mischievous grin. Another little girl with long dark hair in a ponytail over her shoulder, a sailor dress, and a shy smile. A teenage boy with dark hair and eyes, shoulders back, sitting straight, on the verge of manhood.

They had died.

All twenty-six.

I moved the flashlight around, trying to take them in. All their faces.

Heroes, the article called them.

For Jehovah, these youth had been willing to make the ultimate sacrifice. I remembered reading the article when it was first published, thinking – I could be this good if I had the chance. I could be a hero in God's eyes.

This summer, I'd had the chance. Rushed to emergency surgery on a gurney, it was this article that surfaced in my memory, the faces of these kids, the ones who loved Jehovah more than their own life. Remembering them had made it easy for me to sign that No Blood form.

I took a breath, closed that volume, and pulled out another, kept searching.

I found out, it wasn't just blood. For a while, it was also organ transplants.

From 1967-1980, the Watchtower Society degreed organ transplants cannibalism. But after 1980, they pivoted, changed their stance, stating that organ transplants were sanctioned as *a matter of conscience*. But in that thirteen year span organ transplants were considered a sin, many Jehovah's Witness brothers and sisters had refused new livers and hearts, sometimes dying.

Is getting an organ from someone the same as eating them?

If organ transplants are now a matter of individual conscience, shouldn't blood transfusions be the same?

I sat back, clicked off my flashlight.

These questions weren't Keegan's.

They were mine.

***

That afternoon, Mom and I stepped into the bright, warm outside, standing together on the porch to wait for Keegan. I was tired from missed sleep, and too much thinking. The sunlight felt like kindness on my skin.

"Arkansas weather can't make up its mind." Mom shook her head. "One day we're drenched in cold rain, the next sun and sweat. I can't get used to it. I talked to Grandma this morning. Snow in Wisconsin. Up to the chin. That's what I miss, believe it or not. Well, at least here we have the gardens to enjoy for a while longer."

"How's Grandma? Did you tell her about Keegan?"

"I'll let *you* do that, June." She elbowed me, with a sly look.

I was amazed at this small act of grace. I thought for sure she'd already have bragged to Grandma, up one side and down the other, like he was hers now, same as the yellow roses. That was okay. I was just so thankful she liked him.

Keegan's car appeared, cresting the hill, and as he sailed ever closer to our house, my joy rose. I waved, and Mom waved, and he honked at us, tires crunching down our gravel drive. He got out of his car, as he walked toward us with his long and graceful strides, I saw his face. So tired. Worn. Mom saw, too. "Is Keegan okay? He looks unwell."

"He's been working overtime," I said. "He's trying to get a promotion to cover his Dad's medical bills."

"That poor kid. Such a tragedy." She stepped down the porch, solid, strong, and reached out to Keegan, her arms held wide. Seeing her, his face changed, melted into relief, like he'd found a sanctuary. He wrapped her up, lifted her right off the porch, and spun her around. She squealed. "Keegan! Put me down. I'm too old for that!"

"You're not old," Keegan said, setting her on her feet.

"You're new."

"Oh, you!" She swatted his arm, pleased as could be.

Keegan turned his gaze to me. "Hi, June."

"Hi, Keegan."

Around us, the birds trilled and sang, like a spring day.

"Okay, you two, that's enough of that. Keegan, lets go." Mom hooked her arm through his, pulled him with her, ahead of me. "You said you wanted to work in the garden with us. Today is perfect. Maybe the last warm day of the year. What do you think?"

"Heck yeah!" He did a little dance. Mom threw her head back, laughed.

We heard Grits before we saw her, barking frantically. We all turned. Mr. Bad Flannel's truck was gone, but he'd left his garage door open, a reckless crack. We watched Grits scoot on her belly, pull herself under, inch by inch.

"Come on, Grits," I said.

"You can do it," Keegan said.

She broke free, tore toward us. Keegan knelt, and she zoomed straight into his arms. "Hi, Grits. You did it!" She knocked him right on his butt, licking and licking his face. "I love you, girl," he said, wrapping her up in his arms.

"Oh boy." Mom held her face between her hands. "Not you, too, Keegan."

***

Together, we wintered the rhubarb patch.

We sank our knees, side by side by side, into the earth.

Mom showed Keegan how to press the mulch in. "Like a blanket," she said. "It protects rhubarb's crown before the first big freeze."

"Her crown? Like a queen." Keegan pulled on Dad's gardening gloves. "This is so cool. I've never had rhubarb in my life. I thought it was poisonous."

"Only the leaves. You chop them off, cook the stalks. You've never had rhubarb? You hear that, June?"

"What?" I looked around in a daze. "I think I fainted."

Keegan grabbed a gloveful of mulch, tossed it at me. I ducked.

Mom wiped her forehead. "Come summer, we'll teach you how to make our pie."

"Your pie?"

Mom's jaw dropped. "June hasn't told you all about Rhubarb Pie Day?"

Keegan nudged me. "What's that?"

"Fourth of July," Mom said. "We don't celebrate that. We've made our *own* day. The highlight is rhubarb pie."

"You can make pie out of this stuff?"

"The most beautiful pie in the world," I said. "Mom's masterpiece."

"*Our* masterpiece." Mom leaned into me. "June's gotten so good, I think she could teach you how to make it all on her own."

"Nah. I can chop and simmer and roll out the dough. It's Mom who makes the magic."

Keegan watched us. His eyes grew very soft. "I've never, uh," he stopped, shook his head. "Sorry. Dad was such a great Dad. We didn't have much money. But he was always home. Reading his Bible. Working in his shop, making chairs and bookshelves, cabinets and tables. He was always there. You know? Rory and I always joked about Dad's music. Not the music he listened to.

The music he made. You know? It was *bam! bam!* when he hammered together a chair. The *zzzhhhh!* of his sewing machine. My favorite was the *chnk! chnk!* of his staple gun." He laughed. "I never, um. I never missed my mom. Because Dad's music, it filled the whole house. You know?" His chin crumpled. He quickly swiped under his eye, leaving a big streak of dirt. "Sorry."

I sat there, my palms pressed hard into the grass, barely breathing.

Mom took over. She scooted in. She pulled him to her. And he let loose, crying deep, harsh sobs into her shoulder. "Oh sweetheart. Oh honey. It's so sad, so very sad." She held him. She rocked him.

Watching Mom be a mother to him.

I was afraid.

While I drove, Keegan didn't have to talk or think.

I drove us from Hopeton straight to Fayetteville Nature Center.

He looked out the window, and only had to give directions.

Then, we walked.

The rocky path, the stream, the cradle of trees. I already loved this place. It was relief to be here. Our shoes. I liked the way we walked together, kicking at rocks, crunching acorns, slipping on leaves. A side-by-side symphony, our walks.

"Thank you for being so nice," he said, finally.

"Nice? How?"

"That was the first time I've cried for my dad. I didn't know it was in there." We stopped to watch a flock of wild turkeys picking and strutting through the forest. They were riveting, both beautiful and ugly, immensely soothing to watch. Just to stand, and watch together. "I don't think Rory's cried," Keegan said. "He keeps drawing that scary skeleton picture. The one he started a month before Dad...he won't let the picture go. His teacher told me, he draws it in class, instead of doing his work. I called Judge Sanders last night, Dad's friend. He told me, Rory needs to see a counselor."

The turkeys ducked and darted, gobbling, rustling away into the underbrush. Keegan and I walked on, down a boardwalk beside a reedy pond. As we walked, a frog flew from the mud, legs outstretched, plopping into the water.

"How do you feel about that?" I asked.

"So conflicted. I see what Judge means. I'm out of my

depth. It's just, I keep thinking, Dad wouldn't like it. He thought worldly counselors were quacks and phonies, peddling drugs that promote fear, and work against God."

I glanced at him. "Sounds like something my dad would say."

"Yeah?" We stopped on the wooden bridge arching over the pond. I pointed. Two deer, up to their shins in the water, heads bent, drinking. "Your mom is so amazingly good to me. Your sister's super cool. Your dad...he's aloof. Every time I try to talk with him, he pushes me off with this alpha vibe. I get the feeling he doesn't like me much."

On our way out, Dad had driven by us. I'd honked and waved, eager to show off my driving. He'd kept going, like he hadn't seen us. But he had. "It's not you. He's working really hard, trying to grow his practice. He's distant and preoccupied most of the time these days." I stopped there. More would be too much. It was my job to hold the delicate threads of these newly forming relationships together.

As we crossed the bridge, something broke loose in me. "Who's Abby?"

"My girlfriend."

"What?"

"Ex-girlfriend. We broke up before school started." We arrived at a bench, overlooking a scraggly fall meadow where some butterflies still flit like loose petals. "Want to sit?"

We sat together. The sinking sun glazed the meadow in orange light. We both sunk our hands into our jacket pockets. "She plays violin at our church. The first time I saw her play, I was captivated."

I flinched, on the inside. "How long were you together?"

"Over a year. I thought we'd get married. Dad did, too. He

adored Abby."

Jealousy stacked upon jealousy. "Oh, wow," I said. "What happened?"

"Abby has a lot of ambition. She wanted to pastor a church."

"You didn't support that?"

"I did. I know it's controversial, women in church leadership. Personally, I'm all for it. She was the one who broke things off."

"Why?"

"One night we were at youth group, and one of the leaders got up and said, *Is there anyone here who's never spoken in tongues?* I raised my hand, along with a few others, and he had us stand up. He said, *so we're going to make this happen for you tonight!* He had the members who had spoken in tongues lay hands on those of us who hadn't, and start praying for us. He said, *ok, guys, just close your eyes, and start speaking, say anything, say words, say gibberish, it doesn't have to make sense, just let the spirit move through you.*"

I leaned in. "And?"

"And in my head I thought, *fake.*"

I smiled. "That's so you."

"Dad always told me, either the Lord speaks through you, or He doesn't. It's not a game you play. It's a serious thing. It should be genuine, not forced. He thought the authenticity of Gifts of the Spirit had been sullied. One time, at church, someone stood and delivered a prophecy for the congregation in tongues. Dad thought God had given *him* the translation. He was about to stand up and speak. But someone else did. After the service, dad approached the person, said, 'I'm confused, the Lord gave me the translation, but you spoke.' And the guy just shrugged, said, 'it was taking too long, things were getting awkward.' Dad was hurt. He said, that kind of dishonesty was a form of robbery. Dad's take was always more right to me than any preacher. That night at youth group, when I refused to pretend, Abby was seriously disappointed in me. She said I wasn't committed, wasn't trying."

I listened, engrossed. I'd been taught that Pentecostals were crazy delusional wild-eyed snake-handling holy-rolling extremists, and I'd had enough bizarre encounters with them in door-to-door work to confirm that idea. I didn't agree with Keegan's beliefs. But I'd respected, from the beginning, his thoughtfulness. A reasoning, rather than blinding, form of passion. "What happened then?" I asked.

"I wanted to prove to her I was just as dedicated to God as she was, and get back together. We were still trying to work things out, actually, the day you came up to me on the steps."

A jolt. "You were? I should've asked if you had a girlfriend..."

"The day after we talked, I stopped trying with Abby."

"You gave that up? But...you didn't know I was a Witness." My throat ached. "Do you regret it? Me coming up to you? Because, like Rory says, we're 'crookedly yoked'. We can never be what you and Abby could have been."

Keegan glanced at me. "It's the other way around, June. Abby and I could never have been what you and I are." The woods around us hushed, like the trees were listening. "My favorite part of the whole Bible is the story of David and Jonathon. They had such a trusting, intimate bond. When I was a kid, I longed for a friendship like that. You talk about you, being up in your tree, lonely and dreaming, and I'm like, hey, that was me. Only, I never had a place where I went to be lonely. That was just my life."

I burst into laughter. He did, too.

Then some strange grief cracked my heart open. The tears slid out, left and right. I couldn't wipe them away fast enough. "For me, it was Ruth and Naomi. Every time we read that story at kingdom hall, my heart tore in two. *Why can't I have a friend like that? Why can't I love and be loved like that?* I always imagined a girl. A Diana Barry kindred spirit. But it's you." I elbowed him, tenderly.

"I'm more handsome than Diana Barry." He winked.

"I think you even like my hair."

Keegan smiled. "When I first saw you, the light was filtering in from the clerestory windows of the lecture hall, into your curls. My very first thought was, *angel hair*."

"See what you do?" I licked tears from my lips. "Stop. Just stop."

"Never." He leaned in, pulled a twig from my hair.

He looked at it, like he'd found gold.

the purse

"June, twirl! No, not like that. Not like a prissy prairie girl. Like a *diva*."

Rain had swiped Dad's new camcorder from his desk. She'd had the brilliant idea to record our shopping excursion for Grandma, who was in the hospital after a heart scare that turned out to be her gallbladder. *What gall!* she'd joked to me on the phone, trying for her old booming belly laugh. She was currently very frustrated she couldn't meet the tall, good-looking Irishman who was taking her Juney to the big college dance.

I twirled, diva-like as possible, arms spread. The dress fanned out around my ankles. Lavender, with pearl buttons, and three-quarter length sleeves. I shimmied toward the camera. "What do you think, Grandma? Is it me?"

"Turn around. Turn, turn, slowly," Rain directed, twirling her finger, getting the most out of her role as cinematographer. The dressing room had cleared out. The stage was ours.

I said, "Grandma, remember our big all-day shopping excursions? Remember how we'd hijack the entire dressing room with our fashion shows?"

"Ooh, I'm digging how the fabric clings," Rain said. "1800's romantic, with a rockstar edge. Right, Grandma? Am I right?" I laughed, then let loose, shaking my butt at the camera.

Rain wolf-whistled. I spun around, then dropped my arms, looked down, and sighed.

Rain paused, lowering the camera. "What? You don't like the dress?"

"I do. I love it. I mean. I don't know. It's just. I have this old dream...”

Mom swooshed in. She fell, dramatic, against the dressing room wall. Her long sweep of black hair was in a pony-tail, now pushed sideways. “The *last* one!” She held up a dress. “I went to battle for it.”

“Shield your eyes, Grandma.” Rain zoomed in on the conquest. “This ritzy little number could blind you.”

My hand flew to my mouth. “Mom!” I stomped my feet.

“I know you,” she said, wagging a finger. “I know what you like.”

I floated to the dress, like in a dream. I touched it, just one finger, to see if it held, if it was real. I turned, faced the camera, eyes wide. Mom stood beside me, holding up the dress.

“Grandma.” I gazed deep into the camera. I imagined her blue eyes, growing soft with love. “Just look at your little ostrich.”

***

Handing off the camcorder with a bow, Rain took off for class.

Hooking arms, Mom and I headed down the mall to Piccadilly Cafeteria. We had a date with Keegan on his lunch break. I was elated, flying, my new dragonfly wing dress in plastic, draped over my arm.

Mom though, was worn down. Her mood plummeting. She was worried about Grandma. She needed to eat. Every baby’s cry or loud group of shoppers jangled her nerves. I steered her expertly around all possible provocations. Keegan would revive her. I knew it.

Sure enough, soon as she saw him, leaned against the wall,

waiting for us outside Piccadilly, she lit up. She flew to him, pinching his cheek. "Aren't you a sight for sore eyes, young man. I'm so tired. It's too crowded! Wait until you see June in her dress. I can't take all this noise!" She clapped her hands over her ears as a store alarm shrieked. "I need to sit."

Keegan took over. Hooking his arm through Mom's, he guided her through the cafeteria line. He readjusted her purse strap when it fell down her shoulder. He asked the servers for the food she wanted. She looked up at him with gratitude. I watched, from behind, with equal gratitude.

At the booth, Keegan slid in beside me, across from Mom.

Mom sipped her coffee. "Ahh, much better. I need to call Ma. I feel so guilty I'm not there to help her. All she has is my sister, and boy, do they go at it. My sister, Rena, can't be nice. If Ma was dying in front of her, she'd start a fight. Keegan, is that a measuring tape?" Mom squinted, taking another sip.

Keegan lifted the measuring tape from around his shoulders. "Sure is!" He coiled it around his finger, beaming. "Today, it was *my* turn to get fitted for a tux." We caught eyes, and I dipped my head, smiling. "Also, I have good news to share. Guess who's the new assistant manager at Luca's?" He spread his arms.

Mom thunked her coffee cup down onto the table. "Congratulations, young man! Well done!" She lifted her hand in the air. Keegan high-fived her. They laughed together.

Assistant manager.

Some old hurt stirred. Somewhere deep. Crawling up from my belly.

"...proud of you," Mom was gushing. "Such a good guy! No one more worthy..."

Keegan turned to me, his dark blue eyes brimming with

light. "Good job," I said, pushing past the lump in my throat. I took his hand, giving it a squeeze. "I am so proud of you, Keegan. You've worked hard for this." I clinked my glass to his. Joy for him, combined with this sadness coming up, pulled my ribs together, too tight. I struggled to breathe.

"We'll have a party. What do you want to do to celebrate?" Mom asked.

"I want to learn how to make a Flamaggio's steak. Finally!"

"I don't know how they make their steak. But I can teach you how I make mine. It's a skillet garlic butter herb steak."

"Did you say garlic butter? Oh, I'm in."

My head spun. I pinched my dress again, making sure it was still there. Then I realized, feeling around the booth, patting around me, frantic. "Mom," I said. She was still gushing. "Mom."

"What, June?" An irritated look. "What's the matter?"

My heart lodged in my throat. "My purse."

"No, you didn't." Mom slapped her hand over her face. "How many times have I told you?"

"I'm sorry."

"What happened?" Setting down his drink, Keegan glanced between us.

"Keegan." Mom met his eyes, sighing and shaking her head. "June lost her purse and it's not the first time. I've told her time and again. You probably know this by now, but her head's in the clouds. She doesn't pay attention to her surroundings. She's *spacey*."

Keegan wrinkled his forehead. "She's – what?"

"I think it's in the dressing room," I said. "Can I get past?" I tried edging out of the booth.

"Hey." Keegan set a warm hand on my knee, squeezed.

"Hey. It's okay."

Mom's eyes narrowed. "I beg to differ. Her Dad works his butt off to make that money. You know how that is, now that *you're* the dad. And when she doesn't listen to me, we all pay."

"It's not that big a deal," he said. "Everyone messes up."

I froze. *Wrong.*

Mom's face hardened. "Are *you* telling *me* what's a big deal and what isn't?"

"I'm saying, June cares. She can be trusted to take care of things."

"Oh, is that so?" Mom turned to me with a smirk. "Well then. I guess she can do no wrong."

Under the table, I kicked Keegan's leg. "Mom's right. I need to do better. Can I get past?" He stood. I slid out of the booth, charging past him, out of the cafeteria.

"June, wait!"

Outside, in the mall corridor, I swiveled. "What are you doing? Go back!" I pressed my hands to his chest, shoved. "You have to go back!"

Keegan blinked. "Why?"

I scraped my hands through my hair. "I did this. I need to fix it. If you want to help me, stay with Mom. Stop arguing, okay? Don't defend me." I tore off, weaving through the crowds of shoppers.

***

On the way home, Mom raged at traffic. *Morons! Losers! Rednecks!* She tailgated, stomped on her brakes, drove too fast, swerved around other cars with a screech.

Each time I jolted forward in my seat, or shoved sideways,

the side of my head knocking into the window glass, I understood the car had become in her hands a rod – *spare the rod, spoil the child* – and I was being punished.

I took it, squeezing my eyes shut, holding my purse tight.

We exited onto a quiet country backroad. No idiot hillbilly drivers in sight.

Mom turned on me with words. *You got lucky, little girl. Someone honest found your purse. Next time, you may not be so lucky. I guess Keegan thinks you're perfect, huh? He'll learn. You can only keep up the innocent sweetheart act for so long.* Her face, so mean.

I turned to the window, my eyes seeking the refuge, the consolation of pine trees. *June, look at your hair. It' s full of tangles! It embarrasses me. Do you even take care of it anymore?*

It's angel hair. I fought back, silently.

What does he see in you, huh? What kind of spell did you cast? You want to know what I think? I think he's buttering you up, using you to help him take care of that kid brother of his.

I wondered what it would be like to open the car door and throw myself out. I'd roll down the ditch, careen into the woods, bury my red, raw, burned alive heart in soft moss, and cool leaves.

At home, Mom thrashed and crashed around the kitchen, slamming pans, drawers, and cabinets. She charged after me, to my room, throwing my door open after I'd gently closed it. She came right up to my bed, got in my face, seething and sneering. *What if I take that tape of yours? That's what I should do! Maybe I'll just take that dress back, too. Humiliating me in front of Keegan. How dare you! He has no idea how selfish you are, how lazy...*On and on, merciless.

I rolled over, slipped the tape from Dad's camcorder, tucked it inside my bra. I curled up in bed, protective around my new dress.

Finally she left, ranting and stomping, all the way down the hall.

"Keegan, Keegan, Keegan..." I sobbed his name, over and over, like a prayer. "Keegan, Keegan..."

More alone than I'd ever been.

homecoming

Stars clung to me.

They dripped from my breasts, my stomach, my hips.

I twisted in my gold sequin dress, and glittered like a galaxy.

I'd foraged in Rain's forbidden stash of magazines, finding diagrams that uncloaked the mystery of makeup application. For the first time, I'd done it myself. I pouted. Red lipstick, I'd discovered, was maybe my thing. Also smoky eyes, batting my lashes. Rain had been right about the magic of mascara. I'd taken her advice and scrunched mousse into my curls. It was a little bit life-changing, how my dandelion frizz now spiraled, neat curls bouncing just above my bare shoulders. I stooped to admire my cleavage. In *Cosmopolitan*, I'd found a mind-blowing use of makeup in an article with an arresting title: "How to Boob Contour".

"Knock knock!" I snapped upright. Mom entered, and her mouth fell open. I braced.

But she came towards me with a smile. "Juney. Is that you?" Her gaze trailed up and down my sparkling hourglass figure. She pressed her hands to her face. "I can't remember. Did the dress look *that* sexy in the dressing room?"

Across the hall, Rain shut her door, too hard. I checked Mom's face for a reaction.

A few days earlier, Mom had discovered a stinking mountain of filth in Rain's room. For some reason, Rain had been hoarding weeks of dirty clothes and dirty dishes...in her bathtub. Almost like she'd wanted Mom to find it. Wanted to provoke a blow-up. Mom had expressed her outrage to me, but did not confront Rain. Instead, she had cleaned the mess herself, eerily calm.

Ever since, Mom had been *extra* nice to me.

Now, she fussed with my dress, tugging up the front, adjusting the straps, pulling at the hem. "Don't mind her. She's jealous. Big sister should be going to the dance in a pretty dress with a handsome guy. Not little sister. Don't let her snit ruin *your* night." She lifted my chin so I had to look her in the eye. "Promise?"

"Promise." I swallowed, her two fingers pinching my chin.

***

I slung on one of Dad's coats, and headed to the garage.

Wearing safety glasses, Dad ran a jigsaw through wood. *ZZZHHHHTTTT!*

I shut the door, leaned back against it. I thought about Keegan, coming home every day to his dad's dark, empty workshop. How strange it must be for him, to see the floor, still golden with wood shavings. The tools still bright and glinting. But the music, gone.

Plunk! Plunk! Dad hammered now. He picked up a smaller hammer, tried it. *Clink!*

I soaked up every note.

Then my breath caught. My old work stool was still out. He hadn't stuffed it back in the corner. I crept over and looked. *He'd fixed it.* The tear had been patched up. No more stuffing poking out like a puff of white beard. I reached out, tracing the rough contours of the new vinyl. *He'd fixed it.*

I sat on the stool, wrapped in his oversized coat, and spun. Legs out. Sleek and shapely in magic panty hose from Grandma.

Dad looked up, pushing his safety glasses up into his thick, dark hair. I kicked my high heels against the stool. "It's good as new! Thank you."

"Yep." He lifted the wood post, tugged at a bracket.

"You're working on the white picket fence."

"Trying." He didn't look at me.

I twisted my hands together. "Remember that funny old song? The one we used to sing in the car?"

He shook his head. "Nope."

"Yes you do! The one about the bucket." I sang the words, soft, off-key. "*There's a hole in my bucket, dear Liza, dear Liza, there's a hole in my bucket, dear Liza, a hole.*" I waited for him to catch the refrain. Silence. I sang on, kicking my heels against the stool. "*So fix it, dear Henry, dear Henry, dear Henry, so fix it, dear Henry, fix it.*"

Plunk! Plunk! Plunk! The sound of the hammer buried my voice.

I trailed off, a lump rising in my throat. "Can I help?"

He smirked, tossing the hammer down with a clatter. "I don't think you're dressed for it."

"I could still help. I want to!" High-pitched, hopeful. Nine-years-old.

"Nah. You've got a dance to go to."

"Aren't you going to look at me, Dad?"

"Don't want to."

My eyes stung with tears. "Why? You don't like me anymore?"

He toweled his hands, with a little laugh. "I don't like your choice."

"Which one?"

"Friends, huh?" He glanced at me, shook his head.

"He is my friend. He's good and kind to me."

"Satan comes disguised as an angel of light."

Heat rose in my cheeks. "That's really mean."

Dad threw the towel down, pointed his finger at me. "I tried to warn you when you first started school. I told you it was full of temptation and you'd have to guard your heart, every step of the way. And what's the first thing you do? You make *friends* with some guy steeped in false religion. You have no idea what a dangerous path you're on." His nostrils flared. "I thought you'd know better. I thought you'd *do* better."

"Keegan and I talk about God and the Bible constantly. I'm – I'm witnessing to him. I wish you would reach out to him, talk with him, too. He could be a brother in the faith someday."

Dad scoffed. "Is that the delusion you've talked yourself into? You think you're going to change him? Boy oh boy. You're in for a world of hurt, kid."

I was about to break down. I was right there, on the edge. "Dad. I know you don't like my choice. But can't you just love me right now? I'm all dressed up, Dad. I'm going to my first dance. I'm happy, Dad. Can't you just look at me and love me right now?"

He blinked, set his palms on his workbench, looked away.

I watched his back rise and fall.

"Dad?"

The door-bell rang. He bowed his head. "Time for you to go."

***

Keegan stood in the foyer beside Mom.

I walked in, heels a melodic click across the tile. "Wow," he said. And then, hushed, "*Wow*." He pressed his hand to his heart.

I stared at him, transfixed. Tall and glorious in a tux, his tumble of auburn curls gleaming, framing his face, the dimple in his chin and cheek.

Mom pushed us together in front of the mantel. She thrust the bouquet of luscious red roses into my arms. She ordered us to move a little this way, a little that way. Picture after picture flashed, dazzled. My smile ached. It was surreal, in my head, as I compared this dance to the last one. I had a vision of myself, as though from a different world, some far off life, tearing up the hill toward a blue pickup, my teeth chattering in the heat.

Finally, Keegan hooked my arm through his, and we were off, out the door, sweeping together down the sidewalk. "You should live in a tux," I told him.

"And you in sequins," he said.

"Agreed."

With a clatter of toenails on concrete, Grits bounded up beside us.

Our favorite girl, come to see us off.

Keegan and I knelt. At the same time, together, we wrapped her up. She went wild in our arms. "Guess what, girl? I'm going to a dance. A real dance. Can you believe?" I opened my coat. "Sequins, Grits. A whole dress of them." She licked my hand, tail wagging furiously. Keegan's hand met mine in her fur. He clasped my fingers. "Let's take her with us."

I looked up. "What?"

He slid his hand into the pocket of his tux jacket, removed something, held it up to the moonlight. It looked like it was throwing off sparks. A gold sequined collar, perfectly matched to my dress.

My hand flew to my mouth. "You didn't."

"Far better than a corsage. Don't you think?"

"Yes! But..." I craned my head toward Bad Flannel's driveway.

"He's not home." Keegan fastened the collar around Grit's neck, her body waggling.

"The thing is, she won't do it, Keegan. She won't go with us. She won't even go in the garage! Two years now, I've tried and she's just too..."

Keegan swung open the car door, made a grand sweeping gesture toward the backseat.

Grits jumped in. She turned, cocked her head at me. Absolutely sparkling.

"...scared."

***

"Okay, kids, stand against the mantel. Yeah, right there. Oh come on, closer, you two. *Closer*. Don't be shy!"

Homecoming pictures, round two.

Rory was the photographer. Decked out in his Friday night finery of Ninja Turtle COWABUNGA! pajamas, wavy chestnut hair standing on end, he lowered the camera. He studied us, like a pro, tilting his head left, then right. "Hmm. Something's missing..." He tapped his lower lip. Then, snapping his fingers. "I got it! Don't move." He tore off, feet thumping up the stairs.

Keegan's arm around my shoulder was heaven. I dared a glance. He smiled at me from beneath his eyelashes. "This is nice," he said. He pulled me a bit closer. I never wanted to move. Not ever. "Should we bring in Grits?"

"If Rory meets Grits, we'll never get out of here."

More thumping feet, this time down the stairs, and Rory

reappeared. "Here." He thrust Intrepid into my hands. I held her up. She stuck her head out, and her legs. "Perfecto." Rory kissed his fingers, knelt, snapped a picture. I sat Intrepid on Keegan's shoulder. Keegan crossed his arms, leaned back, jutted his chin, James Bond style.

"Yes!"

I set Intrepid on my head. Rory moved the camera away, eyes wide. "June, watch out. She'll get stuck in your hair!"

"Hey now. I used mousse."

"Hold on a sec. We're missing someone vital." Then Keegan took off, thumping up the stairs. Rory and I exchanged glances, shrugs. A few seconds later, Keegan returned with Rory's baby-sitter, a middle-aged woman with glasses, hair in a pony-tail, and a glinting cross necklace. Keegan introduced her as Madeline, from his church. He handed Madeline the camera, and motioned for Rory to join us.

"Keeg, *no*. I'm in pajamas."

"Since when are you fashion conscious, bro? Come on now. I have a turtle on my shoulder. Biting my ear."

Rory grinned. He dashed in between us. The three of us vogued for the camera, one goofy pose after another. Intrepid made her way between our hands, and finally, laughing unstoppably, we slung our arms around each other's shoulders.

The camera flashed one last time.

"Aww," Madeline said, lowering the camera. "You make such a beautiful little family."

I was too overcome to speak.

I felt it though, the way the three of us pulled closer.

***

Grits kept surprising me.

In a swarm of rowdy college kids, she not only held her own, but soaked up every scrap of attention lavished on her. Girls in fancy dresses, shiny hair in ornate twists, stooped to pet her, hug her neck, kiss her on the nose. Guys in tuxes pressed long-stemmed roses into her sequined collar. *Oh my God. Your dress and her collar! Can we take your picture?*

As we posed, I whispered in Grit's ear, a quote from Anne Shirley. *It's delightful when your imaginations come true, isn't it?*

Even a small dream realized, could nearly break your heart with joy.

We moved away from the crowded dance floor, the spinning lights and loud music, to the gymnasium below. Only us. After nosing around the basketball court, Grits curled up on the glossy floor, beneath the player's bench, abloom with her flower offerings.

Keegan strode off and within seconds, the lights grew dimmer, softer. Keegan walked back to me. He held my gaze as he crossed the gymnasium. From upstairs, the lyrics to a love song drifted down, *You make my world, a summer day...*

He held out his hand, and taking it, my knees went weak.

"Do you feel that?" I asked him. Slowly, I slid my hand from his. Then slowly, with an ache, I slid it back. "Click click," I said.

He smiled into my eyes. "From day one."

He laced our fingers together, pulled me to him. Oh, suddenly, we were very close. The scent of him. The heat. And then we were dancing. His arms around my waist, mine looped around his neck, we moved together, swayed.

He had asked me one night, on one of our walks in the trees, what my oldest dream was. I'd answered, to dress up in sequins and go to a dance. He'd said, Will you go to Homecoming with me? And I'd said, Can friends go to dances together? He'd shrugged. Why not? Why can't friends dance.

Was *this* how friends danced?

I lay my head on his chest, and I breathed. *I could breathe.* I could dance. I could let my body sink into his, sway with his. I could nestle ever deeper into his heartbeat. I had permission.

"Keegan," I said. "Our chaperone's asleep." I tilted my face up to his.

"What should we do?" He whispered. Not waiting for an answer, he leaned in, pressing his warm cheek to mine. His stubble brushed my skin as he turned his face, ever so slightly, kissed my cheek. Soft, warm, a summertime raindrop. Then, he kissed my chin. Then, the corner of my lips. My body zinged and zapped, then melted. I grabbed his face, kissed his chin, the dimple in it. Kissed it again, and again.

He took my face between his hands.

Our lips brushed, faint at first, back and forth, little whisper kisses.

And then we kissed for real.

Slow, deep, tender, sweet.

Harder and faster, building heat.

Making fire.

I was ready.

I'd learned all about it in *Seventeen*.

It was called French kissing.

I parted my lips.

And when our tongues met, they twined like flames.

Hand in hand, Keegan and I walked fast in the cold starry night to Hiller Hall.

To our steps.

Our step.

Grits left a trail of rose petals glistening on the sidewalk behind us. My chin and cheeks burned from kissing. My lips were swollen, hungry for more. We sat on the step where we'd begun. *Keegan and June.* And we read to each other. Because we'd brought our books to the Homecoming dance. Of course we had.

So much for not being weird.

Keegan read to me from *The Lion, The Witch, and the Wardrobe.* He reclined against the wall, his tuxedo jacket off. His dress shirt rolled to the elbows. He draped his arm around Grits, and read to me about Lucy meeting Mr. Tumnus. Mr. Tumnus, the notorious faun, was meant to see Lucy, a human, as an enemy. But after tea and conversation, he liked her so much, he couldn't bear the thought of betraying her to the White Witch. Poor Mr. Tumnus was inconsolable.

Keegan set the book down, looked at me. "Your turn." He closed his eyes, settling in for the story.

I wanted to kiss his eyelids, each one, but instead I opened my well-loved copy of *Christy.* As I leafed through the pages, I saw the little pink crepe myrtle flowers pressed in the creases, from the first day of school, which now felt like a dream. Or the beginning of one. I found my place, and began to read. Christy couldn't endure the smell of the unwashed mountain children as she leaned in to help them read and do math. She'd use a handkerchief soaked in perfume, covering her nose and mouth. Then one day she realized, she didn't need the handkerchief anymore. Their hygiene hadn't improved. But she *loved* them. Nothing else mattered. I choked up, had to pause.

Keegan reached for my hand, gently caressing my skin with his thumb. He said, "This book moves you so much."

I looked away, blinking. "I'm a sap, is all. Mushy-hearted, my whole life."

"It's more than that. It's deeper. I've been wanting to tell you, the way you've connected with Rory is something special. He's taken to you like I've never seen him do with anyone."

"I've taken to *him*."

Keegan squeezed my hand. "Yesterday at work, I got another call from Rory's teacher. I braced myself for more bad news. But she was beside herself. He was reading in class. You know what he was reading?"

What? Grits rested her head in my lap, and I set my hand on her face.

"That turtle book you brought him. He takes it everywhere now. He can't get enough. I have to pry it out of his hands at night." He laughed. "Dad tried. I've tried. It's the first time I've ever seen him want to read a book."

My heart filled and filled. "It's his comfort book..."

Keegan grabbed his tuxedo jacket, fished in the pockets. "I found this notice on campus." He withdrew a folded up piece of paper. "I know you have your mind made up about college. But just, I think you'd be so great for this. Here. Take a look."

Wary, I took the paper. My mouth went dry, reading it. *Green Tree Elementary Is Currently Seeking A 5th Grade Teacher's Assistant. Part-Time with possibility of Full-Time. Must Be Enrolled In*

At Least 3 Credit Hours Of Education Courses.

"Oh no. I can't do this." I folded the paper back up and held it out to him.

He didn't take it. "Why not?"

"I'm not eligible, for one thing. I'm not enrolled in education courses."

"Good news. The position doesn't open until January. If you register for the spring semester, you could get Intro to Teaching, which is three credit hours. I already checked."

"That was so nice of you. But no."

"June. Your heart belongs to flashcards. And highlighters. Also, when you read *Christy*, about being a teacher, you get tears in your eyes. Every single time."

I turned away, pained. "I don't think it's a good idea."

"Because of your mom?"

I whipped to him. "Why would you ask that?" My heart just pounded.

"I don't know." He scratched his temple. "Maybe I'm overthinking things. But it's been weighing on me ever since we met up at the mall. Do you realize that every time I'm around your mom, you kind of freak out?" He looked at me. "Like, you control my behavior. I've seen that. You kick me under the table to shut me up, if you think I might upset her. You feed me lines to say to make her feel good, and it's like, you don't trust me. You have to hand me a script. I tell her thank you, and you make me thank her ten more times. If I hug you, you push me away, tell me to hug her instead. Or like, at the mall, when I tried to go with you to get your purse, you made me go back and sit with her. You told me not to defend you."

"She was stressed." I held my elbows in my hands, pressed the toes of my high heels together. "She's been through really bad things in her life. You don't even know."

"I know how much you care about her. I know how loyal you are. But that day in the mall, June. Some of the things your mom said." He stopped, shook his head. "They didn't sit well at all. You lost your purse. And the way she looked at you. She acted like you'd done it on purpose to hurt her. Like she had to get revenge, or something. I don't know," he raked his hand through his curls. "It made me mad."

"Please don't be mad," I said, touching his arm.

"When I got home that day," he went on, like he hadn't heard me, "I was alone in my room at my desk, studying, with some Christian music on the radio. I swore that I heard you calling for me. Your voice was desperate, full of pain. I fell to my knees onto the floor, praying so hard for you. Like I said, maybe it's just me, making things up..."

I held my breath, remembering the way I'd called his name, over and over in my bedroom, heart and spirit broken after Mom's attacks. But how could he have heard me? He couldn't have. It didn't make sense.

I shook his arm gently. "Keegan, you and Mom have such a beautiful bond. You love her. She loves you. *Adores* you. Do you know what she says to me? She says, you're the son she never had. She called Grandma the other day and I heard her say, *I have three kids now, and Keegan's my favorite.*" Rain had rolled her eyes, hearing this, while I had celebrated.

Now, Keegan smiled, and to my great relief, I saw his bad feelings melt away. "That means so much to me."

I changed topics, nudging his shoe with mine. "What about you? Are you registering for next semester?"

"Yes, but not here. I'm transferring to Fayetteville Bible College. The Lord is calling me to get into church leadership.

That summons has become even stronger since being promoted at Luca's."

I went quiet. "What's it like? Being an assistant manager?"

Keegan caressed Grits, her head now resting on his knee. "It's tough. I can see all the broken parts of the business. The things that don't work. And I can't just retreat to the back, like before, to my sewing machine. I have to face things and solve problems. Like when the western attire goes to the wrong wedding party and the groom, who ordered a simple black tux, gets a vest, a bolo tie, and a suede fringe jacket."

I scrunched my face. "Yikes."

"Yeah, yikes. But I'm learning so much, it's crazy. And I get to carry keys." He grinned.

I absolutely ached. "Lucky! Do you jangle them importantly?"

"Heck yeah. That's at least half the fun of being a manager."

"Yeah." I hugged my knees. "I imagined it would be."

"It's cool, too, you know, because I see myself differently now. In school, I was like Rory, the quiet kid. Only instead of drawing, I read books. I never saw myself as leader material."

"You are." I thought about the other night, watching him cook a pot roast with rosemary and thyme from Mom's garden, pay bills, and help Rory with fractions, all at the same time. I'd offered to help with laundry. Were you supposed to feel such bliss, rolling up boy socks and underwear at the dinner table? Such warm, deep joy, watching Keegan carefully check the roast in the crock-pot, then swoop over, leaning in beside Rory to untangle a word problem. That precise moment, in fact. I'd looked at him, and thought, *leader*. It's the moment I'd known, I loved him.

What?

I turned to him now, stunned, electrified. "Keegan. What

did we do tonight? What did we do? We kissed. *We kissed!* We shouldn't have kissed." I stared at him. "Should we have kissed?"

Keegan's eyes held mine, steady. "Yes," he said.

"Yes? But no. Keegan! We can only be – friends."

"That we are."

Oh, the way he smiled.

The way he took my hand, pressed it to his lips.

The way he pulled me right up onto his lap, kissing my neck.

The way I pushed my hands into his curls, lifted his face to mine, and whispered into his mouth as we kissed, "*Best* friends."

large fire

From the first moment, the day had a strange, sad feel.

It was mid-December, steely cold, overcast. The gardens were finally gone. *Asleep*, mom insisted. *Not gone.* But that day, brown, withered, and still, they gave me the feeling of gone.

Maybe it was because my class was ending. Final exam, then winter break. For me, college would be over. *Gone.*

Leaving to school, Rain and I passed Mr. Bad Flannel fetching his mail. He turned sharply, and when he saw us, he practically stepped in front of the car. Rain slammed on the brakes. "Holy shit, what's his deal? Should I roll down my window?" She asked this, even as she was rolling it down. Just enough for him to slant his head sideways and push his big, tobacco-smacking lips in. "Don't bullshit me, girls. Where's my dog at?"

"Sir, we have no idea. Please excuse." She flicked her hand, dismissing him. "We need to go take finals." With her finest eye-rolling, Rain released the brake. We started rolling.

He kicked the side of the car!

Rain pushed on the gas and we peeled off.

He stood in the middle of the road in his big, puffy flannel coat, screaming, "Fuckin' lesbos!"

"Lesbos? We're sisters!"

"It's Arkansas."

"Whatever." Rain gripped the wheel, checking the rear-view. "God. What the hell? This town sucks. I do not need this backwoods drama right before a statistics final." Then, sending me a glance. "You know where Grits is?"

"Nope, sure don't." I slunk down, dipping my chin deep

into the warm, scratchy wool of my scarf.

***

On the way to my final, head down, cold wind whipping my scarf this way and that, I paused outside School of Art, saying a silent farewell. My first day, I couldn't imagine the sprawling University of Arkansas campus ever feeling like mine, belonging to me, the way it did Rain. Only one class, but I'd grown attached. My heart was even more tender toward the art students pushing through the doors with their portfolios. I wondered if Rory would go to art school. He was certainly talented enough. I wondered what he would look like, what he would be like, when he reached college age.

I wondered, with a knot tightening in my throat, if I would still be part of their lives.

Because I wondered, ever since Homecoming night, how Keegan and I would make it work. How could a Jehovah's Witness missionary be with the pastor of a Pentecostal church? How could the pastor of a Pentecostal church be with a Jehovah's Witness missionary? Sharing bread at Flamaggio's wouldn't be enough. Could we even stay friends, if we had to watch each other fall in love with and marry someone else?

You're in for a world of hurt, kid.

Dad's words haunted my brain.

As I turned toward Hiller, the sight of familiar long, dark, curly hair stopped me in my tracks. *Rain.* My sister threw open the doors to School of Art, heading inside. I vividly remembered that day. Finding her with him. Gray hairs. How he carried an art portfolio. His eyes, the way they lingered on her body.

I pivoted, and followed her.

The School of Art shone with polished concrete floors, and smelled sharply of acrylics and clay. Oil paintings lined the walls, experimental self-portraits, distorted features, asymmetrical faces intensifying the surreal feeling inside me as I crept up the stairs. At the top, I peered around the corner. My sister went toward him.

Gray Hairs.

He leaned against the wall, outside a classroom, wearing a paint-splattered apron over a t-shirt and jeans. He was good-looking, in an artsy old guy way, with that bit of beard, touched by silver, and square, black-framed glasses.

As Rain approached, he straightened, smiled at her in a way that made my stomach feel funny. From the pocket of his apron, which bloomed an array of paintbrushes, he pulled out an envelope, handed it to her. She ripped it open, checked something, nodded, then stuck it in her bag. He swung open the classroom door, ushered her in.

He closed the door behind them with a click.

***

That night, the phone rang, shrill, startling me awake from a finals-induced nap. I sat up straight, my book falling off my chest, tumbling from the bed onto the floor. "Hello?" I rubbed my head, groggy, and hoped for the reviving warmth of Keegan's voice, calling me from Luca's.

Not the husky, brusque, "Who is this?"

I woke up fast, clenching the phone. "Who is this?"

"Rain, that you? Or June?"

"Who is *this*?"

"Aunt Rena, sweetheart. Remember me?"

An image formed. Hair, jet-black like Mom's, only short, with bangs teased out sky high. Dark eyes, heavily made up. A smoky laugh, and sour cigarette breath. Fingernails long and red, like bloody spears. "This is June." Suddenly cold, I pulled the quilt over my legs.

"Juuuuuuune!" She sang, and her voice crackled. "Aww, honey. You probably don't remember me. I remember *you*. I used to drive by your house every day on the way to work. I always saw you outside on your swing. You were always there, nose in a book. Aww, poor little thing, you looked so lonely. I'd honk and wave. But you didn't know who I was..." she coughed, harsh and hacking. "Your mom don't speak to me."

My mind went nuts. Aunt Rena, the witch. Aunt Rena, the devil. Why was she calling? Terror-stricken, I clutched my quilt. "Grandma. Is Grandma okay?"

She drew in a wheezy breath. "Ma's fine, honey."

I fell back against my pillows, exhaled, shaking head to toe.

"She loves your tape, sweetheart! She just got it in the mail. I went to pick her up for her doctor's appointment and she don't answer the door. I'm thinking the worst, she's had that heart attack. I get the door open and there she is, in her skirt and blouse, sitting on the edge of her bed. I say, 'Ma, what's wrong? You sick? You need an ambulance?' She points to the TV. And it's you, honey. You in your pretty sequins. She couldn't even talk. I never saw Ma cry like that."

I tasted my own tears as they slid onto my lips. *Oh, Grandma.*

"She'd be calling instead of me, but she's riding in the ambulance."

The hairs on my arms rose. "What?"

"Hate to be the bearer of bad news. The Old Man got into a brawl. Or some asshole thought it'd be fun to beat up a poor old drunk. Ma found him in a snow bank. Bleeding and damn near froze to death."

***

"Come here, come here."

Late that night, Keegan picked me up and drove me back to his house. There, behind the antique pocket doors, on the blue couch, he held me. The most comforting place. Arms wrapped around me, he whispered into my ear, "I'm so sorry. Are you close to him?"

"No. But in a way, yes." I pushed my face into my hands. "Mom shut down when she got the news. I've never seen her look like that. She and her dad have all this...unfinished business. If he dies, I just don't know..."

Keegan fell silent, thinking. And then, "Is he Jehovah's Witness? Or a Christian?"

I bristled. "Jehovah's Witnesses *are* Christians."

"I'm sorry." Keegan let a soft kiss fall on my neck.

Anger hit my bloodstream like a drug. I pushed from his arms, twisted to face him. "Why did you even ask that?"

"I don't know. Because I'm dumb."

"No, you're not. Tell me why."

"I'm just tired, June." His face was drawn and sad. His faded t-shirt depicted a cross, along with the words in fancy script, *madly in love with Jesus my Savior,* which only spiked my anger. It was so disrespectful, speaking like that about Jesus, like he was a crush in a teenage love song.

"It's been a long day," Keegan said. "Finals, then work..."

"I'm not letting you off the hook. Why did you ask about my grandpa's religion?"

Keegan tilted his head back, exhaled. "Because if you'd told me he was Christian, I could comfort you. I could tell you that, if he passes, he'll be in heaven, safe in the Lord's arms. At peace."

"And if I told you he was Jehovah's Witness?"

He swallowed. Said nothing.

"You'd think he was going to hell. Is that right?"

He looked to the side. The muscle in his jaw jumped.

"You do. You do think that. Does that mean..." I pointed to my chest, my heart going berserk. "You think *I'm* going to hell?"

He closed his eyes. "June..."

He did!

"I can't believe...I can't...I thought you were my friend."

"I *am* your friend. Okay? This isn't personal. This is what I believe about *everyone* who isn't saved." He pushed his hands into his hair, held his head.

"So if I died, and Rory asked you where I went, you'd look him in the eye and say, *June's in hell?*"

Keegan dropped his hands. He swung his legs off the couch, found his shoes, leaned over to pull them on. "You know what? We're not doing this. We're both worn out. Today's been rough. We're not having this conversation right now."

"Stop being a coward!" I grabbed a pillow and hit him in the side of the face. So hard, his curls flew up.

He touched his face, turned to me, eyes churning. "I can't believe you did that."

"Me? What about you? You think I'm going to burn for eternity." I exploded to my feet, ran outside to the car. Inside, I tried to buckle the seatbelt, and failed, my hands shaking too hard. Everything was nightmare. Then Keegan was in the car. We were pulling out. We were bumping down his pot-holed driveway. We were driving and driving. Past the Fayetteville skyline, a blur of lights, onto the black ribbon of country road. Pulling over, parking at a convenience store, too bright. Keegan twisting to me, grabbing my hand, holding it to his wet face.

"For being Jehovah's Witness," I said.

He looked at me, broken. "They're not my rules, June. I didn't make them up."

I yanked my hand from his. He stared at the empty space. Then dropped his head down on the steering wheel.

I was crushed.

But there was also power.

Being the angry one.

Being the one to leave.

Being the one to cause pain.

pajama party

The phone ringing jerked me from sleep. A week later, the Old Man was still in the ICU. Grandma said she'd call with any new news. Mom did not come out of her room much. When she did, she plodded around the house with eerie, unseeing eyes. Dad cautioned us to give her space. He brought her coffee and food on a tray, along with something he called 'rescue remedy,' drops he administered to his chiropractic patients who'd been in car accidents. He claimed the vibration-frequency of certain flowers in the drops helped people recover from shock. I accepted his explanation, but didn't really understand. The graveness on his face, it was like Mom was the one in the ICU. Now, dreading, I pressed the phone to my face. "Hello?"

"June?"

"Rory," I said, sitting up.

"Are you ever coming back?"

My throat ached. I gripped the phone, hard.

"Intrepid misses you," he said.

I started to cry.

"What did my doofus of a brother do? I'll beat him up! Swear."

I laughed, wiping my face with my pajama sleeve.

"Can you forgive him? He's just...he's *dumb*, June. I have to forgive him all the time! Like when he makes me listen to Amy Grant." Rory shuffled the phone around and whispered, "Moronic as he is, he misses you."

I took a breath. "Is he there?"

"KEEEEEEGANNNNNN!!!!"

***

He drove out to my house. I didn't even bother to change out of my pajamas. Just slung on a coat and got in his car.

In the car, enroute to Fayetteville, I was the first to speak. "I was mean."

A beat passed. "You? I'm the one who was mean."

"No." I shook my head, voice soft. "You weren't mean. You were telling me the truth. I didn't like it. I don't like it. I hate it. It's awful. It hurts me so badly I – I can't even tell you. But it's not *mean.*" I gazed out the window at the tops of pines, dark and stately, pointy as steeples against the deep violet of nightfall. I'd spent the past few days, in the lonesome, solemn quiet of our house, thinking this through. "There's a difference, you know? Hurting someone's feelings because you're being real, and hurting them because you're being mean. There's a difference."

"Thank you for saying that."

"What came out of me though. I called you a coward. I hit you in the face with a pillow." An anguish in me, so bad I wanted to die. "I didn't know I could do that."

"It's okay, June. You were going through a lot."

"No." I turned to him, fierce. "No matter what, it's *not* okay. Please, Keegan. Don't let me off the hook. It's good for me to be hurt about this." I wedged my hands between my knees. "There are some hurts you don't want to take from people."

Keegan flicked the turn signal as we approached his street. "In that case. You acted like a big, foul, stinking, warty toad head. Don't do it again."

"Haha." And then, I did the next hard thing. "I researched more about blood transfusions. I read a bunch, and...I'm still not sure how to answer your questions. I'm thinking it over."

"Cool." He sniffed, and there was a smug note to it.

I said, "Did you know that the Hebrew word for hell, *Sheol*, and the Greek word for hell, *Hades*, both translate to *grave*? As in, the literal common grave of humanity?"

We turned into his driveway, bumping along the potholes. "I did not know."

"Ecclesiastes 9:10 says, *there is no work nor devising nor knowledge nor wisdom in Sheol*. And Romans 6:7 says, *he who has died has been acquitted from his sin*. Death is the penalty for sin. Not eternal torment. The Bible says death is a state of unconsciousness. Ecclesiastes 9:5, *for the living are conscious that they will die, but the dead are conscious of nothing at all*. According to the Hebrew word *nephesh*, the soul is the *living being*. The whole person, not a separate, immortal part that goes somewhere. I believe that after Armageddon, Jehovah God will usher in a New Earth. Paradise, the way earth was intended to be. There will be a resurrection of the dead. Until then, the dead, good and bad alike, are asleep, unconscious in the grave. I guess this is a topic for another day," as we parked.

"It sure is." He switched off the engine. "Maybe we could discuss at Flamaggio's? We'll be the sexiest couple there, having our candlelight religious debate."

"Just like the first time."

We traded smiles, and I said, "Could you do it, Keegan?"

"Do what?"

"Throw me in a fire?"

He winced. "Don't say that."

"Why not? You couldn't watch me burn?"

"Stop. Of course I couldn't."

"Think of someone you hate then. Someone you think of as evil. Think of Hitler. Could you do it to him?"

Keegan shook his head. "No. I'd just want him dead and gone."

"If you, a sinful human, couldn't inflict that kind of agony, even on someone you think of as despicable, how could your God, the one you pray to with such love?"

***

Keegan went upstairs to make cocoa and a split second later, Rory tore downstairs. He was in his pajamas, too. "Pajama party!" I said, flinging my arms open wide.

We hugged by the fireplace. "It's like swapping howdys all over again," he said.

Thump-thump-thump down the stairs. And then...

A yellow head looked in at us.

I fell to my knees on the carpet, opened my arms. She trotted over, her glitzy collar sparkling up a storm. She licked the tears off my face.

"Oh yeah," Rory said. "I forgot to mention. Grits missed you, too."

Rory sank down beside me. We petted her together. "I wasn't expecting much for Christmas this year. But Grits...she's the best Christmas present I've ever gotten." I didn't bother to correct him about Grits being a Christmas present. I carefully ignored the Christmas tree they'd set up, tall and twinkling in the corner of the room. It was, every year, a real challenge for me to ignore the sequined shimmer of that tree, the whole gorgeous spectacle of a tainted hybrid holiday, Christian (Son of God) and Pagan (Sun God) cleverly but irreverently fused. *What about weddings?* Keegan's question, stuck like a thumb tack in my brain. Rory glanced at me. "Keegan said she was your neighbor's dog. But I know she was really yours. So, thank you."

My heart cracked open. "She couldn't have found a better home than with you, Rory."

He jumped up, padded over to the tree, and came back with a present. Shiny silver paper decorated with Ninja Turtles in Santa hats. "From me. You can open it now. If you want."

"Oh, Rory. It's beautiful. But I don't celebrate Christmas. I can't accept a gift."

His face fell. "Oh yeah."

"I should've told you."

He thunked his forehead with his palm. "Duh! I forgot."

"You can give it to me later. A day that's not a holiday?"

A small smile. "Okay. Yeah."

He sat again, checking on Intrepid, her cage set on the floor near the fireplace. She munched beet shreds with calm concentration, beak outlined in what looked like glamourous red lipstick. She was brave *and* a knock out. Grits rolled over on the soft carpet, and Rory rubbed her belly. She had a home now. She had this great little human to love her. She had everything.

Rory watched me closely. "Are you and Keegan made up? He still won't tell me what he did. I bet it was about religion, wasn't it. I swear, when the Lord put you two together, He was on acid."

"Rory!" I stifled a laugh.

"Before he turned Christian, my dad was a hippie. He told me once he did acid and saw a spider this tall." He raised up on his knees, held his hand over my head.

"Really?"

"Yeah! The spider was in the bathtub." He sat back down, hugged his knees.

"Soaking in a bubble-bath?"

"Yep. With candles, drinking champagne."

I laughed, ruffling his hair. "Where do you come up with this stuff?"

He tapped the side of his head. "Believe it or not, I'm a pretty quiet kid. Ask Keegan. The only person I ever liked to talk to before was my dad." He set his chin on his knee. "Did you know? My mom's a drug addict. She left when I was a baby."

"That's sad."

"You're lucky to have a mom. She makes you cookies! I didn't even think that was a real thing, moms making cookies. They're good, too. Tell her thanks, from me, for all the cookies she sends home with Keegan. I even kind of like the weird plant things she puts in them. And tell her," he dropped his voice, "her cooking lessons *saved* me. I don't have to stuff bean concrete in my pockets anymore!"

"I'll tell her." Then, "You put bean soup in your pockets?"

He grinned. "Do *I* get to meet your mom soon?"

"Well, someday. She's sad right now. Her dad's really sick."

"Oh." Rory's face darkened. He looked down, pet Grits harder. "Did you know my dad died in this room?"

The air punched out of me. "I...no."

"Well, it's true. He died. Deader than a door nail. Did you know he told us Jesus would heal him? Well, guess what. That didn't happen. Do you know how I know? Because I'm the one who found him down here on the couch. He wasn't healed. He was dead. I mean *cold*, and deader than dead."

I couldn't breathe. "Rory."

He jumped up, ran into the adjoining workshop. Grits stood, trotted after him. After a moment, I got up, too, and followed. I found Rory sitting cross-legged on the concrete floor, in a little pile of wood shavings. He gazed up at the unfinished rocking chair on its platform. The little shiny tools in a patient row, waiting.

I sank down on a stool behind him. My eyes roved the walls. For the first time, I noticed the artwork pinned everywhere, like a personal gallery. Crayoned stick figures and animals, messy watercolor landscapes, rough sketches of furniture being built, a pencil drawing of a man with a beard, hammering together a golden bookshelf.

Rory's art, the collection.

On the floor, Grits nuzzled Rory's arm until he gave in, hugged her close.

"Did you know? Dad was making that chair for me." He turned. His eyes, the tears on his face, shone bright in the dark. "Did Keegan tell you? Dad was making the chair for me. So I could sit and draw in his workshop. Did Keegan even tell you? It was supposed to be for Christmas!" With a cry, he shot to his feet. He shoved the chair off the platform. It crashed onto the floor.

Grits slunk, tail between her legs, beneath the work bench.

Rory kicked the chair. It spun, smashed into the wall. "I *hate* Jesus!"

I slid from the stool, and went to him. I held him in my arms. He broke down sobbing into my pajama shirt. His shudders felt like my own heartbeat. I rubbed his back.

Keegan, holding a tray of drinks, watched frozen from the doorway.

He met my eyes, and I watched his face harden.

***

"I think it was a good thing," I said, latching and unlatching my fingers in the passenger seat as Keegan drove me back home.

"A good thing? Are you serious? He said he *hates* Jesus. Why would he say that?"

The way he looked at me. Accusing. "Because I've brainwashed him? Obviously."

"I didn't say that."

"But that's what you think."

"It's more complicated than that. This past week, June, when we weren't talking, all I wanted was to drive to your house and set up camp beneath your window. I want to be near you all the time. I want to touch you. Kiss you. Talk with you. Every second. But I also want you to be free, to make your choices. I thought, after we talked about hell, you didn't want me. I was trying to come to terms with that. Then Rory. He keeps pushing me about you, about us. He won't back off. One morning over breakfast, he announced, 'June was right. Jehovah *is* God's name. I've been researching. How can Jehovah be God, and also Jesus?' Then we go to church. He starts pushing my buttons. Questioning everything our pastor says. Why this and why that. He's been listening to us. He thinks he can start doing what we do."

"Can't he?"

"No, he can't! He's nine-years-old. He's a kid."

"He's not *your* kid though."

"I still have a responsibility to him. This Sunday, Rory refused to get up for church. He said he didn't want to go. Said it was his choice." Keegan rubbed his temple with his thumb, let out a laugh. "Yeah, no. Dad never let church be our choice. We argued, and when he wouldn't budge, I forced him out of bed. He fought back. He hit me, screamed in my face. I yanked down his pants. I *spanked* him, June. Hard." His voice broke.

"Keegan." I set my hand on his knee.

"He hates me, and he's turning his back on the Lord. I can't let that happen." He shook his head. "I can handle our conversations. But Rory? He needs my protection."

"What are you saying?"

"I think…I need some time to think."

broken

A broken heart could make you sick.

I knew that already, though, didn't I.

I was trying my best to stifle the sounds, my head hanging over the toilet, when the phone rang. I flushed the toilet, curled up, knees to chest, on the bathroom mat. The phone rang and rang.

"Somebody get it!" Mom yelled from her room. "Get it, please!"

Dad was at work. Rain was taking her last final. I tried to move. My body was weak, fragile. The phone kept ringing. I sat up, head swimming. I held onto the cold toilet.

Mom's door burst open. She stomped down the hallway. "Where are you people!"

A few minutes later, the house filled with the chilling sound of a low wail. A sound, like something from a bad dream. I pulled myself to my feet, gripping the sink. I washed my mouth out. I opened the door, peered into the dark kitchen. Mom was on her knees, on the kitchen floor, long hair falling around her like a black curtain. She'd dropped the phone and it dangled, off the hook. I crept toward her, down the hall-way. On her knees, her head pushed into her hands, all she could do was make those terrible sounds. I grabbed the phone where it had fallen, pushed buttons in a daze.

"Dad? I think you need to come home."

***

That evening, Rain and I huddled together on her bed, her quilt drawn around us.

Mom was in the bath. The house reeked of bleach. Dad had conferred with us briefly. *The Old Man passed*, he told us. *Your mother's having flashbacks to her childhood.*

He told us he'd drawn her a bath doused with Clorox bleach. This was one of the new therapies he'd learned. *Bleach baths pull toxins trapped in the cells, including old trauma.* The poison of Mom's past, dispersed through the house. *Press a towel under the door, so you don't breathe it in.*

We pressed a towel under the door, but it didn't help. Bleach stung my eyes, the back of my throat. Rain rubbed her head. "I'm getting a headache. Are you getting a headache?"

I shook my head, numb all over. "Do you think bathing in bleach – do you really think it heals trauma?"

Rain closed her eyes briefly. "I think Dad's in denial and, like always, he wants us to play along..." she bit back the rest, glanced at me. "I think he's desperate. That's what I think." We sat in silence. Finally, she turned to me with a solemn face. "There's something I should tell you. I got a job on campus. I'll be working at the coffee shop in Arkansas Union. I won't be here most of the week. I don't want you to be here alone with them right now. Can you stay with Keegan?"

"No. We're not – he said he needs time." I stared straight ahead. I didn't even have the wherewithal to blink. "He's never coming back, Rain."

"Are you sure? June, are you *sure*? Maybe it's not code. Maybe he actually needs time to think. Maybe, hard as it is to fathom, he's not just abandoning you?"

I shook my head firm, then dropped my forehead onto her shoulder.

"God," she said. "It's all crashing down."

***

The next morning, Dad opened my door, looked in at me while I slept.

Clorox slammed my senses.

I woke up fast, tugged my shirt up over my nose. I didn't want the toxins inside me. "Mom's taking another bath," Dad said. His face was haggard, full of new lines. "You might hear her crying, or even yelling. I gave her a washcloth and told her to hit the bathtub if she gets angry. It's called a release. Don't be scared. Bad memories are leaving her body. Get her a towel, stay with her. If you need me, page me. Here's my emergency number."

He left a slip of paper on my desk.

***

I stayed in my room, rolled up a sweatshirt and pressed it under the door. At my desk, I revolved my globe, pausing at Ireland, touching my finger to the little green island I loved. I could go there. I could try. I closed my eyes. There I was. On the Cliffs of Moher. Gray sea. Gray sky. It was raining. A soft rain. I looked up into the sky. The rain grew furious, drenched me. I was all alone in the world again. I didn't want to dance. I spun in circles, close to the edge. I hurt. I hurt. I hurt.

Rain's door creaking open startled me. I snapped up, at my desk, alert, listening.

Drawers opening, then slamming shut.

I stood, yanked my sweatshirt from beneath the door, threw it aside. I twisted the knob, opened my door, very slowly. Rain's door, ajar. The *whisk!* of her closet, thrown open. I crept across the hall, peered into her room.

Mom wore a t-shirt and jeans. Her hair was still wet, though neatly braided down her back. The room stank of Clorox, mingled with lavender. On her hands and knees, she pulled a box from Rain's closet, opened it, dumped the contents onto the carpet. "I'm cleaning," she said, out of nowhere.

I startled. I didn't know she knew I was there.

"Yes, *June*, I know you're there, *June*. You're not that sneaky." She sent me a look over her shoulder. She plucked up a fancy necklace, looked it over. "What's this? Did you get her this?"

"No."

Mom laughed. "Dumb question. You don't have any money, do you?" She threw the necklace back in the box. She picked through the other stuff on the floor. "Your sister thinks she can live here, rent free, and treat us all like crap. Do you know what princess did this morning? She left a huge pile of dirty dishes in the sink. For me. After my dad dies!" She looked up at me, spat through her teeth. "I've had *enough*! I'm done tip-toeing around her, trying to play nice. She's hiding something and I know it." She shoved the box back into the closet. "What's that look on your face?"

"Nothing."

"Bull! You know something." She rose to her feet, coming towards me.

"I don't know anything."

She stood in front of me. "Well *I* know something. You want to know what *I* know?" She pushed her chin in the air. She circled me, looked me up and down, triumphant. Like a little girl on the playground, parading a secret. "I know you and Keegan *stole* the neighbor's dog."

All my hairs stood on end. My mouth opened. The words shot from me. "The only thing I know about are Rain's magazines."

"Magazines?"

"Under her bed."

"Is that so? Well, let's take a look, shall we?" Mom got down on her hands and knees. I felt sick, watching her pull out Rain's secret stash. *Promise not to tell,* Rain had said. *I promise*, I had said.

"What the *hell* are you doing in my room?"

Rain walked in, stood beside me, car keys clenched in her fist.

Mom jerked her head up. Her eyes glittered. "Oh, girlie. No, no, no. You see, this is *my* room. Everything in it, I've bought. Except for this!" She held up a copy of *Cosmopolitan*, the big-haired, full-lipped model on the cover, silky black shirt falling seductively off her shoulders, lacy black bra and ample cleavage on display. "You bring this filth into *my* house?" Mom stood, nostrils flaring. She jabbed a finger at Rain. "I knew you weren't a good person. I knew it! You're sneaky and two-faced, just like my sister, Rena. I've been trying to tell people that for years!"

Rain stared, colorless, shaking her head. "What did I ever do to you?"

"You *use* me! You make me your slave!"

"We're your slaves." Rain muttered it.

"What did you say?" Mom's eyes turned to slits. She stepped closer, curled her hands into fists.

Rain's face shook. "You don't care about us. You care about the power you have over us."

"How could you." Tears rose in Mom's eyes. "You've hurt

me so bad. You've ripped my heart out." Her chest heaved.

"Ripped *your* heart out? All you ever see is your pain. What about you yanking out your blue suitcase like a weapon, threatening me with it. I'll never forget you packing, telling me it was my fault." Tears fell left and right down Rain's face. "I was five!"

Mom staggered, like she'd been shot. "You *lie*. I did no such thing! What is wrong with you? Ever since you were a kid, you've been mean to me. Horrible. Now you look me in the eye and make up a story, try to destroy me in front of your little sister." Mom turned to me, and her face grew soft, pleading. "June." She held out her hand. "You don't believe her, do you?"

I became aware of my body, standing beside Rain's. I became aware of our pinky fingers. How they had found each other, and entwined. Now, I felt hers tighten around mine.

"June," Mom said again. She clasped and unclasped her outheld hand, summoning me.

I tugged my pinkie from Rain's. I put my hand in Mom's hand. She pulled me close. Pressed to her chest, I screwed my eyes shut. "Look," Mom said, squeezing me to her. "You can't turn June against me. You know why? June has a good heart. A *pure* heart. An evil heart can't turn a pure heart."

Sickness crawled up from my gut, sat in my throat.

Mom said, "It was your sister who found your dirty magazines. Your sister who led me to them."

I turned my head to look at Rain. Her two big eyes touched mine, full of shock, brimming with pain. *June*. She mouthed it. *June*.

I would see that for the rest of my life.

Mom kept talking. "June doesn't know the truth about you, see. She doesn't know you can't be trusted. I watched you strut around Keegan, all that makeup, boobs stuck out for the world to see. Putting on a play for him. The same way you did with your dad."

A lightning strike. The whole room lit into a blue-white blaze.

Rain screamed. She threw her keys across the room. They smashed into her dresser. "You are sick! *Get help*!"

In the middle of the night, Rain packed her bags and left.

A few days later, after some furtive detective work, I found out where she was staying.

The house was small and gray, bungalow-style, within walking distance of campus. I walked up the cement porch steps, knocked on the door. Braced. Fortunately, I had years of practice waiting tensely on doorsteps.

I knew that when the door opened, it would be him.

"May I help you?" He stared at me, pushing his black, square-framed glasses further up on his nose. Blue paint speckled his hair and beard, along with the silver streaks.

"I'm here to see my sister." I wedged my hands deep into my coat pockets. A bitter wind blew. I pulled my shoulders together against the cold. "I'm June."

***

In a cozy, bright living room, near a fireplace emitting a soft glow, Rain reclined on a plush orange love seat, supported by a plethora of elaborately embroidered and tasseled pillows. A textbook was spread open on the coffee table, with a notepad and calculator nearby. She wore an oversized red Razorback Hogs hoodie with sweatpants. Her hair was up in a big, curly top knot, with a pencil stuck through it. She looked beautiful. Comfortable. Most of all, safe. She held an earthenware mug between her hands. Steam escaped from it.

"Who brought you?" Her first question, rising up to look

out the window.

"Me," I said. "I did."

"You?" She lowered herself, wide-eyed.

"Dad took Mom somewhere. I don't know where. He said they'd be gone all day. They left in his business van. So I took Mom's car."

Rain blinked. "Wild." She took a sip of tea. She didn't ask questions. She didn't invite me to sit. She drew her legs in closer, stared out the window.

I perched on the edge of the orange couch, my hands still stuck in my pockets. I thought about things I could say. They were all wrong. The worst of all, *I'm sorry*. I rooted around, and couldn't find, in any of the crevices of my brain, the words that mattered. So I just sat there, and we both looked outside, into a whole gray world, now hissing sharp bits of ice against the window pane.

All at once, she started to cry. Little, soft sounds. I glanced at her. On the coffee table, near her textbook, sat a box of Kleenex. The box had daisies on it. I picked it up, set it between us on the couch. After a minute, she took one, wiped her face. "Why are you here, June?"

"I wanted to make sure you were okay."

"I'm not okay. I'm never okay. But thanks for asking. A few years too late. Why don't you go? You should go. You don't know how to drive and the weather's bad. If Mom comes home and finds her car gone..."

"I'm not going."

"Aren't you noble."

"I didn't say I was."

"But you think you are. You're The Good One. In your heart, you've always believed it. Been *proud* of it. Clung to it like a trophy."

I dipped my chin deeper into the folds of my scarf. The fire in the fireplace spit and popped.

"I saw how differently you were always treated. I thought it was because I was defective. I thought if I worked at it, if I tried harder, if I were *better*, I could make her love me. So I cooked dinner. I did the dishes. I did the ironing, even Dad's. You'd run outside to play, and I'd be inside. Vacuuming. Dusting. Cleaning the whole house, wiping the crumbs off your chair. She'd be happy with me for a minute. Not for long. I always messed up, set her off again. The worst was, the way you'd look at me. I could see it on your face. You blamed me for the fights. Maybe, you still do."

I latched and unlatched my fingers. Sometimes Rain was mean, sarcastic and cutting. Sometimes she had a spiteful attitude. She could roll her eyes like no one else. Sometimes she did things, like the silent treatment, on purpose. Some of the things Mom said about her, were true. My head was a tumult. "I can't even think," I said.

"This summer, when it happened to you, I had hope. I thought you'd finally understand. I thought, I'll have an ally. We can help each other. Then Mom came home, and I had to sit there and watch you run right back into her arms. I knew exactly what that meant for us, for me." She met my eyes, and her face twisted with pain.

It made me frantic. "Mom came home. I got sick. You and I went to school. And then I met Keegan. There was so much to process and then it felt like...everything could get better."

Rain sat there while I talked, shaking and shaking her head. "You and Dad. The two of you." She flicked her eyes at me. "When I was sixteen, I grew boobs. It was weird. It freaked me out. I went from an AA, wearing boy undershirts, to a double D, overnight. That's what it felt like. Mom acted embarrassed, jealous even. I had no one to help me make sense of it. At school, guys flirted with me. I felt excited, and so ashamed. I didn't know what to do. At kingdom hall, I was told to cover up, be modest. Otherwise, I was an evil temptress, like Potiphar's wife. I felt so shitty about having boobs! I got my first bathing suit on our trip to Myrtle Beach. It was a one-piece, and I wore a jacket over it. Just to be sure I was modest enough. But then one night I overheard Mom and Dad arguing. Mom accused Dad of *looking* at me in my bathing suit. She told him I was wearing a jacket because of him! After that, he ignored me. Not just on the trip, but for years. He really only talked to you. You hung out with him in his shop and he took you on fishing trips. But he stopped talking to me, stopped taking me places, or being anywhere with me alone. Haven't you noticed, Dad and I *never* talk?" Her voice cracked.

My gut roiled. "I didn't know any of this."

"You don't want to know! You want to think you live in a book. Just like Dad with religion and his big Mom-healing mission. It's the same way you escape into your books or stupid daydreams."

"Rain," I said. "I've had to survive, too."

The words hung between us. Then she lowered her eyes and shifted away. I kept trying.

"Rain, I haven't had your experience. I'm sorry, but I haven't. I'm not you. I can't think like you. I don't even know... what I think."

A hard smile. "You don't have to know. Most of the time, you get what you want from her."

Because I give her everything. Sharp words I didn't say. Instead,

I rested my hand on her sock foot, squeezed. "Who is he? The guy you're staying with?"

"Hank."

"*Hank?*"

"*Dr.* Hank, okay?" She laughed. And my heart flew in circles. Laughing had always reunited us. "There," she pointed to an easel in the corner I hadn't noticed a pencil drawing propped up. It was a sketch of a nude woman with curly hair, and large breasts.

"Wait." A shock zipped up and down my spine. I clapped my hands over my eyes. "Holy crap. That's *you!*"

"Watch your mouth." She smirked. "Hank's an art professor. I met him on the job. Posing pays really well."

My hands still over my eyes, I danced my feet up and down. "I thought you worked at a coffee shop."

"I do. Part-time barista. Part-time nude. Seeing a professor thirty years older than me."

My mouth fell open. "That's...a lot."

Rain shrugged. "I would tell you not to tell, but I know better. And I guess it doesn't matter now, if you go blab."

My stomach sickened. I dropped my hands from over my eyes. "Rain. I did wrong. I was so scared."

"Yeah," she said, picking at a fingernail. "It's my fault really. I should've known. It's what we do, isn't it? Our own little family tradition." She raised her eyes to mine. "Throwing each other into the volcano."

***

On the way home, I drove by a kingdom hall. It was a meeting night, and the parking lot was packed. My first thought was, *it's true, no windows.* I laughed to myself. My second thought was, *I can go.*

I went.

In my jeans and boots, my heavy coat, I strode toward the doors. They would think I was a worldly person, drifting in to listen. I'd get lots of looks, and lots of love.

Well, I needed that.

So, for the first time in six months, I stepped inside a kingdom hall, my heart thudding. An Elder shook my hand, welcomed me warmly, took my coat. The talk was just starting. I sat in the back. I swept my gaze around, melting with recognition. Brothers and sisters, dressed up in suits and dresses, sitting in rows of metal folding chairs. The crinkling of pages as everyone turned to Revelation 19:15.

Down the aisle, hand to hand, an extra Bible was passed to me.

A brother with a handlebar moustache, wearing a tan felt cowboy hat that matched his suit, smiled, winked, nodded. *Thank you,* I mouthed. I thought about Sister Finn, the way she'd always cared for me. Maybe she still did, a little. Maybe I would call her. Maybe I would try. Tears pricking my eyes, I turned to the scripture. *From His mouth comes a sharp sword, so that with it He may strike down the nations, and He will rule them with a rod of iron.*

"On the Last Day, brothers and sisters, one headline will dominate."

I looked up at the Elder on stage, delivering the talk.

"Death and Destruction!" He thundered into the microphone, throwing his arms out wide. "In America and Antarctica, Death and Destruction. In the Fiji Islands, Death and Destruction. In Costa Rica, Spain, Iceland and China,

Death and Destruction." He dropped his arms, gripped the sides of the podium. "Armageddon, brothers and sisters. God's War. When the evil, the immoral, the unbelievers will perish! When those clinging to their sin, their False Religions and False Gods, must face the sword! When fire rains from the sky, their screams will fill the earth. Jehovah's ears and heart now closed to them, there will be no safe place for them. Nowhere to run. Nowhere to hide. Death and Destruction! World-wide. And the birds shall fly from near and far to feast upon their flesh."

The congregation looked up another scripture, while I gathered my things.

I left the Bible on my seat, grabbed my coat from the closet, and walked out.

The day after the Old Man's funeral, Grandma called. She talked to Mom for a long time, then asked to talk to me. I steeled myself. Grandma had a bad cold. That, along with a heavy heart, suppressed her usual gusto. She said, in a hoarse voice, "Juney. I've been wanting to talk with you for ages."

"Hi, Grandma. Are you okay?"

"I'm tough as an old ox! At least, I have a butt like one." She laughed, then broke down coughing. "Himmel, himmel," she said.

I wanted to reach through the phone and hold onto her forever.

"Thank you for the tape, Juney. It's the most beautiful gift anyone has ever given me. I'm *obsessed.* Do you know what? I make everyone watch it. Everyone! The other day, I made the mail-lady watch. By the way, you have a new fan. Aunt Rena thinks you're the best thing since sliced bread. It's the only thing we've ever agreed on. Don't tell your mom. How was the dance, sweetheart?" She blew her nose.

"It was a beautiful dream come true, Grandma." Sparks of pain flew around in my chest. I rubbed my hand over my heart. I hadn't told Mom about Keegan and me. I couldn't. Even though, she was calmer now. Dad was treating her with what he called "brain tones," sounds at different frequencies, another therapy he'd learned. He claimed that the sounds rewired a traumatized brain. Mom listened to them faithfully, while cleaning and making dinner. The day before, I'd wandered into the kitchen to get lunch, only to find Mom sitting in a chair with a blanket around her, ashen, shaking from head to toe. Dad stood behind her, massaging her shoulders. In the background, brain tones played, like a giant mosquito solo. Dad had pulled me aside, and with sharp, excited eyes, confided that she'd had a major emotional break-through.

I didn't know what that meant. Did he think she was healed now? I wished I could believe it.

None of us talked about Rain. It was surreal. Like she hadn't left. Like she hadn't *existed*.

"Keegan's the dream come true. Those dimples! Those curls. Why, he's better looking than Elvis Presley! Never thought I'd say that." Grandma paused. "The most important thing, does he treat our June like the treasure she is?"

"Yes, Grandma, he does." *Did*. It was true. Even if it was past.

Grandma sniffled. "That's not my cold. This crabby old lady's in tears. I told you, didn't I? I told you all along. I get premonitions, see. Your mom says, Keegan's a book-worm, just like you. Didn't I tell you? One day you'd turn the corner and, there he'd be, nose stuck in a book."

"Your premonition was spot on."

"Thank God for magic panty hose!"

I smiled. "Thank God for magic Grandmas."

***

Mom scrubbed the dishes, her back to me. "'You and Keegan had a fight."

I was sitting at the kitchen counter, lost in the final pages of *Christy*. Christy was deathly ill. The passionate Scottish physician, Dr. Neil MacNeill, was trying desperately to save her.

Christy was a Christian. Dr. MacNeill was an atheist. They battled about this. He was deeply in love with her. And about to lose her. Once again, my tears plopped onto the pages. I imagined they'd always be there. Like the pink crepe myrtle blossoms, stuck in the creases, from way back in August. Moments before I turned the corner, into Psychology 101, and everything changed. *Seat Thief.*

Mom came over, whisked the dish towel at me. "I know who those tears are for."

I wiped my face. "It's my book. I'm at a sad part."

"Then where's Keegan? Why hasn't he called, or come over?"

"Christmas Break." I stared at her, stricken.

Propping her elbows on the countertop, she studied me. "You know, June. Your big green eyes are a world. They lay your whole soul bare, ever since you were a little girl. Besides that, you're my daughter. You can't hide from me. I *see* your pain."

Those words. They broke me in two. I cried the truth, "We didn't fight, Mom. We just can't be together. We can't make it work." I doubled over. There'd been no room, no space to feel this, not even on my own. And now I could. Mom pulled me to her. She held me. She patted my back. She said *there, there*. She smelled like dish soap. Her hands were in my hair. *Her hands.* I loved them. I loved them in my hair.

She said, "Are you sure, June? Are you sure you're not jumping to conclusions? You do that, you know. You assume the worst. Do you want to walk? Just the two of us? I've been wanting to go down to the forest, collect vines and berries, make some winter wreaths. Will you help me? We can talk."

We can talk! Words I suddenly felt I'd been living for, growing ancient in my yearning, moss-covered, a million years.

In the laundry room, we helped each other wrestle into our coats and boots. We set off down the yard. The small ice-storm had left the grass crunchy.

"Crunch, crunch, crunch!" Mom sang, hip-bumping me. She pointed up. "Look at those angel clouds. That soft glaze of winter light." The light. The clouds. I loved her like this most of all. The way she saw beauty, and wanted to share it.

We reached the edge of the forest. Mom lifted a branch, so I could duck under. As I did, I felt her eyes on my face. She stepped in behind me, let the branch drop. It bounced, shaking off a dusting of snow. We walked down the narrow, winding path Dad had carved out and lined with wood chips. "I have to ask you something, June." Mom's voice, behind me. "Have you seen your sister?"

My heart sped up. I walked more briskly, tried to stay ahead of her on the path. "No." I dodged a grasping branch, one of the thorn trees. This forest was crammed with them. They were pretty, but once they got hold, they'd tear you to shreds. "Careful, Mom. These trees!"

"I know about the trees, June." Mom crunched closer behind me. "What is it? Did you hear something from Sister Finn?"

She sounded worried. "No. Why would I?"

"Well, good riddance to her. To both of them. *Fakes*. Who needs 'em?"

I didn't say anything. A thorn tree tried to grab my hat. I ducked, held it on my head.

"Don't fool yourself, June. Your sister treated you like dirt. You think I didn't see? She made fun of you. She mocked your looks, your hair. Got mad and wouldn't talk to you for days. She made you suffer, June, and you always forgave her. Just let it go. You were weak, and she took advantage."

My upper lip broke into a sweat. I tried to stay clear in my head. I imagined what I might say to Keegan, if I were telling him about this moment. *Rain can be hurtful, even mean, but she doesn't deserve to be cast into hell.* I breathed, in, out, in, holding that truth, protecting it in the safety of my own head. Mom pushed ahead of me, rough, her braid bouncing. I hadn't spoken up. But in a way, I had. Staying silent, instead of rushing to agree, or placate, was a way of speaking.

Mom stopped abruptly. I collided with her. "That one! I want it." She raised on tip-toe, reaching for a graceful coil of vine, swinging from one of the thorn trees. "I can't quite..."

"Here, Mom. I've got it." I jumped, grabbed the vine. I held it out to her. She whipped it from my grip, so hard, I stumbled backward. I held my raw, burning hand. "Guess what I found." She reached into the pocket of her jeans, produced a folded up piece of paper. She shoved it at me. "I wasn't going to say anything. But now I feel like I have to."

My mind raced, unfolding the paper. It took a minute for the words to unscramble. It was my first psychology exam. The big 98% in red at the top. Dr. Freeman's kind words. I choked on my own wild heartbeat. I'd stuck it in the top drawer of my desk, deep inside my journal. Mom must have gone through my things, the way she had Rain's.

"You wrote about me!" Mom said, jabbing her thumb to her chest. "You had no right, *no right*. To tell my secrets. To shame me." Her lips trembled. "My life. My dad. *Mine*. Not yours."

"I wanted to understand."

"Understand *what*?"

"You."

Her eyes darted across my face. "What on earth do you need to understand about me?"

Everything. "Why did you leave last summer?" I gave her the world inside my eyes. I let the broken pieces rise to the surface. For the first time, I let her see it all.

Her face only grew harder. "I left to protect myself. From *you!*"

She ripped my exam from my hand. She crumpled it. I saw my scrunchie, crushed in her fist, my frizz still clinging to it. I saw the Pocahontas doll, my violets poem shredded in her hair. I saw all the things we'd never talked about, but hadn't gone away. No matter how many make up cookies. *Nothing. Was ever. Forgotten.*

"I saw the truth about you, June, the moment you walked out the door on that *date*. You knew how hurt I was and away you went. Didn't look back. Walked right out the door. Not a care in the world! Had yourself a high old time. Came back and had a gossip session with my mother, didn't you? Made me look like the villain. I've tried to get over it. But I can't. I will *never* forget what you did."

"Mom, listen, please." I tried again. *Mom.* I know you're in there. *Mom.* Somewhere deep, buried under all your pain and fear like an avalanche. *Mom.* You see me. Your June. June Namid. *Mom.* Remember? I'm your Star Dancer. "Mom," I said. "I love you."

She stepped very close.

Peering deep into my eyes, she said, "I hate you."

As my cells exploded left and right, I believed her.

Footsteps in the forest behind us. Barking. I knew that barking. *Grits!*

"June? Are you down here?" *Keegan.*

Mom's head snapped up. She stepped backward, so fast she stumbled, almost fell.

Bounding around the corner, Grits appeared. She saw me, and tore down the path, wood chips flying in her wake. Keegan, right behind her, waved a bouquet of flowers, bright and bold against the dark of the woods. "June!"

Mom and I locked eyes. *Run*, she mouthed.

I ran. I bolted off the path, wildly, blindly, clawing my way through the thorn trees.

"Run, June, run!" Mom called. Her voice had turned high-pitched and playful. "Get her, Keegan! Go get her!" She laughed and clapped like a kid, like we were all playing a game.

Behind me, the crash and snap of branches, brambles. "June!" Keegan yelled.

Crying hysterically, I ripped free from a cluster of thorns. I emerged, gasping, panting, into the yard. I sprinted, arms pumping, jaw clenched, thumping up the back porch steps. I threw open the front door, fled to the bathroom. I slammed the door, twisted the lock.

Not long after. A gentle knock. "June?"

Keegan's voice.

"Go away!" I screamed it, face pressed to the door. I bashed my fist against the door, once, twice. "I hate you! *I hate you!*"

Silence. For a long time.

Then, the creak of the floor. The front door opening, closing.

Quiet. Quiet. Quiet.

I opened the door. Just a crack.

Enough to see the bouquet of pink, yellow, and orange gerbera daisies, deposited on the floor.

Their petals, shredded.

"See? Told you, didn't I? Jumping to conclusions. He's crazy in love with you as ever." Mom drove me to Keegan's house. She sped. "Tell him he shouldn't sneak up on you though. Tell him gentlemen don't drop in on a lady. They call first. What if she doesn't have her makeup on?" She laughed, a strangely pitched giggle, and nudged my knee. She wanted me to laugh, too. "That boy needs a mother!"

I directed her down the Fayetteville roads I now knew so well. "Boy oh boy," mom said, ducking to peer at the neighborhood. "He sure lives in a rough area. You never told me that." She did all the talking, and it was as fast as her driving. I picked my lips to skin-splintered pieces, tasted blood. I pointed at the tall blue house with the lace curtains in the windows. We pulled in.

"Tell him he and his brother are *both* invited for dinner tonight." She said this as I swung open the car door, climbing out. "Tell him I'll get rib-eyes for everyone. I'll teach him how to cook a steak." I didn't respond. She grabbed my arm, yanked me back inside the car. Her fingernails dug in. "Now you listen to me, little girl. You better get ahold of yourself," her voice, low and fierce. "Stop that." She shoved my hand from my lips. "Nasty habit." She whipped away, pinched the bridge of her nose, inhaled, then exhaled, shakily. She turned to me, and said in a controlled voice, "I know you care about my relationship with Keegan."

I nodded.

"He is vulnerable right now and needs a mother."

"Yes," I said.

"If you talk about me, you will ruin things between us. Do you want that?"

I shook my head. "No."

She squeezed my knee. "Tell him, steak's on at 6."

***

I knocked on the door. No one answered. I knocked again, waited. I jiggled the doorknob, realized the door wasn't locked, and walked in. "Hello?" I called in the entryway. "It's June."

"In here." Keegan's voice, from his dad's workshop.

I walked in.

He sat on a stool at his dad's workbench.

He looked up as I entered.

I stopped in my tracks. Ninja Turtle band-aids crisscrossed his face. "What...?" Then, under my breath, because I knew, "What happened?"

"What happened? I came over to see you. I thought we could go for one of our walks and talks. I called first, to make sure it was okay. No one answered. I couldn't wait. I drove to see you, and brought Grits to see you, too. I rang the doorbell. No one answered. Grits ran off, toward the forest. I followed her. You saw me, and split. I chased after you." He shook his head. "The way you and your mom acted, I thought we were all playing some sort of game. Except, no one warned me about the thorns." He looked at me. "And you screamed *I hate you.* Twice."

"I didn't mean it. I was...you snuck up on me, you startled me, and..." My eyes followed his hand to the bottle of hydrogen peroxide, open on the workbench. A little pile of cotton balls.

He plucked another from a bag. “Mom wants…tonight…she wants… to teach you how to cook steak…”

Keegan dabbed a cut under his eye, winced. “You know? I think I’m too hurt to make steaks.”

Too hurt.

I rubbed my hand over my heart, watching him affix another band-aid to his scratched up face.

Rib-eyes are make up cookies.

The truth of that bombed me.

No one warned me about the thorns, he’d said.

I’d been teaching him. How to be part of the family. How to take care of her. How to be me. But if he loved her like me, he’d be hurt like me.

I sank to the floor, but at the same time, something inside me rose up. “Keegan. I have to tell you something.”

Keegan slid off the stool and knelt beside me, his hand on my back. “It’s okay. You can tell me.”

“I can’t!” I shrieked it into my hands, spit dropping out. The fear inside me wanted to devour the truth.

Keegan rubbed my back. “I’m here,” he said.

“Mom and I were fighting.”

That wasn’t the truth. I had to dig deeper. I had to be honest in a way I never was, not even inside my own head.

“It wasn’t a fight,” I told him. “Mom was enraged. She’s enraged all the time. Even when she seems fine, or happy. Deep down, she’s enraged.”

Close.

“My mother is a person full of landmines. It doesn’t matter how hard you try, eventually, you’ll trip one. She’ll blow. You will *lose* things.”

Keep going.

"Her dad, my grandfather, was an alcoholic. She thought she protected us from him. But she didn't. Because she does to us, what he did to her. Only not with liquor. With rage."

How terrible, how real, and how it hurt!

The truth sliced me open, so that I bled stories.

"Look!" I lifted my shirt. I showed him my appendix scar. I threw my head back. And I wailed. Endless grief, let loose, flying around that room.

And truth, so much of it.

I wiped my face, nearly hysterical, then grabbed onto Keegan's arm. "She'll name you Namid. She'll call you her Star Dancer. She'll feed you violets. She'll write you love notes on butterfly sugar cookies. She'll take care of you when you're sick. She'll teach you to read. She'll massage lavender on your wrist. She'll dance with you, barefoot in the grass. She'll point at the clouds and call them angels. And one day a year, she'll bake you the world's most beautiful pie." I looked at him. My friend. My best friend. My Naomi, whom I loved. "Keegan, she'll make you love her, and then she'll *hurt* you."

Keegan took my hands in his. He bowed his head, touching his forehead to our hands.

I whispered, "Don't hate her."

He didn't say anything. "Please." I shook our clasped hands. "Keegan, please don't hate her. Her dad just died. Her heart is good. She's gone through horrible things..."

He looked at me, pained. "I don't hate her, June."

"Don't tell her I told you. Don't let on you know. *Please.*"

He shook his head. "June..."

"Please, Keegan!"

"June." He took my wet face between his hands, held it steady. "Your mother abuses you."

Silence grew thick between us.

And then, I threw that word from me like fire.

"No." I scooted backward across the floor, away from him. "No. You didn't listen. I said she *never* hit me. Didn't you hear?"

"I heard." He held my eyes, even as I pressed my back against the wall.

"Then why! Why are you using that word!" I pounded the floor with my fists. I'd learned about abuse. I knew what abuse was. Parents who lost it. Slammed their kid against a wall. Punched them. Hit, kicked, slapped. Broke their child's arm or nose. Black eyes. Later, they lied in the emergency room, coached their kids to lie. *Abuse*. It was horrific. Beyond comparison. How could he?

Without a word, Keegan's eyes drifted down, down. I followed his gaze. To the bottom of my shirt, rolled up.

I saw what Keegan saw.

A scar. Only three inches long. Pink now, neatly healing.

Beyond the scar, a deeper truth.

Pain.

Something broken.

Hurt, inside.

Hurt, never the same.

Keegan's car wasn't even halfway down our drive when I set my hand on the handle, prepared to jump out. On the way to Hopeton, We'd fabricated a story. We'd tell her Rory was sick. The flu. Keegan had to stay home with Rory. Keegan was getting sick, too.

Maybe that was too much. She'd know. If it were too much, *she'd know.*

I couldn't get out in time. Mom must have been watching for us. She stepped onto the porch, waving her heart out. "No. Oh no. Oh no." I buried my face in my hands as she walked across the yard to meet us, her long black hair whisking this way and that in the wind.

Keegan rolled down the window. "Come on, kids!" She motioned for us to get out. Cheeks pink in the cold, she danced her feet up and down. "Brrrr, hurry, let's get inside! Keegan, I've got four of the dreamiest rib-eyes..." her eyes flicked to the backseat. "Your brother didn't come?"

Keegan said, "He's got a fever. I think it might be the flu." His lower lip trembled.

I watched her face change as she registered Keegan's band-aids. His anxiety. *She knew.* I knew she knew. We locked eyes. Both of us, knowing.

She slid her eyes from me, back to Keegan. "Keegan," she said, sweetly. "Come inside, will you, please? Let's talk. Just you and me."

"Sure." Keegan slid the keys from the ignition. He understood not to look at me, not even a glance. Climbing out, he let her hook arms with him as they crossed the yard. I sat, reeling, watching them step through the front door, into the house.

With his impeccable timing, Dad drove down the driveway. I slunk low in the seat. He parked and after a minute, the door swung open. He climbed out with his briefcase and stack of paperwork. He strode toward the house. He looked in high spirits, whistling.

I stayed put. The sky grew heavier, grayer. The air, colder. I hugged myself, starting to shiver, and in my head, counting down. *Five, four, three, two, one...*

Dad stalked out of the house, still clutching his briefcase and paperwork.

No more whistling. His face was drawn and grave. He jumped back into his van, fired the engine. He crept up the drive, turned onto the neighborhood road, and was gone.

Escaping, again.

And again, I could not.

I flung open the car door, pressed out, into a surge of cold wind that tasted like snow. I let myself into the back door, through the laundry room, and stepped up into the kitchen. I gazed around, taking in the skillet and steaks, along with the cutting board and several pearly cloves of garlic. Keegan's gingham apron waiting on the back of the chair. The dining room table set beautifully, with candles lit, melting down. Into my awareness crept a low steady hum. Mom's CD of brain tones, playing. I wondered if she'd been listening to it while preparing everything, or if Dad had pressed 'play' before running out the door.

Mom's voice came from the living room.

I crept into Dad's study, and listened.

"Keegan. It's not fair. You've only heard *her* story, *her* side of things. You don't know the whole story."

"Okay, tell me," Keegan said.

"Oh, I'll tell you, all right."

The mean in her voice. I went rigid. My scalp prickled.

"She's self-centered. She only thinks about what *she* wants. You think you can trust her? She'll hurt you in a heartbeat to get her way."

"That's not what I've seen."

"Of course you haven't! You're her boyfriend. Do you think she's going to show you her bad side? I'm her mother. I'm the only one who really knows June. You've known her a few months, Keegan, and you think you know her better than her own mother?"

"Yes," Keegan said.

Yes. Just like that. Calm and firm. I knew him. I knew he'd looked her right in the eye and said it. He had no idea. He was going to die.

"June and I talk constantly," he said.

"I don't care what you do! You don't have to live with her. And you *spoil* her. I watch you! I've spent all these years trying to help June be the best person she can be. I'm honest with her. I set her straight. I point out her flaws. Then you come along and make her think she can do no wrong. You're ruining her, Keegan. Behind your back, she's angry. She's out of control!"

A beat passed. "Are you talking about June, or you?"

Like before a tornado, the air went silent, lethal.

And then.

"HOW DARE YOU!"

I flew into the room. "No! Stop!"

Mom had her chair raised over her head. She brought it crashing down on the coffee table.

SMASH!

Keegan's arm flew across his face as chair fragments flew.

Before I could act, Mom dropped hard onto her knees. She crawled. On her hands and knees, she crawled like a baby across the floor. To Keegan on the couch, leaned away, breathing hard, shielding his face.

Mom set her hands on Keegan's knees. Dropping his arm, he stared at her, the band-aids bright against his ashy skin, his eyes open wide.

She bared her teeth, and hissed, "From now on, no matter what I say or do, know this. *You are my enemy.*"

***

Keegan drove too fast.

I couldn't see straight.

The world was spinning away.

A garbage bag was tucked between my feet, torn, spilling the things I had thrown in. Mostly books, a lake of books spreading around my feet. "Keegan," I said. "I think I might be sick. Can we pull over?"

Keegan flicked on the turn signal and we slid into a space in a parking lot.

I breathed, slow and deep, in and out.

Keegan still had no color in his face. "June," he said, looking around in a daze. "What *was* that?"

I stared out the windshield, unseeing. *What was that?* The unsolved mystery of my life. *What was that?* No one else's mother. *What was that?* Not even in a book. *What was that?* Not even the holy tree that held and consoled me knew the answer. *What was that?* I didn't think, my whole life, I would ever know the answer.

I sat there, whimpering.

Keegan grabbed me in his arms. We held onto each other. We stayed that way for a long time. "Hey," Keegan said finally, "isn't that your dad's van?"

My eyes opened, gripped by a bright white graphic of a vertebral column, and the words *Good Spine*.

I pulled away. "I'll be right back."

***

I stood in the entry, looking and listening, feeling this place that had once been mine.

The crackling basket of french fries, swooped fresh and glistening from the grease. The swish and flurry of cashiers in blue Polo shirts, straight black slacks, and visors. The callback to the cooks, a song. The cooks sliding burgers into the warming bin. And there, gleaming at me. *My old register.*

Behind it, a cute freckled girl with sandy hair in a pony tail pulled through the back of a visor, tapped the keys, then swiveled to briskly cap a drink. I flexed my fingers, feeling in my own hands the soul-satisfying crinkle of the lid.

I craned to the kitchen, looking for a familiar glower and bristly chin. Of course she wasn't there. None of them would be. This was the night crew. I sank to my feet, and allowed the grief to rise.

Becky, and Janet.

Maggie, and Mikey.

Old Farmer Henry.

Family.

I turned, swept my eyes around the restaurant.

He was sitting alone in a side booth. One with a wall phone, for the truckers who wandered in, more homesick than hungry, at midnight. When I slid in across from him, he startled. Set his pen down. "What are you doing here?" Thick eyebrows drawn together. Recently, along with a sudden sprouting of gray in his unruly sideburns, he'd acquired a pair of reading glasses. He glowered at me from behind them.

"What are *you* doing here?"

Dad took off his glasses, cleaned them with a corner of his rumpled red work shirt. *Good Spine*, and *Phil Taylor, DC*, stitched in shiny white thread above the pocket. I took in his large coffee and ten-piece McNuggets meal, crispy golden fries spilling from the grease-stained container. Forms fanned out neatly across the table. He was in the middle of paperwork, and clearly set up for the long haul. My skin went cold and clammy with a sudden knowing. "Dad. Is this your second office?"

"What?" Voice brusque, he turned his face away, eyes following an 18-wheeler, lit up like a city as it whined into the fuel station outside.

"Do you ever come here, instead of home? Or, do you ever leave home and come here?"

Dad bit down on the inside of his cheek, eye twitching.

"I get it, if you do," I whispered. "This place was my sanctuary, too."

His face cracked. He thunked his elbows down onto the table, pushed his head into his hands. He cried. He cried so hard, his shoulders shook.

I sat paralyzed.

I'd never in my life seen my dad cry.

And he was suddenly so small. So alone.

I'd never once in my life seen him with a friend.

I didn't think he even had a tree.
Did he?
I moved to his side of the booth.
I patted and patted his back.

I woke up, cradled in warmth.

In Keegan's arms, my head on his chest. His hand, resting gently on my stomach. His heartbeat, singing to me. This boy. This friend. This comfort. This connection. This safety. This joy. I lay so still, soaking in the immensity, the wonder, my heart full of mountaintops.

Then, from another room, the phone rang. My body shrunk, turned into a knot.

Each ring drilled terror deeper into my gut.

The answering machine played.

You've reached the Callahan's, leave us a message!

I waited. A soft click. Then, the reprieve of silence.

I let out an exhale from the bottom of my soul, and sat up. Keegan and I were on the blue couch downstairs. Keegan's head, propped up on pillows. Auburn curls falling across his forehead, he looked like a sunrise. I wanted to kiss him, warm, soft, and deep, melting into bliss. I wished, how I wished.

Instead, I rose, went to the windows. The raw agony inside me was also waking up. So vibrant, it felt alive, clawed. I had to go back. There was no other choice. I pulled aside the long, lace curtain. A breathtaking swirl of fat snowflakes fell, whirling, from a castle of gray-blue clouds. The driveway was already a glorious bank of white, Keegan's car completely enclosed.

The realization. We weren't going anywhere.

I let the curtain fall, and sank, shaky-legged, into a chair. I drew my knees to my chest, rocked back and forth.

Rocking chair.

My eyes flew open. The rocking chair! The half-finished one on the platform. The one Rory's Dad had been making for him – was *made*. A big, shiny red bow was tied through the back slats. My eyes went to Keegan, still sleeping on the couch. I slid my hand over the seat, absorbing every little roughness and imperfection.

The thump of feet down stairs, and the jingle-jingle of tags.

I threw my arms around her, held her face, kissed her and kissed her. She was getting round, her fur warm and sweet-smelling. Attached to her bedazzling collar, a new gold tag, heart-shaped. I picked it up. Her name, what was always her real name, engraved. *Grits*.

"June?" Rory peered at me from around the corner, rubbing his eyes. "Is that you. Or am I dreaming?"

"It's me," I whispered. For as long as it lasted, I decided I would give myself to joy. "We've got a snow day."

***

Bundled up in coats, hats, and boots, we all ran outside, jumped off the porch, shrieking, into the snow. The sky, so dark at 3 pm, the streetlights flickered on. No cars. No people. The whole world, ours.

We dashed into the empty road.

Rory wheeled round and round, arms out. He'd stuck a knit hat on his head. It was too big, falling over his eyes. *Dad's hat*, he'd said. He broke into a sprint, and Grits chased after him, kicking up snow with her hind legs, like a deer.

Keegan slid up beside me. He pulled me close. The giant and the garden gnome. Even so, our hips locked. "Feel that?" Keegan said.

"Click click."

We walked like that, down the middle of the snowy, empty road, our hips perfectly nestled. I looked up at him. He looked down at me. He, too, wore a knit hat, one with a funny ball on top. His curls pressed, dark and damp against his face. The beautiful dimpled square of his chin. The deepening blue of his eyes, lashes glistening with snowflakes.

"You are my tree," I told him.

"What?" He stopped walking.

I took off my mitten, and with one finger, gently touched the cleft in his chin. "I woke up cradled by you. You've become my favorite place in the world. The warmth, the solace. It was why I always went to clapping tree. You, Keegan. You are warm and strong. You are more like a tree than any human I've ever known."

Keegan looked at me with an intensity of tenderness that might have melted the snow. My body. The whole world. I backed up, struck shy, uncertain. I loved him. I would always love him. I wanted to love him with all of me and everything I had to give. But I didn't know what we were to each other. What we could be. I slid my mitten back on, kicked at the snow. "You finished the rocking chair for Rory."

"Well, let's say I tried. I'd built some chairs with Dad before. I had some idea how to do it. Still, it's pretty imperfect."

"Can he sit in it?"

"Yeah. But I don't think he'll sit in it and talk to me, the way he did with Dad."

"He'll talk to you, the way he would with *you*."

"You mean, tell me all the ways I don't stack up?"

"Maybe. And then someday, he'll unfold himself from that very chair, tall like you. Growing a beard to hide his freckles.

He'll be on his way to school, to study psychology, so he can be a strong, wise presence for kids like him, teaching them to fly. But before he goes, he'll turn to you. He'll say *thanks, bro, for the bean concrete*. You'll look at each other, for a long time."

Keegan's eyes shone. "That's a beautiful prophecy. One thing though. Will you be there, too?" He caught my hand, pressed it to his cheek. The rough bandage there, covering his wounds, a kick in the heart.

"I don't know what's going to happen, Keegan. I think she meant it." I looked in his eyes. "From now on, you'll be her enemy."

"She was becoming like a mom to me."

"I know. I'm so sad, and so sorry..."

He tucked his hand under my chin. "Look at me." I did, through tears, and he smiled. "I'm grateful to you. Our conversations have pushed me to be honest, even when it's terrifying. The last couple weeks, I've tried telling *myself* the hard truth. Rory, too. I drove us out to the cemetery where Dad's... where Dad's buried. We sat together for a while. Then I said the words. 'Dad died.' I said them out loud. I said, 'Dad told us Jesus would heal him. He believed that. He believed so powerfully that faith would protect us, he didn't have insurance, or savings, or a plan for the house, or for you. He wasn't healed. He wasted away before our eyes. And he died. Now we have each other, a mortgage, and medical debt. This is our reality.'" Keegan wiped his face. "It sucked to say it. It hurt so bad. But also, it's been better. Rory stopped drawing that picture. He untied Dad's cushion from the chair at the head of the table. He still won't let me sit there. That's Intrepid's new place." He laughed, then looked me full in the eye. "I know it was brutal, telling me about your mom. And it hurt me to hear. But it would have been worse, later. I'm starting to see. Truth removes pain from the world. And I'm grateful to you."

We held onto each other's eyes.

I raised up, as he leaned in.

Our lips brushed, shy, sweet, and then...

... *Whoomph!*

I lurched, let out a shriek.

"Ten points!" Behind me, Rory threw his fist in the air.

"Oh! It's *on*!" Keegan dipped down, packed a snowball. He reared back, leg up like a baseball player, and...*whoosh!*

Rory screeched. The well-aimed snowball swept his hat clean off. Grits dashed over, scooped the hat from a snow bank. She shook it wildly between her teeth.

We scrambled. We packed, we flung, we ran.

Grits darted from one of us to the other. She chased our snowballs. She leapt, biting them. Rory, smacked in the chest, fell backward into a snow bank. "Ya got me! I'm in heaven now!" Sweeping his arms and legs, he made an angel.

Grits pounced.

She licked Rory's freckled face.

He laughed and laughed.

His laughter made the moon come out.

***

Twinkling white lights beckoned us.

We stomped our boots outside, shaking free the snow.

At Nonna's Italian Cafe, we were the only ones, at a table made for three.

Since no one else was there, they let Grits come inside. They brought her water and a bowlful of steaming scraps. She wolfed it down, tail thwacking my legs. All around, shimmering strings of lights, the perfume of garlic and olive oil, and lovely violin music serenading us from a crackly radio.

Rory swept his dad's hat off, his chestnut hair sticking up in staticky spikes. "I can have *anything*, Keeg? Are you sure? What about..." He closed his eyes, let his finger choose. "Lobster Fra Diavolo? Is that how you say it? However you say it, it's a whopping eighteen bucks."

"You want it? Get it."

Rory narrowed his eyes. "Is the rapture happening? Am I about to be left behind?"

"Don't push your luck. Just order."

Our server deposited a tray of warm, crusty bread, along with a little plate of olive oil. Keegan dragged a slice through the oil. He held it out to me. I smiled into his eyes, taking it. I picked up a piece of bread, and did the same for him.

Rory watched us, patting his hair down. "Okay. What's this all about. Why are you two being so goofy?"

"Our first date," I told him. "We liked each other. And bread."

"Bread," Rory said flatly. "A love story for the books, right there."

I swooped a slice through oil, held it out to him. "Try." He glanced at me, took it. One bite and he swooned, slumping in his chair. "Sweet bread of love."

Keegan and I laughed.

The server swept over with our food, smiling at each of us in turn.

For Rory, a heaping plate of spaghetti and meatballs, lavished with parmesan cheese. For Keegan, a giant square of lasagna. For me, something new, never before tried. Clam linguine with a white wine sauce.

We tucked in. We didn't talk.

Even our quiet together, was rich, full.

Snow left sparkly gauze trails down the windows.

I discovered an undying love for tender clams. I twirled the noodles round and round my fork. They fell off. I made a mess. Garlicky oil smeared on my chin, my fingers, my jeans. We all snuck Grits chunks of bread under the table. Her rough tongue licked olive oil off my fingers. Peace flowed through me. Peace. And I remembered Rain, wishing that word into her future. She was right. Peace was more life-giving than blood.

"So, um, June." Rory swirled his fork in his spaghetti noodles, eyeing me. "It's January. Not a single fun holiday in sight. Can I give you my not-Christmas present now?"

"You brought it?"

Grinning, he leaned over, withdrew the gift from his little backpack. The Santa-turtle wrapping paper was worse for wear, the edges of what looked like a picture frame poking out at the corners. I tore the wrap away, revealing one of Rory's drawings, framed.

"Personally, I think it's my best work to date." He kissed his fingers.

He'd drawn the family portrait that sat on the mantel, with a few notable additions. Their dad, robust and bearded, dimpled smile, Bible tucked under his arm. *Dad*, etched in a soft cursive halo above his head. Keegan, auburn curls swept playful across his forehead, arm slung around his dad's shoulders, flashing his dad's same dimpled grin. *Brother* across his shirt. Rory squinting, freckles lighting up his face, chestnut hair tousled...holding up a turtle in a green cape. On the cape, *Intrepid*. At Rory's feet, a yellow dog, owning her real name at last. *Grits*.

And someone else.

"It's from Homecoming," Rory said. "Can you tell?"

He'd drawn me in my sequined dress. He'd added *glitter*.

"Oh yeah," Rory pointed to my elaborately drawn frizz. "I didn't think it would be you without something in your hair."

I looked closer. A word in tiny script ... stuck in my hair.

Sister.

Rory watched me intently. "Do you like it?"

"Rory, Rory." Oh, I was going to cry, terribly, here in the middle of serene Nonna's with the snow falling gently outside. "Rory." I pressed the picture to my heart.

"Told you it was good." Rory winked at Keegan. "Can I get tiramisu?"

I looked out the window again. *Snow, please snow forever.*

I was happy. And it mattered.

My own happiness mattered.

Under the table, I curled my finger into Grits sequined collar, took a breath. "Keegan. I have something to tell you."

He wiped his mouth with his napkin. "What's up?"

"I registered for Intro to Teaching."

"June! No way. Are you serious?"

"There's more." I said, in a rush, "Starting next month I'm going to be a 5th grade teacher's assistant."

Keegan set his fork down, and we locked eyes.

I broke into a smile. "I got the job."

PART III
CHOICE

You've always had the power, my dear. You just had to learn it for yourself.

-Glinda, the Good Witch

January 7th, 1996
Fayetteville, Arkansas

"That's the part of my story that brings me here. To you, Judge Sanders."

I'm exhausted, but strong.

Stronger than I thought I would be.

I'm sitting straight, looking into Judge Sander's eyes.

His chin rests on folded hands. There are two crumpled Kleenex by his elbow. He smiles. Then, he takes me by surprise. "You're not *quite* done though, are you?"

"What do you mean?"

He leans back, taps his pen on the desk-top. "When do you turn seventeen, June?"

"Oh, um, soon." My mind races. "I'm sorry. What is today, Judge?"

"January 7th."

Prickles unleash. I can't quite catch my breath. "Today. Today. I turn seventeen today." I blink in wonder at the bookshelves. The evening light gives the wood a halo. "I knew it was close. But time, the past few weeks." I rub my arms. "Time's gotten so weird."

"That's understandable, June, considering."

"Funny, isn't it? How things work out..." I trail off, look down at my sparkling gold sequined Homecoming dress. The only dress out of all my dresses I'd thrown into the garbage bag when I ran.

When Mom got this dress for me, she had no idea, she was buying me my wedding dress.

Judge Sanders watches me. "It's a special day. May I say it?"

I startle. "Say what?"

Judge tilts his head, wiggles his brows. I've heard the words, countless times. But never, not once in my life, for *me*.

Judge Sanders begins to sing. "Happy Birthday to you, happy birthday to you..." His voice, so sweetly off-key. "Happy birthday, dear Juuu-nne," cracking on the high note, he shakes his head, laughing. "Happy Birthday to youuuuuu!" He belts it out, throwing his arms wide.

My hand finds my heart, stays there.

"Ah, that was atrocious!" He rubs his face with a chuckle.

"It was the most beautiful birthday song anyone's ever sung to me."

He meets my eyes, smiles. "I guess that's the truth, isn't it." And then, he lifts his spectacles from the beak of the wooden owl, sets them on the bridge of his nose. This action signals his eyebrows to draw together, his mouth to turn downward, and his pupils to sharpen. Just like before. "And so," he says, peering at me, "the mean judge returns. But I know you better than I did before. I think you know yourself better, too. I think you know how tough you really are. I think we both know, a measly pair of spectacles can't subdue you. Why are you here today, June Taylor?"

This time, I don't hesitate. "To marry Keegan Callahan."

He glowers at me. "So! The two of you have figured out,

marriage laws are lenient in Arkansas. However, even here, even on your 17th birthday, young lady, you are still a minor. You *cannot* get married without parental consent. Where is it?" He holds out his hand.

"I can't get it. You know that."

Judge Sanders withdraws his hand. "Keegan told you his dad was friends with a judge. Now you know. That judge was me. Those bookshelves you so admire?" Nodding to the wall. "Patrick Callahan made them for me. And you're absolutely right, they *do* glow." His voice grows a little husky. I gaze with him at the floor-to-ceiling shelves, ever deepening in gold as the sun sinks. "I'm the judge who has advised Keegan since his dad passed. I've helped him sort out finances and legal issues. I'm the one who helped him become Rory's guardian. Although, as he told you, I tried my best to talk him out of it. I feel a great responsibility to that family." He pierces me. "June."

"Yes, Judge." I focus on him very intently.

"Rory lost both his parents before the age of ten. Do you understand? He's at risk. He's going to need so much support. You and Rory have developed a bond. Your great friendship, with both these boys, is an answer to my prayers. But life will only grow more challenging. Have you thought about that? Are you ready, June? For life with a teenager?"

I give him a look. "Is anyone ready for life with a teenager?"

A small smile. "Touché." He lowers his spectacles, rubs the space between his brows. "It's not just Rory, of course. It's all of you. Sorting out faith, family, trauma...and marriage on top of it?" Judge meets my gaze, weary, but tender. "I don't question your love for Keegan, nor his for you. You've made your case. Together, you and Keegan are a force. I've never believed in soul mates. But the story of Seat #25 almost," he lifts a finger, "*almost* makes me believe. What I believe in most, are two people willing to work extraordinarily hard and be terribly brave for one another. Age isn't the real issue here, June. Truth be told, I've married old folks I've thought far more inept and doomed. What is it then?" He's talking to himself now, rubbing his chin.

"What, Judge?"

He points his pen at me. "Let me be clear, young lady. As you lack written parental consent, there are only two conditions upon which I can grant you permission to marry. One, you are pregnant. Two, you are being abused."

That word.

A boulder slamming against my heart, rolling down to the pit of my stomach.

I swallow, stay silent. My hand finds my violet earring, and clings to it.

Judge Sanders slams his pen down. "Good grief. I find myself at the end of our time together asking the same question as at the beginning. Why are you here today, June?"

"I want to marry Keegan..."

He holds up a hand. "Listen. Really listen. What is *your* story, June? What do *you* believe is true?" His face is red, and it trembles. "If you make this decision based on what someone else thinks, or tells you is true, you are still a victim. You will look back, you will feel that, and you will never forgive yourself."

I'm so confused. "What do you want from me?"

"Are you pregnant?" His voice is calm.

"No, Judge."

He rises just slightly, plants his palms on his desk, stares me down. "Are you being abused?"

In the dead quiet that follows, it's her hands I see.

They are rolling out the dough for our rhubarb pie. Strong

and firm, weathered and work-worn. I see her child hands, tucking her dolls into a cradle, hidden far up in her favorite tree. She is protecting them. I see her hand, stroking the soft newborn cheek of her June Namid, seventeen years ago this very day. I see her hand, holding out a violet in the warm bright summer sunshine. Two summers before, when she'd rolled out our pie crust, I'd noticed for the first time, the veins popping out in her hands.

Someday, she won't be here.

Someday, she'll be gone forever.

***

Keegan, dressed in a beautiful suit from Luca's, a rosebud tucked into the buttonhole on his lapel, slides into the driver's seat. I had run past him, straight out of the judge's office. Now, Keegan waits for me to speak.

"Take me home," I say, without looking at him. "I want to go home."

He watches me. He is grappling for the right words. The question I need.

"Don't," I tell him. "Don't speak. I only want to go home. Please. That's all I want."

Swallowing words, Keegan draws his keys from the pocket of his suit coat. He starts the car. My mind is a boiling cauldron of contradicting wishes. *I can't go back. Yes, I can. No, I don't want to go back. Never again! Yes, I do. With all my heart, I do.*

"Can we just...could we drive around town?" I latch and unlatch my fingers.

Keegan glances at me, turns at the next signal. Here we are then. Still in Fayetteville. Still fifteen solid miles away from

Hopeton, all that black star-filled sky. *I can stay here with Keegan and Rory.* My heart spins to joy. *How can I betray my mother? How can I leave my dad all alone?* My heart spins back to anguish.

"Okay." I wipe my sweaty face with the sleeve of my jacket. "Can we take the next exit to Hopeton?"

Keegan takes the next exit.

On the interstate, sick dread roars back. *You're my enemy.* It's true. It's terrible, horrible, head-wrecking, heart-wrecking *truth.* She never forgives. She never trusts. She never absorbs love, or loves. She can't seem to. No matter what we give...or give up.

"Keegan!" I shout, startling him. "I'm sorry. Can we exit? Head back to Fayetteville?"

Quiet, he takes the next exit. We loop back around to the city. The Fayetteville skyline, silvered with snow. The city offers itself to me. Not as an easy way out. Oh no. It will be *hard.* We'll be orphans. We'll be poor. It will be hard.

But not hard like it has been. Not *eat-me-alive* hard. Not *shreds-my-heart* hard.

There's a difference.

I pull my garbage bag onto my lap. The one I ran away with. I rummage inside it with trembly hands. I don't know what I'm looking for. I pull out a book.

A book.

I grasp the book like it will save me.

Haven't they, all my life?

Jane Austen and Charlotte Bronte. L.M. Montgomery. Catherine Marshall. Oh, so many! Trooping into my world, transcending the grave, their minds and hearts captured in print, on a page. Loving me. Teaching me love. Teaching me courage. Teaching me who I want to be in the world. Giving me strength, giving me solace. These writers. Whispering me wisdom. My countless lighthouses in the endless dark. *Family.*

I flip the book, read the title. *Poets in Love.* That library book! The play about Elizabeth Barrett and Robert Browning. The one I'd forgotten about, and never returned. The fee must be enormous. I flip to the end. I have to find out.

I flick on the overhead light, read with hunger.

Elizabeth eloped with Robert. They moved to Italy. Her health revived. She and Robert traveled the world together.

Elizabeth's father never spoke to her again.

I read and re-read those words.

Her father's estrangement hovered over her life like a dark phantom.

When he died, she returned at last to her old house.

There, she found all the letters she'd ever written him.

Tied in a bundle, unopened. *Unread.*

I drop the book. "Keegan. Take me home."

***

It's 3 am when we roll down the gravel driveway.

We sit in the car for another hour.

I can't move. Can't speak. Can't go.

Keegan rests his hand on my leg. He turns on soft jazz, keeps the engine running for heat. He rolls his head back on the seat, closes his eyes. I search the darkness of my yard.

I have to go.

I jiggle the door handle, then pull back. The snow is thick.

Down the hill, I can just make out her outline.

Clapping tree.

This spring, she'll return. Little future-clapping buds bursting out.

Nearby, rhubarb, resting like a queen under the snow. Next Rhubarb Pie Day, we'll have a party! All of us, there together. In the kitchen, Mom and I, in our matching blue-checked aprons, teaching Keegan how to chop the rhubarb and roll out the crust. My dream of a family, come true.

Only if I went back, and tried.

I set my hand on the door handle.

What if I didn't?

I pull back. Soft jazz carries my mind. To the future.

Instead of a flash back, a flash forward.

Mom. She will stop speaking to me. She will cut me out of her life. She will ignore my flowers, my gifts, the cookies left on the front porch steps in the night. My own special recipe. My own version of make up cookies. Every day, I will break in some new way. Time won't teach me not to want my mother. When the light splashes across my garden, and she's not there to swoon with over the thousand small, sacred treasures she's taught me to see, to love, I will splinter at the center. I will hope, *someday*. Hope will take me captive. Hope she'll change. Hope she'll heal. Hope she can love me now. *Hope!* This beautiful gift of the spirit will become my poison, and yet, one day, when she tries to return, I will have to keep her away, protect my family, just like she had to do with the Old Man.

Rain. We'll go watch *Sense and Sensibility* half a dozen times. Each time, in the dark theater, we'll sob, tissues balled in our laps. When Elinor clasps the foot of gravely ill Marianne, whispers, *Marianne, please, don't leave me here all alone.* Rain and I will grasp hands. We know this love. We have this love. It won't save us. One minute my sister and I will laugh, like our old, best selves. The next, we'll be at each other's throats. We will never truly be alone together. Mom will always be between us.

Our relationship, hobbled. My sister and I, the saddest thing. A beautiful bird, with a broken wing.

Dad. He will change the locks. Just in case I try to come back. *Honor thy father and mother.* I broke Jehovah's commandment. He will say I divorced them. Divorce is a sin, he will say. Jehovah sanctions them to cut me off. I will drive by his clinic, honking and waving to a closed door. He will drive by the tall blue house and not know, that's the house where his June Bug lives now. June Bug will be out on the porch, reading, jolted to her feet by the bright shock of vertebra on the side of his van. June Bug will wave and wave. "Dad!" She will call. "DAD!" He will keep going, until he disappears.

Grandma. We will have loved each other to the last breath. That, I will know. I will know that forever. Grandma loved her little ostrich with all her razzle-dazzle heart, and her little ostrich loved Grandma right back. Kindred spirits to the end. I will grieve for her in dressing rooms. Alone, trying on sparkly things, I will look in the mirror. I will turn side to side without seeing. *Where are they?* The sequins of my heart. I will miss them for the rest of my life. *The girls.*

"No!"

I fling the car door open, and dash into the snow. The furious cold soaks my panty hose. I scramble up the back porch steps. They are icy. I slip and slide.

Once I'm inside, the decision is made. No going back.

I fumble for my key. I find it, jam it in the lock.

Inside, a movement, a shadow. *What was that?*

CRACK!

I pivot, launch myself right off the porch.

I run, hard as I can, arms pumping.

When I stop, I'm standing in the middle of the yard, in the

snow. I stare at my house, breathing so fast, my heart about to explode.

Mom. Mom. I'm so scared she's there! Of what she'll do.

I look down. And my eyes fix on my knees.

They are doing something strange.

Something I've never seen them do before.

They are knocking together.

I watch the terror of my knees, and they speak to me.

They are my voice. They are telling me the truth.

My knees save me, when my heart can't.

Watching them, and listening, I know now, what I will say to Judge Sanders.

Crunch, crunch. I look up. Keegan stands, hands in his coat pockets. At the top of the hill, he is there. He is waiting for me.

He is there. He loves me. No matter what I decide.

I think about the way he drove me back and forth, all around. Listening. Only listening.

More like a tree than any human I've ever known. More like... a home.

I want to be the same for him. And I will be.

I run to him. He holds out his hand. I take it. And it feels like this.

Click click.

Together, we walk to our car. My hand on the door, a breeze stirs.

There are no leaves.

But I hear her.

She is clapping for me, even as she lets me go.

Acknowledgments

You either face your demons, or they raise your children.

I came across this quote recently on social media.

It punched me in the gut, and left me breathless.

It's a tragedy, how many of us were raised by our parent's demons.

This book is a love letter written to us, the children, and especially the daughters. The tribe of lonely girls sitting in trees, reading their books, quietly nursing a broken heart. Losing your mother before she dies is a grief few talk about, and many live through.

Along with our demons, growing up requires that we face our gods.

Leaving people, places, and beliefs we never thought we would leave is a shock, another complicated grief that ripples down through the years.

You won't be alone though. There will be lighthouses.

Thank you to the women writers, Beverly Cleary, Jane Austen, L.M. Montgomery, Catherine Marshall, the Bronte Sisters, Elizabeth Barrett Browning, Fanny Burney, and Deb Caletti, whose books showed up at critical points along the way – you are my mothers, my sisters, my aunts.

Thank you to the many trees who have loved, nurtured, and

watched over me throughout my life, especially clapping tree and great grandma tree.

Thank you to the animals who have protected and guided my heart including Scooter, Katie, Charlie, Buster, Hope, Maggie, Meeko, Cocoa, Fatty, Hecate, Penny – and Yellow Dog, whom my heart adopted.

Thank you to Keith Coley and Paul Fraser who gave me the greatest gift on the planet – health.

Thank you to Pooja Patel – light in my life before you even knew.

Thank you to Matthew for Road Rash, Ru Paul, and most of all, when my heart needed it most, calling me *sister.*

Thank you to Clyde Edgerton for telling me that it's okay if the story is a tragedy, and that he wished he could be my agent.

Thank you to Robert Siegel for shouting "That's a piece!" every time I told a story about my life.

Thank you to Rebecca Lee for the crucial words – *never stop trying to get this book in print.*

Thank you to Dawn Serna, for all the letters sent across the Cape Fear, for showing up there, my Forest Family.

Thank you to Jan Lily Welch for sending me a fairy crown of jasmine to wear on my graduation day – Anne of Green Gables would christen you *bosom friend.*

Thank you to Kathy Morgan for lovingly reading my stories and showing me the way, saying, *you help us process our grief, alongside yours.*

Thank you to my Crockett High School students and fellow teachers for championing me, and this book journey.

Thank you to the Apprentice House Press team and Kevin Atticks at Loyola University Maryland for giving this book a place in the world, a chance to meet its kindred spirits, and for making my lifelong dream come true. Thank you to Riley Mitchell for tenderly caretaking with your edits.

Thank you to Kim DeMaddis – *if only we were allowed to say, instead of a tiny, polite thank you, the truer – you just saved me. If only...we could fall to each other's feet.*

Thank you to Aly, my seat thief, for being my tree, and annoying me with the hardest questions. You helped me get free. I love you, my one, forever.

Thank you to Grandma Millee for magic pantyhose, sequin dreams, and dear beloved grandma, the courage you gave me for a lifetime!

About the Author

Summer Hammond grew up in the rural Midwest and Ozarks, one of Jehovah's Witnesses. After parting ways with the faith, she went on to earn her BA in Literature and teach ninth grade reading. Summer earned her MFA in Fiction from the University of North Carolina–Wilmington. Her fiction has been recognized as a finalist for the *Missouri Review* Jeffrey E. Smith Editors' Prize, among other honors. She won the 2023 New Letters Conger Beasley Jr. Award for Nonfiction and her work was selected for publication in Best American Essays 2025. Summer lives in Austin, Texas, with her kindred spirit, Aly, and their many books.